STABILITY ISLAND

ALSO BY THOMAS KELSO

Fractured

Hyperion's Fracture

STABILITY ISLAND

MARK THURMAN SERIES
BOOK 3

THOMAS KELSO

JOLLY ROBIN
PRESS

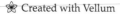 Created with Vellum

For Vicky and our children

The prediction I can make with the highest confidence is that the most amazing discoveries will be ones we are not today wise enough to foresee.

—Carl Sagan, *Billions and Billions*

Map of Isotopes

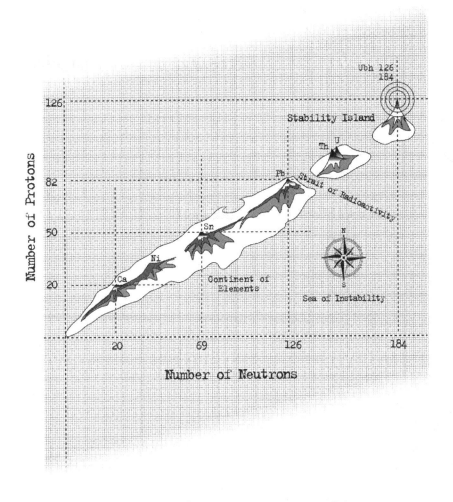

STABILITY ISLAND

FOREWORD

Batteries must improve if we are to achieve a world powered by clean energy. Scientists and engineers have been making batteries better since Alessandro Volta invented the first one in 1800. However, advances in energy storage technology have plateaued, and many problems continue to plague progress. It takes only a few minutes to fill an automobile fuel tank, but it can take hours to fully recharge an electric vehicle. Batteries are heavy, electrode degradation limits lifespan, and EVs have limited range before recharging is required.

We are approaching maximal performance with current battery technology and rapidly running out of strategies for improvement. Every element on Earth has been investigated. So, what is the next step?

What if someone manufactured a new element, one never known to exist, created for the first time—an element possessing extraordinary properties? Could this happen?

I believe it is possible. In fact, it has been done for decades. Scientists began creating new elements and extending the periodic table in the 1940's as a spinoff of the Manhattan Project. In the 1960's the media dubbed these researchers "the atom smashers." These atom smashers developed machines called particle accelerators and ion colliders that enabled scientists to take two atoms and smash them together with enough energy that their nuclei fused, forming a new element. This is how elements larger than uranium have been discovered.

One of the scientists who made a career of smashing atoms was Glenn Seaborg, PhD. He invented or helped to invent ten new elements, modified the periodic table, and proposed the existence of the Island of Stability. For his work he received the 1951 Nobel Prize in Chemistry.

Stability Island is the story of what happens when a scientist makes such a discovery.

CHAPTER 1
YURI'S SURPRISE

YURI DRAKE RESISTED the force coming from the metallic sphere clenched in his right fist. It pried at his fingers, working upward, struggling to escape. He released it. A sharp crack echoed throughout the empty locker room. It bounced and rolled across the ceiling, coming to rest against a light fixture. Adrenaline surged through his body as he stepped onto a bench to retrieve it.

Marvelous. He pinched the gleaming marble-sized orb between his index finger and thumb, holding it to the light while gazing at his miniature reflection on its mirrored surface. Then he stepped down and laughed. "Incredible."

He opened his locker and placed his creation under the top shelf, where it remained suspended. He stepped out of his coveralls, compressed them into a ball, and made a ten-foot jump shot into the hamper. He changed into street clothes and reached for his motorcycle gear. The smell of new leather clung to his Kevlar-lined jacket. Yuri slipped it on and hugged himself to stretch the stiff fabric. It felt like armor. He tucked the sphere into the jacket's breast pocket and closed the zipper then reached for his secured phone and made a call.

"Is everything all right?" Noreen Chase asked.

His grin made him squint. "The battery works."

"Are you serious?"

"I just left the lab. It's gone over a thousand miles without recharging."

"Yuri, that's wonderful. You've done it."

"This calls for a press conference, say, day after tomorrow?"

"That's a little hasty, don't you think? You'll blow your cover."

"I know what I'm doing." He lifted the motorcycle helmet and gloves from the top of his locker. "It's the only way."

"He'll find you."

"I suspect he already has."

"Impossible," said Noreen.

"Nothing is impossible with Stanov."

"How could he know about us? Are you sure?"

"Not a hundred percent, but something's wrong."

"Then why make an announcement?" asked Noreen.

"If I break the news, he can't steal it and hold the world hostage. And if he can't profit from it, then he has no use to come after me. It'll be safer for all of us."

"You don't know that. It could make things worse. We need to think this through. At least give me a couple of days to check with my sources before you go making any announcements."

"Fine. Three days."

"What are you going to do in the meantime?"

"Pray I'm wrong."

"Yuri, you're scaring me. I don't want to lose you."

"Don't worry. I'll be fine. Walters will be back with the car in a couple of hours. So far everything is right on schedule. I'll call and let you know how it went."

"All right," Noreen said. "Be careful."

"Always."

He slipped the phone into his pocket as he exited the locker room.

Yuri left the main research building and strode through the employee parking lot. Light towers illuminated the grounds of Angstrom Industries like a night game at Yankee Stadium. He straddled the motorcycle, engaged the ignition, then slipped on his helmet and checked to make sure the Bluetooth connection was paired with his phone. The engine growled as he shifted it into gear, let out the clutch, and twisted the throttle. He struggled to keep his speed under the limit on campus and anticipated the backroads where he could lean into curves and turn the Kawasaki loose. The pull at his breast pocket and the rumble between his legs filled him with a rush of anticipation. This heart-pounding exhilaration almost matched the thrill of transforming science fiction into reality.

A silver half-moon rose over rolling hills surrounding North Carolina's Research Triangle Park. Yuri waved at the guard as he passed through Angstrom's main gate and left his work behind. The road's interrupted yellow centerline soon blurred to solid as he wound through the gears. He voiced commands to call his wife, Aliya. She picked up just before her phone went to voicemail. "I'm on my way." He eased into a turn and then hit the throttle as the bike exited onto a long stretch of open road.

"Speak up, I can hardly hear you. Why can't you drive a car like everyone else? I hate that thing. You're going to sell it when the baby comes, aren't you?"

"Of course," he lied.

"You promised," she said. The irritation in her voice was plain.

"Maybe I'll get a new one in a few years," he said. "One that really flies."

"Don't you care about us?"

"No, I mean one that actually *flies*."

"Watch your words, someone could be listening."

He sighed and changed the subject. "I have a surprise for you."

"What is it?"

"The sphere." He padded his jacket pocket.

"You have it with you?"

He shifted and accelerated. The engine roared. "You have to see this. It's everything we dreamed it would be."

"Oh, Yuri, why take such a risk?"

"It's worth it," said Yuri. "You've worked hard for this too."

"I could have seen it when I came back to work."

"It will be safer with me. I don't know who I trust anymore."

"Just get home in one piece." She ended the connection.

He shook his head. *Can't she just be happy for me, for us? Why does she always make things so difficult?*

The suburban landscape whipped by as the stoplights became less frequent. The Old Chatham Golf Club appeared on his left as the motorcycle sped into farm country. A few minutes later Yuri turned onto Highway 751, opened the throttle, and hung on. The pull from the thousand-cubic-centimeter engine sent his heart racing. The cool evening air pummeled his body. He leaned forward into the wind. The motorcycle's headlight spot lit the pavement. A few miles later he glanced in his rearview mirror and noticed a car approaching. It would be gone in a few seconds. He twisted the throttle. The bike surged. The front wheel came off the pavement. *See ya.* Up ahead, a pickup truck turned into his lane from a dirt road on the right. Its red taillights grew larger. *Damn it.* He considered passing, but a car approached from the other direction. He let off the gas and braked. The headlights in the rearview mirror became brighter. The oncoming car in the opposite lane flashed by. *Now I'm out of here.* He swerved into the left lane, accelerated, and almost made it to the late-model pickup when it changed lanes and cut him off. *What the . . . ?* Before he could move back, the vehicle in the rear pulled next to him. *What are you doing, asshole?* Then he realized the car had been two cars following close together. The trailing vehicle switched lanes and closed the gap from behind. He was boxed in. The pickup truck braked. He glanced to his right and did a double take.

How did they find me?

The driver motioned for him to stop. Yuri had two options, pull over or make a run. He chose the latter. He drove off-road, gunned it, and would have escaped if not for the signpost that caught his handlebars, sending the bike into a spin and launching Yuri's body into the night air.

CHAPTER 2
TRAUMA ALERT

DR. MARK THURMAN walked into the new St. Matthew's Medical Center about the time a Duke Life Flight helicopter landed on the rooftop. Thurman entered the trauma center and watched EMS techs wheel his latest patient from the heliport elevator into Trauma Bay 1. The motorcycle accident victim cried out and reached for him as the gurney went past.

Once the patient arrived in the room, the trauma team performed their initial assessment. Afterwards, Thurman began his job, stabilizing the pelvic fractures, where knife-edged bone fragments had slashed arteries and veins that now filled the deep recesses of the patient's abdomen with blood.

The physician's assistant standing next to him pulled off her sterile gloves and grabbed the ringing phone clipped to her waistband. Her expression froze. A moment later she replied, "Right now? I'm helping Dr. Thurman . . . Yes, sir, I'm on my way." She stepped back from the treatment table. "I'm sorry, I have to go. Dr. Naylor needs me."

"You're kidding?" Thurman gestured to the patient who lay before them. "What about him?"

Consternation showed on her face. "What do you want me to do?"

"What did the Hands of God say?"

"And I quote, 'I need you right now! Get your butt to Trauma 3 pronto.'"

"He really said that?"

The PA's eyes rolled. "Naylor isn't known for his bedside manner. You can handle this, can't you? It's just an ex-fix."

Thurman took a deep breath. *Just an ex-fix.* His mask billowed as he exhaled. "Go on, but send someone to help me as soon as you can."

"Will do," she said over her shoulder.

The cacophony intensified. Fluid from IV bags drained into both arms. Personnel scurried about trying to keep the motorcyclist's heart and lungs working so his brain wouldn't die.

Thurman picked up an unloaded scalpel and slid a new size 10 Bard Parker blade onto the handle while mentally rehearsing the surgical steps of the task at hand. The intensity of the ER didn't help the situation. Thurman preferred to construct a pelvic ex-fix in the controlled environment of an operating room, but situations like this one made that luxury impossible.

He pressed the scalpel into the flesh above the left hip and drew it toward him. A two-inch-long crimson line appeared as if marked with red ink from a Sharpie. On the second pass the blade sliced all the way to bone. Blood filled the incision. He jammed a lap sponge into the hole, wished for a Bovie, and glanced at the instruments on the Mayo stand.

Monitors beeped. The shrill ping of an alarm repeated over and over. An anesthetist squeezed the Ambu bag attached to the endotracheal tube while slapping additional EKG leads onto the patient's chest. A nurse clamped an oxygen saturation monitor onto his index finger. When Thurman leaned close to the victim, he whiffed the coppery metallic odor of blood and the musty smell of damp dirt.

Wall-mounted video monitors displayed x-ray images of multiple shattered bones. Thurman studied the pelvic fracture pattern like it was a puzzle to be reassembled. Multiple breaks disrupted the sacrum at the base of the spine, and in front, the pubic symphysis was splayed so far apart it looked as if the patient had just given birth. *What a mess.*

Thurman looked for assistance as he contemplated the next step. A woman in blue scrubs standing on the other side of the instrument stand caught his attention. *Who is she?* He nodded in her direction then glanced at his incision and pulled the sponge, preparing to proceed.

She walked closer for a better look. "That's a nasty open-book pelvic fracture."

Thurman looked up. "Technically, it's an *open*, open-book fracture," he said, pointing to indicate where the splintered bones had penetrated the skin. "Check it out." He reached down and removed a saturated red sponge from a large laceration in the groin, then replaced it with a dry white one.

"That's some bad . . ."

"Luck," he finished.

"Need some help?"

Thurman inspected the woman. Strands of short dark hair snuck out from under her surgical cap. Steely azure eyes arrested his gaze. "Do you know what APC means?"

"Yes, sir, it's an anterior-posterior compression fracture. Which implies the deforming forces came from front to back, according to the Young-Burgess pelvic fracture classification system. This patient has a type three—the most severe, with complete pelvic ligament disruption and vertical instability." The mask hid the smile, but her eyes gave it away. "And, since it's an open fracture, possibly contaminated with fecal matter if there's a bowel puncture, it's at high risk for infection, so he'll have to be taken back to the OR a couple of times next week for washouts."

"Show-off." He returned a masked smile and pointed to a glass-windowed cabinet containing boxes of sterile gloves. "Put on a pair and hand me the drill."

She followed his instructions then picked up the device and passed it to him, handle first.

"Now give me a Steinmann pin."

She reached for a pointed rod, threaded like a screw, a little less than a foot long and about as thick as a pencil. "This?"

He loaded it into the drill chuck.

"What happened?"

"Motorcycle accident."

Thurman took a clean sponge and dabbed the incision he'd made minutes ago. He picked a starting point, placed the tip of the pointed pin on the crest of the bone, then pulled the trigger. A moment later he handed the drill and the chuck key back. "Load another one."

"How fast do you think he was going?"

"To do this?" He shrugged. "Who knows, fifty, sixty miles per hour?"

She winced. "Was he drunk?"

"I don't know."

She sniffed and handed him the loaded drill. "He doesn't smell like it."

Thurman paused and looked at her. "Want to walk through what we're doing here?"

"Pardon me?"

"Tell me what we're doing. Show off your knowledge. Instill me with confidence."

Frown lines appeared between her eyebrows. "You're inserting external fixator pins into the pelvic crest in order to construct a frame to stabilize the fracture."

Thurman nodded and drilled the second pin. "Not bad. By the way, its iliac crest, not pelvic crest. Why is it important to do this?"

"To compress the intrapelvic space to stop bleeding."

"And . . . ?"

"Stabilize the fracture, preventing bone fragments from causing further blood vessel damage."

"There's one more."

She paused to collect her thoughts, then said, "To keep both halves of the pelvis aligned so he doesn't end up with one leg longer than the other."

"Correct, excellent answers." Thurman held out the drill. "Well, what are you waiting for? Let's do the other side, load another pin." They repeated the process so that two six-inch parallel silver rods protruded from each iliac crest, on both sides of his waist.

"Well, did I?"

"Did you what?"

"Instill you with confidence."

"Most definitely, very impressive. You're better than most orthopedic junior residents. Where did you learn all that?"

"Reading and watching videos. I like trauma."

"It shows."

Thurman reached for a nylon suture and began closing the incisions around the pins. A masked face, wearing a green surgeon's cap, appeared from over his right shoulder, followed by an invisible cloud of garlic and stale cigar smoke. Thurman coughed and held his breath as a familiar voice growled, "Stop pimping the ER resident and get your Tinkertoys put together. We haven't got all damn night!" Dr. Richard Naylor had a knack for making his presence known. The effects usually lingered in the air longer than his signature cigar smoke. "We want this patient to live!"

"Relax, Rich. He's almost yours." Thurman snapped a clamp on each pair of pins and connected them with carbon fiber rods that came to an apex a foot above the patient's belly. Before proceeding he paused and looked at the woman, recalling Naylor's words. *ER resident?* "Have we met?"

She shook her head. "It's my first day. I'm Carmen Black, third-year emergency medicine resident doing an ortho trauma rotation on loan from Walter Reed. Dr. Emerson sent me to find you."

"Is that so? I didn't know we took residents from Walter Reed."

"We normally rotate through Shock Trauma in Baltimore."

"So why the switch?"

She shrugged. "Ours is not to reason why, . . ."

Thurman chuckled. "Ah, yes, I spent time in the military too."

"I know. I think that's why I'm here."

"Why do you say that?"

"I may be in combat one day. The military values your experience."

"I doubt they know anything about me."

"You're being modest."

"Well, I hope you're never in combat." He held out his gloved hand and she shook it. "I don't think we've formally met. I'm Mark Thurman. I run the orthopedic trauma service here at St. Matthew's. So far, you're doing a great job. We've got one final step." He handed her a T-handled socket wrench. "When I squeeze his pelvis back together, you tighten the clamps. We want this frame rigid. Got it?"

She gave a quick nod. "I'm ready, sir."

Thurman put one hand on each side of the patient's waist and felt bones grind together as he compressed the pelvis close to its original shape. "Tighten them—and stop with the 'sir' stuff."

She turned the wrench.

"All the way. We don't want it coming loose."

Carmen's brow creased as she gripped the tool with both hands.

Naylor called from the other side of the room. "Can you two please hurry up!"

"Ignore him, you're doing great, just be careful not to strip it. That's it."

She rotated the wrench clockwise until each nut wouldn't turn further.

"Nice job." He grasped the frame and pulled. The patient's body rocked with his effort. The pins and bars created a solid frame, stabilizing the broken pelvis. Thurman wiped his sleeve across his forehead and looked at Naylor. "That's a damn fine pelvic ex-fix."

The green-capped surgeon turned and walked away.

"Thanks," said Carmen.

"Let's find Dr. Emerson."

"The last I saw him he was in Trauma Bay 4 putting a femur in traction."

"What for?" Thurman double-checked the clamps.

"There's an MVA with a dislocated hip."

"Did he reduce it?"

"I did."

His eyebrows rose. "Not bad. How'd you do it?"

"The Captain Morgan method. You know, like the pirate on the label of the rum bottle. I placed my foot up on the gurney, draped his leg over my knee, and pulled it down while raising my heel. I felt it pop back into place."

"I'm familiar with the technique." He ripped off his gloves and rubbed the back of his neck. "You're really interested in orthopedics?"

"That's why I'm here." Her eyes smiled above the surgical mask as she removed her gloves.

"Thurman, are you finished?" Naylor boomed from across the room. "Can we transport?"

He gave Naylor the thumbs-up.

"Excellent. Let's get this patient upstairs, he needs his belly explored. The blood bank's ready and they're waiting for us in OR 10."

Thurman gripped the backboard and helped transfer the patient onto a gurney. He yanked off his mask and looked at Naylor. "Keep the Philly collar on, neurosurgery hasn't cleared his c-spine. Do me a favor and order a pelvis x-ray when you're done. We can adjust the frame after he's stabilized."

"If he makes it," Naylor barked.

Thurman stared at his assistant. "What's your name again?"

"Carmen Black." She removed her mask, revealing an unblemished olive complexion and a bright smile. When she pulled off the surgical cap, a bob of wavy dark brown hair tumbled free. She shook her head and brushed the bangs to one side, tucking longer loose strands behind her ears. She had the look of a gymnast, energetic and lean.

"It's nice to meet you, Dr. Black. On my service we dispense with academic formalities, feel free to call me by my first name."

"You can call me by mine."

"Okay, Carmen, let's see if Steve needs our assistance." They followed the gurney as attendants rolled the patient into the hallway. Thurman held the door as they turned toward Trauma Bay 4. A couple of steps down the hall, Carmen stopped and looked at her hand, then her waist. She began to pat her pockets.

"Go on, I'll catch up. I think I left my ring."

"I'll help you." Thurman walked with her back into the now-deserted treatment room. "When did you take it off?"

"When I was putting on my gloves. I tied it to my drawstring." She looked down at her scrub pants and held out the ends of the material. "It must have fallen off." She walked toward the trauma table. A pile of filthy shredded clothing lay on the ground. She kicked through the garment remnants, then got down on her hands and knees and looked under the base of the metal OR table that stood perhaps an inch off the floor. Her hand disappeared beneath the structure. She squeezed a piece of trapped clothing and pulled. Portions of a muddy, blood-smeared jacket came free along with the sound of something metallic rolling across the floor. Carmen smiled. Her ring sparkled as it came to a stop two feet away. She reached for it and slid it on.

"Find it?" Thurman asked.

"Yep." She stood up and held out her right fist. A gold college ring decorated the fourth finger. Around the onyx stone were two words and the year she graduated.

He bent closer and read the inscription. "You're a West Pointer?"

"Part of The Long Gray Line." She smiled and glanced at the floor. "It must have come loose and rolled under the table."

That's when they both noticed it. The jacket, now partially protruding from under the metal base of the OR table, lifted a few inches off the floor as if it were trying to float away. Carmen squatted and pushed it down. It sprang back when she removed her hand. "Did you see that?"

Thurman walked over and stepped on the leather material, pinning it to the floor. As he stood with his foot on the sleeve, he noticed the shoulder patch. A yellow shield trimmed in turquoise. Across the lemon colored background a green caterpillar wearing a crown crawled on the stem of a rose. *Not exactly biker's colors.* He quickly forgot about it when he felt the force under his shoe. *Bizarre.* When he removed his foot, once again the jacket recoiled upward. "What in the world? Are we seeing the same thing?"

Carmen reached out and pressed it back to the floor. "It's trying to float away."

"The sleeve is caught." Thurman unlocked the trauma bed and gave it a shove. It rolled a foot sideways. They jumped as the shredded jacket flew straight up and snagged on an OR light. "Why didn't anyone see this?"

"Four or five people armed with trauma shears stripped him when he first rolled in. Someone probably threw it on the ground and kicked it under the table." Carmen reached above her head and gripped a dangling cuff. She had to pull with surprising effort to bring it down.

"There's something in the pocket." She opened the zipper and probed with her fingers. "It feels like a marble." The sphere slipped from her grasp when she pulled it out. Their heads rocked back as the gleaming orb shot to the ceiling, then bounced and rolled. "Is it a magnet?"

"I don't think so. The roof's not metal. A magnet would have stuck to the OR table."

"Then what is it?"

Thurman climbed onto the table, reached up, and plucked it from the ceiling. He clenched it in his fist and climbed down.

"Let it go."

He opened his hand. The sphere flew straight up. His jaw went slack as he peered upward and laughed. "That's the weirdest thing I've seen in a long time." He retrieved it from the ceiling and put it in his shirt pocket. But it worked its way loose and zoomed up, ricocheting off the OR light. This time they had to reposition the table so he could step up and grab it. He held it in his fist and grinned as he hopped to the floor. "What is this thing made of?"

Their smiles faded as a voice blared from the intercom: "Attention, all trauma personnel. ER code silver! ER code silver!"

Carmen glanced at the speaker as it repeated the warning. "Is that an armed intruder alert?"

"Let's get out of here. There's an exit past the scrub sinks." Gunshots and screams sounded in the hallway. Thurman noticed several people running past the small window in the corner of the room. He froze and held a finger to his lips. Carmen nodded understanding. Her biceps tensed when he gripped her arm as the door burst open.

CHAPTER 3
CODE SILVER

A MAN DRESSED in scrubs and a long white coat stood in front of them. Close cropped black hair protruded from the edges of a surgical cap. Dark eyes glared at Thurman. He leveled a semiautomatic pistol aimed in their direction. "Where is it?"

"What?" asked Thurman.

"The sphere."

"What sphere?" Thurman replied.

The muzzle flashed. The report hammered the air. Shards of glass rained from a shattered OR light. "The next one won't miss. Start talking."

Thurman stepped back, moving the two of them away from the intruder and closer to the heavy metal surgical table. The antigravity force radiated in his left hand.

The gunman pointed at the pile of blood-soaked dirty clothes. "Where did they take him?"

Thurman took another step back. "He's upstairs, in an OR, fighting for his life."

"What did you find in his pockets?"

"We don't dig through the pockets of—" Thurman began.

The intruder pointed the pistol at Carmen. "She dies in five seconds unless you hand it over."

Footsteps sounded in the hallway. Thurman moved in front of Carmen. *Got to get to the table.* The man stepped forward with the gun aimed squarely at Thurman's chest.

"Two seconds."

"Oh, you mean this?" Thurman held out his left fist and opened it. The chrome sphere shot to the ceiling. The man's head followed it upward as Thurman charged. He vice-gripped the gun as their bodies crashed to the floor. Thurman's right fist jabbed the gunman's larynx. He gasped. The pistol clattered across the room. The man bucked Thurman off him. The gunman rolled to his belly and scrambled for the gun, but Thurman grabbed one of his legs and pulled. The man's fingers clawed at the gun, grasping for control. Thurman leapt onto his back, then reached into the front of his scrubs and extracted a pistol, placing the barrel to the gunman's skull. "Move and I'll blow your head off!"

Carmen sprinted from the OR table and kicked the intruder's gun across the floor.

A man in a hospital security uniform burst into the trauma bay. "Security, drop your weapon!"

Thurman kept his gun pressed to the assailant's head. "Don't shoot! We're medical staff."

"I said, drop your weapon."

The assailant cried out, "I'm a doctor. Get this lunatic off me."

"Shut up, asshole." Thurman pressed the barrel harder into his scalp. "Get over here and cuff him. What are you waiting for? You've seen me a million times before."

"I don't know you from Adam. All I see is you holding a gun to that man's head. Drop it and put your hands up or I'm going to shoot you."

"He's telling you the truth," said Carmen. "We're hospital staff."

"Shut up," said the officer. "Put the gun down and back away." He reached for his radio and spoke. "This is hospital security, seven echo. I'm in Trauma Bay 1, I need backup."

"All right, relax. I'm going to slide the gun to you. Don't shoot anyone." Thurman placed his gun on the floor and slid it toward the guard, then climbed off the intruder and stood.

"Put your hands on your head and kneel down."

Thurman did as requested. The gunman stood and straightened his coat. "Thank you, officer, great job."

"Get over there," the policeman said, motioning to the man.

"Look out!" said Thurman as the intruder lunged, grabbing the security guard's weapon then splitting the guard's nose with his fist, sending the navy blue ballcap flying to the floor. Thurman pushed Carmen toward the OR table and dove for his weapon that lay on the floor. A gunshot echoed. The uniformed man stumbled to the floor, clutching his abdomen. Thurman gripped his Sig and turned, searching for his target. Too late. The gunman's white coat disappeared through the door and into the hallway. *Damn it.* Thurman holstered his firearm and called in the trauma alert on his cell phone. As he inspected the injured security officer, another man, in a coat and tie with a gold police shield clipped to his belt, entered the room. He held his firearm up, scanning the area.

"I'm Sergeant Jerry Hairston, Durham PD. What happened?"

"Your man's getting away."

"Let me worry about that. What happened?"

Thurman briefly explained, leaving out the sphere, as two more uniformed police officers entered. One of them addressed Hairston. "The ER is secured, sir. Multiple units are responding."

"The gunman is dressed in scrubs and a white coat. He left this room less than five minutes ago," said Thurman, then added, "He's armed."

The detective stood over Thurman, who knelt by the wounded man. "Anything else you can tell me?"

"The intruder wore Rick Mason's physician's coat."

"Who's Mason?"

"One of our surgical chief residents."

"Any idea what the shooter wanted?" Hairston said.

"He wanted to know about the trauma victim they just took to surgery," Thurman replied.

"Name?" Hairston asked.

"Don't know. They'll have it up front."

"That's it? No mention of drugs? Money? Anything like that?"

"Nothing." The security guard groaned as Thurman applied pressure to the wound. He looked at Carmen. "Grab some ABDs from the dressing cabinet."

While the detective finished jotting notes, Carmen knelt on the other side of the guard. As she took over holding pressure on the abdominal wound, her eyes caught Thurman's and moved upward. He returned the stare, and almost imperceptibly moved his head a few millimeters from side to side.

Hairston finished writing and tucked his notebook into the breast pocket of his jacket. He stared at them for a moment, like he had another question, but either the thought escaped or he changed his mind. He smiled and said, "Thanks for your cooperation. I'll need you to give formal statements at the precinct."

"That will have to wait, we're on call."

"And try not to touch anything. This is a crime scene."

"Detective," said Thurman, "this is a level 1 trauma center. We have to touch things."

"Then wear gloves."

Thurman glared. Trauma team members flooded into the room and gathered around the victim.

The security guard's owl eyes blinked. "I screwed up," he whispered. "I'm sorry."

"You have nothing to be sorry about. Try to be calm." Thurman nodded toward the charge nurse. "Call the surgery team. Get an OR ready. Tell Naylor he has another ex-lap waiting."

Hairston thought for a moment, then said, "Do me a favor. If you get a break tonight, write down what happened. Everything you can remember. It will keep the details fresh. Then come down to the station in the morning. Will that work?"

"Sure," said Carmen absently as she started an antebrachial IV.

"Thanks."

"If you don't mind me asking, how did you get here so fast?" Thurman asked.

"I was visiting my mom. She broke her hip. You guys replaced it yesterday."

"You're Mrs. Hairston's son?" said Thurman.

"Thanks for taking good care of her. See you tomorrow."

Thurman nodded as the detective turned and walked toward the door.

Two hours later, after a pause in the trauma action, Carmen gripped Thurman's bicep and pulled him into the breakroom. She scanned the room, making sure they were alone, then closed the door.

"You okay?" she asked him.

"Sure, why?"

"For starters, some lunatic almost killed us."

"Oh, that. That's just a typical Thursday," Thurman teased.

"I don't know about you, but that's more excitement than I like during my shift." She exhaled as she raked her fingers through her hair. "I didn't plan on staring at the wrong end of a nine millimeter."

"Did you see his eyes? He meant business."

"I'll say, and where in the hell did you get that gun?"

He reached into the front of his scrub pants.

Carmen's eyes popped. "What are you doing?"

He ignored her. "A couple of tours in Iraq and Afghanistan taught me to be prepared for all contingencies. This is a Sig Sauer P365." He drew the compact semiautomatic pistol from its concealed holster. "The magazine holds ten nine-millimeter rounds, and there's one in the chamber."

"You carry it in your underwear?"

He pulled down his scrub pants so an inch of his underwear showed. He snapped the elastic band. "It's called Thunderwear, perfect for concealed carry under scrubs."

"They make those for women?"

"Of course, but not briefs." He holstered his weapon and retied the drawstring.

Carmen folded her arms across her chest. "What's up with your story? Why didn't you tell him about the sphere?"

"I have my reasons."

"You're withholding information from the police."

"Maybe."

"There's no maybe about it. You didn't tell him, and that implicates me in your shenanigans."

"We're not withholding information. We're just not saying anything for now. In the heat of the moment, we forgot. Relax, everything will be fine. When we make our statements, don't mention it. Agreed?"

Carmen let out a sigh. "I guess, but why?"

"That sphere is unlike anything we've ever seen. I've got a feeling it's important and probably top secret. I want to make a few phone calls before we say anything. Make sense?"

"Not really, but what are you going to do with it in the meantime? What if that guy comes back?"

Thurman frowned. "I don't know yet. We need more information about the patient—who is this guy, and what's in that marble? Trust me, okay?"

"Don't leave me out on a limb."

Thurman turned and looked straight into her eyes. "I'd never do that. By the way, you did great."

Her cheeks flushed. "Thanks, you weren't too bad either."

Their wristwatches began to vibrate, indicating another incoming trauma. Thurman walked toward the door. "I have to attend a conference tomorrow afternoon on Duke campus. How do you feel about nanomaterials?"

She raised an eyebrow. "Fascinated, I guess . . ."

"Great. Meet me after shift change and I'll give you the details."

Three hours later, after activity in the ER lulled and the crime scene investigators finished their work, Thurman returned to Trauma Bay 1, climbed onto the OR table, and plucked the sphere from the ceiling.

CHAPTER 4
ELECTRIC WONDER CAR

ROBERT WALTERS SQUIRMED in the driver's seat of the modified Tesla Model X, trying to relieve the pain shooting down the back of his left leg. He could no longer feel the outside half of his foot, and twitching hamstrings foretold a muscle spasm. *That's all I need,* thought Walters as he slid the driver's seat as far back as possible and stretched his aching leg. *At least the security van's taken care of. Let's get this over with.* The ping of an encrypted phone call sounded, and Walters touched the computer screen.

"How's it going?" David Moore asked.

"Not good. My sciatica is getting worse. There's no way I was going to wait around for another support vehicle."

"I can't believe it. That van has less than a thousand miles on it and practically everything needed for any repair."

"Weird," said Walters as he massaged the back of his thigh.

"The driver called in ten minutes ago. They towed it to a service station in Florence, South Carolina."

"Must be a software glitch," said Walters. "I'm just glad we're close enough to make the final leg on my own without security."

"It's a risk we'll have to take. Hang in there, you're almost home. Only another hundred and fifty miles."

"Easy for you to say."

"It's dark, lay the seat back and relax, the car will drive you home. You're in the bottom of the ninth."

"Kiss my aching buttock." He read the vehicle's instrument data while flexing his knee to relieve the pain. The car stayed in the right lane as he glanced at the speedometer. It remained pegged at seventy miles per hour, just as it had for the entire day, with stops only for restroom breaks and security vehicle pit stops. Walters's main task had been to stay awake. The test vehicle drove itself. He only had to monitor the car's performance and touch the steering wheel every few minutes. The sun had set a couple of hours ago, and in the early evening darkness the computer dashboard glowed like a multicolored Christmas tree, displaying data from twenty sensors. Walters read the remaining battery charge. "Hey, Mo."

"What is it?" Moore asked.

"Nothing wrong, but it looks like we're not going to make it all the way home without a recharge. The battery is down to half a percent, and we're a hundred and thirty miles out."

"That's funny, it looks fine on this end. My instruments say over 25 percent left."

"Not according to the dashboard."

"Send me a photo of the reading and the odometer."

"What, you don't believe me?" he said, glancing at the dashboard charge meter, which read 25 percent.

"I believe you. I want it for the report. It's probably a bug."

"Are you disappointed?"

"Heck, no, I'm excited. We've gone over twice as far as anyone else." Moore paused, then said, "There's a charging station in Lumberton."

"I'll stop there."

"It shouldn't take long."

"I'll charge for five minutes, then see what we've got." A green sign flashed by. "The exit is in one mile."

Forty-five seconds later Walters took over manual control and activated the right turn signal. He exited the interstate and continued onto Highway 211. The Tesla Supercharger station was fifty yards ahead.

Walters got out and stretched his stiff back, then bent over and touched his toes. Pain shot down the back of his left leg. His sciatic nerve screamed. He grimaced while attaching the charging cable, then set the timer on his work phone and limped toward the restroom. Before he got there, the other phone rang. He pulled it from his pants pocket; a FaceTime call. A man with black hair and a cropped, grizzled beard with wrinkles around his eyes appeared.

"Dr. Walters, how has the experiment gone?" His voice was deep and rough, like a smoker whose vocal cords had been coated with decades of tobacco smoke residue. His English was excellent, but Walters detected the trace of a Russian accent.

"Fine, just like I said it would."

"Did you get the sphere?"

Walters shook his head. "I told you, he keeps it locked in a safe in his office."

A scowl etched lines over the man's face. "Very disappointing."

"Forget about the sample, the battery is all the proof you need."

"I want the sphere."

"It would be easier to rob a bank."

"Do you have the car?"

Walters turned his phone so the vehicle appeared on screen. "When do I get the rest of the money?"

"Once it's delivered, the money will be wired. You have my word."

"No money, no car. I can recharge and keep heading up the road."

"I wouldn't advise that. We have an agreement."

"You owe me ten million dollars."

"When I get the car, and you show me how the battery works, you'll get the money."

Walters gripped the back of his left leg as a spasm of pain reached a crescendo. Sweat beaded on his forehead.

"Dr. Walters, do we still have a deal?"

Walters didn't answer.

"Professor, think of your wife and daughter. We wouldn't want anything to happen to them, would we?"

Walters froze. "What have you done with them?"

The Russian chuckled as he lit a cigarette, its tip glowing as he inhaled. Smoke streamed from his mouth and nostrils as he spoke. "Nothing, they are safe at home. Call them if you don't believe me."

"All right, I'm trusting you. Don't screw me over."

"A wise decision."

———

Angstrom's vice president of research and development, David Moore, took a sip of coffee and glanced at his watch. It would be close to eleven o'clock by the time Walters returned and they finished securing the vehicle. Moore settled into his chair in front of the computer screens and reached for the phone on his desk. Walters answered on the third ring.

"What now?"

"How are you feeling?"

"I'll make it."

"You're almost home. A scotch and an ice pack will do you wonders."

"Make that a double and a heating pad. Maybe a Vicodin."

"How high did the battery charge?"

"Seventy-two percent."

"In five minutes?"

"Five minutes and eight seconds, to be precise."

"Will it hold?"

"What, the charge?"

"Yeah."

"What do you think?"

Moore smiled and lowered the coffee cup from his mouth. "Just drive it home. Next week we'll add another battery and start for San Francisco, see if we can get across the country."

Not with this car, my friend, thought Walters.

"Without recharging."

Walters squeezed the back of his left butt cheek. "You're driving."

"We'll tag team."

"Hey, Mo, I'm getting an error signal. I'm going to check it out."

"I don't see anything on my screens."

"Well, it's on mine. I'm going to run some diagnostics. I'll call you back in a few minutes."

"Hey, you missed the I-95 on-ramp. Turn around."

Walters ignored his friend, felt the burn of acid reflux, and turned off the phone. He opened the glove box and reached for a Pepcid while the car continued on Highway 211 toward Wilmington, North Carolina.

———

Walters headed east for five miles until he spotted the deserted gas station. He almost turned around, but instead turned in. Gravel crunched as the car came to a stop. He felt palpitations as his heart rate surged. He took several deep breaths and slowly exhaled. Then he took out his phone and tapped the Libre app. He reached for the back of his left arm and touched the phone to the sensor. The phone vibrated and he glanced at the screen. *No way, a hundred and ninety-five! You've got to be kidding me!* He swore as he processed the magnitude of the blood glucose spike. He glanced at his reflection in the rearview mirror. *Relax, this will all be over soon, and you'll be set for life.* So far, his type 2 diabetes could be managed with oral medications, but insulin loomed in his future if he couldn't manage stress better. Walters hated needles.

A tractor trailer loaded with a shipping container was parked next to the old gas pumps. The rig's diesel engine idled. The man inside opened the cab door, climbed down, and walked toward him. Walters noted the oversized high-cube container on the flatbed and surmised it was probably because of the electrical shielding needed to conceal the vehicle. The trucker wore jeans, a sweatshirt, and a dirty Atlanta Braves baseball cap. Walters powered down his window.

"This good enough? Do I need to move it?" A gust of cold wind rattled the desiccated leaves still clinging to the trees surrounding the old station. Walters hated what he had to do, but what choice did he have? Mounting medical bills from his daughter's multiple pediatric heart surgeries sealed his decision; still, he wondered if he'd struck a Faustian deal with the devil. *God forgive me.*

"You're fine, buddy, let me get these ramps in place. You think you can drive her on in?"

Walters nodded.

"How you gonna get out?"

"Let me worry about that." Walters watched as the trucker set up two thirty-foot ramps, each a foot wide, that led up into the shipping container.

"I'll line you up. Go slow."

Walters stopped when he felt the front tires touch the ramps. He got out and checked the position of the vehicle. Satisfied with the car's alignment, he got back in and crept up the ramps into the metal container, steering the car as far to the right as possible and leaving clearance on the driver's side.

"All right, that's good, put it in park. Don't forget the emergency brake."

Walters complied. *Thank God for these vertical-opening doors.* He scrambled into the back seat and squeezed out of the car, sidestepping toward the rear until he cleared the taillight.

"Good job, man," the trucker said, tipping his ballcap. "Now jump on down. We'll get this baby secured and hit the road."

Walters walked down a ramp and removed his phone. "Thanks, man, you got it from here. I've got things to take care of."

"Let me give you a lift."

"Not a good idea. I have a plane to catch, and you have a delivery to make. In a couple of hours every cop in the state is going to be looking for that car, so climb into the cab and hit the road. I'll be fine."

The trucker chuckled. "I'm not making myself clear. You're coming with me."

"I don't think so."

"I do. Those are my instructions." The trucker approached. Walters turned to flee as he fired the taser. The twin wires penetrated his left thigh.

"My leg!"

"Sorry, dude." Walters's body toppled to the turf, depolarizing into a grand mal seizure. The trucker walked over, pulled the wires, and injected the ketamine. "Sweet dreams, partner."

———

Thurman reached for the phone on his nightstand. He'd just returned home from the trauma center and crawled in bed when John Bristow returned his call. He looked at Bristow's smiling face on the screen. *Thank God, not another trauma.* "Thanks for calling back."

"No problem. What's going on at this hour?"

Thurman explained the evening's events. "Any ideas?"

"It sounds like you stirred up a hornets' nest."

"More like one fell into my lap. That guy knew right where to go and came in with his gun drawn. I almost took a bullet for that damn marble. Then the lunatic gets away."

"Calm down, pretty boy. I don't have all the details, but something's going down. The wife of one of our assets called a few hours ago. She said the police reported her husband had been in a motorcycle crash. He'd been taken to a local hospital. It sounds like you found him."

"Got a name?"

"Drake, Yuri Drake."

"That's the guy. Why is he so important?"

"The admiral will have to fill you in. You still have the magic ball?"

"It's in a safe place."

"Keep it there, and keep your mouth shut. No one needs to know about that little gem but you and I for now, capisce?"

"C'mon man, tell me something."

"Let's just say a lot of resources have been invested in this guy for a number of years. Keep him alive."

"I'll do my best, but tell the admiral to be prepared for the worst. I doubt if Drake's Glasgow Coma Scale is much above ten."

"What's that mean?"

"He has a serious head injury along with a lot of other problems. He's in critical shape and may not make it."

"Work a miracle like you did for me."

Thurman tensed recalling the events of a year ago when Bristow had been a bullet-ridden trauma patient at St. Matthew's. "You better hope Naylor can stop his internal bleeding."

"He's in good hands–the best. Work your miracles. I'll talk to you soon."

CHAPTER 5
THE MEETING

THURMAN ROSE before dawn Friday morning and checked the home security images on the CCTV feed. Eight cameras provided surveillance of the house and grounds. He half expected to see someone snooping around. *All clear.* He reset the security codes, showered, and left for morning hospital rounds. At 6:00 a.m. he met with Carmen; Steve Emerson, an associate professor of orthopedics; and John Wynn, an orthopedic surgeon doing fellowship training in trauma. They gathered at the surgical ICU nursing station with the rest of the orthopedic trauma service, which included residents, medical students, physical therapists, nurses, and respiratory therapists.

Thurman received a text from Carmen as one of the fourth-year medical students began presenting the first patient to the group. *How did you sleep?* it said.

Nightmares, he responded.

Me too. She looked at him out of the corner of her eyes and smiled.

An hour later the trauma team arrived outside Yuri Drake's room. Thurman addressed his partner. "Dr. Emerson, can you give the team a brief synopsis of last evening's events and what's happened since he came back from the OR?"

Emerson rattled off Drake's injuries and the procedures performed thus far, finishing with the story of the armed intruder. "The patient's identity is being withheld; he's been given an alias in case anyone else comes looking for him. Only essential personnel will be assigned to this John Doe. A police guard has been posted outside his room. So, you medical students get a break, one less person on your patient census. Furthermore, he's not in his room. Dr. Naylor took him back to the OR a couple of hours ago." He looked at Thurman. "I'll get details and fill you in this afternoon."

Thurman concluded rounds with a couple of remarks. "All right, everyone has their assignments. Dr. Emerson and Dr. Wynn have cases this morning. Those of you assisting them, head to the ORs. Dr. Black and I have meetings in Durham. The rest of you have a good day."

"See you in a couple of hours," replied Emerson. "Are you presenting your research?"

"Noreen Chase is giving the presentation. She's the lead investigator."

Thurman and Carmen drove across town and gave their statements at the Durham police station. Afterward, Carmen headed to the conference center and Thurman went upstairs in search of Detective Hairston. A clerk directed him to an office with a hallway window. The blinds were open. Hairston sat at his desk. He took a sip from a coffee cup, then went back to pecking at his keyboard. Thurman stood in the open doorway and knocked on the jamb. "Good morning, detective."

Hairston looked up and smiled. "Dr. Thurman. Come to give your statement?"

"Just finished."

"Excellent. What can I do for you?"

"Just wondering if you found our intruder yet."

"We're checking hospital security cameras. He slipped out a back door and took off down an alley. We found Dr. Mason's white coat in a dumpster."

"Other leads? What about his clothes? Any prints on his gun?"

"The evidence is at the forensics lab." Hairston scooted his chair back. "Why aren't you back at the hospital? You looking to join my team?"

"I just wanted to know if you apprehended the suspect. He knows who I am."

"What are you worried about? He wanted your patient, not you."

"Maybe he didn't like what I did to him."

"Like I said, he got away. I'll let you know when we find him." Hairston interlocked his hands behind his head. "Thanks for stopping by. Anything else you forgot to tell me?"

Thurman shook his head. "It's all in my statement. We went over it ten times last night."

"By the way, how's Dr. Mason?"

"Mason's doing all right. Aside from a concussion and a mild headache, he'll be fine. I think he's at work today if you need to speak with him."

"He said the guy came up to him in the utility hallway and pulled a pistol." Hairston paused to sip some coffee. "Forced him into a storage room and asked if a motorcycle accident had been admitted. How would the shooter know that? The helicopter just brought him in, right?"

"Yeah. I arrived as it landed."

"The guy made him take off his scrubs, beat him unconscious, and tied him up with a couple of zip ties. That makes him a pro. Your average psycho mass shooter doesn't bind people with zip ties."

"And he knew how to handle a gun."

"I can't help but wonder, why would Dr. Mason be in a back hallway?"

"It's a shortcut to the stairs that lead up to the ORs. We use it all the time."

Hairston made a note on the legal pad next to his keyboard. "Dr. Mason and I have an appointment after lunch to go over the details. Oh, there's one thing I forgot to ask. One of the nurses said she heard him mention a place."

"Who, the shooter?"

Hairston shook his head. "The guy he was looking for. Before they stuck that breathing tube down his throat, he mentioned an island, stability island. Ever hear of it?"

"Funny, that's what Dr. Black said. He muttered it several times."

"I looked it up. There's no place with that name as far as I can tell."

"I've never heard of it either," said Thurman. "What's this guy do for a living?"

"He's a freaking nuclear physicist, works in the Triangle at a place called Angstrom Industries."

"You're kidding?"

"Is that surprising?"

"I do research there with one of their scientists. It's just a hell of a coincidence is all."

Hairston reached for his pen. "Who do you do research with?"

Thurman told him about his project with Noreen Chase.

"That is interesting. You've got my number, right?"

Thurman held up his phone. "Right here."

"Good, send me Chase's contact information and call me if you think of anything else. I've got to go." He stood and shook Thurman's hand. "Thanks for stopping by. You know how to get out of here?"

Thurman stood in the doorway and scratched the back of his head.

"Need something, doc?"

Keep your mouth shut. Bristow's words echoed in Thurman's mind.

"Nope. Just trying to remember which way I came."

"That way," Hairston indicated.

"Thanks," Thurman said, starting down the hallway.

"We'll be in touch," Hairston called after him.

———

Noreen Chase sat at a table in the back corner of the bar, but every eye in the room was on her. A fact she appreciated most of the time, but it had its drawbacks. Across from her, Terrance Morton occupied a seat on the wall-length bench facing the entrance. He loosened his tie, finished the last of a Johnnie Walker Black, and watched the doorway like something dangerous was about to enter. "Any word about . . . ?"

"No. He's in critical condition. That's all I know," she whispered.

Morton's elbows rested on the table. He leaned forward, massaging his temples. "It's not your fault, Noreen. You can only protect people who want to be protected. He's been a problem from day one."

"That's the job," she said, sipping chardonnay.

Morton swirled the half-melted ice cubes and held up his glass, motioning to a waitress. "He actually said he wanted to have a press conference?"

"I talked him out of it and bought us some time." She shook her head. "Now . . . this."

"What a shitstorm. First the car, now Drake. Stanov's making his move. If we were smart, we'd cut our losses and get out of the game."

Noreen shot him a startled look. "What are you saying?" she said.

A waitress stopped at their table. She reached for Morton's empty glass and replaced it with another round. She looked at Noreen. "Can I get you anything?"

Noreen waved her away. "Not now, thanks."

"I'll check back later." The waitress said as she retreated.

Noreen shot Morton a look. "What do you mean? We can't walk away now, we're in too deep. Drake is depending on us."

"I don't care about Drake. I'm thinking about you and me." Morton gripped his glass. "This isn't my first rodeo. One thing you notice after a couple of decades in this game is that the case officers who survive are the ones who know when to get out. Those addicted to the job, who make it personal, they end up dead. That ain't happening—I intend to make it." He picked up his glass and downed half. "You better get moving. Your talk is in fifteen minutes."

"I'm ready," she said. "Meet me here after the session. I have a few more things we need to discuss."

Morton checked his watch and took another sip. "Gimme a key, I'll meet you in your room."

"Forget it. It's safer here in public. And slow down on the Scotch," she said, gathering her purse. "I need you to be functional tonight."

CHAPTER 6
NOREEN

THE FIFTH ANNUAL International Symposium on Biomedical Applications of Nanomaterials took place at the Washington Duke Inn on Duke University's campus. After leaving Detective Hairston, Thurman drove from the Durham police precinct to the conference. He parked and walked to the entrance. The hotel resembled an English country estate with its surrounding acres of manicured grounds and well-managed forest.

Thurman felt the vibration of his phone and read the text message as a bellhop opened one of the ten-foot oak doors that led to the lobby. A small sign next to the check-in desk directed him down a hallway. Along the way he passed portraits of leading Duke family members dating to the nineteenth century. At the end of the corridor, he entered the conference facility, where a large blue-and-orange banner welcomed attendees to the symposium.

Thurman smiled when he spotted Dr. Carmen Black standing exactly where her text message indicated he'd find her. She wore a white blouse, navy pencil skirt, matching blazer, and black pumps that made her a couple of inches taller. She spotted him, smiled, and waved.

"You upgraded your outfit."

"That tie and sport coat aren't too shabby either," she said while adjusting her tortoise-shell frames.

Thurman took a step back, giving an admiring glance. "I always find it surprising when I first see someone outside the OR in regular clothes. It's a big change from baggie scrubs and hair covers."

"We weren't in scrubs at the police station."

"I know, but I didn't get a chance to tell you how nice you look."

"So, no trouble finding me in the crowd?"

He raised an eyebrow as he scanned her outfit. "Your text was spot on, and you're drawing a lot of attention in those civvies."

Her cheeks blushed slightly. "Is that a compliment?"

"Civilian clothes."

"I know what it means, remember?" She poked out her fist, displaying the West Point class ring.

Thurman responded with a light fist bump. "I remember, and yes, it was meant as a compliment. You look great."

"Thank you." She smiled and tucked a lock of hair behind her ear. "You want to see what's on the schedule?" She removed a conference program from her shoulder bag and stood closer to him. "This stuff is Greek to me."

He glanced over her shoulder. "Don't sweat it, there's no test. This is super technical and cutting edge. No one expects you to understand it all. Hell, I don't and I've been studying the field for a while. Nanotechnology is changing medicine. That's the take-home message. For the moment, we're only interested in this one." He pointed to a presentation.

"Hey, you're one of the authors."

His eyes widened in mock surprise. "Shocked?"

Carmen closed the program and tucked it into her shoulder bag. "Of course not."

"A little?"

"No . . . well, maybe. I read your CV. It didn't list anything about nanomaterials research. It listed you as a coauthor with a Dr. Hodgson on a bunch of papers about 3D biological tissue printing and fracture healing."

"We had a good thing."

"What happened?"

"Long story short, a fire destroyed our research lab. The whole project had to be halted. Claire," he paused, "Dr. Hodgson, my research partner, is on sabbatical while repairs to her lab are completed. She's on the West Coast working on a new project."

"I'm sorry about that," said Carmen.

"There's nothing to be sorry about. That's the way things go sometimes."

"So, how did you get involved with nanomaterials?"

"About six months ago someone from Angstrom Industries contacted our department to see if anyone might be interested in developing products that could improve orthopedic implants."

"Hip and knee replacements?"

Thurman nodded. "Low-friction, scratch-resistant ceramic materials that could double the life of a total joint. How could I refuse an opportunity like that?"

"Good timing."

Thurman nodded. "I needed a research project. The Department of Defense funded our grant, and we started running experiments."

Carmen glanced at the program. "With this woman presenting the paper?"

"Noreen Chase, she's a nanomaterial engineer."

Carmen bit the end of her pen while scanning the program. "What did your results show?"

"I'll let Dr. Chase explain. She's up next." He led the way into the conference room as the overhead lights dimmed. They found two unoccupied chairs midway to the front. Carmen took a legal pad from her bag. Thurman looked around, then leaned over and whispered, "Have you seen Steve?"

Her eyebrow rose as she leaned away.

"Sorry, I didn't mean to intrude into your space."

She smiled. "It's okay, he's two rows in front to the right."

Thurman spotted Emerson fighting to stay awake, his head rocking back and forth like a bobblehead doll.

Carmen leaned close and whispered, "We were on call last night. We did a few cases early this morning."

"Were you scrubbed in with him?"

She nodded.

He whispered, "You're not dozing off."

She shrugged and said, "Coffee?"

They held each other's gaze, perhaps a moment longer than necessary. Then she turned her attention back to the podium. Her scent lingered. *Lilac?* He wasn't sure. She was older than a typical third-year resident. He guessed early thirties—ten years his junior.

The sound of applause drew his attention toward the front of the room. Following her introduction Noreen Chase commanded the stage.

"Wow, that's your research partner?" said Carmen as she turned to Thurman. "She's gorgeous."

"She's more than that."

At the end of the afternoon presentations, Carmen excused herself. "I'm heading back to the hospital."

"Saturday morning rounds are at seven. I won't be there. I have another obligation."

"Okay, I'll call you if there are any problems." She smiled, then scooted down the row and blended with the crowd leaving the conference room.

He followed her until she disappeared and thought of Claire. He hadn't seen or heard from her in so long, he wondered if she'd moved on. *It would be nice if she'd come out and say it.* Thurman caught up with Emerson where the conference sponsors had their product displays.

"Crazy last night, huh?" Emerson said.

It hadn't been the first time Thurman had been assaulted in a hospital. He shook his head in disgust. "Gun-toting lunatics are everywhere these days. We were lucky. It could have been a lot worse. You look beat. Carmen told me you two operated all night."

"We had a few breaks, but the ICU nurses kept us busy between cases. Some of our patients are train wrecks."

"C'mon, I'll buy you a drink." They followed the music and laughter toward the hotel entrance and entered the bar adjacent to the lobby. A five o'clock happy hour crowd filled the room. Walls of televisions played a variety of muted sports channels and music streamed over speakers in the background. Every table and booth appeared occupied, so Emerson pulled out a barstool. "This okay?"

"Sure." Thurman sat next to him and scooted closer to the polished mahogany bar.

"What can I get you, gentlemen?" asked the bartender.

"Vodka and tonic," Thurman said.

"A pint of your best lager." Emerson reached for a fistful of peanuts.

"What did you think of the symposium?"

"Interesting, I guess," he said while stifling a yawn. "Ask me when I haven't been up for thirty-six hours."

"Yeah, I get that," Mark said. He knew the life all too well. "I thought you were going to sprain your neck with all that head bobbing."

"Notice how I perked up when your research partner took the stage."

"I noticed."

"You actually work with her?"

Thurman nodded. "She's brilliant."

Emerson sipped his beer, then added, "She has a career in modeling if she ever gets tired of research."

"That's not her style. She'd be bored to death."

"I'm just saying." Emerson glanced at the mirror behind the bar and followed the reflection of a woman approaching from across the room. His eyes widened. "Speak of the devil."

The bartender returned with their drinks, blocking Thurman's view. "Who, Noreen?"

"There she is."

Thurman turned around on his barstool. She waved while weaving through the crowd. "I asked her to join us."

"Genius move," Emerson said with a wink. "It's about time you faced the facts. How long has it been since you heard from Claire?"

Thurman tensed at the sound of Claire's name. It hurt to be tuned out of her life after all they'd been through. "Let's talk about something else."

"You don't mind if I chat up Dr. Chase?" Emerson said.

"Be my guest," he replied as Noreen stepped up beside him.

Thurman stood and gave her a customary double cheek kiss. "Great job today. I tried to congratulate you earlier but couldn't get through the crowd of admirers."

In high heels she almost stood at Thurman's eye level. She brushed blonde hair over her shoulders and looked directly at him. "It helps when you have a brilliant colleague assisting." She stepped forward and smoothed the lapels of his jacket. "You bring out the best in that jacket." Then she leaned close and whispered, "Who sat next to you this afternoon?"

He gave a half grin. "You mean Dr. Black?"

"Does Dr. Black have a first name?"

"It's Carmen, why?"

"Just wondering."

Thurman gave a tight-lipped smile. "She's an ER resident. We just met yesterday."

"Be careful, darling, you're vulnerable."

He ignored the comment. "Can I get you a drink?"

She remained close and straightened his tie. "Not right now. I'm meeting a friend, but I'm free later." Steve raised his eyebrows.

"I'd love to, but I'm taking it easy tonight. The ER's been busy lately."

"I'll say," Steve interrupted. "Aren't you going to introduce me to your colleague?"

"Pardon me. Noreen Chase, this is my cousin and orthopedic partner, Dr. Steven Emerson."

He slid between them like someone cutting in line. "Please, call me Steve, and the pleasure is all mine. Great presentation today."

Noreen smiled and glanced around his shoulder at Thurman. "You two are cousins?"

"Our mothers are sisters," Thurman said.

"How lovely. Oh, if you gentlemen will excuse me, there's someone I need to talk to." She moved Emerson to the side and kissed Thurman's cheek. "Watch out for Dr. Black."

His face flushed as she sauntered between the tables. *Damn, I meant to ask if she knows Drake.*

Emerson followed her retreat in the mirror as he sat at the bar and nursed his beer. "Oh my God, she's stunning—drop-dead gorgeous." Every ten seconds he glanced at Noreen's reflection in the mirror. "Who's she's talking to?"

Thurman followed his gaze. She sat in profile at a table across the room, talking to a man in his late thirties or early forties with reddish-blond hair and a deep bronze tan. "No idea."

"Dude looks like he just got back from the Keys. Probably owns a tanning bed."

"Who cares?" Thurman sipped his drink and watched the man stand and stride from the bar.

Emerson glanced at Noreen's reflection for several minutes, then changed the subject. He looked away from the mirror and turned toward Thurman. "I'm worried about Drake. He's circling the drain."

"I've seen worse who survived." Thurman sipped his vodka.

"It's not looking good. He spiked fevers all night, so Naylor took him back to the OR. He found another bowel leak and a bleeder."

"That explains the fevers," said Thurman.

"What's up with that freak trying to hunt him down? What the hell is going on?"

"You want my opinion?" Thurman motioned for the check. "Someone chased him. He crashed. They came after him when he reached the hospital."

"If they're trying to kill him, why not do it at the crash site?"

"Maybe they want him alive, maybe he has something."

"Like what?"

Thurman shrugged. "Money, information, who knows?"

"His wife says he's reckless, a risk-taker. Always has been. She's been begging him to get rid of the motorcycle for years."

"How do you know that?"

"I overheard the cops questioning her when I checked on him last night."

"Have they contacted you?"

"Not yet."

"Get ready for it."

"Why?"

"They'll want to talk to everyone who's made contact with the crash victim. You look tired, ready to head home?"

Emerson stifled another yawn. "Whenever you are."

"You've had a beer and no sleep, I'm driving." Thurman left a tip and looked over at Noreen. She was alone at her table and motioned for them to join her. Steve led the way.

"I'll take you up on that drink," she said.

Before Thurman could respond, Emerson sat in the chair vacated by the man. "Excellent."

Thurman took a seat.

"What happened to your friend?" Emerson asked.

"He had to get back to his wife."

"Darn, that's too bad," said Steve, snapping his fingers. "But his loss is our gain."

Noreen smiled.

"We can't stay long," Thurman said. "I have to get this guy home before he falls asleep."

"Speak for yourself, cuz. I just got my second wind."

Noreen reached out and touched Thurman's cheek. "Just one drink, to keep me company. I'm meeting someone in half an hour for dinner. You don't want me to get lonely, do you?"

"Loneliness isn't an option while I'm around." Emerson took out a pen and wrote his number on a napkin. "If you ever feel that way, call this number." Thurman pinched the bridge of his nose while shaking his head.

Noreen smiled then unsnapped her purse and dropped the napkin inside.

"What would you like?" Emerson motioned for a waiter.

"White wine, please," she replied.

"Do I know your friend?" Thurman asked.

"I don't think so, why?"

"Just curious. Is he a celebrity or corporate exec?"

Noreen laughed. "No, he's just a friend. Why do you say that?"

"Because I know you."

"You don't know me that well." Noreen removed a compact from her purse and checked her makeup. Her ruby earrings perfectly matched the color of her necklace and nail polish. Apparently satisfied, she closed it and deposited it back into her handbag.

"Are you staying here?" Emerson asked.

"Just tonight."

"Perrier for me," Thurman said to the waiter, then pointed across the table. "A pint of the draft lager and a prosecco for Dr. Chase."

Noreen frowned. "Water? Mark, you're so straitlaced."

"Someone's got to drive. Do me a favor and give me a copy of your PowerPoint presentation from this afternoon. I want to use it for an upcoming department lecture."

"I'll get it to you. By the way, I may be leaving on a trip soon."

"Where?"

"Tahiti, I think."

Thurman's head tilted. "You don't know?"

"I haven't decided. Want to come?"

"Tempting."

Steve looked up. "I'll carry your bags."

Noreen reached out and placed her hand on his wrist. "I need someone to do more than that."

Emerson's neck flushed. "Whatever you want."

Thurman kicked him under the table and looked at Noreen. "When are you leaving?"

"Not sure."

Thurman leaned back in his chair and crossed his arms. "You're not sure about a lot of things these days."

"It's complicated. I'll call you tomorrow with details. I'll know more then."

Thurman nodded. *What is going on? Is she in some kind of trouble?*

After pleasantries they talked about future experiments and research projects. When the waiter returned with their drinks, the conversation drifted to non-work-related subjects. Emerson's eyes widened when she began discussing football and the upcoming college basketball season.

"I wouldn't have guessed that a nanomaterial engineer would be such a big Duke fan," Emerson said.

"Really, why not?" she replied.

"I don't know. It's unusual."

"Stick around, I'm full of surprises."

That you are. Thurman checked his watch and cleared his throat. "I think it's time for us to hit the road. What do you say, Steve?"

"Why? We haven't finished our drinks."

"She has a dinner date, remember?"

Emerson frowned. "Some other time, then, soon."

"Come on," Thurman said as he stood.

Emerson looked at Noreen. "Can we get together for dinner sometime?"

She sipped her wine and smiled. "Maybe."

Thurman stood. "I'll call you tomorrow. Great presentation." As they were about to leave, he turned to his cousin and pulled keys from his pocket. "I'll meet you at my truck. I need to talk to Noreen for a minute."

"That antique shouldn't be hard to spot." Then he looked at Noreen. "I'll call you soon if you don't mind."

"Not at all. Mark has my number."

Emerson grinned and waved as he left.

Thurman sat back down. "Do you know anyone by the name of Yuri Drake?"

She looked up at him quizzically. "Should I?"

"He works at Angstrom. I thought you may have run into each other."

"It's a big place." She started to take a sip of her wine but set it down and stared at him. "Why do you ask?"

"Just curious, since you both work at the same place. He was in the worst motorcycle accident I've seen in a while." He stood and started to leave.

"Wait." Noreen rose from the table. "He's your patient? How is he?"

"I thought you didn't know him," said Thurman.

"I don't, I'm just concerned about a fellow employee, that's all." She sat back down, eyeing him closely.

Thurman pulled the chair next to her and leaned in. "Look, Noreen, if you know something, you need to tell me. Some psycho came looking for him and pulled a gun on me. I need to know if there are going to be any more." He took out his phone and opened a video. "What do you know about this?" It showed his hand releasing the sphere. The camera followed it to the ceiling. It recycled in an endless loop, hand opening, sphere rising to the ceiling.

Noreen's jaw tightened. "Where did you get that?"

"Yuri's motorcycle jacket. What can you tell me about it?"

"Delete it. If anyone sees that video, your life will be in danger."

"It's already in danger."

"This is serious, Mark. You're in over your head."

"Then tell me what I've gotten myself into."

"I can't. Just give it to me. I'll keep it safe. You're better off not being involved."

Thurman laughed. "Not a chance."

Noreen's eyes went wide. There was something in them he'd never seen before. Fear.

"If you're not going to give it to me, then get rid of it."

"Seems to me like you're the one who's in over their head," Thurman said.

"I have to go," she said, getting up. She bent down and kissed his cheek. Then she whispered in his ear, "Be careful." She turned away and walked to the elevator. The doors opened, and she disappeared.

Thurman walked outside into the cool night air. Steve sat in the passenger seat of his vintage pickup parked curbside.

"C'mon, let's get out of here."

"What was that all about?"

"Nothing important."

"Look, there she is," Emerson said, pointing at the hotel entrance. Despite the evening twilight, the striking figure of Noreen Chase was unmistakable. She paraded past several parked cars and got into the passenger seat of a large European sedan with tinted windows. Her long legs moved together as she pulled them into the vehicle. The valet closed the door behind her, and the car pulled away. "Who's driving?"

"I can't see," said Thurman.

"That dude in the bar must have come back."

"Don't be disappointed. She's not your type."

"Oh, yes she is. She's definitely my type."

Thurman checked in both directions as they reached the intersection, then turned right. "Trust me. You don't want to get mixed up with that one."

"How well do you know this woman? I saw the way she came up to you in the bar. It looked like more than just *lab buddies*."

"We keep it professional." Thurman turned onto the entrance ramp for the Durham Freeway heading south, then merged with traffic.

CHAPTER 7
THE GARDEN OF GOOD AND EVIL

EARLY THE NEXT morning Sergeant Hairston parked his car near the gift shop at the Sarah P. Duke Gardens and buttoned his navy blue mackintosh. Dark gray clouds blocked the sun. A steady bombardment of rain blurred the windshield. He grit his teeth, anticipating a cold, wet walk to the crime scene.

He cursed the weather for the tenth time as he opened the car door and raised his umbrella. The rain slackened to a steady drip, pattering on the fabric and spilling from its edges. He avoided puddles in a futile attempt to keep his cuffs dry. *The watch commander said to go to the koi pond.* He followed the path and descended a flight of steps into a circular graveled area dominated by a seven-foot-diameter dogwood flower sculpted from stone. He paused to read the inscription at its base, a quote by Francis Bacon: "God Almighty first planted a garden. And indeed it is the purest of human pleasures." The detective doubted if he'd agree with Sir Francis in a few minutes.

He followed directions to the pond, walking down a gravel lane lined with dripping elephant ear plants. Twenty yards in the distance yellow tape marked off a crime scene.

From the other side of the barrier a younger man in a suit and rain-coat called out, "Jerry, over here."

Hairston kept his left hand in his overcoat pocket and marched toward him, dodging puddles. He handed Detective John Floyd his umbrella as he ducked under the tape. "Thanks."

"No problem, sir."

Hairston reclaimed his umbrella but stood close enough that it could shield them both. "Congratulations on making the homicide unit. Is this your first assignment?"

"Yes, sir."

That's just great. I'm stuck with a greenhorn on a high-profile case like this. Hairston studied the area, memorizing details. Through the pond's rippled surface, he observed orange-and-cream-colored fish, the size of his forearm, swimming beneath Amazon water lilies whose turned-up edges resembled floating green cake pans. Patches of aquatic sedges and rushes grew at the water's edge. Irises, milkweed, and other species thrived even this late in November. The setting looked fresh and clean except for the ivory arm protruding from the vegetation on the opposite side of the pond, twenty yards away. At first glance it could have been part of a marble sculpture. The hand's fingers were barely touching the water. A fish broke the surface and nibbled at a fingertip, perhaps attracted by the ruby nail polish.

"Any ID?" Hairston asked.

"Not yet. I'd guess early thirties, maybe thirty-five."

"Has the crime scene been locked down?"

"The CSI team has been here since before sunrise. They packed up and left just before you got here. The ME is on the way to pack up the body."

"Hold this again." He handed Floyd the umbrella and struggled to squeeze his wet hands into a pair of latex gloves, tearing a wrist cuff in the process. Hairston ignored the damage and walked around the edge of the pond, carefully moving branches out of his way. Floyd followed with the umbrella. It was obvious there had been activity in the area. Marsh grass lay flat where the crime scene investigators had performed their work. On the opposite side of the pond, he moved branches aside and abruptly stopped. She lay facedown, naked in the tall grass. The dorsal half of her body appeared statue white while the ventral half displayed shades of deep purple. Lividity. She'd been dead for hours.

"No ligature marks on the wrists or ankles." He gently pulled the platinum blonde hair from her face. "Or her neck. Any stab wounds or bullet holes?"

Floyd shook his head. "No, sir."

"So, no obvious cause of death. We'll let the ME earn his paycheck this week," Hairston replied. "Any sign of her clothes? She didn't just walk in here buck naked."

"We haven't found any yet."

"Get a diver out here and check the pond. Any sign of her purse or a phone?"

Floyd shook his head. "No, sir, just the body."

"I don't see any security cameras around."

"Just at the entrance," said Floyd.

"Let's go talk to the campus cops. Maybe they can shed some light."

Hairston began walking up the path. After several steps, he stopped and squatted.

"What is it?"

"Hand me a plastic bag." He reached out with the stylus of his pen and snagged a small silver object from the gravel.

"It looks like one of those things that holds an earring in place," said Floyd.

"A butterfly nut."

"A what?"

"That's what they're called. Look around for an earring to go with it. Did you notice earrings?"

"No, sir," said Floyd.

They returned to the body. Hairston squatted and once again gently pulled back her hair, this time until it revealed an unadorned pierced ear. "I want to see the other one. Help me turn her head." The body felt stiff as a mannequin. They had to roll her onto her back to view the other side of her face. The lobe held a dazzling ruby in a silver setting surrounded by diamond chips. Hairston got out his phone and took several pictures, then looked at Floyd. "Start looking for the other one. I'll call CSI. Maybe they found it."

CHAPTER 8
NIGHTMARES

SWEAT BEADED THURMAN'S FOREHEAD. Damp sheets clung heavily to his body. A nightmare, some variant of PTSD, jolted him awake. His phone displayed 3:50 a.m. He sat up and swung his legs off the side of the bed and reached for the light switch. *It's a dream, just a dream*, he told himself. Iraq and Afghanistan had been tough, but they paled when it came to the apocalypse of cancer and the perpetual terror of a relapse. *Please, Lord, not again, never again.*

He stepped into the bathroom and reached for the running clothes he'd laid out the night before. His reflection in the mirror above the sink revealed a rugged, forty-year-old body with more scars than he cared to count. Some were the result of injuries, others from surgeries. He turned at an angle. The four-inch scar on his right hip reminded him of the titanium rod inserted into his femur after chemo and radiation destroyed the final Ewing's sarcoma cell. It had almost killed him —the cancer, and the cure.

When they'd been together, Claire witnessed the writhing and heard his anguished dream-state cries. Once, she made an appointment for him to see a therapist. He'd refused to go.

Maybe if I'd gone we'd still be together. He stared at himself in the mirror. *Nah, to hell with that. Best not to dwell on the past. Maybe Steve's right. Maybe it's time to move on.*

There would be no getting back to sleep. He put on his running gear, grabbed the sphere from the nightstand drawer, then stepped on the bathroom scale. *Whoa.* It read twenty-two pounds less than yesterday. He released the sphere and his weight returned to normal. *Maybe it will help me run faster.* He stepped up on the edge of the bathtub and retrieved it from the ceiling. *I'd better not drop this thing.* He went to the kitchen, grabbed a water bottle from the refrigerator, and downed half before placing it on the island. Before leaving he duct-taped the sphere to the palm of his left hand and clenched his fist. After stretching, he exited through the back door and took off. Running always helped make problems feel farther away.

It was almost six o'clock when he returned and pressed the timer on his watch, then did a double take—a new PR, over twelve and a half minutes better than his previous record. An endorphin high surged through his body until the light framing the back door grabbed his attention.

The door automatically locked when closed. He remembered pulling it shut. He approached it, climbed the steps, and crossed the deck. Splinters lay on the threshold where the doorjamb had been sprung. He entered and listened. Silence. He crept into the laundry room and opened the handgun safe in the cabinet above the washing machine. He unwrapped the tape and exchanged the sphere for a Glock 19, then locked the door. A one-man house-clearing operation violated everything he'd been trained to do, but he had no time to wait for backup. Holding out the gun, he peeked into the kitchen. Every light had been turned on and the room was ransacked. Drawers lay on the floor or were partially open, their contents strewn everywhere. He froze when footsteps came from the hallway, followed by the creak of the front door opening. Within seconds a car engine started. Thurman sprinted into the great room and peered from the edge of the curtains. The car pulled away from the curb. Taillights disappeared as a large black sedan drove through the streetlight and turned the corner at the end of the block. He couldn't read the license plate. It looked like the car Noreen climbed into the night before, but he couldn't be sure. He thought of the video and her reaction to it. *Damn it. Did she send someone to steal the sphere?*

The bedroom looked worse than the kitchen. All his clothes lay in piles on the floor. Shoes and personal items were tossed haphazardly across the room. Every drawer was pulled and dumped. He calmly searched the rest of the house and convinced himself no one remained.

Before he could call the police, his phone rang. An unknown number appeared. He considered not answering it but given the situation, he tapped the screen. "Hello."

"Oh, thank God, you've gotta help me." Desperation resonated in the plea.

"Steve?"

"Yeah, it's me."

"What's going on?"

"She's dead."

Thurman held the phone between his neck and shoulder while bending over to remove his running shoes and shorts. "Which patient?"

"Not a patient. Noreen . . . Noreen is dead."

Thurman stopped as he walked through the living room, then he went to sit on the ottoman. His thoughts became scrambled. "What did you say?"

"They think I killed her!"

"Noreen is . . . dead?" He recalled their conversation in the bar when she denied knowing Yuri and her abrupt travel plans, then fought back the sick feeling expanding in his gut.

"That's what the cops are saying. Hell, I don't know. I don't remember."

"They think you . . . did it?"

"It's insane. The cops practically broke my door down and hauled my ass to the station."

"But why? You hardly know her. I dropped you off before seven o'clock. You went to bed."

"She called me," Steve said.

"Damn it. What did you do?"

"Nothing. We had a few drinks and went back to her room. I fell asleep and woke up alone. That's all I know. Look, I don't have time to explain. This cop's telling me to hang up. Just get down here, please."

"Where are you?"

"The police station."

"Which one?"

"Durham. You work with these guys, talk some sense into them."

"I'm not a member of the Durham force. I'm auxiliary Raleigh PD."

"Call your detective friend, Ingram."

Detective Jackson Ingram was a senior member of the robbery and homicide division of the Raleigh Police Department. He commanded the SWAT team where Thurman served as medical officer. They'd been close friends for several years after Thurman operated on him following a line-of-duty shooting.

Thurman processed the information. "I'll call him as soon as we hang up. For right now, get a hold of yourself. Sit tight and keep your mouth shut until your lawyer gets there."

"Lawyer? I don't have a lawyer."

"You're about to."

The line went dead.

"Hello? Steve, you there?" Silence.

Thurman called Ingram's number.

Ingram answered on the fourth ring. "It's a little damn early for a phone call. This better be good."

"It's not, but it's important."

"All right. What's going on?"

"Who do you know at the Durham PD?"

"I have a few contacts. Why?"

"Remember my cousin Steve Emerson? I introduced you a couple of months ago."

"Tall guy, black hair?"

"That's him. He just called me from the Durham PD lockup."

"He's in jail?" Ingram let out a chuckle. "What did he do? Pick up a hooker?"

"This isn't funny. They think he killed someone."

"What? You serious?"

"They have him downtown in Durham."

"Sorry about the joke. Give me some background and I'll make a few calls. Jerry Hairston runs their homicide unit. He's reasonable."

"I know, we've met."

"I read about the ER shooter. You didn't piss him off did you?"

"I don't think so."

"That's a first. Now, what happened with your cousin?"

Thurman quickly summarized the events at the bar and the drive home.

Ingram grunted. "What's his story?"

"I don't know all the details yet."

"I'll call Hairston. Meet me at the Durham station. Has he been detained for questioning or have charges been filed?"

"He didn't say."

"I'll see you there in an hour. We'll get to the bottom of this."

"Jack, there's one more thing. Someone broke into my house during my run this morning."

"Jesus, what's going on with you?"

Thurman sat and rubbed his eyes. "I wish I knew. I couldn't sleep, so I went for a 0400 run and got back just after six. When I got home I noticed someone had crowbarred the back door. I got my gun and started searching the house."

"By yourself? Did you call for backup?"

"There wasn't time. I heard someone run out the front door as I came in from the garage."

"That was dumb. What were you thinking? If he had a partner you'd be dead. You can't clear a house by yourself. We've gone over that a hundred times."

Thurman exhaled. "I got it, it wasn't protocol. By the time I reached the living room, their taillights were halfway down the block. I couldn't see the license plate."

"One guy or two?"

"Not sure. I didn't see anyone."

"Strange timing. It sounds like they waited until you left the house. Someone must be watching you."

"That's comforting."

"I'll send some guys to look into it after we get done. One thing at a time. Don't touch anything and meet me at the Durham precinct."

"I'll see you there." Thurman retraced his path to the laundry room and opened the handgun safe. The sphere remained stuck to the top. He went into the kitchen to finish the water he'd started before his run. Numerous objects cluttered the surface of the island, but no bottle. He checked the floor and the countertops and shook his head. *I left it right here.* He grabbed another water from the fridge then stepped through the laundry room and into the garage, where he grabbed a claw hammer and three sixteen-penny nails. He went to the broken back door and pounded them through the stile into the jamb. *That ought to hold it.* He headed to the shower, locked the bathroom door, and placed the Glock by the sink. He didn't need any more surprises today.

———

A police officer escorted Thurman to a room separated from an interrogation room by a two-way mirror. Unobserved, he watched Steve, who sat at a metal table facing him. He looked twenty years older. The fluorescent lights gave his uncombed hair a grayish tint, and his dehydrated skin had the appearance of parchment. Bags sagged under his eyes. Thurman recalled the lyrics to the early eighties tune *Maneater* and wished he'd given his cousin a stronger Noreen Chase warning. He turned at the sound of voices in the hallway. The door handle rattled, and two Black detectives entered. The first stood a little under six feet tall with a medium build. His tight military haircut and his dark suit blended with the shadows. Thurman immediately recognized him—Jerry Hairston. Jackson Ingram, dressed in black SWAT BDUs, a couple of inches taller and looking as fit as an NFL strong safety, followed behind.

"Mark, I believe you've met Detective Hairston, senior investigator for Durham PD's homicide unit. I've given him some of your background."

"We're acquainted. I didn't expect to see you again so soon," Hairston said.

"Me neither. Thanks for arranging this." Thurman extended his hand.

Hairston gripped it with authority. "It's the least I could do for Ingram's SWAT team medical officer and a former SEAL. Why didn't you say something the other night?" The detective pointed to the gold police shield clipped to the left side of Thurman's belt.

"I guess the guard with the bullet in his belly distracted me." *Among other things.*

Hairston nodded. "Understandable."

"And just for the record, I'm not a SEAL, I served as their orthopedic surgeon for a couple of years. I put them back together and kept them mission ready."

"He may not wear a trident, but they trained him well. He can outshoot any cop, and you don't want to meet him in a dark alley," Ingram said. "I guarantee it."

Thurman shook his head from side to side. "He exaggerates."

"You sure handled the situation admirably the other night," Hairston replied. "I'm just sorry you have to put up with Ingram all the time."

Thurman smiled. "You know him well."

"We go back a few years."

"So, what's the situation?" Ingram asked as all three faced the two-way mirror. On the opposite side Emerson sat facing them with hands clasped and head bowed as if in prayer.

Hairston pulled out a pen and pocket-sized notebook and opened it. "We received a call at 4:50 this morning from the Duke campus police saying they'd found a body in the Sarah P. Duke Gardens. The victim has been identified as Noreen Jacqueline Chase, thirty-five years old, single, employed by a company called Angstrom Industries. You mentioned you worked with her."

"We partnered on a research project."

"Interesting," said Hairston.

"What's that supposed to mean?"

"Nothing. When's the last time you saw her?"

"Yesterday evening. I attended the symposium where she presented our latest research findings. Steve was there. We had a drink with her at about five at the hotel bar. We left afterward, and I drove him home."

"That's what Dr. Emerson told us," Hairston said. "What happened after that?"

"I made dinner, watched some Friday night college football, and went to bed about ten thirty."

"You don't have much of a life."

"I like it that way. Work keeps me busy."

"Anything else? Did you have any contact with Ms. Chase or Mr. Emerson later that night?" Hairston asked.

"It's Dr. Emerson." Thurman shook his head. "That was it. We had SWAT training scheduled for eight this morning, so I went to bed at a decent time. I got up early and went for a run. Emerson called around six thirty."

"Anything else?" asked Hairston.

"Tell him about your morning visitors," said Ingram.

"Does that concern the Durham PD?" said Thurman.

Hairston looked from Ingram back to Thurman. "Why don't you let me make that decision?"

Thurman repeated the events of earlier that morning.

"Nothing stolen?"

"I didn't take inventory."

"Why would someone break into your house?" asked Hairston.

"Good question, detective," said Thurman. *Probably because I have the sphere.*

Hairston stroked his chin for a moment. "Let me see if I can put this together. An armed intruder invades an emergency room where you're on duty, looking for your patient. The next night a woman you work with winds up dead, and a few hours ago your house was broken into. What the hell is going on with you? What's the connection?"

Thurman remained silent. A vision of Noreen's exquisite face appeared in his imagination, soon replaced by a feeling of profound sadness. *Dear Lord, did my having the sphere lead to her death?*

"Did you report the break-in to the police?" Hairston asked.

"Just Ingram."

"Do you mind if our guys take a look around the scene?"

"You mean my house?"

"Yeah, any problem with that?"

Thurman shook his head. "I'll take you there when we finish."

"What about Emerson?" Ingram asked.

"He claims to have met the victim yesterday, as Dr. Thurman just corroborated. She called him last night about nine thirty." Hairston looked at Thurman. "Any idea how she got his number?"

"He wrote it on a napkin for her at the bar."

"At the Washington Duke Inn?" Hairston asked.

"Correct."

Hairston continued. "He claims she called him, and they made plans to get together later that evening."

"She called him?" asked Thurman. *Why would she do that?*

Hairston nodded. "According to Emerson's phone, she called at nine twenty-eight. He said she asked him to meet her at Cody-Q's near the ballpark on Blackwell Street at ten thirty. Because you drove him home, his car was still in the parking lot at the inn. He called for a car and met her at C-Q's. That checks out. They had a few drinks and danced until about midnight when she offered him a ride back to the hotel to pick up his car. When they arrived, she invited him to her room."

Thurman tilted his head.

"Once in the room she went to the bathroom for a few minutes. When she came out Emerson says they had sex."

"Then what?" Ingram asked.

"He claims he fell asleep."

Thurman interjected. "The guy was on call the night before and had been up for almost thirty-six hours."

Hairston made a note and continued. "He says he got up to use the bathroom around 2:30 and noticed she wasn't in bed. He looked around, but she'd left the room. He needed to be at the hospital in a couple of hours, so he got dressed and drove home. That's where we found him a few hours ago."

"How did his car get there?" asked Ingram.

Thurman spoke up. "He drove it there from the hospital to attend the conference. After we had drinks at the bar, he looked dog-tired, and I didn't want him driving home so I gave him a ride. We left his car in the hotel lot."

"What did you find in the woman's room?" Ingram said.

"Clothes, makeup, and a variety of drugs and paraphernalia scattered on the bathroom counter."

"What about the victim? Is her tox report back?"

"Not for a couple of days."

"Emerson's?"

"His BAL is legal," said Hairston. "He consented to a tox screen. It's pending."

"Why are you holding him? There's no crime in going to a beautiful woman's hotel room at her invitation," Thurman said.

"Drugs in the bathroom, and he's the last one to see our murder victim alive."

"Someone planted the drugs."

"That's what they all say," said Hairston.

"What about her clothes?"

Hairston raised an eyebrow. "You can't make this stuff up. They were found a few hours later in the Garden for Peace."

"Why am I not surprised?" Ingram scratched his grizzled chin.

"I kid you not, that's the name of the garden. Chase's driver's license and a room key were in her purse. We found Emerson's phone number on the napkin you mentioned. We ran the number, woke him up, and brought him in for questioning."

"Wait a minute," Thurman said. "There's no way Steve kills this woman, drags her body across campus, then leaves it in the garden."

"Someone did. You just told me he had his car there and she invited him to her room."

"There must be fifty security cameras on the hotel grounds. Have you checked them?"

"Standard procedure," said Hairston. "Look, I didn't say he killed her. At this point in the investigation, we're gathering information. He's an intelligent guy who's big and strong enough to lift and carry a body. He could have loaded her up, driven to the garden, and dumped her."

"Or given her the lethal dose once they got there," Ingram added.

Thurman glared. "Whose side are you on?"

"The truth," said Ingram. "Don't get testy, I'm just thinking out loud."

"That's my cousin in there. He didn't kill anyone, so start thinking about who did." Thurman walked to the two-way observation mirror. His cousin sat with his head on the table. "This is ridiculous. Steve's not a liar, and he's no killer. After he fell asleep, she got up and left the room. Someone else killed her."

"I hope you're right, for your cousin's sake."

"What about the other guy?" Thurman asked.

"What other guy?"

"Noreen met a guy in the bar and had a drink with him. After he left, she invited us to join her. She said he was married and had to go home."

"Description?" Hairston readied his pen and notepad.

"I only saw him from across the room." Thurman gave the details.

Hairston repeated, "About six feet, two hundred pounds, reddish-blond hair with a dark tan. People with red hair don't usually have dark tans. Did it look fake?"

"Looked real to me."

"Freckles?"

Thurman shook his head. "Negative."

"Weird. Anything else?"

"When Steve and I were in my car leaving the hotel, we saw Noreen come out and get in the passenger seat of a big black BMW sedan. It drove off right in front of us."

"I'm guessing you didn't get a look at the driver."

Thurman shook his head. "Tinted windows, too far away, it was getting dark. Steve will confirm."

"License plate?"

Thurman shook his head. "Never crossed my mind to look."

Hairston tucked the notepad and pen back into his jacket pocket. Then he put his hands in his trouser pockets and stared at Thurman. "I spoke with Dr. Mason yesterday."

"What did he say?"

"He said the gunman asked where the guy who'd been in the motorcycle accident was."

"That's how he knew to come to Trauma Bay 1."

"He also said the shooter asked for you."

"What?" Thurman stepped back. "For me? I never saw that guy before in my life."

"Interesting, isn't it? Now your house gets broken into. What is it about you that's so interesting to this guy?"

"I wish I knew."

"That makes two of us."

A noise came from the interrogation room. The three observers turned their attention to the two-way mirror. The door opened and a police officer escorted a tall, handsome gentleman dressed in a tailored three-piece suit. The man in the suit introduced himself to Emerson and placed a business card on the table. "I'm an attorney, Mark White-house. I specialize in criminal defense. A friend, Mark Thurman, called and said you could use my help. If you're interested, I'll take your case."

Emerson rose and steadied himself, then shook the lawyer's hand. "Thank you."

Whitehouse turned toward the mirror and waved. "That's all, folks. Charge him or release him. No more questions unless I'm present. Understood?"

Ingram and Hairston looked at each other, then turned to Thurman. Hairston's back stiffened. His hands went to his hips. "Son of a bitch. Did you call that shyster?"

Thurman imitated the detective's posture and stood his ground. "Damn right I did. That's my cousin you're holding, and Whitehouse is the best defense attorney in the city."

Hairston massaged his temples, then exhaled. "All right, there's nothing else to be done here." He opened the door and spoke to the officer standing in the hallway, then returned. "I told him to release Dr. Emerson, but he's to remain in the city. If he tries to leave without my permission, I'll have him arrested. Understood?"

Thurman breathed a sigh of relief but kept his arms crossed. "Understood."

"He's still a suspect. Now, if you don't have any objection, I'd like to take a look at your house."

"Sure, let's go."

———

Thurman leaned against the kitchen island among the scattered utensils and broken dishware. Ingram stood next to him while Hairston and two officers combed the house for anything the intruder may have left behind.

Hairston called from the master bedroom. "Hey, doc, do you have pierced ears?"

Thurman glanced at Ingram, then replied, "No."

"Come here. I've got something to show you."

When they entered the room, the detective had his phone out, taking pictures of the contents of a dresser drawer. "What is it?" asked Ingram.

Hairston reached his gloved hand into the drawer and produced a silver and red object pinched between his thumb and index finger. "Take a look at this."

"It looks like an earring," said Thurman. "It's not mine. I've never seen it before."

Hairston pinched the post and spun it, displaying a single brilliant red gemstone haloed by bright silver and sparkling clear stones. "I'm betting this is a two-carat, near-perfect ruby set in platinum and diamonds."

"Maybe," said Ingram. "It could be silver. The stone could be garnet or fake."

"No, it's ruby and platinum. Those are real diamonds, not zirconium. I'm sure."

"Since when did you become a jeweler?" asked Ingram.

Hairston took out his phone and flipped through several pictures. He found one and brought the phone over for Thurman and Ingram to view. "This is the other one. We had it appraised."

Thurman's eyes narrowed. His jaw clenched. "I've never seen that earring before."

"Wow," said Ingram.

"Another interesting coincidence." Hairston enlarged the image. The lifeless face of Noreen Chase looked back at them. Her blonde hair fell behind her ears. The right earlobe was undecorated while the left held a brilliant red earring exactly like the one in Hairston's hand. "I'm betting this is a perfect match. Gentlemen, this is a crime scene. Please vacate while I call CSI."

"That earring was planted by whoever broke into my house." Thurman folded his arms across his chest. "I'm being framed."

"I'm going to go over every inch of this place to see if they left anything else. If you want, I'll get a warrant."

"That won't be necessary." *The sphere isn't in the house.*

"You already know the drill, but I'm going to say it anyway. Don't stray too far, and keep me informed of your travel plans, Dr. Thurman."

CHAPTER 9
NEUROSURGICAL ICU
ROUNDS

THURMAN FROWNED at the text message. *This can't be good.* The chairman of orthopedics wanted to see him in his office first thing Sunday morning. Thurman felt like he was being summoned to the principal's office. Harold Codman Vogler, MD, MBA, had been appointed the department head when the new hospital opened six months ago, replacing Thurman's longtime mentor and friend, Martin Mile.

Thurman entered the large corner office. Vogler motioned to a seat on the opposite side of his desk while speaking into his phone. The Sunday edition of the *Durham Herald Sun* lay on the desktop, displaying a front-page exposé about the Duke University murder and the ER shooting.

Thurman glanced at the surroundings. Diplomas and framed academic certificates covered the walls along with photographs of Vogler with various high-profile politicians and celebrities. He spotted no images of wife and family, then recalled rumors of a messy divorce. As the phone conversation went on, Thurman's ire grew. The Sunday summons had already irked him, then to be ignored while Vogler talked on the phone ticked him off even more. He took a deep breath, exhaled slowly, and recalled one of his favorite quotes. *You have power over your mind—not outside events. Realize this and you will find strength.*

Vogler's blinking habit had become the stuff of medical student lore. Thurman watched for it while observing the phone conversation. There it was. He counted six or seven rapid-fire flutters. Thurman smiled.

Vogler blinked another volley, then switched the phone to the other ear. "I agree, it's the right course of action." His head bobbed up and down in the favored motion of sycophants. "We have to get out in front of this . . . yes, of course. Decisive action. The medical system is lucky to have someone with your experience and leadership. Thank you for your input. I'll see you at next week's board meeting. You do the same." He hung up, straightened his tie, and placed his folded hands on the desk.

"So," Vogler began. "I guess you've seen this?" He shoved the newspaper in Mark's direction.

Thurman nodded without looking at it.

"Well, what do you have to say about it?" Vogler asked.

"I've had better days."

"That's it?"

"What do you want me to say?"

Vogler leaned forward. "Let me summarize things from my perspective. A lunatic enters this facility looking for you. He assaults one of your chief residents and shoots a security officer. Your research partner is murdered the following day, and your cousin, a surgeon employed by this institution, is a prime suspect—and all you can say is you've had better days?"

Thurman glared. "Noreen Chase's death is a tragedy, but Steve had nothing to do with it."

"I spoke to the police this morning." Vogler spat the words at him. "They tell me neither you nor Dr. Emerson are allowed to leave the Raleigh-Durham area. I have two surgeons involved in a murder investigation who aren't allowed to leave town."

Thurman felt his heart rate increasing. *You are pathetic, Vogler. You're more worried about your image than your people.* His fingers interlocked as he leaned forward. "Get this straight, Hal. Steve and I had nothing to do with her death or anything illegal. Am I clear on that? We are innocent."

Vogler scoffed and threw his hands in the air. "What about the police finding evidence in your home implicating you in the murder investigation? Who am I supposed to believe?"

Thurman's eyes went to the newspaper for the first time. *Would Hairston leak that to the press?* "Excuse me, what?"

"It's right here in black and white." He flipped the paper around and fingered the headline, LOCAL DOCTORS INVOLVED IN MURDER INVESTIGATION.

Thurman stared at the paper, trying to read the article. He felt the heat in his face and neck as he absorbed the inaccurate and mostly false accusations. He flipped it over. There beneath the picture of Duke University were photographs of him, Steve, and Noreen. "You don't actually believe this nonsense?"

"It doesn't matter what I believe. It's damaging the reputation of this institution."

"Two-thirds of that article is garbage."

"The public doesn't know that."

"And what do you intend to do about it?"

Vogler leaned back and crossed his arms. "I'd watch my tone if I were you."

"Just spit it out."

"The board of directors has decided to place you both on administrative leave until further notice. You're not to have *any* patient contact or step foot on hospital grounds. Clear out your office immediately."

Thurman resisted the urge to reach across the desk and slap the smug look off Vogler's face. "Who's going to handle the orthopedic trauma service?"

"That's not for you to worry about. I'd start worrying about getting your names cleared so you can be reinstated."

"Does Steve know this?"

"I have an appointment with him later this morning. I plan to tell him then."

"This is ridiculous," Thurman fumed. "You know we didn't do this."

"For all I know, you did it together."

Thurman sprung across the desk and filled his fists with Vogler's lapels. "I ought to knock you out."

"Let go of me or I'll have you arrested." His eyelids began fluttering.

After a moment Thurman laughed out loud and released his grasp.

"You've gone mad," Vogler sputtered.

"No, Harold, I just don't appreciate your bureaucratic bullshit. If you want to fire me, then just do it and quit trying to act like you're an alpha dog—which you're not."

Vogler's eyes bulged. "You're out of line!"

"Where's your spine, Mr. Orthopedic Department Chairman? Show us some leadership. Defend your staff."

"I will not risk the reputation of this institution. It's my job. That is all I have to say, Dr. Thurman. Security will be here shortly to show you out per hospital protocol. I have things to do." Vogler stood up, buttoned his white lab coat, snapped the latch of his briefcase, and scurried out the door.

———

Thurman shoved open the mammoth oak panel doors and strode from the hospital administration offices to the stairwell opposite the elevators. He charged up the stairs two at a time. *I'm not leaving this hospital without checking on Drake.*

He entered the ICU and approached the nurses' station, passing the policeman guarding Yuri's room. He slowed his pace and nodded, trying to appear casual. *What if Vogler already told everyone?*

Carmen spotted him as he came around the corner. "Hey. I was wondering where you were."

Nope. Not yet. "Good morning. Sorry for the delay."

"You almost made it on time, only two minutes late," Carmen replied. A white coat covered her clean dark-blue scrubs, a stethoscope draped over her shoulders.

Thurman pulled up a chair in front of a computer. "Recovered from Thursday night?"

She nodded. "I went online and ordered some Thunderware."

"Now all you need is a Sig P365."

"I have a Kahr 9 that will work just fine."

"Nice."

"We missed you on rounds yesterday."

"Did you read this morning's paper?"

She turned to face him. "I'm a resident. No time for a life, remember? What's going on?"

Thurman leaned closer, placing his forearms on his knees. "You're not going to believe this, but someone murdered Noreen Chase early yesterday morning."

Carmen's face went slack. Her pen fell from her grasp and clattered on the floor. "Murdered?"

"Here's where it gets crazy. Dr. Emerson is a suspect, and I've been implicated."

"Dr. Emerson and you? This is a joke, right?"

Thurman repeated the key events. "I can't say much more, and I'd appreciate it if you wouldn't either."

Carmen's jaw tightened. "This all has to do with the thing we found, doesn't it?"

"It's a possibility."

"This is a nightmare. What are you going to do?"

"I'm not sure yet. I've got a few ideas." *I need to talk to Bristow.*

"I just came from a meeting with the department chairman," he continued. "My privileges have been suspended until this is sorted out. I'm not allowed in the hospital and can't see patients."

"Both of you?"

Thurman nodded.

"I'm in shock."

"So am I. I almost punched him out."

"That wouldn't have solved anything."

Thurman leaned forward and rubbed his temples. "You and Dr. Wynn will have to run the service for a while. I want to go over Drake with you before I check out."

She stared at the computer screen for a moment, then retrieved her pen and jotted a few lab values on a five-by-seven notecard. "It's going to be weird without you around."

"Let's try to forget about that for a while. What's going on with Drake?"

She swallowed hard and looked at the notecard on the top of her stack. "Motorcycle accident victim: Yuri Drake, forty-one-year-old male, no chronic medical problems . . ."

"C'mon, you can give me the report while we check his wounds."

She led him to room seven and pulled open the sliding glass door.

Thurman's nose wrinkled when the unmistakable odor of bowel contents greeted them upon entry.

"It's not what you think," said Carmen. "The nurse just changed his colostomy bag." The patient lay on his back with arms and legs spread like da Vinci's Vitruvian Man. The white towel covering the middle of his torso draped over the connecting rods of the pelvic external fixator like a pup tent covering his genitals. He lay half submerged on an air mattress designed to protect his skin from developing pressure sores. Thurman counted a half dozen tubes, each with a function of keeping him alive. Video monitors displayed a series of numbers and graphs.

"His vital signs look stable."

Carmen checked her notecard. "They have been, though he briefly spiked a temp to a hundred and two last night. It dropped to ninety-nine an hour ago."

"What about his heart rate and blood pressure?"

"They've been good since the ICU staff started the dopamine drip. His pressure has remained at about a hundred over sixty, and his heart rate has been in the mid- to upper seventies."

"The dopamine hasn't affected his intracranial pressure?"

"Not so far."

"H&H?"

"Hemoglobin ten, hematocrit thirty."

"Then he shouldn't need another transfusion."

"As long as he remains stable. There are four units available in the blood bank if needed."

"Any worry about infection?"

"Not since the diverting colostomy. He's had white cells in his urine and bilateral pleural effusions."

"ARDs?"

"Not yet. They're covering him for everything."

"What's he on?"

She looked at her notecard and found the place for antibiotics. "Ceftaroline."

Thurman's eyes widened. "Bringing out the big guns. Blood cultures negative?"

"Yes, sir. Sputum cultures are pending."

"Did you check the x-ray of his pelvis?"

"It looked good to me, but you better double-check."

"His bandages look clean."

"They were just changed. He's on the OR schedule for a washout of his pelvis wound and nailing of his lower extremity fractures tomorrow afternoon."

"If he stays stable." Thurman inspected the patient and took inventory: intracranial pressure monitor, endotracheal tube, chest tube, nasogastric tube, triple-lumen central venous catheter, arterial blood pressure line, and a Foley catheter. "Naylor will need to put in a PEG."

"The feeding tube procedure is scheduled for tomorrow after we finish."

"That's ambitious. I hope he holds up."

A nurse dressed in scrubs stepped into the room and approached the bedside. "He needs nutrition if he's going to live." The nurse went to the IV fluid pump, hung a new bag, and adjusted the flow rate. She turned and said, "You have a guest at the nursing station who wants to speak with you, Dr. Thurman." Carmen shot him a nervous look.

Busted. Great. "Time to go." He stepped out into the hall and Carmen followed. The only way out was past the nurses' station. *Might as well get this over with.* Thurman walked down the hall with Carmen by his side. As they approached the center of the unit, a smile spread over his face. "Angie." They briefly embraced. "What are you doing here?"

"Taking over care of our patient, Mr. Drake," she said and winked.

"What have you been up to?"

"Traveling," she said, then smiled. "You know, special assignments wherever I'm needed."

"Carmen, meet Angie Speers, the best ICU nurse I've ever worked with. She's an ex-Army Special Forces medic. We worked together about a year ago."

"That was an interesting experience," Angie said as she shook Carmen's hand. "Get him to tell you about it someday."

Angie turned to Thurman. "I sent the other guests to your office. I hope you don't mind."

"Guests? Who are they?"

"Oh, you'll recognize them," she said.

CHAPTER 10
REUNION

THURMAN SAID goodbye to Angie and Carmen, exited the ICU, and walked to his office. He broke into a wide grin when he recognized his good friend, former SEAL sniper John Bristow, and their former commanding officer, retired vice admiral Zachariah Jaggears, standing in the hallway next to the door. Bristow strode toward him with a smile that grew with each step.

"Doc, I was hoping to never see the inside of this hospital again." Bristow greeted him with a backslapping embrace. "How have you been?"

"All things considered, not bad. You?"

"Been good. Surprised to see Angie?"

Thurman nodded. "She confirmed my suspicions."

Bristow chuckled. "I knew you'd figure it out."

"How did you get Angie assigned to Drake?"

"The secretary of defense can pull a few strings, Commander Thurman. Sorry to intrude like this. We appreciate your time," said Jaggears, who always addressed him by his service rank even though Thurman hadn't been on active duty in years.

"It's no problem, sir." Thurman said, resisting the urge to salute. Instead, he shook his hand. "Step into my office. What brings you to the hospital?"

"I think you have a pretty good idea," Jaggears said.

"I'm assuming it has to do with Yuri Drake and what happened the other night."

"Affirmative."

Thurman sat down behind his cluttered desk. Jaggears took a chair on the opposite side while Bristow bent over and adjusted his ankle holster, then leaned against a wall, keeping his eyes on the door. Thurman noted no imprint of the primary weapon Bristow always carried, a Glock 19 holstered on his right hip under his jacket. "My life's been turned upside down in the last seventy-two hours. What's this all about, admiral?"

"What can you tell us about Yuri Drake?" Jaggears said.

"At the moment, he's in critical but stable condition."

"Will he live?"

Thurman shrugged and rattled off the usual ICU clichés. "We'll have to wait and see. Only time will tell."

Jaggears leaned forward. "What are his odds?"

"I'm lousy at predictions, sir."

"Guess. Fifty-fifty?"

"The probability changes day to day. I can promise, he's getting great care and we're doing everything possible. There are too many things that could go wrong for me to give you accurate odds. For now, he's doing about as well as can be expected."

"I expect a daily report."

"Angie will have to handle that. Because of this whole mess I've been placed on leave from the hospital." He briefly explained the situation.

"I'll see what I can do," said Jaggears. "My apologies for not giving you more warning."

"When was the last time that happened?"

Jaggears smiled. "We've all been caught off guard by recent events, so I'll cut to the chase. Yuri Drake and his team at Angstrom Industries are working on several projects with direct bearing on national security."

Now comes the part I've been waiting for. Thurman leaned forward, placing his forearms on the desk. "What are they doing?"

Jaggears turned in his chair and motioned toward the door. Bristow shut it, then returned to his post by a bookshelf. Jaggears locked eyes with Thurman. "I checked your security clearances before making this trip. You're good. What I'm about to tell you stays in this room. It's classified, understand?"

"Yes, sir," Thurman answered.

"The Department of Defense and the Department of Energy are funding Drake's work. They have a vested interest in his medical treatment."

"I'm listening." *Tell me about the sphere.*

Jaggears continued. "Last Thursday night a group of men tried to take Yuri Drake hostage. They botched it, causing him to crash his motorcycle. It wasn't a hit-and-run."

"Why take him hostage?" Thurman asked.

Jaggears crossed his legs and unbuttoned his jacket. "Ever heard of Senator Preston Penfield?"

Thurman shrugged. "I don't follow politics."

"He chairs the Senate Committee on Commerce, Science, and Transportation, and heads its aviation and space subcommittee."

"What's this have to do with me?"

"I received a phone call from Senator Penfield this morning. He wants information about Yuri's medical condition."

"Why?" Thurman said.

"Yuri Drake and his wife, Aliya, are scientists who came to the United States from Russia five years ago. We provided them with new identities as Ukrainian scientists and arranged for them to work at Angstrom. Yuri recently made a remarkable discovery with direct bearing on the future of worldwide transportation and energy. Senator Penfield wants to make sure Drake recovers and is protected during his convalescence."

"Why does he need protection?"

"Because the Russians know about his discovery," said Bristow. "That guy you got into it with in the ER is a Russian intelligence agent, SVR."

Thurman stared at Bristow then looked back at Jaggears. "A spy?"

The admiral nodded. "He's not the only one after Drake."

"Whoa, hang on a minute. Let me get this straight. Yuri defected, made some fantastic discovery, and now the Russians want him back."

"They never wanted him to leave," said Jaggears. "The CIA helped him relocate here and gave him a new identity, but his cover has been compromised and they want him, and his wife, returned. Most importantly, they want what he has discovered."

Thurman stroked his jaw. "So does the US."

"Uncle Sam has funded him to the tune of a hundred million taxpayer dollars. We want a return on our investment. That doesn't happen if he dies."

"I wish I could help, but my department chairman just fired me."

"Let me worry about that," said Jaggears. "I'm sure there are other fine doctors that can pinch-hit for you for a while. We need your services for another problem."

"There's a mole at Angstrom," Bristow said.

Thurman looked at the admiral. "Just what has Drake been doing?"

"What do you know about superheavy metal?"

Thurman didn't miss a beat. "I can't listen to it. It makes me want to break things."

Jaggears scowled. "We're not talking about rock music. Cut the crap and get serious." He nodded to Bristow. "Yuri Drake's research partner, Dr. David Moore, is in the waiting room; he can explain. Please, ask him to join us."

CHAPTER 11
THE ISLAND

DR. DAVID MOORE'S sharp ectomorphic features resembled an academic version of Ichabod Crane complete with a receding hairline and thick, wire-rim glasses. He extended his bony right hand. "Nice to meet you, Dr. Thurman."

Thurman released the scientist's silicone grip and motioned to the chair next to Jaggears. "Please sit down."

David Moore sat perched on the edge of his seat with hands clasped and elbows on his knees and began his story. He spoke slowly as if he were giving a lecture. "Until five years ago, Yuri and his wife were part of a research team working at the Joint Institute for Nuclear Research in Dubna, about an hour north of Moscow. Their work focused on a specialized field of chemistry called superheavy elements —we just say superheavies. Have you ever heard of this?"

"I've heard of it, but I'm no expert on the subject," Thurman replied.

Bristow's face was blank.

"If you look at a periodic table of elements—"

"Excuse me." Bristow raised his hand. "I could use a refresh, and keep it simple; they don't teach nuclear physics in sniper school."

Moore pointed to the computer. "Can you pull up a picture of it?"

Thurman turned to his desktop machine. A few seconds later a picture of the periodic table of elements filled the large screen. He rotated it so everyone could see.

"With a couple of exceptions, elements with atomic numbers up to 92, which is uranium, are found in nature. Those with larger atomic numbers aren't."

Bristow walked over to the computer screen and inspected the periodic table. "Hold on . . . let me get this straight. These elements larger than uranium don't exist on earth?"

Moore nodded then said, "They can exist but they're not naturally occurring. You can't mine plutonium or californium. They're synthetic, made in a laboratory."

Bristow scratched his head. "How do you make an element?"

Moore looked at Thurman and reached for the keyboard. "May I?"

Thurman turned the keyboard toward him.

Moore began typing. Pictures of the Lawrence Livermore National Laboratory in California appeared on the screen. "This is an atom smasher. We call it a nuclear collider. It's used to make two different atoms join to form a new one. It takes a huge amount of energy and a lot of luck to get the nuclei to stick together, but it can be done.

"Since the 1950s over a dozen new elements have been created." He switched back to the periodic table and pointed to several elements. "Californium, einsteinium, fermium, and nobelium are some of the newest. Unfortunately, once created, they exist for only microseconds before they decay. We've been trying to make a superheavy with a long half-life so it can be collected and studied."

Thurman asked, "You've built an ion collider at Angstrom?"

Moore nodded and said, "Several."

"I thought those things were miles long and cost billions of dollars."

The engineer brought up a picture of the Large Hadron Collider in Geneva. "The older ones are monstrous and profanely expensive. This one is seventeen miles in circumference. Yuri knew this wasn't the answer. New discoveries require innovation. Yuri designed and built a new straight-line, linear version that's more powerful, orders of magnitude smaller at a fraction of the cost."

Bristow looked up from the screen. "You made one of these?"

"Eight of them, connected in a parallel array, each one twenty feet long," Moore answered.

Thurman sat up and leaned forward. "When Yuri arrived at the hospital, some people heard him mention something about an island of stability. Does this have anything to do with what you're talking about?"

Moore smiled. "It has everything to do with it." He reached for the keyboard and typed *map of isotopes* in the web browser. "Yuri became obsessed with reaching the island. For two decades he's been designing particle accelerators to try to prove its existence. His early experiments failed. The collision products would instantly blow apart and decay." Moore pointed to the photograph of a man on the screen. "In the 1960s an American chemist, Nobel Prize winner Glenn Seaborg, speculated that somewhere beyond element 110 scientists would find a combination of protons and neutrons that would yield stable elements. He drew a graph with protons on the y-axis and neutrons on the x-axis and called it the Map of Isotopes." A picture of the graph appeared on the screen. Moore rotated the monitor so all could see and pointed to the image. "The Continent of Elements represents all the stable isotopes. It is separated from the radioactive elements by the Strait of Radioactivity. To the far upper right is Seaborg's Island of Stability, an isolated group of stable superheavies. Yuri is the first to reach stability island. He proved it by creating element 126, unbihexium."

"What?" Bristow said.

"Un-bee-hex-ee-um," Moore replied. "You won't believe what it can do."

"I think I have an idea," said Thurman. At that moment his phone vibrated. He glanced at the screen. "Excuse me, I need to take this one."

CHAPTER 12
WEIRD SCIENCE

CARMEN'S PHOTO appeared on the phone. Thurman accepted the call. "What's going on?"

"Dr. Vogler came into the ICU asking for you. He looks pissed," Carmen whispered.

"Thanks, I'll call you back when I'm done here." He ended the call.

"Everything okay?" asked Bristow. Thurman nodded.

Moore continued. "Seaborg called the area around the island the Sea of Instability. Atomic numbers in this area are too unstable to form elements, but here," he pointed to the Island of Stability on the graph, "the forces are balanced. The nuclear shells are filled with the appropriate number of protons and neutrons, and energized electrons orbit with velocities near the speed of light, resulting in properties unheard of on Earth." Moore rubbed his bony hands together.

"Weird science," Bristow said.

Thurman smiled.

Moore's hatchet face remained unchanged. "Superheavy elements within the Island of Stability have long half-lives and amazing properties."

"How long?" Thurman asked.

"We don't actually know. There's only one isotope from the island of stability; it has 126 protons and 184 neutrons. Ubh-310 appears to be totally stable. Yuri thinks its half-life is over a thousand years."

"What did you call it?" said Bristow.

"We refer to unbihexium by its abbreviation, Ubh, and the specific isotope by its atomic mass, in this case 310, the sum of its protons and neutrons."

"What's so amazing about it?" said Bristow.

"We designed a battery made of this material that powered a car from here to Florida and back," Moore said. "It recharges in minutes and doesn't react with oxygen. If the battery is damaged in an accident, it won't ignite like current batteries can."

Jaggears interrupted. "Unfortunately, the car and the engineer piloting it, Rob Walters, are missing. They disappeared last Thursday night just before returning from the car's first test run. We believe the people who tried to take Yuri hostage are responsible."

Thurman rubbed his chin. "You say this unbihexium has strange properties. What do you mean?"

"For instance, you'd expect an element with a nucleus that large to weigh a lot," said Moore. "I know it sounds crazy, but it's not heavy at all, it resists gravity. That's why the battery, and anything made from it, is so light."

Thurman opened the middle drawer of his desk, reached in, and withdrew a clenched fist. "You mean like this?" He presented the chrome orb at the tips of his fingers.

"How did you get that?" Moore reached out.

Thurman released the sphere. Everyone's eyes tracked the object. It made a sharp crack when it struck the ceiling. It bounced and settled near a light can, its mirror finish glinting from reflected rays of light.

"What the *hell*?" Bristow blurted.

"Where did you get it?" Moore flashed an angry expression.

Thurman ignored the question and stood on his desk to retrieve the sphere. "Is this unbihexium?" He handed it to Moore.

It held the engineer's gaze like the One Ring. "It's a very small sample, less than a milligram. Yuri encased it in stainless steel with a cobalt-chrome-polished surface."

Bristow was hypnotized. "What's it worth?"

Moore shrugged. "This is the only sample in existence. It's price-less. He kept it in his office safe at the lab. How did you get it?"

"Yuri had it in his motorcycle jacket pocket the night he crashed."

"Why would he carry it around in his pocket?" asked Bristow.

Thurman shrugged. "Who knows?"

"Do you mind if I take a look?" Jaggears asked.

Moore passed it to him.

Thurman looked at Moore. "Can you make more?"

Moore raked his fingers through thin strands of hair. "That's the problem. No one else knows the process. Yuri designed and built the linear accelerators. He is the only one who can program the ion beams and run the SHIP."

"Ship?" Jaggears asked.

Moore nodded. "It's the *separator for heavy-ion reaction products*. We call it the SHIP. It uses helium jets and inert gases to collect the unbihexium once it's created."

"No one else knows how?" said Bristow.

"It's complicated."

"Most scientists are required to keep detailed notebooks that are signed and witnessed by their colleagues. Where did he keep his?" asked Thurman.

"They're missing."

Thurman crossed his arms and leaned back in his chair. "If he planned to patent his discovery, I doubt if he kept the information in his head. His results have to be witnessed and attested."

"Aliya, Walters, and I attested them, but they're not in the lab or his home," said Moore. "Aliya checked their bank safety deposit box —nothing."

"What about his computers? Did you find any files?"

Moore spoke to the floor. "They've all been erased. There's no trace of anything to do with unbihexium."

"Then he suspected something," said Thurman.

"And prepared for it." Bristow put his hands in his jacket pockets and leaned against a bookshelf. "C'mon, professor. You must have some idea what he was doing."

"Of course I knew what he was doing. I'm his boss, but I didn't keep copies of his data. I oversaw the project. He and Aliya ran their lab together until she got pregnant. She took early maternity leave because of concerns about radiation exposure."

"Did he file for a patent?" Jaggears asked. "If he did, the documents should explain how the machines work."

"I begged him to submit a patent application, but he hadn't done it the last time we talked. He didn't discuss his methods either. I can't run the machines. He has a specific process he kept to himself. I don't know how he did it. If I did, we wouldn't be here."

"If he dies," Jaggears said, "it will set us back years."

Bristow walked to the window. "What a CF."

Thurman steepled his fingers. "Dr. Moore, did you know Noreen Chase?"

Moore's posture stiffened. "How do you know her?"

Thurman caught Jaggears glance at Bristow. Both said nothing. Thurman looked back at the scientist. "So, you know her?"

Moore nodded. "She's worked at Angstrom for about five years, in the nanomaterials department."

"That's how I know her. We collaborated on a research project. Did she know Yuri?"

"Yes."

"Were they friends?"

"More than that," Moore said, squinting and rubbing his forehead. "They were having an affair."

Thurman's eyebrows raised. "You're certain?"

Moore nodded. "Positive."

Jaggears remained silent. Bristow guarded the door.

Thurman continued, "When I asked her, she denied knowing him."

"Then she lied," Moore said. "I can't imagine why, but that's Noreen for you."

Jaggears tensed and looked at Moore. "Tell me more about their relationship, this woman and Drake."

"They met last year, at the company Christmas party. Yuri and I were talking when his friend introduced them."

"What friend?" Jaggears said.

"Terrance Morton."

"Who's that?"

"Her ex-boyfriend."

Thurman leaned forward. "She never mentioned a boyfriend to me."

Jaggears said to Moore, "Explain."

"Terry Morton dated Noreen. He owns the local Kawasaki dealership. He sold Yuri his motorcycle. They're friends and ride together. She brought Morton to last year's Christmas party."

Jaggears folded his arms. "Go on."

"Yuri and Aliya were there. Morton introduced Yuri to Noreen. The next thing I know she and Yuri are hanging out at the lab." Moore shrugged with outstretched palms. "I couldn't believe it."

"Did you know her before this?" asked Thurman.

"Not really. I'd seen her around the place. She's hard to miss. We all work in isolated labs on projects that we're not allowed to talk about. Management keeps everyone separated as much as possible. There are people who've worked there longer than me that I've never met."

"And because she started visiting him at the lab, you think they slept together?" asked Thurman.

"Well, not right away, but eventually they did." Moore looked up. "He practically admitted it."

"That's hard to believe. Yuri's not exactly Noreen's type."

"Believe what you want," said Moore. "He told me he planned to leave his wife."

"How did Noreen and this motorcycle guy, Morton, meet?" Jaggears asked. "How long had they been together?"

"I don't know." Moore shrugged. "Like I said, Noreen was just around. I didn't know her well."

Thurman typed on the keyboard and a minute later his jaw dropped. "Bingo."

"What?" asked Bristow.

Thurman turned the screen toward the group. It displayed the Raleigh-Durham Motorsports website with a picture labeled OWNER AND GENERAL MANAGER. "Is this the guy?"

Moore nodded. "That's him."

Thurman leaned closer to the screen. *The guy in the bar.*

"You've seen him before?" Bristow said.

Thurman raked his fingers through his hair and leaned forward. "Someone murdered Noreen Chase early Saturday morning. I saw her Friday evening talking to this guy." Thurman pointed at the screen.

The room became silent.

"What?" The color drained from Moore's face.

"The Durham police identified her body Saturday morning. They're calling it a murder." Thurman told the story, including his home invasion.

"This keeps getting better," Bristow said.

"I'm betting," Jaggears said, holding out his hand with the sphere in it, "whoever's after this stuff killed her."

"They know I have it, and now they're after me." Thurman looked at Jaggears. "I'm going to need your help."

"And we're going to need yours. I'm putting together an operation to recover the stolen battery, and the missing engineer. Senator Penfield and the secretary of defense have made this a top priority. Can I count on you?"

"Yes, sir." *I can't do much here thanks to Vogler.*

Jaggears stood and held out the sphere. "Excellent. I'll hang on to this. We'll be in touch soon. We're on a rapid timetable. Gentlemen, this meeting is adjourned." Before leaving he looked at Thurman and added, "Remember your oath, tell no one about this meeting."

"I understand, sir."

The rest of the men stood and followed Jaggears to the door.

Bristow grabbed Thurman's arm. "Keep your eyes open. If those guys think you have the sphere, they may make another try for it."

"I already thought of that." Thurman stopped at the door. "I'll call you tonight. You remember how to get out of here?" The men stepped into the hallway, and he looked at the text message he'd just received from Vogler.

Vacate the premises! Your ID badge has been deactivated.

CHAPTER 13
TELLTALE TAILLIGHTS

THURMAN READ Vogler's text again. *Deactivated? Locked out and kicked to the curb after everything I've done for this hospital. What a total jerk. It's time to start looking for other opportunities.* He gathered some personal items from his office and left the hospital. When he turned onto his street, the yellow police tape across his front door was visible from halfway down the block. He phoned Ingram. "Can I go in my house?"

"Yeah, we're finished. They packed up and cleared out about an hour ago."

"Find anything?"

"A few fingerprints, including Chase's."

"She's been here before. How'd you get results so fast?"

"Expedited preliminary results. There were several unidentified fingerprints on drawer handles and countertops."

"They belong to the intruder," said Thurman.

"I believe you. Be patient. We'll get this cleared up."

"Easy for you to say. Someone leaked information to the media about the investigation and got me kicked out of the hospital."

"Fired?"

"Administrative leave."

Ingram let out a chuckle. "You need a break."

"It's not funny. There are patients depending on me."

"Sorry about that. I'm not sure who leaked it."

"I've got a pretty good idea," Thurman said. "Tell Hairston thanks."

"Jerry's a good guy, he wouldn't do something like that. He hates reporters. He'd rather have a tooth pulled than talk to one."

"I doubt it."

"Trust me, he's on our side."

"I'm not convinced."

"Believe it. Look, I got to go. Call me if you need anything."

Thurman slipped his phone into his pocket and pulled down the crime scene tape. *Maybe it's for the best. After this gets cleared up, I'll start looking for a new job. Life's too short to work for egomaniacs like Vogler.*

———

Three hours later the house still looked like the aftermath of a tornado. At half past six he picked up Emerson at his apartment on the way to Aris Pizzeria. When they entered, the smell of fresh wood-fired pizza reminded him that he'd missed lunch. They sat across from one another in a booth toward the back. A waiter brought a pitcher of beer and took their order. Emerson attacked his first glass while Thurman finished bringing him up to speed on their patients and gave him a rundown of his meeting with the department chairman. By the time he'd finished, the pizza had arrived. Emerson reached for a slice.

"Vogler gave me the same bullshit speech. What a jerkoff. Never in my darkest dreams did I ever imagine I'd be a suspect in a murder investigation."

"That makes two of us."

"I get it, he thinks he's doing what's best for the system, but c'mon, there's no way I'd ever lift a finger to harm Noreen, or anyone for that matter."

"Don't kid yourself. The only person Vogler cares about is Vogler. Why do you think his wife left him? She figured that out a long time ago."

Emerson raised a hand to cover his mouthful of pizza. "Hot," he mumbled and cooled it down with a gulp of cold beer. "Thanks for the invite, by the way. For the first time in fifteen years, I have more time on my hands than I know what to do with. Being stuck in that apartment is driving me crazy."

"You're not under house arrest. Go do something."

"I know, but it's hard to get motivated. My life just went to hell. Vogler's suspension ruined my chances for board certification this cycle."

"Don't worry about him. He's just covering his ass while climbing the corporate ladder. A year from now we'll look back and laugh."

"We won't laugh about Noreen."

Thurman's smile faded as he watched steam rise from the square slice of Greek pizza he held in his hand. He bit off a corner and chased it with beer. After a moment he looked across the table at his cousin. "I've never met anyone like her."

"You're lucky. You got to know her."

"Not as well as I thought."

"Does anyone?"

Silence.

"Did you have a thing for her?" Emerson asked.

Thurman took another drink and paused before answering. "No. Claire may be in California, but I haven't given up completely."

"Were you tempted?"

"In spite of what you may think, there was no physical attraction between us."

"It didn't look like that in the bar the other day. She came on to you."

"No, she didn't. We focused on the research. Nothing more than that. We did everything to make it successful."

"How could you resist? She was the most beautiful woman I ever met." Emerson wiped the sweat from the sides of his empty glass. "She messed me up."

"You're probably not the first person to feel that way." Thurman topped off their glasses and changed the subject. "What's Whitehouse say about your case?"

"We're supposed to meet tomorrow. This could go on for a long time. We could be out of work for months if this thing goes to trial. Maybe a year. I don't know what to do. I've got bills to pay."

"I can lend you some money if you need it. Don't worry about that. Finish the grant proposal you're working on. Catch up on your reading. Get back in shape."

"Vogler must think I'm a moron."

"Forget about him."

"I can't. My whole career, everything I've worked for, just went up in smoke."

"Knock it off. You didn't do anything wrong. Things will work out."

"Easy for you to say. How do you know?"

"Truth always wins," Thurman said. Steve looked up.

"Wait a minute. You've been hanging out with Ingram. What did he say?"

"Nothing I can talk about. Trust me."

"Oh, come on. We're family, for Christ's sake. You have to tell me something. I'm going crazy over here."

Thurman looked around. "Not now. Not here. We'll get this behind us and move on. Don't lose sleep over it. We can take our dog and pony show somewhere else. There are plenty of places looking for two solid orthopedic trauma surgeons."

"What about you? Now that you have all this time on your hands, maybe you should pay Claire a visit."

Thurman sipped his beer and looked down at the table. "I doubt if Hairston will go for that."

"He might."

Thurman shook his head. "She's too busy."

"Are you nuts? What's wrong with you?"

"Nothing."

"Then what happened?"

"Between us? There's not much to say. She's in California doing her gene-editing stem cell research."

"That's so important she'd wreck your relationship?"

"It's not that. Her work is going well. She's figuring out how to cure cancer. You know as well as I do the implications of that. I'm not selfish enough to make demands on her time. She'll let me know when she's ready."

"What are you, a saint?"

Thurman laughed. "That's funny. I've been called many things, but no one's called me a saint. I know what it's like to almost die from cancer. If she can figure out a cure for Ewing's sarcoma, then who am I to interfere?"

Steve set down his pizza. "Is she coming back?"

"I got an email. No mention of returning." He signaled for the check. "I got this. Let's get home. I have work to do. My house is still in shambles."

As Thurman pushed open the restaurant door, lightning split the sky, followed by a crack of thunder. The rain slanted as they hustled across the parking lot and jumped into Thurman's pickup drenched.

"Where'd that come from?" Thurman asked as he wiped rain from his face and dug his keys from the pocket of his wet jeans. His truck was into its second decade of use but still ran like new. He turned the ignition, then flipped on the windshield wipers and peered through the streaks arcing across the glass.

"You could use some new wipers," Emerson commented as he fastened his seatbelt.

"Feel free to get some the next time you borrow it."

"If it's raining, I may have to. How many miles on this thing?"

Thurman checked the odometer. "Two hundred twenty-seven thousand and some change."

"Why do you keep it?"

"Sentimental reasons. Dad gave it to me when I graduated from college."

"It's a truck. Get a new one."

"I don't want a new one. This one runs fine."

"I almost forgot." Emerson dug into his pocket, then lifted the lid to the storage console between them and placed an object inside. "I didn't have a chance to give this to you the other day."

"What is it?" Thurman leaned forward without looking at the object and wiped condensation from the inside of the windshield. He adjusted the defrost to max and turned onto Peace Street.

"A thumb drive, Noreen gave it to me in the hotel room. She said it was the copy of her slide presentation you asked for."

"I'd almost forgot about that."

After ten minutes and several stoplights, the downpour slackened. Thurman turned left onto Saint Mary's Street. Five blocks later he turned into his cousin's apartment complex.

Emerson unbuckled his seatbelt and gripped the door handle. "Thanks for dinner."

"No problem. I'll call you tomorrow. You want to come over and help me?"

"Do what?"

"Clean up after that douchebag and the cops ransacked my place."

"Sure. There's nothing else on my social calendar."

Thurman reached over and placed his hand on Emerson's shoulder. The raindrops rattled the roof. "It's not your fault. We're caught in the middle of something we don't fully understand."

"Why did she leave the room in the middle of the night? It makes no sense."

"The police will figure it out."

A car turned into the parking lot. Thurman watched it stop in front of the walkway leading to Emerson's front door. "That's a BMW 7 series."

"Why's he parked in front of my apartment?"

"Let's ask him." Thurman opened the driver's door. As he approached the BMW it accelerated out of the lot and turned right.

Emerson jogged around the front of the truck, stopping next to his cousin as the car turned onto the street. "Did you see that?"

Thurman watched red taillights disappear into the night. "Yeah. It looked like the one Noreen got into after the conference. Did you get the license plate?"

"I tried . . ." Emerson looked at him. A lightning flash illuminated his face.

"What?"

"The license plate light was out. A brand-new, hundred-and-fifty-thousand-dollar car and the plate light doesn't work."

I couldn't see the rear plate the other morning either, Thurman recalled. "You think it could've been Morton?"

"I don't know, maybe. Why would he be here?"

Thurman shook his head. "I'm calling Ingram. It could be the guy who ransacked my house. If that's the case, then they didn't find what they were looking for. They may think you have it."

"Have what? What are you talking about?"

Thurman gripped the steering wheel as he stared into the rain. "How should I know?"

"That's bullshit. I'm being framed for a murder. If you know something, tell me."

"It could put you in danger."

"Like I'm not now?"

Thurman thumped the wheel. "Look, I don't know who we're dealing with, but I can tell you the stakes are high. We're not taking any chance on those guys coming back. You're staying with me tonight."

Thurman opened the console and found the memory stick. *I'll bet this thing has some answers.*

CHAPTER 14
EXPLODING HEAD

THE CLOUDBURST, having spent its fury, transformed into a steady pitter-patter on the windshield. Periodically Thurman flicked on the wipers to clear the view. Lights from downtown Raleigh illuminated the night sky less than a quarter mile away as he turned the truck into his neighborhood, where most of the houses dated to the seventies and eighties. Mature trees lined the streets, giving it stately charm. He turned into his driveway and passed under the canopy of branches from the twin live oaks and crepe myrtles that formed an arch leading to his house. Their ancient roots had long ago burrowed beneath the pavement, cracking and tilting its surface. He parked in the garage and pulled the thumb drive from the console. The engraving on its metal surface read USB 3.0, 128 GB. He looked at his cousin. "Whatever is on this drive stays between us, understood?"

"Understood," Steve said.

"All right, then, it's showtime. Let's see if Noreen left us anything." They climbed the stairs to his study over the garage. He sat down at his desk and Emerson pulled up a chair.

The memory stick contained two untitled files and one labeled NANOMATERIALS CONFERENCE. The largest untitled file required a password. Thurman tried their password at the lab. "No luck there." Next, he tried to open the unprotected file. A video appeared on the screen. He clicked play. Noreen sat perched on a kitchen barstool with legs crossed. He recognized her apartment. She smiled and looked into the camera.

"Damn," said Steve, his voice quivered. She wore the same outfit she'd had on at the conference on Friday. After taking a sip of bottled water and brushing a lock of blonde hair from her eyes, she began to speak. Thurman's breath caught in his throat. The earrings matched the pair Hairston found.

"Mark, I did my best to keep you out of this, please remember that. I don't have much choice now. If something happens to me, I need an insurance policy, and you're it. Yuri Drake is in grave danger. If I fail, then please do all you can to help him. This will come as a surprise, but I've known about Trident Sentinel International for some time."

Thurman sat up straight. *What?*

"Show this video and the other file to Zachariah; it's important he sees them."

He went rigid. *She knows Jaggears?*

Emerson's head turned from the screen to his cousin. "What's she talking about? Who's Zachariah?"

Thurman held up a hand as Noreen continued.

"I'm making this video Friday night after our meeting in the hotel bar. I'm sorry that didn't go well and I couldn't tell you more. The video clip of the sphere you showed me is a top-secret discovery. There are many interested parties that will kill for it. It must be protected at all costs. I don't know who, but we suspect someone has betrayed Yuri."

"What the hell?" Steve said. "Our patient?"

Thurman nodded, not taking his eyes from the monitor.

"I'm making this video because it's too dangerous for us to meet. I'm under surveillance. I plan to get this to you through Steve. Someday, when this is all over, thank him for me."

"Whoa, pause," said Emerson. "She invited me into her room just so I could deliver this?"

"Sounds like it."

"That's cold."

"I tried to warn you."

"Who's Zachariah and Trident Sentinel?"

"Will you *please* stop interrupting? I'll explain later." Thurman clicked play.

Noreen continued, "You may be wondering how this started. I've asked myself the same question. It's too late to second-guess now. What's done is done." Noreen paused for a moment.

"About seven years ago I began working at Thyssenkrupp in Essen, Germany. Early in my career I'd been part of several successful projects but felt like my life was on autopilot. Wake up, go to work, come home, sleep, then repeat. It became boring. I wanted a change.

"Then I met Richard Gross, a handsome American executive who'd been transferred from the Berlin office. He swept me off my feet. I felt like a schoolgirl with a crush."

Thurman smiled, thinking of the implausibility of that scenario.

"After a few months, he asked if I'd do him a favor. He asked me to pick up a package in a locker at a rail station. It was, of course, a dead drop." She laughed. "After several months of these sorts of things, we realized I had a knack for it. Plus, it cured my boredom. One thing led to another, and before I knew it, I'd been recruited into the agency and sent to the Farm. After my CIA training, Richard and I were tasked with getting the Drakes out of Russia. We ended up sneaking Yuri and Aliya onto a plane and staging an ocean crash so no one would come looking for them. Unfortunately, things didn't go as planned, but it worked. We got them out."

"Stop the video before my head explodes," said Emerson as he rose from his chair. "A spy? I slept with a spy."

"I'm sorry. I had no idea." Thurman clicked to continue.

"I worked out of Essen until a couple of years ago, when I got a phone call about a new operation back on US soil. As you know, federal law prevents the CIA from operating within the US, but my background and relationship with Yuri made this a special circumstance, so the director farmed me out to Trident. They landed me the position at Angstrom, and I became Yuri's handler. Then about a year ago when Yuri's research began paying off, the station chief in Moscow reported message traffic indicating Yuri might be alive. The CIA suspected someone in the lab was feeding the Russians information.

The director called Jaggears. They decided it would be wise to have additional manpower close by if things went sideways. Given our mutual interest in nanomaterials and your previous work with TSI, Jaggears immediately thought of you, but he didn't want to read you into the program at that time. The fewer people who knew the situation, the better. So, he came up with the idea that I approach your orthopedic department and propose a research collaboration. Fortunately, you took the bait."

Thurman's jaw tightened. *That sneaky son of a bitch.*

"That explains how you started working with her. They set you up."

Thurman paused the video.

Emerson clapped him on the shoulder and leaned back in the chair. "At least I wasn't the only pawn."

"I can't believe I fell for it. He played me."

"Who is this Jaggears dude?"

Thurman didn't answer and restarted the video.

Noreen resumed her story. "He wanted someone he could trust as my backup. You fit the bill perfectly. If the need came, you would be read into the operation. Things worked out until last night when they tried to kidnap Yuri. Dimitry Stanov is responsible, he's a billionaire Russian oligarch who's been looking for Yuri and Aliya since their disappearance. Stanov has a mole inside Angstrom. I don't know who, and I can't trust any of my usual contacts, not even his wife. That's why I'm recording this and giving you what I have of Yuri's files. He only gave me half. Find the rest of them. Don't let me down."

Thurman felt a tightness in his chest. *Too late.*

"Stanov wants to steal the technology and monopolize Yuri's discovery. He's hired several scientists who used to work with him. The most important of these is an Italian physicist, Dario Benedetto. If anyone is capable of replicating Yuri's discovery, it's him. Stanov wants element 126, and he's bet a sizable part of his wealth on it. Plus, he's just an evil son of bitch. Don't underestimate him. He is as intelligent as he is ruthless."

Noreen paused and took another drink from her water bottle. "Yuri planned to go public and give the technology away. The US government wouldn't let him. They tried to confiscate his research. He copied and then erased all files containing design plans for his linear collider and the formula for Ubh synthesis. You have copies of everything he gave me, but it's incomplete. He told me to 'look inside the artist's portrait.' It's some kind of clue. I have no idea what that means; you must figure it out.

"Stanov has problems in Russia. Other oligarchs have poisoned government leaders against him. Element 126 threatens their interests. He knows that if he returns to Russia with Yuri's discovery, they will arrest him, confiscate the technology, put him on trial, and ship him to a gulag. We've received reliable information that Stanov is building a Ubh production facility in Italy. The stolen car and Walters are there. Jaggears will explain. First find Dario Benedetto. He is the key.

"The file with Yuri's information is password protected. I can't risk saying it on this video. You know me well enough to put it together. The first clue is in my apartment in my favorite book. Good luck; this won't be easy. A storm is coming, and you may not be able to withstand its fury."

Thurman clenched his fists. *I am the storm.*

"If I end up on that wall at Langley, pay me a visit every now and then. Ciao, love."

Thurman closed the video file. He thought about her star and the trip to Langley he'd make as he tried to open the remaining file. No luck.

Emerson swiveled in his chair. "You've got a lot of explaining to do."

"You think I know what's going on? This is the first time I'm seeing this."

Emerson rose and began pacing the room. "Who is Jaggears and TSI?"

"On your honor, this stays between us. I could go to jail if you mention this information to anyone."

Emerson raised his right hand.

For the next few minutes, Thurman told the story of meeting Jaggears when he commanded DEVGRU and their recent missions. He ended with the current situation.

Emerson stopped pacing and sat down. "Help me understand—Jaggears runs this company, Trident Sentinel International."

"We call it TSI."

"It has some kind of role in covert CIA operations?"

"It's a cutout."

Emerson stared at him. "What exactly does that mean?"

"There are times when the agency needs a job done but doesn't want anyone tracing it back to them. When that happens, they call someone like Jaggears who runs an organization that can handle the task discreetly."

"But isn't TSI a corporate security company?"

"That's what a cutout is, a dummy company set up to look legit to the IRS but carries out whatever the director wants."

Emerson pinched the bridge of his nose and let out a sigh. "We're in deep kimchi."

"That's why I'm going to Noreen's apartment."

"Now? What for?"

"To find that password."

"I'm coming with you."

"No chance." Thurman held out his palm. "The police won't let you near her apartment."

"I can't stay here and do nothing."

"Yes, you can. Take a shower and hit the rack early."

"Fine. I need to borrow some clothes for tomorrow, though."

———

Thurman pocketed his truck keys and went to the garage. As he backed down the driveway he recalled Noreen's words, *The first clue is in my apartment in my favorite book.* Then he thought of Jaggears and his parting words from their meeting, *Remember your oath, tell no one.* So much for that. He reached for his phone.

Jack Ingram answered on the fourth ring. "You okay?"

"Hanging in there."

"What's up?"

"I need a favor."

"Is it going to get me in trouble?"

"Maybe. I need to get into Noreen's apartment."

"Now? It's almost nine o'clock. Plus, technically you're a suspect. Hairston will blow a gasket and claim I let you contaminate his crime scene."

"Is it still a working crime scene?"

"Well, no, but . . ."

"Then I can't contaminate it. Besides, if you can't help me, I'm going there on my own."

"Relax, settle down, bro. What's the emergency, anyway?"

"I'd rather not say. I need you to trust me."

Ingram snorted through the phone. "Really? I already trust you. You know that."

"I appreciate that."

There was a pause, then Ingram said, "I received some news today."

Silence.

"What news?"

"Your boy Emerson has big problems. Hairston called this afternoon. The Durham PD received Chase's preliminary toxicology report. She died of an overdose. The report lists multiple substances in her system—fentanyl, cocaine, and MDMA."

"It confirms what we suspected. Someone gave her an overdose. Steve's innocent. He's not a user and neither was she. His report came back clean, didn't it?"

"Still, his prints are all over her and the hotel room."

"No surprise there."

"For the record, I don't think he did it, but between you and me, it's going to be a rough road."

"When's the autopsy?"

"This morning—"

"Damn it, Jack," Thurman interrupted, "you were supposed to let me know. I wanted to be there."

"Sorry, someone expedited it. They didn't call me until afterward. I'm guessing Hairston didn't want you there."

"Were there any needle tracks? Anything to make you think she used drugs?"

"He didn't mention needle tracks, but the ME reported a couple of fresh puncture wounds. They don't think she self-administered the drugs. It looks like someone incapacitated her in the hotel room. When she was out of it, they took her to the garden, stripped and raped her, then injected a lethal dose and left her to die."

Thurman let out a five-second string of profanity.

"Now you're talking like a cop. There's hope for you."

"Someone will pay. Any clues at the scene?"

"Nothing I can tell you over the phone."

"They can't get away with this."

"They won't. Be patient. Sometimes the wheels of justice turn slow."

"I'll be at your office in twenty minutes. We'll go together—or I'll go by myself. Either way, I'm searching that apartment."

"Way to be patient," Ingram said. "I'll give Hairston a courtesy call. He may want to be there."

Thurman signed off and dialed John Bristow. "I have more intel."

"Care to share it?"

Thurman explained the files on the thumb drive. "Find out all you can about a Russian by the name of Dimitry Stanov and an Italian physicist, Dario Benedetto."

"Jaggears will want to see that video."

"I'm on my way to her apartment to find the password."

"Who's got your six?"

"Ingram."

"Roger that. I'll be waiting for your call."

CHAPTER 15
RESIGNATION

THE ELEVATOR STOPPED at the twenty-fifth floor of the PNC Plaza building in downtown Raleigh. Ingram led the way down the hall to the doorway with crime tape dangling from its entrance like yellow party streamers. He brushed them aside and they entered.

"Sherlock and Dr. Watson have arrived." Detective Hairston chuckled at his joke while sitting on the same kitchen barstool Noreen had occupied in her video.

Thurman raised an eyebrow and looked at Ingram. "He does standup too?"

"Jerry's a regular Dave Chappelle," said Ingram.

Hairston slapped his thigh and rose to greet them. His smile vanished. "Gentlemen, can we get on with this? It's getting late."

The apartment was contemporary, austere in its matte and glass décor. The open kitchen flowed into the living room. A gunmetal-gray faux-leather sectional sat opposite a flat screen that occupied most of one wall. Ceiling-mounted halogen beams illuminated abstract original art pieces like a gallery in the Guggenheim.

"Strange stuff," said Hairston's partner John Floyd as he gazed at a poster-size framed ink drawing.

Thurman approached the detective and studied the piece. "It's a famous work by the artist M. C. Escher called *Relativity*."

"What's it worth?"

"This isn't an original, but if it were, I'd guess millions. It emphasizes the effect of different points of view. Noreen liked his work." He pointed to another smaller framed reproduction displayed in the built-in bookshelf. It showed two hands holding ink pens and drawing each other. "This one's called *Drawing Hands.*"

"Kind of cool," said Floyd.

"Most would describe it as genius." Thurman approached the glass bookshelves. Sadness swept through him as he scanned the collection. Multiple books on modern art lined the shelves along with several framed photographs of Noreen with others.

"She liked pictures of herself," Hairston commented.

"If you looked that beautiful you might too," Ingram remarked, "but you don't have to worry about that."

Floyd chuckled.

Hairston's lip curled. "Now who's the comedian?"

"Sorry, just kidding." Ingram picked up a five-by-seven framed photograph of Noreen standing between two men. "Who're these guys?"

Thurman stood next to him studying the composition and pointed to the taller man with black hair. "This is Yuri Drake. I've never seen the other guy." The sharply focused picture captured Noreen standing between Yuri and the stranger. It had been shot on a steep narrow street. Sunlight flooded the tight space, making the subjects squint. Mustard-colored stucco buildings with arched doorways and green shuttered windows lined both sides. Pedestrians walked on rectangular flagstones laid in a herringbone pattern. The stranger looked to be Yuri's age with a full head of shaggy dirty blonde hair. All three appeared happy and relaxed. Yuri had an arm around Noreen's shoulders. The trio stood outside a doorway under a green-and-yellow flag that jutted upward at a forty-five-degree angle. Thurman took out his phone and took a picture of the picture. *Noreen, Yuri, and perhaps Dario Benedetto?* "Where is this?"

Hairston came over and took the frame. "It looks old world, European. If we can't locate it, I'll send it to the Bureau. Someone in Quantico will figure it out."

Thurman continued to walk around the apartment.

"What exactly are we looking for?" asked Hairston.

"Clues to a password."

"To what?"

"I'm not sure, maybe her computer." Thurman stopped in front of a bookshelf. "I'm betting it'll be in her favorite book."

"What's the title?" said Hairston, who began scanning the bookshelves.

"That's the problem, I can't remember. I think it's about the artist M. C. Escher." A splash of color on the bookshelf grabbed his attention. On the bottom shelf he spotted a stack of vintage *Scientific American* magazines from the nineties. The December issue from 1996 lay on top of the pile. He knew it well. It contained the article that Noreen used to convince him to form their research partnership. The piece began on page seventy-four, "Creating Nanophase Materials," by Richard W. Siegel. He and Noreen had discussed it many times.

"What is it?" asked Ingram.

Thurman explained the significance of the magazine and how metals and ceramics made from nanophase materials resulted in highly durable and nearly frictionless surfaces ideal for orthopedic artificial joints. The ideas put forth in the Siegel article had influenced their scientific research at Angstrom. He had a copy of the same issue in his study at home.

"I thought we were looking for a book?" said Ingram while shaking his head.

"We are," said Thurman.

"Give me something to work with. You got a title?"

"I can't remember, but I'll know it when I see it." Thurman scanned the bookshelves. Her collection varied from academic books published by the large scientific houses like Springer and Elsevier to classics by Shakespeare, Austen, and Beckett. "It has to be here."

Thurman read the titles starting at the top and working down. On the third shelf, three books lay flat, stacked on top of each other. The bottom title caught his eye. *Gödel, Escher, Bach: An Eternal Golden Braid*, by Douglas R. Hofstadter. Thurman reached for it. "Now I remember, she mentioned this book a couple of months ago. It was a gift from her father. She read it as a teenager. It sparked her interest in computer languages and the works of Escher. We both love Bach."

"Nerds," muttered Ingram.

Thurman opened the cover and began turning pages. He stopped at illustration number five on page eleven, *Waterfall* by Escher. It showed a waterfall fed by a stream of water flowing uphill in an aqueduct system back to the waterfall in an endless, gravity-defying loop.

He thought of Yuri's magic marble bouncing off ceilings.

Noreen had written an inscription in the margin: *Reverse transcribe the name of the Japanese scientist mentioned in the article by RWS.*

"Reverse transcribe?" Ingram said. "Sounds like cloak-and-dagger-type stuff."

"I think she means write it backward." Thurman reached down and picked up the *Scientific American* issue, flipped to the nanomaterial article, and began reading it. "Here it is. Give me a pen and something to write on."

Ingram pulled a pen and notepad from his inside jacket pocket.

"On the second page of the article, Siegel mentions the work of a Japanese researcher at Tokyo University in the early 1960s. His name is Ryogo Kubo. If you write the letters of his name backward, you get o-b-u-k-o-g-o-y-r."

"What is that?" asked Hairston.

Thurman shrugged. "I think it's the password?"

"To what?"

"I don't know, a computer, a website?" *The file on the memory stick?* "It's brilliant. You need both things to figure it out, the book and the article. Like phone authentication plus a password for a website."

"And, you had to know her favorite book to piece it together."

"Which I almost forgot," Thurman said.

"Good work. You can stick around," said Ingram as he slapped Thurman's back.

"Hey, you two geniuses," Hairston called from the bedroom. "I hate to break up your party, but it doesn't work on her laptop."

Thurman tried it. Nothing.

"Does she have another computer?" Ingram asked.

"There's one in her office at Angstrom."

"Let's check it."

Hairston held up his hands. "Hold on, boys. I'll save you the trouble. I already searched her work computers. There's nothing on them, she erased all the files."

"You could've missed something." Ingram held up the notebook. "You didn't have the password."

"Suit yourself. Let me know if you find anything. I'm going home." Hairston grabbed his coat and headed for the door. He and Floyd stepped through the tape and were gone. Thurman turned to Ingram.

"Feel like going on a little field trip?"

———

Ingram stopped at the guardhouse and flashed his shield. Thurman presented his Angstrom photo ID badge.

The gate remained closed as the uniformed guard bent over and looked at Ingram. "I'm sorry, but you aren't authorized to be on this property."

"Excuse me?"

The guard repeated the denial.

"Look closely at this badge." Ingram shoved it out the window. "I'm a Raleigh homicide detective investigating the murder of an Angstrom employee. This is official police business."

"Employees only. No exception, sir, those are the rules. You'll need a warrant before I can let you through this gate."

Thurman opened the car door and walked around the hood. "I'm an employee." He showed the guard his ID card, then turned to Ingram. "Wait for me." He began jogging across the parking lot.

Ingram leaned his head out the driver's window. "Where're you going? Get back in here."

"I'll be back in half an hour."

"You better call Uber 'cause I'm leaving your ass."

Thurman could still hear Ingram ripping into the guard as he passed the motorcycle parking area twenty yards from the building. The empty spaces kindled memories of Yuri's broken body being wheeled into Trauma Bay 1. *This is where it all started.*

At the entrance he scanned his ID card and pressed his right palm flat on the bio reader. The device scanned fingerprints and analyzed the pattern of hand veins. The polycarbonate bulletproof door slid open with a swoosh, and a cool wind flowed across his face generated from the positive-pressure ventilation system used throughout the facility. He took the elevator to the third floor and hurried down the gleaming tile hallway to the office Noreen had graciously shared with him for the past six months. The arrangement had worked well since he needed to be there only once or twice a week. The office door looked unchanged. He inserted his ID card, but the indicator light remained red. He stared into the darkness through the door window, then tried his ID again. Same result. *What is going on? They must have deactivated it.* He reached for his phone and dialed security.

"This is Dr. Mark Thurman. I'm standing outside my office and can't get in. Can someone please come and open the door?"

"What's the number?"

"Office 321."

The response came a moment later. "I can't let you in, sir. That office is a restricted space."

"Not to me. I work here. That's the office I shared with Dr. Chase."

"I'm sorry, but since her death the space is off-limits. If you have objections, take them up with the head of security."

"Call them."

"Not available, sir."

"What do you mean, not available? Who's in charge?" he demanded. The phone went dead on the other end. *Seriously?* Thurman's pulse quickened. *I'm getting in there.*

He marched down the hallway and entered a men's restroom. In the corner he spied what he needed. He dumped the contents of the trash can on the floor and hefted it with both hands. *This should work.*

A minute later he stood in the hallway outside Noreen's office and hurled the metal canister at the door window. It spiderwebbed. He gripped his makeshift battering ram at both ends and hammered the glass. It shattered after the second blow. He tossed the trash can down the hall, reached through the window, and turned the deadbolt, then the door handle.

He powered up Noreen's computer. The ninety seconds seemed like ten minutes. A password prompt flashed. He entered the one discovered in her apartment. A dozen files popped onto the screen. The file labeled DIMITRY STANOV caught his eye. He clicked on it and read for the next ten minutes.

That explains a lot. Thurman clicked on another file. The screen exploded with engineering diagrams. *This is a gold mine.* Hurried footsteps echoed down the hall. He turned to face the door. A guard burst through.

"Put your hands up! Move away from the computer." The guard pointed a taser at Thurman's chest. "I'm not going to ask again."

Thurman raised his hands and rolled the chair back from the desk. "Relax, this is my office. I work here."

The guard glanced at the shards of glass strewn over the floor. "You broke into an office and destroyed private property. The police are on the way."

"You're making a mistake. I work here. Check my ID."

"On the floor. Put your hands behind your head."

Thurman knelt and then laid on his stomach with his hands behind his head.

Two more men charged into the office.

"I'm Detective Ingram with the Raleigh Police. What's the situation?"

The security guard stepped forward. "I called; this man broke into this office and is stealing corporate information."

"Stand up," said Ingram, pulling out a pair of handcuffs.

The shackles bit into Thurman's wrists. "Hey, knock it off."

"Shut up." Ingram pushed him toward the door. "I've got this from here, guys. Good job." He turned to his prisoner. "You have the right to remain silent . . ."

Ingram's grill lights flashed blue at the curb by the entrance doors. Thurman ducked his head as the detective shoved him into the back seat.

"Uncuff me."

"That's what you get for leaving me at the gate with numbnuts."

"How'd you get there so damn fast?"

"The call came over the radio while I waited for you. I told Barney Fife to show me where to go. He unlocked the gate and took me right to you." Ingram laughed. "What did you find?"

"I don't know what Hairston's trying to pull, but Noreen's computer is loaded with files."

"He's not trying to pull anything. I've known him a long time. He's a good cop."

"Then he probably couldn't see them without the password."

"What did you find?"

Thurman squirmed in the back seat with his hands cuffed behind his back. "Not much, they got there too fast."

"Don't lie to me."

"I'm not. There wasn't time."

"You're a terrible liar. What did you see?"

"Jack, I didn't get a chance. They got there too fast. There are at least a dozen files on that computer. We need that information."

"We'll have to get a warrant. It may take a few days."

"Pull over and get these cuffs off me."

Ingram laughed a good minute before he finally pulled over.

Thurman silently watched the Raleigh city lights flash by the cruiser's passenger window and thought about the file on Stanov as Ingram drove him back to his truck. Carmen's text message broke his trance.

I need to show you something.

Where? When?

Now. She included her address.

CHAPTER 16
DELTA VARIANT

THURMAN RETRIEVED his truck at police headquarters, and to his frustration, caught nearly every traffic light on the way to Carmen's apartment. The information obtained from Noreen's office computer kept his mind busy while waiting for the lights to turn. She'd clearly been interested in Stanov for years and had built an extensive cache of photographs and newspaper and magazine articles, along with various government reports detailing his life. The file Thurman had read summarized his bio. After the fourth intersection he'd figured out what he wanted to tell Bristow and picked up his phone.

"Dimitry Stanov is the only child of Nikolai and Elena Stanov. Get this—Nikolai rose to political power as an ally of his childhood friend, Boris Yeltsin. He took advantage of his position and acquired a fortune during Yeltsin's Western economic reforms, becoming one of the original oligarchs. That's where Dimitry gets his money. Unfortunately, his father's political position collapsed when Yeltsin resigned in 1999. Putin had Nikolai arrested on trumped-up charges and thrown into Butyrka prison. He never came out."

"He died there?" asked Bristow.

"Interrogated and tortured. No one ever saw him again. Up to that point Stanov lived a life of privilege and earned a degree in physics from the University of Moscow. He did graduate studies in particle physics at the Joint Institute for Nuclear Research, but left without a degree to run the family businesses after his father's arrest. He knows Yuri and understands his research. Dimitry Stanov wants element 126.

"If he controls the production of 126 and figures out how to make the Angstrom battery, the world's reliance on oil shifts to electric."

"You think that's possible?"

"One-hundred percent. Maybe not right away, but in a few years fossil fuels will become obsolete, and when that happens what do you think that does to Russia's political power?"

"It would be totally undermined," Bristow said. "Their geopolitical influence is based on natural resources, and most of that is oil and coal."

"Time for a regime change," said Thurman. "Stanov wants to take down Putin."

"Sounds like some sweet revenge."

———

After ending the call with Bristow, Thurman merged onto Interstate 440. Vehicles driven by lunatics whizzed by doing over eighty on the well-lit four lanes. Thurman ignored them, lost in thought. *Maybe she copied the files from her computer onto the memory stick. I hope that password works.*

Thurman checked his mirrors, looked over both shoulders, and changed into the far-right lane, where rational drivers migrated. He switched off the turn signal and peeked at the rearview mirror. A black sedan caught his attention as it tucked into his lane a few cars back. He eased off the accelerator, tightening the gap. The two cars between them pulled out and sped by, and one driver gave him the finger. Thurman waved. *Sorry, dude.* The sedan closed the interval between them, and its reflection now took up most of the rearview mirror. Shadows shrouded the driver's face. The car didn't have a front plate. Thurman reduced his speed to fifty-five miles per hour. It seemed like a crawl. The car maintained its distance. Thurman slowed to fifty. *Damn it, pass—I want your license number.* It was the same model and color as the car at the Washington Duke Inn and at Emerson's apartment. He considered pulling onto the shoulder and letting it go by to get a look at the rear plate. *C'mon, asshole.* He voice-called Ingram.

"There's a black BMW 7 series sedan following me."

"There're probably a thousand of those in the metro area."

"It's the car. It's staying right on my ass no matter how much I slow down. I can't get the plate number. Are there any patrol cars in the area?"

"How are they going to justify a stop?"

"It's the car from the hotel. I'm sure of it. This could be Noreen's killer tailing me. Stop him for faulty equipment or something."

"Forget it. He'll probably video the whole thing, and we'll get charged for harassment."

"Then I'll give you something to stop him for." He took his foot off the gas until the car was within fifteen feet.

"What are you doing?"

Thurman slammed on the brakes. His head rocked as the BMW impacted the rear of the pickup. The truck spun ninety degrees to the flow of traffic and came to rest with the tailgate against the guardrail. The BMW sat stalled on the shoulder with a crumpled front right quarter panel and single working headlight. Thurman opened the door and stepped onto the shoulder. *Let's see who you are.* The BMW's turbocharged V-8 engine roared to life. The driver turned his head to check for oncoming cars. Gravel flew from the rear wheels as the car shot into the lane and merged onto the interstate. Its red taillights mingled with others until he lost them in the distance. *Shit!* Thurman pulled out his phone and called Ingram. "He fled the scene of an accident, but I got what I needed." Thurman gave him the plate number.

"You're a determined son of a bitch, I'll give you that much. Wait a sec. I'll alert units in the area." He came back on a moment later. "Sit tight, they'll be there in a few minutes."

"Call them off, I don't need them. Just find that BMW." Thurman checked the rear of his truck. The driver's side rear bumper hung at an unusual angle, but otherwise the tailgate looked undamaged. The low-slung hood of the BMW had wedged underneath the pickup bed when it struck. Thurman patted the tailgate with affection. Before he hung up he asked, "anything back on Noreen's DNA?"

"Still pending. You know the drill."

"Ridiculous. A polymerase chain reaction analysis doesn't take weeks."

"Chain of custody, my friend. Handling evidence is not the same as running a hospital lab test. I'll let you know if anything comes up on the BMW. Now we have a reason to stop him."

"It shouldn't be too hard to find."

Carmen's call came through as Thurman merged onto the interstate. "Where are you?"

"On my way. It's been an interesting evening."

————

Thurman parked half a block away and walked up Mulberry Street. A sign next to the sidewalk read RIDGEWAY APARTMENTS, ESTABLISHED 1976. He counted four stories. The main structure sat back twenty yards from the street. Two wings jutted from each end so that the brick building had the shape of a U. Few windows remained lit. He strode up the walkway into the building. Thurman found the correct mailbox and pressed the buzzer. The door to the stairs clicked open. He walked up to the third floor, stopped at an end unit, and knocked. He heard the chain rattle, then Carmen opened the door.

"Come in and make yourself at home."

"Very nice," he said, looking around. The main room, kitchenette, and dining area were to the left. A short hallway to the right presumably led to the bedroom. The living room had a television mounted on the wall between two large bookcases.

Despite the hour, she still wore a V-neck sweater and skinny jeans. The outfit defined her lithe body. A gold necklace shimmered on her olive skin and disappeared in the cleft beneath the sweater's neckline. Even after medical school and three years of residency, she still looked like an athlete.

His eyes undressed her. She smiled and held his gaze.

"Why am I here?" he said.

"Because I asked you; there's something you need to see." She walked to the small table and chairs just off the kitchen. On the table sat a computer. She leaned over and entered a password. "This is my army-issue encrypted laptop. I received an email this morning from my former CO."

Thurman pulled the chair and sat in front of the computer, his arms crossed. He leaned closer to the screen. "It's signed Col John Fitzgerald, Commanding Officer, 1st Special Forces Operational Detachment – Delta."

Carmen stared at him, mimicking his crossed arms.

Thurman blinked, then finger-raked his hair. "You're Delta?"

"I've been authorized to tell you I am a member of 1st SFOD-D."

Thurman's eyes narrowed. "I'll be damned."

"I'm slated for a fellowship in tactical medicine at Johns Hopkins next fall. The army is training me to be part of Delta's medical operations unit."

"What's a tactical medicine fellowship?"

"Just what it sounds like, advanced leadership and field support training for law enforcement and special operations. Hopkins has one of the best."

"Never heard of it."

"It's only been around for the last ten years or so, since the world started going crazy."

"It's always been crazy. The weapons are just more advanced."

Carmen pulled a chair at the table and sat next to him. "So you see, no ER shift work for me. I'll be supporting Special Operations."

"That explains a lot." He paused and looked around. "You got anything to drink?"

"What do you want?"

"Something stronger than coffee."

"Johnnie Walker?"

"Neat, please."

He moved to the couch while she went to the kitchen. A minute later she returned with two glasses and sat beside him, perched on the edge, back straight, knees together.

Thurman knocked back half a shot and wiped his mouth with the back of his hand. "So, is this a mission? Are you on orders?"

She shook her head. "The email directs me to inform you of my Delta affiliation and to stand by for further instructions."

Thurman sat on the couch. "When did you get the email?"

"Right before I sent you the text, a couple of hours ago—it's the sphere, isn't it?"

"That's part of it."

Carmen shook her head. "Stop with the bullshit. Noreen is dead, Yuri is in the ICU, we almost got shot in the ER, and I just received a cryptic email from my CO, who I haven't heard from since starting residency. What the hell's going on?"

That memory stick probably has a few answers. He drained his drink and resisted a cough. "My CO told me to keep my mouth shut."

"You're not in the military."

"My ex-CO."

She tossed back her drink and rose from the table. She placed her hands on her hips. "Do you think I just showed up in the ER the night of Yuri's crash?"

"I did until a few minutes ago."

"My original clinical rotation schedule had me doing orthopedics next spring. That all went out the window last week. I received a phone call from my residency director telling me there'd been a change, and to immediately report to your team. I packed my car and arrived Friday morning."

Just in time to meet Yuri, Thurman thought, rubbing the back of his neck, *and almost get shot.*

"Why would he do that?" she asked.

"I don't know. We have residents and fellows rotate through this program all the time. I thought you were a new resident on Emerson's team."

"My director said he'd sent you an email informing you of the change."

"It's possible."

"Did you see the email?"

Thurman acknowledged the oversight with a quick smile. "Sometimes things get buried in my inbox."

"It ticked me off and wrecked my calendar."

"You gotta appreciate the excitement."

"Don't try to be funny."

"I can't help it."

"I'm a good soldier, I do what I'm told." She took a sip of scotch and placed her glass on the coffee table.

"From what I can tell, you're also a damn good doctor." The ringing of his phone interrupted the conversation. The screen displayed Steve Emerson's photo. "What is it?"

"A big black SUV just backed into your driveway."

Thurman's spine stiffened. "Get out of there. Use the back door. Call 911. I'm on my way." He tapped the screen then called 911. "I'd like to report a home break-in." He gave the required information, then hurried to the door.

"Wait," said Carmen, "let me get my coat." She ducked into a room and returned with her coat on and a semiautomatic handgun. She sent a magazine up the mag well and slapped it in place, then racked the slide and placed the weapon into her jacket pocket. "Let's go."

CHAPTER 17
TALKING HEADS

EMERSON CALLED 911, then hurried to the foyer and peeked out. The SUV remained in the driveway with its rear doors open. It looked empty. Emerson darted back to the guest room and dressed. *Who the hell are they?* He grabbed the tablet on the coffee table and tapped the screen. A panel of six images from security cameras popped up. "This is not good," he whispered. A man with a crowbar approached the side entrance while another knelt by the back door. *Shit. Shit. Shit.* He thanked the Lord for Mark's paranoia. The outside entrances had solid hardwood doors, each with multiple deadbolts. It would take a few minutes for them to get through. He ran through the kitchen and up the stairs to the study over the garage. The thumb drive remained in the USB port. He snatched it and jammed it in his pocket, then ran downstairs and peeked out a living room window. *Clear. They must be around back.* He unlocked the front door, swung it open, and sprinted across the yard.

A man dressed in black burst from the SUV. "Stop!" He raised a pistol.

Emerson kept running. The suppressed gun report coincided with the pain he felt in his shoulder. The second bullet pierced his right thigh and pitched him to the ground. "Help! Help! I've been shot."

The man pounced and pummeled his head. "Shut the fuck up," he hissed.

Emerson fought back. He bucked and twisted. The man went over his shoulder. Emerson tried to stand, but his right knee buckled. Pain shot through his skull, and he collapsed to the turf.

Solo stood up as one of his men arrived. "Let's get him into the truck."

Emerson's eyes blinked as the men pulled him across the lawn by his ankles. His two hundred and twenty pounds made their task difficult. One man swore in Russian. Emerson's right shoulder throbbed. He got his fingers into his pants pocket and grabbed the thumb drive. Then he screamed and thrashed. The men dropped him. Emerson kicked out, striking one in the face. As he did, he tossed the USB drive into the darkness. The man's head snapped back, then he touched his mouth and looked at the blood on his fingers.

"He busted my lip." He pounced on Emerson, hammering his face with meaty fists.

"Enough," said Solo. "We need him alive. Get the stuff. Now!"

The man reached into the SUV and produced a syringe. He jammed it through Emerson's clothes and depressed the plunger. Then he stood over Emerson's body and wiped his bloody mouth with his shirtsleeve.

Solo looked up as a light came on in the house next door. "That will shut him up. Get him into the truck and bandage his leg. Hurry up." They carried Emerson to the rear of the SUV and rolled him inside.

Minutes later two other men came from behind the house and jumped into the SUV. One of them clapped Solo on the shoulder. "Get moving. There won't be much left of this place in a couple of minutes." The SUV accelerated out of the driveway. Emerson's limp body rolled as they turned onto the street. The first explosion rocked the house. More followed in close succession. Three blocks later a cop car flew past in the opposite direction with lights flashing. Solo smiled as he lit a cigarette and cracked the window.

Thurman turned into the neighborhood. An orange glow appeared above the treetops. Steve's phone went unanswered.

"Oh, God," Carmen said when they parked across the street. The fire engulfed the entire house.

Thurman bolted into the front yard, halting thirty feet from the door. He shielded his eyes and scanned the flaming structure. Heat pushed him back, forcing him to retreat. That's when he noticed the streaks on the grass. In the flickering firelight the blood appeared black. He followed the trampled trail marked with blood. Halfway across the yard he spotted a small metallic object reflecting firelight. It felt sticky. His finger came away red, stained with blood. *Steve's?* He placed the USB drive into his pocket and went over to a fireman standing near his mailbox. "I live here. My cousin was staying with me. Any sign of him?"

The fireman shook his head. "I haven't seen anyone. I hope he made it out."

Carmen placed her arm in Thurman's and gently pulled him toward the street. "Come with me."

He resisted for a moment, and they stood together, staring at the inferno. Sirens wailed in the distance. Neighbors stood on front porches in bathrobes and jackets, taking pictures with their phones. At that moment he felt the vibration of his phone. He didn't recognize the number.

"Hello."

"If you want to see your cousin alive, then I'll be needing the sphere and Yuri's files."

"Let me talk to him."

Steve's drugged voice came through the phone. "I've been shot."

The stranger's voice returned. "Now listen closely. Do not involve the police. If you do, I'll put a bullet through his head. Am I clear?"

"Clear," Thurman repeated.

"You will receive a phone call tomorrow. Make sure you answer." The line went dead.

Two and a half hours later they sat in Ingram's office. The wall clock read a quarter to two in the morning. Their statements had been taken, but before they were released, the homicide detective had more questions. He leaned back in his desk chair with interlocked fingers resting on his belt buckle.

"What's the real story?"

"C'mon, Jack," said Thurman.

"Why would anyone torch your house?" Ingram asked. "What's the motive?"

"I don't know."

"Don't give me that. I'm trying to help."

"I appreciate that." Thurman crossed his legs and brushed ashes from his jeans. *Steve, where are you?*

"It's related to the recent events. Let's start with the ER shooter?" Ingram looked at Carmen.

She nodded. "He's probably Russian."

"Well, that's just great. The Russians are invading. I got a Russian scientist almost killed in a motorcycle accident. Now I have a Russian hit team shooting up ERs and burning down houses on American soil."

"Yuri Drake is Ukrainian," Thurman said, correcting him.

Ingram scowled. "I don't give a damn where he's from; his associate is dead, and your home is a pile of rubble. What are they after?"

Thurman looked at the ceiling. An apparition of Jaggears sitting across from his desk formed in his consciousness and he recalled his words, *This is an issue of national security.* "Jack, I wish I could help, but you know everything I do."

Ingram snorted. "That's a crock of shit. After all we've been through. I've stuck my neck out—on more than one occasion—for your sorry ass, and now you're withholding information from me!"

"You have to trust me."

"Who's calling the shots, the president?"

Thurman exhaled and leaned back in his chair. "There's something else."

Ingram massaged his temples. "What is it?"

"Steve Emerson is missing."

Ingram's head shot up. "What?"

"After the drive-by at his apartment, I thought it best if he stayed with me. I left him at my house when we went to Noreen's apartment."

"Could he have been killed in the blast?"

Thurman shook his head. "You won't find remains." He held up his phone. "I added a couple of indoor security cameras after the break-in. Here's the feed until the incendiaries went off." The great room camera showed Emerson dashing out the front door. Thurman fast-forwarded until the screen flashed white, then went blank. "I don't have any footage of what went on in the yard. They took out the outdoor cameras. When I got there, I noticed blood on the front lawn."

"You're telling me whoever torched your house kidnapped your cousin."

"Yes."

"Send me a copy of that video. We have to monitor your phone. Someone may contact you."

"They already have. Right after I arrived. They said not to contact the police, or they'd kill him."

"That's usually the first thing they say."

"I'm supposed to receive a call with instructions," he said, glancing at his watch, which read 2:19 a.m., "later today."

Ingram interlocked his fingers on his desk and leaned forward. "Our phone techs will monitor your calls. Watch what you say. You got a call recorder app on your phone?"

Thurman nodded. "Yeah."

"Use it on any unrecognized number, and let me know immediately. In the meantime, get some sleep. Be back here by nine o'clock." He paused. "You need a place to stay?"

"He can stay with me," said Carmen.

"Suit yourself. You know you're welcome. Diane has been asking about you."

"Thanks, I may need to take you up on that, but I don't want to wear out my welcome."

"Don't worry about that."

"Tell her I said thanks." They shook hands and Ingram closed the office door behind them.

Thurman parked in the same spot down the street from Carmen's apartment. He fingered the thumb drive as they walked up the stairs to the third floor. Carmen opened the door. "Welcome back."

He produced the drive from his pocket. "Where's your laptop?"

She pointed to it on the kitchen table. "Let me put in my password for you," she said, heading toward it.

A few seconds later, Thurman inserted the USB memory stick. He clicked on the file and entered the password. It opened. "Look at this." He scrolled through the files.

"What is it?" asked Carmen.

"Technical stuff. Plans, blueprints, specs. Stuff that's way out of my league."

"Yuri's inventions."

"I'm going to make a copy of this on your hard drive and then hide the memory stick. You got a safe in this place?"

Carmen gave a wry smile. "A little handgun model in the night-stand next to my bed."

"Better than nothing." He shut down the computer and handed her the drive. "Put this in there with your Kahr." He looked at his watch. "It's after 3:00, don't you have rounds in the morning?"

"Not much sleep tonight, plus we need showers. You reek of smoke." She held her nose and led him down the hallway to her room. "There's only one bathroom." She pulled him through the door. Her bedroom smelled fresh. A white duvet and a pile of pillows covered the queen-sized bed. Out of respect he avoided looking at personal items and followed her to the bathroom. She opened the door to the walk-in shower and turned on the water. "Give me your clothes. I'll wash them. Want a beer or glass of wine?"

"Whatever you're having."

A half hour later he sat on her couch, a towel wrapped around his waist. Faint sounds of the washing machine in the laundry room competed with the bedroom shower as Carmen took her turn. He drained his beer, then stretched out on the couch and drifted into sleep.

A floorboard creaked. His eyes opened. He sat up. "Carmen?" He sensed her presence, then felt the touch of her fingers on his shoulder. Light from the bedroom spilled down the hallway, backlighting her body.

CHAPTER 18
GOING GHOST

HE FELT her hand gently touching his face when he awoke two hours later. The sun had yet to rise. A lamp on the nightstand glowed a soft forty watts. Carmen stood before him dressed in scrubs and her white physician's coat. His watch read a quarter to six.

He reached out and swept his hand over the top of the nightstand.

"Your phone is on the dresser. No texts, no calls. I already checked."

"I have to get him back."

"We will. Don't forget, Ingram wants to see you at nine."

"I have other plans." He leaned back on his elbows and lifted the covers. His arm slipped around her. Their eyes met. She bent down. A lock of her brown hair fell onto his face. She leaned closer and kissed him, the delicacy of her lips stirring mixed emotions, both anxiety and arousal. *Is this right?* He brushed strands of dark hair from her face. A long-suppressed surge of desire coursed through him. He drew her to him and kissed her deeply.

She let out a long breath and leaned on his chest. The tip of her index finger touched his chin. "I have to go."

"Stay."

"I'll be home by six, maybe sooner."

"Promise?" he said between kisses.

She sat up and ran her fingers through his hair. "I'm not on call."

"Wait. What if they're watching you?"

"I'm a big girl." She pulled the Kahr 9 from her purse. "I know how to use this. It will be with me at all times."

"Got your Thunderwear on?"

She winked and patted her mons.

"Be careful."

"You too."

"Let me know how our patients are doing," he said, running a hand through his hair.

"Cheer up, I'll make you dinner after I get home."

"If only it were that simple. Let's see how the day goes."

"We can always get takeout."

"Yep."

"Why don't you drop me at the hospital and use the Jeep? I'll catch a ride home." She shrugged her purse onto her shoulder. "Come on, I'm going to be late."

"Where are my clothes?"

She pointed to the chair where they lay neatly folded.

"You better give me the USB drive in case I need it," he said.

"I put it back in your pants pocket."

"Thanks." He pulled her to him and kissed her again.

———

He had driven halfway to his neighborhood when his phone rang. *This could be it.* He pulled to the side of the road and activated the app. "Hello."

"Good morning, Dr. Thurman."

"Who is this?"

"Listen carefully if you want to see your cousin again."

"Go on."

"Today at five o'clock, Umstead Park, take the Sycamore Trail to the Graylyn Trail. Cross the stone bridge. When you come to the tree sculpture, stop. You will be contacted when you get there. Come alone. Bring the sphere and the memory device. We'll be watching. If anyone else is within a mile of the drop, then your friend here is going to have a really bad day."

"If you harm—"

"No threats, doctor, just be there—alone."

The call ended.

He replayed the recording. *"We'll be watching."* He thought about this. *The sun will be setting. Umstead Park is over five thousand acres. They want to make the swap and leave me in the forest in the dark.*

He parked Carmen's Jeep next to the curb across the street from his house. The fire trucks were gone, leaving behind wisps of smoke and steam rising in the cool autumn air. He walked under the towering live oaks and up the driveway, staring at the burnt-out brick shell with its collapsed roof and shattered windows. Dismay and anger grew like tentacles in his mind as he inspected the wreckage of his home. He cursed and stepped over the yellow tape, circling the structure.

He walked into the open garage, leaving footprints on the blackened concrete. The stench of smoke hung in the air. Water dripped from everything. He looked up into the charred space that used to be his study. A creaking noise caught his attention, and the black remnant of a floor joist clattered from the ceiling, landing on a pile of charred wood and brick. He squatted on the wet, soot-covered garage floor, thinking about what had happened. A torrent of emotion pulsated through him as he tallied the recent events that began when Yuri's sphere struck the ceiling in the ER. *Things can always get worse, but I'm due for a break.* He called Ingram and left a message saying something had come up. He would not be there at nine.

———

He exited Highway 540 and drove south toward Sanford. Twenty-five minutes later, he parked in front of the familiar two-story white farmhouse. He crossed the veranda and approached the front door. No one answered the bell. After the second try, he called John Bristow.

"You at home?"

"I'm at the barn."

"I'm standing on your porch."

"Come on down."

"I'll be there in a minute."

Thurman left the Jeep and walked a hundred yards down the dirt lane that ran next to the house. John Bristow's barn sat in the center of a copse of oak and pine trees like an oasis in the middle of hundreds of acres of cultivated fields. The open doors of the new metal barn exposed vehicles in various stages of repair and numerous pieces of farm equipment. Bristow left the hood up on a tractor and wiped his hands on a rag as Thurman approached. A German shepherd stood by his master and began a low growl, his ears perked.

Thurman knelt from several feet away. "Stealth, is that any way to greet an old friend?" The dog recognized him and began wagging his tail. He came over and sat at Thurman's feet, his tongue flopping from the side of his mouth. Thurman scratched his ears and rubbed him down. Bristow shook his friend's hand with a tight grasp. Thurman had yet to meet anyone as tough as John Bristow, but you'd never know it if you ran into him on the street. He looked like a regular guy. Jaggears considered him TSI's best covert intelligence operator.

"Your coat smells like smoke. What happened?" asked Bristow.

"Those assholes torched my house." Thurman sat on a bale of hay and told his story.

Bristow adjusted his ballcap. "I'm sorry, I know how close you and Steve are."

Thurman looked up. "He's like my little brother."

Bristow stuffed the grease rag into his back pocket. "We'll get him back. You have the sphere and the information. They're going to call to set up a swap. We'll be ready."

"They've already called. It's on for today at five o'clock." Thurman played the recorded phone call. "I don't have the sphere, the admiral does, remember?"

"Let's ask him for it."

"There's something I don't understand. Why destroy my house? It doesn't make sense. If the sphere had been there, it could have been incinerated or floated into space."

Bristow shook his head. "Spiteful assholes?"

"Maybe, but I don't think so. They would have taken it if they found it."

"So why try to destroy it?"

Thurman shrugged. "To keep it secret. They didn't have time to do a thorough search, so they burned my house to get rid of any evidence. If they can't have it, then no one else will either."

"It's possible." Bristow nodded in agreement. "Like you said, their entire oil and gas industry could become irrelevant."

"And the world is a better place."

"Human beings don't generally excel at making the world a better place. That's why it needs people like us."

Thurman held out his fist and smiled.

Bristow adjusted his ballcap. "You have the files?"

Thurman pulled the USB drive from his pocket. "Right here, and I know the password."

A gust of wind blew in, rattling the barn doors. "C'mon, you need a jacket and I need to modify your phone. That recording app is a few levels of technology below what we need. I know just the folks who can do the job." Bristow walked to the two large sliding doors. He gripped the handle on the right one and leaned left. His weight provided the momentum to start it rolling. "Those assholes are going to want that drive. Maybe we can use that to our advantage."

"You mean, like to plant a bug?"

"Something like that. We've got news on those names you mentioned, Stanov and Benedetto."

"What did you find out?"

"Jaggears has the details, he's called an 1100 briefing. He said to make sure you showed up."

"Hold on a sec. Got any ball bearings around here? I need one about the size of a marble."

Bristow walked to the back of the barn where a long workbench lined the wall. Several chest-high toolboxes stood next to it. He walked to one, opened a few drawers, found a plastic box, and opened it. He plucked out a chrome sphere. "This one is fifteen millimeters in diameter." He pointed to the one next to it. "That one's twenty. Will they do?"

Thurman read the label on the box, REDHILL PRECISION SPECIALTY BALLS, and selected the smaller of the two. "This one is perfect."

CHAPTER 19
REIDERSTVO

THURMAN AND BRISTOW made the fifty-mile drive to TSI headquarters in just over an hour without any sign of surveillance, arriving a few minutes before the briefing's designated start time. Although officially a civilian corporation, Trident Sentinel's main campus lay nestled on the northwestern border of the one-hundred-and-sixty-thousand-acre pine forest known as Fort Bragg, North Carolina, home of the Airborne, Special Operations Forces, and Pope Army Airfield.

After parking near the main building, Bristow led the way inside. As they walked through a warren of office cubicles, Thurman caught glimpses of men and women hunched over keyboards, their eyes transfixed on computer screens. Purifiers filtered the air and kept the temperature wine-cellar cool to protect the sophisticated electronic equipment located throughout the complex. They hustled down a hallway and entered a familiar conference room. Zachariah Jaggears stood next to a screen at the front of the room and turned to face them as the door opened. He frowned and glanced at his watch.

"You're late, gentlemen, take a seat."

"Sorry, sir," said Bristow.

Thurman kept his mouth shut. He looked around and recognized communications specialist Bill Kearns and several others he'd worked with in the past. They sat around a polished conference table with half a dozen high-backed leather chairs on each side. Electric shades covered the tall windows along the outside wall. Bristow and Thurman took their seats.

Jaggears wore a navy Savile Row suit, a white shirt, and a red tie. He directed his laser pointer to an image displayed on the screen at the front of the room. A photograph of a middle-aged man with a full head of gray-streaked black hair took up most of the viewing space. The man had wide cheekbones, thick lips, and a fleshy chin that merged into broad shoulders and a barrel chest. A close-trimmed grizzled beard couldn't hide a complexion that still carried pockmark scars of adolescent acne. "This is our man, Dimitry Stanov." He advanced the images, showing Stanov in a tuxedo raising a champagne glass, his oiled hair combed straight back. In another he stood shirtless on the deck of a yacht in Speedo swimming briefs, displaying the physique of a former athlete going to fat. A third showed him dressed in a business suit, exiting a limousine in a bustling city. Beautiful women who looked like they just stepped from a fashion runway accompanied him in each image. "He's the one behind all of this." Jaggears advanced to the next slide. "He is one of about fifty men in the Russian Federation who control over 30 percent of Russia's assets."

"What's he worth?"

"Estimates vary, but we have it in the range of twenty to forty billion."

Kearns gave a head shake. "That's with a *B*?"

"Affirmative."

"How do you get that rich in a communist country?" asked Bristow.

"Corporate Russia is run by men who know only one thing, the law of the jungle. They have an organized-crime mentality. There are no rules. No SEC oversight. Respect is earned through strength and intimidation." Jaggears paused for emphasis. "This is how every Russian oligarch views the world, kill or be killed."

"Sounds like another version of the cartels," said Kearns.

Jaggears smiled. "You're getting the picture. At the top of the mountain is the Russian president. Nothing is said or done without his approval. He has absolute power, and anyone opposing him is dealt with severely." The image changed to the current political leaders of Russia. "The Russians have a sophisticated playbook. They have made an institution out of political corruption. The new ruling elite is basically a hybrid of organized crime and law enforcement that practices a merciless form of asset grabbing known as *reiderstvo*"—he pronounced it re-*derst*-vo—"a type of corporate raiding where legitimate businesses are stolen from the people who built them."

"That's bullshit. Why don't people resist?" asked Kearns.

"We're talking about Russia. Citizens fear government reprisals. It's in their DNA. This has been going on for generations."

"Didn't that end with Stalin?" Bristow said.

Jaggears advanced to the next image. A headshot appeared on the screen. "Dimitry Stanov is a principal benefactor of *reiderstvo*. He has an army of thugs who carry out his dirty work. Until recently he's peddled political influence, paying off judges and prosecutors to get the results he wants. Most of his wealth comes from ownership in the primary Russian steel, auto, and chemical companies acquired by his father, Nikolai. He's a cunning, well-educated crook, but he has a big problem: he became a threat. His rivals have moved against him and convinced the Kremlin he needs to go."

"I'm guessing they got wind of his plan," Bristow said.

"You guessed it. Stanov wants to control production of this material." Jaggears removed a metal canister from behind the podium and unscrewed the lid. He caught the marble-sized sphere that shot toward the ceiling.

"What the . . ." Kearns said. "What is that?"

Jaggears pinched it between his thumb and forefinger, holding it up for inspection. "For those of you not familiar, this is a small sample of element 126, unbihexium, or Ubh for short. It possesses properties that have only been imagined before now. Stanov wants to control its production. I suspect the Russian government does too."

"Why?" asked Kearns.

Jaggears looked at Thurman. "Doc, bring them up to speed."

Thurman told the story of Yuri's invention and the events of the last week, then took out the flash drive and played Noreen's video. They watched in silence. When it was over, Thurman looked at Jaggears. "How did you know I would agree to work with Chase?"

"I didn't, but I thought the odds were good. Noreen could be very persuasive." Jaggears unbuttoned his jacket and leaned on the podium. "You needed a new research project, and I needed an asset I could trust inside Angstrom."

"You left me in the dark. I should have known what was going on."

"With all due respect, I think you'll agree your life was better before you found out. There was no need to inform you until now."

"I could have done more, been more prepared."

"It wouldn't have changed anything," said Jaggears.

"I might have saved her life."

"Or been killed," said Jaggears.

Bristow changed the subject. "What's up with this Benedetto dude?"

"We're trying to locate him," said Jaggears.

"This may help." Thurman took out his phone and displayed a picture. "I took this yesterday in Noreen's apartment: Yuri, Noreen, and I'll bet this guy is Dario Benedetto."

Jaggears looked at it. "But you're not sure?"

"I'd never heard of him."

"Send me a copy."

"Done," said Thurman as he tapped his phone. He looked back at Jaggears. "How did Noreen get involved?"

"I don't know the whole story, but Chase began as an associate of a CIA case officer named Richard Gross. He recruited her and they began working together in Germany. She and Gross handled the Drakes. Once they arrived in the United States, our government wanted to keep close tabs on his research and make sure he didn't get homesick. The director asked my assistance."

"You were her boss?" Thurman said.

"If you want to continue the CIA analogy, I'm chief of station. She was a case officer. Yuri is the asset. Now, if that's clear, I'd like to move on." Jaggears advanced the slide on the screen. "This is the electric vehicle doc referred to."

"A Tesla?" said Kearns.

"Not exactly. In a production model, the Tesla battery weighs over a thousand pounds and takes up the entire floor of the car. Fully charged, it supplies about eighty-five kilowatt hours of power. In Angstrom's modified version, the Tesla battery has been removed and replaced with their Ubh-graphene nanobattery. It weighs less than a kilogram, a thousand pounds lighter, and supplies two hundred and fifty kilowatt hours of power, and it fully recharges in minutes."

Kearns's jaw dropped. "Okay, so it's not just any old Tesla."

"Every vehicle could someday be powered by an Angstrom battery. It's a quantum leap forward in technology. That's why Stanov is desperate for it."

"What else do we know?" asked Bristow.

Jaggears related the circumstances surrounding the failed kidnapping. "I spoke with Chase the night Yuri crashed. She believed someone leaked information. The morning after the car's disappearance, a freighter departed the Port of Wilmington bound for Livorno, Italy. There's a good chance it left with the car. Robert Walters, the driver, is also missing. He's probably somewhere in Italy, hopefully not in the Atlantic Ocean."

"What's the plan?" asked Bristow.

"The Italian State Police, *Polizia di Stato,* and the *Carabinieri* have been contacted. Because of the possible Walters hostage situation, the FBI has also been notified. We're working with their New York field office and the FBI legal attaché in Rome. A joint operation is being put together."

Jaggears flipped to the next image. "Last year Stanov purchased real estate in the Tuscany region. He's invested an impressive sum into a manufacturing facility in Poggibonsi, a small city between Siena and Florence." Jaggears turned toward Thurman. "Dr. Chase was scheduled to give a lecture at a conference in Florence next week. We've arranged for you to take her place."

"What?" *Not until Steve is safe.* Thurman folded his arms and leaned back. "I'm sorry, but I'm not going anywhere until I have my cousin back. I need to borrow the sphere and the thumb drive."

Jaggears placed the sphere into its container and tucked it in his pocket. "Negative, doctor. I'm sorry, but this is the property of the United States government. It has become an issue of national security. I've been tasked by the secretary of defense to ensure its safety. It will not leave this building."

———

The freighter docked at the Port of Livorno late in the afternoon and began unloading its cargo. Walters peered through a porthole in his narrow stateroom, watching the dockworkers as the sun began to set. The Atlantic crossing from Wilmington had taken four days and cost him ten pounds, the weight he'd lost retching. He no longer cared. The deck had stopped moving and now he had a stable place to stand.

Shipping cranes five stories tall hoisted containers from the main deck onto the docks. Floodlights illuminated the scene. His concentration was disturbed by a noise at the door as a key slid into the lock. The door handle turned and a man wearing an Italia Marittima work uniform appeared. He handed Walters a tray containing baked chicken, boiled potatoes, and a bottled water. "Try to keep this down," he said in English with a heavy eastern European accent. "We will be leaving again soon."

Walter's heart sank. "Where are we going?"

The man did not answer. He tossed a T-shirt and a zip-up hoodie onto the bed and shut the door. Walters heard the key turn.

After picking at the bland food that wasn't destined to stay down anyway, he lay on his rack and closed his eyes. He awoke to sounds in the passageway and sudden brightness from the overhead light. The man from earlier stood at the doorway. "It's time."

"Where are my wife and daughter?"

"You will see them soon. Don't try to escape. If you do, it will not go well for them. Do you understand?"

Walters nodded. The man turned and walked down the passageway. Walters zipped the hoodie and followed closely. The man walked funny; he didn't push off with his right foot. *An amputee?* They went through narrow corridors and stepped through watertight doors. After observing the man's gait, Walters became convinced he wore an artificial limb. They descended several ladders and exited the superstructure onto the main deck. Men scurried all around them, attaching cables to containers and giving directions to crane operators. Walters stepped to the edge of a massive cargo bay and watched a container being lifted from its depths. The Russian gripped Walters' arm and pulled him next to the bulkhead. "Stay close. I don't want to have to explain how you broke your neck."

The two men walked to the port side of the ship, crossed the gangway, and descended metal stairs to the pier. They dodged transport vehicles. A truck sounded its horn and braked. The driver leaned out his window and screamed an oath in Italian. The Russian gave him the middle finger and hurried across the dock to a flatbed tractor trailer loaded with a shipping container. Walters recognized it.

"Where are we taking the car?"

The man stepped up and opened the passenger side door. He motioned for Walters to enter and followed him up into the cab. "In the back," he said, then looked at the driver. "Let's go."

Twenty minutes later the city lights of the port city were disappearing into the distance. The truck exited onto a main highway and passed a sign that read FIRENZE 85 KM.

"Is that where we're going?" Walters asked.

The two men lit cigarettes and continued their conversation in a language Walters didn't understand. It sounded Russian. The truck drove into the dark Tuscan countryside. An hour later they had just passed a sign that indicated Florence lay fifteen kilometers ahead when an explosion came from the rear of the truck. The trailer rocked, then weaved back and forth across two lanes.

"*Boris! Kakogo cherta.* What the hell?" said the driver. His cigarette fell into his lap. He swatted it to the floor, creating a burst of embers.

The driver braked as the trailer jackknifed. The truck skidded to a halt blocking the rode. He slammed his hands on the steering wheel and turned off the ignition. The men cursed at each other. Boris opened the passenger side door and climbed to the ground. The driver exited and they disappeared toward the rear of the truck. A cell phone lay on the driver's seat where it had fallen.

Robert Walters picked it up and recognized his wife's and daughter's faces on the screen. A smile spread over his face. He tucked it into his pants pocket, reached for the keys, then climbed out and ran.

CHAPTER 20
CHAINSAW LOG

THURMAN STEERED onto the shoulder of the private two-lane road and parked in front of the Graylyn Gate, a secondary entrance into the William B. Umstead State Park. In fading daylight he got out and walked toward the black-and-white crossing gate as a gust of wind shook the pine branches overhead.

Thurman checked his watch, 4:30 p.m. *Better get moving.* He climbed over the chained crossbar gate and double-timed it down the gravel trail.

"You have about a half mile to the spot." Bristow's voice came from miniature bilateral earpieces.

"The reception's perfect." Thurman's heart picked up speed and sweat trickled down his spine. He figured he should be able to make his destination in under fifteen minutes.

"In two hundred yards, the trail forks. Take the left branch," said Bristow, who monitored his progress on GPS.

He ducked under the trunk of a large pine tree that angled across the trail, uprooted from a previous storm, and then he caught sight of Sycamore Creek and a stone bridge. He crossed the span and continued down the trail. About a tenth of a mile farther, he came to a clearing. In the middle lay a gigantic log. As he approached its form began to take shape in the dimming light. The log had been intricately sculpted by a chainsaw artist and resembled an enormous, downed totem.

He didn't have time for art appreciation. He peered into the underbrush, making a three-hundred-and-sixty-degree turn while listening. Nothing but the sound of the forest. His watch read 4:55 p.m. *Where are they?*

"See anything?" Bristow said.

"Negative."

The digital numbers on his watch face blinked 5:00 p.m. A gust of wind rattled branches. Shadows now shrouded the clearing.

A ringing phone broke the silence. His muscles tensed instinctively, ready for action. "Hello."

"Place the items on the fox's head."

"Where is he?"

"You heard me. Place them on the log on top of the fox's head. Then leave the area."

"I'm not leaving without him."

The phone call ended. A minute later a FaceTime call came through. Steve Emerson's battered face appeared distorted with a swollen right eye and mouth. His nose angled to the right, with dried blood crusting his nostrils. "I'm all right, just get me out of here."

Thurman's jaw tightened. "Bring him here and you can have them."

"You just saw him, doctor. Now do as I asked or the next time you see him, he won't be talking."

"Don't do it," said Bristow in his ear.

"You have ten seconds."

Thurman took the three-inch square tin box he'd found in Carmen's kitchen from his back pocket.

"Stop," said the voice from the phone. "Show me the items."

Thurman put the phone on the log and opened the container. He produced the cobalt chrome sphere, then the USB drive he'd copied earlier. "Satisfied?"

"Good. Now put the box on the fox's head and step away. Once we have them, you'll receive a call with the location of Dr. Emerson."

"Give me the location now."

"You now have eight seconds." The screen showed Emerson with a pistol pointed at his temple. "The clock is ticking."

Bristow's voice came through the earpiece. "They're bluffing."

Thurman stared at the screen. "Look, asshole, if I let go, it's going to float into space along with the drive. Do you want it, or is Earth about to get a new satellite?"

Thurman looked around. *How are they watching? Cameras?*

"Make them show," said Bristow. "I have three snipers covering you with night vision. The second they clear we've got them."

Thurman turned and walked to the edge of the trees. As he did so a humming noise grew. He turned and looked at the log. In the waning light he watched as a drone dropped from the sky and hovered over the log, then landed. The rotors stopped.

"Take the box with the items and put it in the cargo compartment of the drone. Then step away."

Thurman stared at the machine on the log.

Bristow's voice came over his earpiece. "Don't do it. You hold the cards. You give them a fake sphere, who knows what they'll do."

The drone sat motionless. The man on the phone spoke. "I'm waiting, doctor. Your cousin needs medical attention. He's been shot. He's lost a lot of blood."

Thurman reached behind his back and drew his Sig P320 XFIVE Legion semiautomatic pistol. He sighted the red dot Romeo optical sight on the drone and fired three rounds. The shots echoed through the empty woods. Two of the four rotors splintered, and the body flew from the log, landing five feet away in a pile of pine needles. Thurman looked at his phone. "I'm waiting."

Another drone dropped into the clearing. The voice from the phone said, "That wasn't very smart, doctor. This is your last chance."

Thurman gave the camera his left middle finger and shot down the second machine. "One more and I'm an ace, right?"

"You idiot! Now your cousin will pay the price." The camera angle widened to show Emerson tied to a chair, arms behind his back, head lowered. A hand entered the picture and grasped his hair, exposing his face. A pistol barrel pressed against his left temple. "And you will witness his execution."

CHAPTER 21
CASTELLO STANOV

DARIO BENEDETTO BRAKED AND DOWNSHIFTED, guiding the Ducati Panigale through the hairpin. The rear end threatened to break loose as he accelerated out of the curve, continuing through the Tuscan hills thirty minutes northwest of Siena. It brought back memories. *Yuri raced these roads like a pro.* He shook his head and checked the speedometer.

His destination, the two-hundred-year-old castle dominating the hilltop directly ahead, belonged to the man who hired him six months ago. *Why ask me to meet him at his home?* A feeling of uneasiness came over him as he contemplated the possibilities. He turned the motorcycle into the macadam drive and stopped at the entrance.

Less than a minute later the twelve-foot iron gates swung inward. *No turning back now.* He took a deep breath, let off the clutch, and accelerated up the winding drive lined with cypress trees. He parked in the designated area to the left of another walled entrance. Vineyards and olive groves covered the countryside. Until recently the castle had been in the possession of the same family for two centuries. He suspected taxes made them sell. *What a shame.* Benedetto removed his helmet and left it on the seat, then rang the bell. The door buzzed. He entered and crossed the courtyard to the main house. A butler answered the door and motioned for him to follow. They passed through several rooms undergoing renovation, then turned down a hallway to another wing. The man stopped at an arched doorway and stepped aside. Dimitry Stanov sat perched in a leather chair on the opposite side of what Dario surmised was once a beautiful library. The shelves were empty. He felt Stanov's eyes studying him as he entered the room. It made him nervous.

Stanov stood and motioned for him to approach. "Welcome, Dario. Thank you for joining me."

"It's my pleasure, Mr. Stanov."

"Please, call me Dimitry."

Dario forced a smile and shook Stanov's extended hand. "You have a beautiful villa."

"There is still much work to be done, but it will be sufficient when it is finished." He walked across the room with a fluid athletic grace that belied his bear-like stature and stopped in front of an antique credenza. "I'm having Scotch, would you like some?"

"No, thank you."

Stanov shrugged. "Bring me up to speed on your progress."

"It's going well, sir. We have almost completed assembling the CO_2 laser and will begin testing next week."

"Excellent." Stanov poured his drink and held the glass to the light, admiring its appearance. "This has been aged for over fifty years and costs a fortune. You sure you don't want some?"

"I'm sure, sir."

"Suit yourself. Any other news?"

"Not now, but very soon."

Stanov downed a third of the whiskey, then stared at his guest. "You may be wondering why I asked you here."

Dario nodded, relieved by the change of subject.

"I want you to see something. It arrived yesterday. Come." Stanov placed his glass on the polished burled wood and walked from the room.

That's going to leave a mark, Dario thought as he followed. Stanov led him to a detached garage. Inside were four bays, each occupied with a car that cost more than Dario's home. "They're beautiful."

The stout Russian smiled and walked toward the back. "This way."

They descended a stairway to a basement. Stanov pressed a button and a metal door slid open, revealing a subterranean garage with a vehicle parked in the middle, its rear hatch open.

Dario walked to the vehicle and peered inside the rear compartment. A container, the size of a carry-on piece of luggage, lay on the floor. Two metal pieces and screws along with a screwdriver lay next to it. "What is that?"

"It's the car's battery. The retaining brackets have been removed. Pick it up." Dario reached inside and lifted it out. It was so much lighter than he expected that he nearly stumbled backward.

"This?" Dario's hands gripped the carbon fiber container at each end. He shook it. "It's empty."

Stanov's laugh resonated within the stone walls. "No, it's not."

Dario placed the case back in the cargo space and opened it. A dozen equal-sized rectangular plastic boxes filled the container. He picked one from the nearest row and it almost floated from his hand. He popped open the lid. It contained a dense array of paper-thin rectangular graphene cards stacked side-by-side with only micrometers of space separating each sheet.

Dario guessed there must be hundreds of the cards precisely arrayed within each small box. "This is the battery?"

"Amazing, isn't it."

"Is it powerful?"

"It powered this car from North Carolina to Florida and back without recharging."

"How far is that?"

"It could drive from Rome to Amsterdam."

Dario shook his head. "Impossible."

Stanov laughed again. "It's true. One of the men who helped build it has accepted my offer to join us and will be arriving soon."

An offer he couldn't refuse? Dario cupped his hands around his eyes and peered through the windows of the vehicle.

"What is it made of?"

"Element 126."

Dario rubbed his temples. "There is no element 126. The periodic table ends at element 118."

"It will need to be expanded."

"If what you're saying is true, and I believe it, there's only one person who could have created this battery."

A wide grin spread over Stanov's face. "Yes, he's alive, but unfortunately not well."

Dario looked up. "How can he be alive? I went to the funeral."

Stanov's eyes flashed. "You witnessed a charade. The CIA faked the plane crash, then smuggled him into the US. Yuri Kogan became Yuri Drake and has been working with Mr. Walters, who will now be joining our team."

My God, now the SVR and the CIA will be after us. "What about Aliya?"

"She's with Yuri. They've been working together these past five years."

"Can I talk to them?"

"Soon, but not now. Yuri is recovering from an unfortunate motorcycle accident. They are being closely monitored. Contact is out of the question at the moment."

"How serious is it?"

"Very. When he is capable of traveling, I will personally bring them here. In the meantime, you will go to America and talk to him. I want you to learn all that you can about how this element is made in the event he doesn't survive."

Voluntarily bring him here? Yuri would never agree to that. Dario smiled. "I will try."

Stanov clapped him on the shoulder. "This engineer, Walters, he knows how to build the battery, but only if you can produce element 126. I'm depending on you."

"I'll need to see Yuri's notes and schematics."

"Walters has copies."

"When can I see them?"

"When he arrives."

Dario ran his fingers through his hair. *What have I got myself into?* "I'll have that drink now."

CHAPTER 22
INFIDELITY

SERGEANT HAIRSTON PULLED into the motorcycle dealership and shifted the transmission of his Ford Taurus into park. He kept the motor running and the heater on while surveying the layout. The thermometer on the dashboard read forty-two degrees, but gusting northern winds made it feel ten degrees colder. He peered at the building through a translucent windshield coated with road grime from this morning's drive on a rain-soaked Interstate 40. Lately, the weather fluctuated like the mood of his youngest teenager, making him long for an Indian summer.

A red neon sign beamed RALEIGH-DURHAM MOTORSPORTS from the rooftop, and the three-story glass storefront reflected a line of clouds scudding across the sky. A phalanx of gleaming motorcycles leaning on kickstands guarded both sides of the store entrance. The Taurus door hinges creaked when Hairston pulled the handle and pushed it open. He shoved his hands into his overcoat pockets, left the umbrella on the front seat, and marched to the entrance.

"Looking for anything in particular?" asked the attractive woman in her mid- to late twenties standing in the middle of the showroom. "Check this baby out." She mounted an enormous touring bike and eyed Hairston. "Think you can handle this? How 'bout a test ride?"

Hairston smiled while inspecting the saleswoman. Her beauty

deflected his concentration. An intricate tattoo of reptiles and vines in greens and yellows decorated the backs of her hands and wrists. The pattern continued across her ample cleavage above the plunging neckline of her long-sleeved white Lycra top. Two delicate gold rings penetrated the flare of her right nostril. Multiple earrings pierced the helices of both ears. Straight black hair hung in a long thick braid over her shoulder. Emerald eyes and perfect white-capped teeth accentuated the exotic face. Her nametag read NATASHA. The detective was momentarily taken back. "I'm looking for Terrance Morton."

"Who should I say wants him?" She took a cell phone from the rear pocket of her jeans and thumbed the screen.

"Sergeant Jerry Hairston, Durham PD." He opened his coat to display the gold shield clipped to the left side of his belt.

"There's a cop here to see you," she said, getting off the bike.

She placed an e-cigarette to her lips and inhaled deeply. A white cloud streamed from her nose and mouth. "Terry says go on up." She jerked a thumb toward a row of offices on a balcony overlooking the showroom floor.

"How do I get up there?"

"Over there." She pointed to a staircase in the far corner of the building. Then she turned and sauntered toward a customer entering the store.

Hairston took the stairs two at a time, walked the balcony, and knocked on the door Natasha had indicated.

"Come in." Morton opened the door and stepped aside. Hairston took a mental inventory. Morton stood about five foot ten in a pair of cowboy boots that probably cost a thousand dollars per foot. His bronze skin contrasted with a full head of strawberry-blond hair cut stylishly over his ears. He wore slacks and a Carolina-blue cashmere sweater over a black crew neck T-shirt. "To what do I owe the honor, detective?" Morton retreated to his desk and sat in its oversized leather high-back, placing his bootheels on the corner of the desktop. He motioned to a couple of chairs. "Have a seat, detective. What can I do for you?"

"I'm hoping you can help me identify several people. I'm working on a murder investigation." Hairston pulled a photograph from his inside jacket pocket. "You know this guy?"

Morton smiled and looked up from the picture. "Yuri Drake. A longtime customer. Has he done something wrong?"

Hairston held up another three-by-five. "What about her?"

Morton's eyes cut away from the photo. His posture tensed. "Noreen Chase. She's a friend."

"When did you last see her?"

Morton paused for a moment before responding. "At a party a couple of weeks ago. They were both there."

"What kind of party?" Hairston pulled his notebook and made an entry.

"Something to do with their work. They were celebrating something Yuri invented, having a good time, acting like they'd hit the damn lottery."

"What were they so happy about?"

"I don't know. I wasn't invited. I was picking up Noreen for a dinner date. She didn't tell me. It wasn't any of my business."

"How about after that? Have you seen either of them since?"

Morton leaned back and gave the question some thought. "Nope, that was the last time."

"Rumor has it you and Ms. Chase have been more than friends. Did you have a relationship?"

"We're friends. That's it. The rest is ancient history."

"How ancient?"

"A year and a half or so," he said.

"What happened? Why did you break up?"

"She fell for Yuri," Morton said.

"You just said you picked her up for a dinner date."

"I also said we're friends."

"After she dumped you for Drake?"

Morton turned and looked out the window. "Look, detective, I don't know what goes on in her mind. She's an engineer. I guess she has a thing for nerds."

"*Had* a thing."

"Excuse me?"

"She was murdered last Saturday."

Morton stiffened. "Murdered?"

This guy's good. "That's right, don't look so surprised."

"What's that supposed to mean?"

"It's been front-page news."

"I don't read the newspaper."

"I guess you don't watch TV either." Hairston studied Morton's poker face, then tried a different tack. "How would you describe your past relationship to the victim?"

"We had a good thing, but not long term. Noreen wanted fun, not a commitment. I knew that the moment we met. I hung in there as long as I could."

Morton's eyes revealed a genuine sadness. *Guilt or loss?* Hairston wondered. "Why did you two break up?"

"She got bored, I suppose. Noreen liked the thrill of the hunt. Once she had you, she lost interest. I don't know, it wasn't because of me. I loved her."

"Was Yuri still interesting to her?"

Morton's torso tensed. His eyes narrowed. "That skinny geek rented a yacht and took her on a ten-day trip to the Virgin Islands a few months back. Does that sound interesting?"

"What did his wife think about that?"

"How the hell should I know? Look, detective," he pointed an index finger at Hairston, "Yuri and I are friends, we ride and have a few drinks, but we're not family. He doesn't tell me his personal business, and I sure as hell don't tell him mine."

"If he stole your girlfriend, why are you still friends?"

"It's not his fault. If I were in his shoes, I'd do the same thing. Wouldn't you? Plus, he's one of my best customers. You understand business, Detective Hairston?"

"Any idea what he's worth?"

Morton put his hands up. His manicured nails were flawless. "I'd guess ten, maybe fifteen million."

"How does an immigrant scientist from Ukraine come into fifteen mil?"

"You invent stuff everyone wants, I suppose."

"How did you meet Chase?"

"At a bar."

"When?"

"About two and a half years ago."

"How did you meet Yuri?"

"He bought his motorcycle here. Natasha hooked him and I closed the deal."

"When?"

"Two summers ago. I'd have to check my sales records if you want a specific date."

"Did you introduce Chase to him?"

"They both worked at the same place," Morton said. "She invited me to the company Christmas party. Yuri came with his wife. I introduced him to Noreen—big mistake. I could see the writing on the wall."

"Just like that?"

"She acted like I had a bad odor. When Noreen put her spell on him Yuri didn't have a chance. He fell for her hook, line, and sinker." Morton looked out the window again. "When's the funeral?"

"To be determined. Her body hasn't been released to the family yet. How long have you owned this business?"

"About five years."

"What did you do before that?"

"I worked in California."

"Where?"

"La Jolla."

"Doing what?"

"Do I need a lawyer, detective?"

"Do you?"

"I just remembered I have a meeting in a half hour in Durham, so if you'll excuse me, I need to be going." Morton stood.

"I have just a few more questions."

"Maybe some other time. It's an important meeting. Just call and make an appointment, and I'll be able to give you my full attention." Morton reached out a hand and Hairston shook it.

"I'll be in touch," Hairston said as he headed for the door. Morton didn't follow. He remained seated and pulled out his cell phone.

———

Hairston's phone rang as he walked across the parking lot to his car. Jack Ingram's name appeared on the screen. "Got any leads?"

"Chase's phone records."

"Verizon wised up."

"They're cooperating, turned over everything we've asked for."

"It's about damn time. Anything interesting?"

"We haven't been through it all, but she made a lot of calls during her last few days."

"Any to a guy named Terrance Morton?"

"A bunch, how'd you know?"

"Just a guess. Anything else?"

"She called Thurman, as you'd expect. There are several calls to a number in the U.S. Virgin Islands."

"Who did she call?"

"It's registered to a business, Island Adventures. Maybe she was planning a vacation?"

"She went there with Drake a couple of months ago. Let's run that down. What else?"

"She also called an international mobile number registered to a German company with an office in London, Thyssenkrupp."

Hairston pulled hard on the driver's side door. He winced at the sound of the metal hinges grinding as he slid into the seat.

"What the hell was that?"

"I need to get this door fixed."

"Sounded like you were in an accident."

"Nope, just the door."

"You need to up your game. That thing's a POS. The Durham PD isn't that broke; get a Charger or something with a little more street cred."

Hairston turned the ignition. "Nah, it runs great."

"Don't use it on a stakeout, the whole damn block will know you're there."

"Anything else with the phone logs?"

"Cell tower logs show IMSI numbers that made several calls and texts in the same location around the time she made calls with her registered cell phone."

"A burner phone?"

"Several."

"Where did the calls go?"

"Washington, DC, Siena, and other areas in Italy," said Ingram.

"I'd like to know what she stored on that phone. We don't have it yet, do we?"

"Your guys haven't found it."

"Something tells me we won't." Hairston watched the dealership's entrance and parking lot exit. Morton hadn't left for his important meeting.

"Why would she call someone in London who works for a German company?"

"We need to know who was on the other end of those phone calls. Who she talked to."

"We're on it. I'll get back to you when something turns up."

Hairston ended the call. Morton was still in the building. As the detective drove away, his phone rang again.

CHAPTER 23
FIRENZE

"WAIT!" Thurman slipped his fingers into the box and held up the ball bearing between his fingers.

The hand on the screen released Emerson's hair. His head flopped forward, chin to chest.

"When do we make the trade?"

"This isn't a negotiation. Give me the sphere and the USB, or he dies."

"He doesn't have what you want, and he knows nothing of value to you. I'll give you the sphere, but if you kill him, this thing flies into space. We understand each other?"

"Then release it, doctor."

Calling my bluff. "No, I'm going to hang on to it. If you want it, then return my cousin, but if he dies, you die."

The man laughed. "We'll be in touch." The screen went black.

Thurman sat on the log thinking about what had just happened and the past several days. Minutes passed. *This is my fault. I never should have left him.* Branches rattled to his right and Bristow emerged from the shadows in full sniper camouflage, resembling a Tolkien Ent. "If anything happens to Steve, I'm going to kill those worthless fucks." Thurman spat on the ground.

Bristow reached out and gripped his friend's arm. "I'm happy to assist, just say the word."

Forty minutes later they reassembled in the TSI conference room. Jaggears played the video from the low-light cameras set up in the clearing and the one worn by Thurman. "They used sophisticated drones of the latest designs. Initial inspection of the ones you destroyed suggest Chinese technology. Two came into the clearing, but four others hovered nearby. They served as decoys, making the target difficult to trace. They're identical but went to different landing zones, where their operators retrieved them and drove away, sort of a high-tech shell game. We tracked the remaining four to their LZs. They switched vehicles multiple times and we eventually lost them. We're not dealing with amateurs."

Thurman stood and leaned over the table, facing Jaggears. "I'm going to need that sphere, admiral. These guys don't mess around."

"I'm sorry, doctor. It's property of the US government. I'm not authorized to give it to you."

"Steve is like a brother to me."

"I understand, and we'll get him back. In the meantime, you have a mission to carry out."

"Forget it. No way I'm going anywhere as long as they have Steve."

"I'm giving you a direct order, commander. Get your gear packed. Your flight to Italy leaves in four hours."

"I'm not a commander anymore, and I don't give a damn about your mission." Thurman's voice rose. "If that was a member of your family, then the whole of TSI would be beating down their door right now, and you know it. You sure as hell wouldn't be leaving the country."

Jaggears stiffened but maintained his composure. "Look. I'm going to be straight with you. Whoever killed Noreen is behind this, and those guys don't play by the rules. They are never going to let Steve just walk out of there. This mission is Steve's best chance. You are the only one with the expertise to pull this off on such short notice. Otherwise, I wouldn't ask."

"And how am I supposed to do this while I'm in the middle of a hostage negotiation? What if they call and want to make the swap tomorrow?"

"My team has some of the best hostage negotiators in the world, and they've analyzed the situation. You gave these guys a good taste of how tough you are. Odds are they're going to make you sweat for at least a couple of days to try and break down your resolve. This operation should take less than forty-eight hours. They'll never know you're gone, and once you get this resolved, then I will have TSI's full resources at our disposal. We'll get Steve back. Do we have a deal?" Jaggears stared straight at Thurman, who remained silent. "Don't make me give you my Nathan Hale speech."

Bristow shook his head. Thurman rubbed his eyes and remained standing.

"I didn't hear you, commander. Are you on board?"

It's the best bad choice. Thurman pulled himself to attention and faced the admiral. "Yes, sir."

"Good." Jaggears flipped to the next image. "As I mentioned in our last meeting, in three days an international conference on medical research in the field of nanomaterials begins in Florence at the Hotel Regency. It will serve as cover for your assignment. Dr. Chase was scheduled to give a lecture at the conference. Commander Thurman will go in her place."

"What? I can't speak Italian."

"Your presentation will be given in English and you'll be accompanied by a research assistant who can." Jaggears changed the photo.

Thurman's head nodded back and forth. "Now I understand. I should have seen this coming."

"Gentlemen, meet the newest member of your team, from the Army Medical Corps, Major Carmen Black. She's a member of Delta Force, fluent in Italian, and will soon begin advanced training in tactical medicine at Johns Hopkins."

Thurman recovered and stared at Jaggears. "You set me up . . . again."

"That's not the phrase I would choose."

"She knew all along?"

"Negative. Major Black is not on active duty. I read her into TSI the night of Yuri's accident. Dr. Black was briefed regarding this assignment earlier today. Angie is filling her in on some organizational details. She has arranged to have time away from the hospital. Her cover is that she's needed in Italy for family reasons.

"All right, then, this will be the usual four-man operation. Team lead is Bristow, Kearns is weapons, Major Black will be logistics and communications. Thurman, you're medical. The mission is to recover Walters and retrieve the battery before the Russians reverse engineer it." Jaggears advanced to the next slide, an image of a hilltop estate surrounded by rolling vineyards and olive groves. Tall, pointed cypress trees lined a road in the distance. "Anyone care to guess where this is?"

Kearns spoke up. "Looks like a scene from *The Gladiator*."

"It's in Tuscany, near the city of Siena. Last year Stanov purchased this two-hundred-hectare hilltop vineyard and estate, Villa Chigi Saracini, situated between Siena and Arezzo."

"What's up with the interest in Italy?" Kearns said.

"We're not sure, but it looks like he's setting up shop in the Tuscany region. If he can figure out how to build what he needs in Italy, he won't have to worry about it being confiscated and getting him thrown in a Siberian gulag. Go home and pack your bags, doc. You and Major Black leave tonight."

"I don't have a home, and these are the only clothes I own."

"Then you'll be packing light."

He looked around the room. "Gentlemen, get your gear together. If there are no further questions, you're dismissed." Jaggears did an about-face and walked out the door.

———

At ten o'clock the next morning, the Alitalia A320 taxied to a stop fifty meters from the terminal at Amerigo Vespucci Airport in Florence. Thurman watched from his rear window seat as men rolled a stairway to the cabin door. The midmorning sun made him reach for his Ray-Bans as he disembarked. Carmen waited for him on the tarmac. They passed through immigration and passport control and collected their baggage. At the rental car counter Carmen collected the keys to their Fiat. As they approached the car, she looked at him. "You want to drive?"

"Are you kidding me? Italians drive like maniacs."

She chuckled and slipped behind the wheel. "No worries, I've done this before." She worked the clutch and stick shift like a native Florentine whipping through working class neighborhoods packed with apartment buildings and small businesses. He white-knuckled the door handle, and his feet threatened to penetrate the floorboard. Motorcycles and small vehicles engulfed them in midday traffic. After several minutes the street sounds calmed as they entered the old city.

"That's the Arno River," Carmen said as she turned left and passed over a stone bridge a couple hundred meters long that spanned a waterway only a kayak could hope to navigate.

"River?"

"With snow melt and spring rains it can flood the city." She took a right and sped along the road next to the river. People crowded the sidewalks. She skillfully navigated between vehicles and pedestrians, shifting gears and braking like a Formula 1 driver. A couple of minutes later she whipped into a piazza and stopped. A hotel attendant opened her door.

"Benvenuti all'hotel Saint Regis."

"Grazie," Carmen replied as she exited the vehicle.

"Do you need help with your luggage, signora?"

"No, thanks," Thurman replied as he pulled the two small suitcases from the hatchback of the car.

"We do need valet service, though." She handed the car keys to the attendant, and he returned with a slip of paper. Another handsome Italian opened the hotel door, and Thurman saw him give her an admiring glance.

A short time later they stepped out of the elevator and followed a bellman to their rooms. He stopped in front of room number 422. "Your room, signora." He looked at Thurman and pointed down the hall. "Yours is 426, signore."

———

Thurman stepped in front of the drapes and peered at the Arno. He looked upriver at the bridge to the far left. Italian graffiti decorated the stone wall on the far side. Teenagers sat on rocks at the river's edge, laughing and smoking. He rubbed his eyes and tried to clear his thoughts. After a couple of deep breaths, he flopped on the bed and reread Claire's email. It was an electronic version of a Dear John letter. He tossed the phone onto the pillows. *Running back to Chris Peterson.* Her final words stung the most: *"For the time being I think it's best if we pause, so please don't call or email."* I don't have time to think about this now. He lay staring at the ceiling thinking of Steve and the mission until overcome with fatigue, he drifted off.

A knock at the door startled him awake. He wondered how long he'd been out. His phone buzzed. A text appeared from Carmen. *It's me, let's go for a walk.*

He heard a knock at his door. He rolled off the bed and opened it.

"Hey, what are you doing?"

"Not much. I'm tired," he said.

"Let's register for the symposium and then I'll show you around," she said, beaming.

He felt like taking a nap, but her enthusiasm was infectious. "All right, lead the way. Are we walking or driving?"

"In the old city, everything is in walking distance."

Thank God for that. When they passed the hotel desk, the attendant looked up and said, "Mi scusi, signore. You are Dr. Thurman, correct?"

"Yes."

"A gentleman left this note for you about an hour ago."

"Who was it?"

He shrugged. "He didn't give his name. He just asked me to give you this."

"Did he say anything else?"

The attendant hesitated. "He first asked for a Dr. Chase. I told him no one with that name was registered."

"Noreen Chase?" Thurman asked.

"Si, he seemed agitated, nervous. He wrote this and asked that I give it to you."

Thurman took the note. "What did he look like?"

The desk clerk gave a description. It didn't fit Dario Benedetto.

"Grazie." Thurman accepted the envelope, tipped him a couple of euros, then walked across the foyer into the parlor, where the concierge sat at her desk at the back of the room.

"May I assist you?" she asked.

"No, thank you." He opened the envelope and extracted a cream-colored piece of stationary. On it was written in small, slanted letters:

Be at the Gates of Paradise at 4:00 pm.

Carmen held out her hand. "Mind if I take a look?" She studied it for a second and handed it back.

"Benedetto?" she asked.

"It doesn't sound like it. The description the guy at the desk gave doesn't match the person in Noreen's photograph." Thurman took a couple of steps toward the window and gazed at the piazza.

"Then we should meet him." Carmen checked her watch. "It's two o'clock. We have a couple of hours."

"I'll call Bristow and let him know what's going on."

"Tell him we'll be at the Baptistery of San Giovanni at four o'clock."

Thurman made the call and then pocketed his phone. "He said they'd be nearby."

She reached for his hand and pulled him toward the foyer. Outside, the clear blue sky greeted them, and a gentle breeze danced across the piazza. The temperature hovered in the midfifties. Carmen led him along the road that paralleled the river. They passed merchants plying their trade in buildings dating to the Middle Ages. Pedestrians and vehicle traffic increased as they approached the heart of Florence. The smells of fresh baked bread and cooked meat wafted from a tavola calda across the street. She pulled him to the right, and they walked toward a bridge. "This is the Ponte Vecchio, *the Old Bridge*. There's a shop I want to visit." They dodged tourists until they crested the apex of the span, and she entered a jewelry shop.

Carmen approached a vendor and began speaking in Italian. Thurman watched the dramatic hand gestures and facial expressions. After what felt like an eternity of haggling and trying on necklaces, Carmen emerged, radiant with a gold filigree chain.

"You had to work for that."

"My grandmother taught me the art of negotiating."

"I thought that poor man was about to start crying."

"It's part of the game."

"You play it well," he said.

She smiled and fingered the delicate prize that now hung from her neck. She slipped her arm through his as they strolled through the shifting crowds. They made several turns and entered a large area thronged with tourists and merchants. To their right was the Loggia dei Lanzi, a covered stage that housed an outdoor sculpture gallery. "Cellini's *Perseus*," she said, pointing out the bronze statue of the sword-wielding warrior holding the decapitated head of Medusa. "You remind me of him."

Thurman inspected the sculpture. A smile appeared as he turned his gaze back to Carmen. "I wish I had a pair of those winged sandals."

She pointed to another bronze statue. "My favorite." It depicted a woman raising a sword, ready to strike the neck of a vanquished soldier. "Judith beheading the Assyrian general Holofernes, by Donatello. She's the symbol of liberty, virtue, and the triumph of the weak over the strong. The Florentines knew the strength of women five hundred years ago."

"I never had any doubts."

Carmen looked at her watch. Her eyes widened. "We need to hustle. It's getting close to four o'clock. We should head that way." A half mile later they beheld the magnificence of the Duomo, the Cathedral of Santa Maria del Fiore. Thurman stared upward in awe at Brunelleschi's dome that had survived for nearly six hundred years.

"C'mon, we don't have time to sightsee." She picked up her pace and headed toward the smaller octagonal building directly across from the entrance to the cathedral and stopped in front of the enormous bronze doors protected by a barred gate.

Thurman surveyed the piazza and saw no sign of Bristow or Kearns. He looked up at the bell tower twenty meters behind him. A man in a dark jacket with a Burberry scarf stood in a third-floor window shielding his eyes, inspecting the crowd. *He doesn't look like one of ours.*

"The artist Ghiberti created these panels. He was one of the first of the great Renaissance artists to master perspective. Michelangelo thought these doors were so beautiful he called them 'The Gates of Paradise.'" She began looking at faces in the crowd. Thurman looked back up to the bell tower. The man was gone. Carmen's watch read exactly four o'clock. His pulse quickened. *Is that him?* Thurman looked around and surveyed the situation.

"There must be five hundred people here."

"Including the Carabinieri." Carmen nodded toward a group of solders carrying automatic rifles.

He felt a tug at his right coat pocket. He turned and saw the Burberry scarf and recognized the face of Angstrom's missing engineer. "Walters?" Thurman let out a deep breath.

"Yes, take this." He stuck a phone in Thurman's jacket pocket. "It has Yuri's plans and lab books. I escaped and now they're after me."

"Settle down. Did you leave the note at the hotel?"

He nodded affirmatively. "I'm in trouble. I need your help."

"What's going on? Where's the car?"

"I don't know, but they have my wife and daughter."

"Did you notify the police?" asked Thurman.

"I can't, they'll kill them if I do."

"And you left them behind?" Thurman said.

Walters bristled. "I don't know where they are. Getting help was the best chance for all of us to make it out of here."

They moved toward the edge of the piazza. The crowd began to thin. Walters stopped next to a storefront, and they huddled together. "I don't have time to explain. I made a mistake and trusted the wrong people."

"Come with us," Carmen said. "I know a place."

Walters looked around. "I can't."

"Why not?"

"When I called my wife, Stanov answered. He needs me, wants me to work for him. I can't do that. I'll play along, but you have to get us out."

Thurman gripped his arm. "We know about Yuri's element, the car, and the battery. We're here to help you."

"He'll never build a battery without the information on that phone. I know enough to build the battery, but only if he can produce 126. If he gets the information on that phone, then I become expendable. Don't let anyone get ahold of it. Tell the authorities. Please, his men are psychopaths."

"How did you find us?" asked Carmen.

Walters's head swiveled as he checked the crowd. "Noreen told me about the conference. She planned to meet up with some guy named Dario that Yuri used to work with. She wanted him to join the team at Angstrom."

"You went to the hotel to find her?"

Walters nodded.

"You know what happened to her?"

"I told you, they're fucking psychopaths."

"How did you know to ask for Mark?" Carmen asked.

"It's not rocket science. The program schedule is online. He's presenting her paper. I figured he'd been sent in her place and was my best chance at getting help."

Thurman pocketed the phone. "What are you going to . . . ?" Thurman caught a flash of movement in the periphery. A man rushed at Walters. Another grabbed Carmen. A woman nearby screamed. Thurman fell backward as an assailant crashed a shoulder into his chest, causing him to stumble into an elderly man. They fell to the ground.

Carmen shoved the man who had grabbed her. "Get off me!" When he charged, she executed a perfect hip toss by gripping his jacket sleeve, then spinning her hip into him while reaching around his waist. His body flew over hers and slammed to the pavement.

Thurman rolled and bounced up into a fighting stance, fists clenched.

"Run!" Walters shouted. Two men dragged him toward a waiting vehicle.

The old man, who fell when Thurman stumbled into him, tried to rise, then grimaced and collapsed on the street. Blood stained his shirt. A knife handle protruded from his belly. People screamed and began running. Carmen grabbed Thurman's arm.

"We have to get out of here."

"What about him?" Thurman said, kneeling by the wounded man.

"There's an ambulance next to the cathedral. They'll be here in two minutes. We have to go. If we get detained, the whole mission is compromised."

Thurman leaned close to the elderly man and opened his jacket. The knife handle moved in time with his pulse. "Don't remove the knife. Help is coming. You're going to be all right." The man responded in panicked Italian.

Carmen explained in Italian. Her words had the desired effect. He relaxed and made the sign of the cross.

Whistles blew. The mob expanded and contracted in all directions. The soldiers in green camo unshouldered their rifles. A group clustered around Thurman and the man lying on the pavement. Thurman stood and backed away with Carmen at his side.

"Voi due, fermatievi!" yelled a soldier, commanding the two to stop. He and several other soldiers ran toward them with weapons at the ready.

"Run," said Carmen as she bolted into the crowd.

CHAPTER 24
DANTE'S CHURCH

THURMAN SPRINTED AFTER HER. She dodged in and out of the crowd, then disappeared down a side street. Even at full stride he had trouble keeping up. They weaved between tourists. She dashed down another alley and turned right, leading him through curving narrow backstreets. They ran into the shadows until she stopped in front of a small building. She glanced around, then twisted the handle and disappeared through the doorway. He followed and closed the door, then looked around and saw the altar. Everything inside was peaceful while just outside, police sprinted through the streets with weapons drawn.

They were in a dimly lit chapel. Carmen stopped by a pew, knelt, and crossed herself. Thurman slid in next to her and did the same. He slowed his breathing. The baptismal font gurgled. It seemed like an eternity, but according to his watch, only a dozen or so agonizing minutes had passed when she nudged his elbow.

"Time to move." Carmen knelt again before leaving the pew, then made her way to the exit. She poked her head out the doorway and glanced up and down the street. "It looks clear." They left the chapel. After several blocks she turned to him. "You hungry?"

"We're attacked, a guy gets stabbed, the police chase us, and you think about food?"

"It's a good place to lie low." She tucked stray locks behind her ears. "Plus, the food's amazing."

"Unbelievable."

"Sorry, excitement makes me hungry." She led him down a cobblestone path.

"How the hell do you know your way around this maze?"

"It's not a maze. These are the streets of history."

"You didn't answer the question."

Carmen continued walking. "Nonina, my grandmother, held my hand and led me through these neighborhoods when I was a child. She taught me the history and culture of Florence. Dante Alighieri lived around the corner. He met his unrequited love, Beatrice, in the church we just left. And da Vinci and Michelangelo created their masterpieces nearby. She told me stories of fear and adventure, of how she and others risked their lives to help refugees fleeing the Nazis. They led Jews to the north passing them to those who delivered them safely into Switzerland. She showed my grandpapa and the men of his platoon the German fortifications around Arezzo, ensuring an Allied victory. She is the reason I went to West Point and why I do what I do. It's because of her I know this city."

Thurman stopped and turned to face her. "Your grandmother sounds amazing."

"She was."

Carmen turned down a narrow street thrown into shadows cast by the surrounding buildings. "It happened exactly at four o'clock. They were waiting for him."

"An informant at the hotel, maybe? Where were Bristow and Kearns? We could have been killed. That knife was meant for me. Plus, now Stanov has Walters."

"He risked a lot to give you that phone."

"We need to find out what's on it. I'll call Bristow."

"I want you to meet someone who might be able to help," said Carmen.

Thurman sensed they were heading back toward the river. Carmen kept to alleys and backstreets, avoiding the main avenues. She stopped in front of an arched wooden doorway with the words ANTICO

FATTORE, DAL 1865 written in gold lettering over the entrance. They entered, and Carmen spoke to the man at the register. Tears formed as he hurried around the counter to hug her, then he turned and began shouting toward the kitchen. A beautiful woman with shining dark hair wearing a knee-length black dress and matching Italian leather heels appeared from a doorway and elegantly strode toward them. Her face beamed with a smile that displayed few wrinkles. They embraced like mother and long-lost child. Thurman stood back and observed. After a minute of unbroken chatter and embracing with various members of the restaurant staff, the older woman wiped tears of joy from her face. Her smile disappeared as she inspected him.

She asked Carmen something in Italian.

"He's my teacher, Dr. Mark Thurman. He's a surgeon, and we are here for a medical conference."

She frowned and shook her head. More Italian. Thurman couldn't understand a word that was being said, but he had the distinct impression that she wasn't impressed.

"This will give you some privacy," the woman said in English as she led them to a table. "We don't open until seven."

"Thank you, Maria."

The woman leaned over and kissed Carmen's cheeks. "I'll be back in a little while. Enjoy your dinner."

Thurman looked around the room. Gold sconces provided a warm atmosphere. Cutlery wrapped in black cloth napkins lay on the white linen covering the wooden tables.

"Maria is my aunt. I haven't seen her since I was in college. This place has been in her husband's family for over a century." A waiter brought them a bottle of sparkling water and returned a few moments later with a bottle of red wine. He opened it and poured their glasses, then retreated to the back. "Take off your coat, relax. We're safe here."

He shrugged off his jacket. Their waiter returned with the antipasto. Thurman took a bite of Manchego and followed it with a sip of Brunello. His right leg brushed against a table leg, causing him to grimace. An ache from their earlier scuffle? He didn't think he'd gone down that hard. He slipped a hand under the table and rubbed his right knee.

"You all right?"

"Mostly." He lifted the tablecloth and looked at the tear in his trousers. "Damn, I have to wear these tomorrow. I'm short on wardrobe these days."

She placed her hand on his knee. "We can work on that while we're here."

Half a bottle of wine later, a waiter entered the room carrying a large plate. A faint cloud of smoke trailed the dish. He placed it on the table while it still sizzled. The aroma of grilled steak drifted from the platter.

"Bistecca alla Fiorentina, enjoy!" Another attendant brought two large steak knives.

Thurman's mouth watered at the sight of the two-inch-thick medium rare porterhouse, coated with Tuscan spices and seared to perfection.

The waiter cut the meat, placing the pieces on a wooden platter, while another server brought roasted vegetables and fresh bread.

"My father is from Kansas City," said Carmen, "but he always said steak Florentine was the best in the world."

"I agree with your dad. This is the best I've ever had." He reached for his wineglass and brushed against Carmen's hand. "Awesome job today."

Carmen smiled and sipped her wine. "Walters said Noreen wanted to recruit Dario."

"We need to find him, before Stanov and his men do."

As he cut another piece of steak, his phone chirped and vibrated. He blinked and stared at it. A text from Bristow appeared: *Get out! They're coming.*

CHAPTER 25
IT'S NOT MATH

HAIRSTON SAT at his desk reviewing Noreen Chase's case file while eating lunch. He bit off a corner of his PB&J, washed it down with a swig of black coffee, then wiped a dollop of strawberry jam from the corner of his mouth. *Would they really still be friends if Noreen dumped him for the other guy?* He thought about Morton for a moment, shrugged his shoulders, and frowned. *The dude is weird. Who wants to hang around their ex and their new lover? That's like torture.* As he leaned forward, his forearm nudged a pile of papers on the corner of his desk. A professional headshot of Noreen taken from the Angstrom website slid from the top of the stack and landed faceup on the carpet. He retrieved it and studied the image. It could have been from a modeling agency portfolio. The camera loved her. He shook his head and put the photo back. *Good Lord, how did a nerd like Yuri Drake punch her buttons?* Nothing about this case made sense. He'd seen a lot in his career, but this one felt different. He couldn't put his finger on why, so he decided to pay Mr. Motorcycle another visit.

An hour later Hairston walked out of the motorsports dealership and crossed the parking lot to his car. Natasha had informed him Morton wouldn't be returning until tomorrow. He didn't believe her. He parked the Taurus in a spot down the street with an unobstructed view of the entrance and waited to see if she spoke the truth. He pulled a worn copy of a Walter Mosley novel from the glove box and began to read. Natasha had lied. At half past three, a car turned into the parking lot with Morton behind the wheel. It disappeared around the rear of the building. Hairston put the book down. Two minutes later the car reappeared with Natasha in the passenger seat and drove past him.

Hairston called in the license plate while making a U-turn and followed from a safe distance in the early surge of afternoon rush hour traffic. After ten minutes on Interstate-40, the sedan exited and drove through downtown Durham. Two turns and five blocks later, Morton slowed and parked in front of Anastasia's, a gentleman's club on Alston Avenue. The Durham PD knew the establishment well. It had the reputation of being frequented by a variety of lowlifes, especially those connected to Russian organized crime. Hairston parked half a block away and observed. Natasha got out and adjusted her miniskirt. She shouldered a gym bag. Hairston watched as she leaned into the window and said something to Morton. Someone opened the glass entrance door to the club. She straightened and glanced behind her at a man in the doorway. She said something and flipped him a middle finger and took a drag on her cigarette. He beckoned to her. Smoke flared from her nostrils. Embers flew when the cigarette butt bounced off the pavement. She crushed it with the tip of a platform stiletto, then strutted through the entrance as Morton drove away. The detective wondered what he'd just witnessed as he pulled from the curb and followed.

Hairston kept a safe distance as Morton cruised west into a suburban landscape that had been farmland a decade ago. He passed cookie-cutter homes and strip malls. As they continued the tract housing gave way to pine forest, and a few miles later the car turned onto Colvard Farms Road and disappeared down the wooded lane. Hairston drove past and pulled to the shoulder. The license plate database search revealed that Morton owned the car and that he lived in the exclusive gated community of Colvard Farms. His home address was displayed with the search results. Hairston stopped at the guard shack.

"May I help you, sir?" asked the attendant.

Hairston flashed his shield. "Checking out the neighborhood. We've had reports of break-ins in the area. Mind if I look around?"

"No, sir, go right ahead."

"Thanks, I won't be long."

The eight-foot-tall wrought iron gates swung open. Hairston proceeded a quarter mile, then made a right turn and stopped in front of 214 Forest View Road, a two-story Georgian white-brick mansion with a four-car garage. Blooming chrysanthemums and camellias interspersed between bare crepe myrtles ringed the circular driveway. Hairston snapped several photographs. A pair of Doric columns supporting the portico and five evenly spaced dormers decorating the slate roof made the architectural proportions perfect. Hairston spotted a pool and pool house in the backyard as he drove past. *This place could be on the cover of* Southern Living. *The motorsports business must be good . . . damn good.* He drove through the bucolic neighborhood bordering Lake Jordan, then returned to Morton's and parked in the driveway. He walked to the front door and rang the bell.

Hairston removed his sunglasses when the door opened, revealing a nubile blonde woman holding a glass of white wine. Black leather pants and a white spandex top clung to her body. Spiked heels added three inches to her height.

"What do you want?" she said with an eastern European accent.

"I'd like to speak with Mr. Morton, please."

"He's not here."

Hairston smiled and badged her. "I think you're mistaken, miss. Get him and say Sergeant Hairston has a few more questions."

She sipped her wine and sniffed like she was fighting a cold. Or an addiction.

"How old are you?"

"Old enough."

A voice from within the house called out. "It's okay, Candy, ask him in." Morton appeared from behind the door and placed his hands on the young woman's shoulders, then kissed her neck. "Give me a few minutes while I answer the detective's questions."

Hairston raised an eyebrow as the woman walked away. "Candy?"

"Her stage name."

"She an actress?"

"She'd like to be, but for now she performs in local productions."

"She doesn't look a day over sixteen."

"That's not what she says. What can I do for you, detective?" Morton remained standing in the doorway. "I thought we'd completed our business."

"As I recall, you had an important meeting and ran out on me. I had a few more questions."

"And you were going to make a follow-up appointment."

"That's why I'm here." Hairston smiled and took out his pen and notepad while glancing around. "Mind if I come in?"

"I only have a few minutes." Morton led him into the living room and motioned to an overstuffed sofa. "What can I help you with, detective?

The cushions enveloped Hairston as he sat. "Nice place. Let me guess, eight thousand square feet?"

"You didn't come here to ask about my house."

"Just curious."

"Try eleven including the guest rooms over the garage, but who's counting?"

The detective flipped through his notebook. "Original art, Parisian décor, three manicured acres in a premier neighborhood . . . you must sell a lot of motorcycles?"

"You want to know about my business?"

Hairston raised an eyebrow. "Just making an observation."

"For your information, the Durham store is one of five in the mid-Atlantic region. Our Greenville, South Carolina, store opened last year, and the one in Tyson's Corner, Virginia, began moving inventory last May. Business is good." Morton walked to the bar and picked up a bottle of bourbon. "Drink?"

"No, thanks, it's a little early for me." Hairston stroked his chin. "You've opened five franchises in two years?"

"Three years."

"That's a lot of capital."

"I've got good bankers."

Hairston redirected. "Ever work overseas, in Europe?"

"No, but I'd be interested if you know of any good opportunities."

"I hear they're hiring at Thyssenkrupp in Germany."

Morton returned and sat on the edge of a chair on the other side of the coffee table. He took a sip of his Woodford Reserve. "I don't have any idea what you're talking about."

"You never worked in Essen?"

"Where is that?"

Hairston chuckled. "C'mon, you know exactly what I'm talking about."

"I'm afraid I don't."

Hairston tried a different tack. "Where does Candy work?"

Morton blinked. "What does that have to do with anything?"

"Just answer the question, please."

"Anastasia's, downtown."

"You have a business interest in that establishment?"

"I may." Morton sipped his whiskey.

"Do you, or don't you?"

"I own 20 percent."

"Who owns the rest?"

"My business partners."

"Who are they?"

"You wouldn't know them. They live in New York."

"I need a list of their names."

"I'll have to get you one from our attorney."

"Can't you give me one now?"

Morton shook his head. "No."

"Why?"

"Because they wouldn't want me giving out that information."

"You got something to hide?"

"No. It's a legitimate, profitable business, but these are businessmen who may not want their names associated with a gentlemen's club, if you know what I mean . . . the MeToo movement and all that."

"I'm not a reporter, this is a confidential police inquiry."

"I'm sorry, detective. You'll have to get the information from my attorney. What else?"

"Noreen Chase. I'm unclear when you met her."

"I told you that already, we met at a bar about two and a half years ago."

"Didn't you meet when you two worked at Thyssenkrupp?"

"Did I miss something? I told you I never worked for that company or anywhere outside the US."

"Well, two and a half years ago, Mrs. Chase was working in Germany, so how exactly could the two of you have met in a bar in the States?"

"Maybe it wasn't that long ago. I don't remember the exact date."

"Think about it, try to recall," said Hairston as he jotted a few notes.

"It's been too long ago. I don't remember."

"Do you happen to remember what bar?"

"Anastasia's."

"You met her at your strip club? Really?"

Morton smiled. "I asked if she was with anyone and she said no, and she offered to buy me a drink. Would you turn that down?"

Hairston gave a tight-lipped smile. "If you don't mind, I'll ask the questions. Did Ms. Chase work at Angstrom Industries at the time?"

Morton nodded. "That's right."

"That little romantic interlude led to you and Chase starting a relationship lasting for, what, a year or so?"

"Sounds about right."

"Then she drops you for a nuclear chemist geek whose idea of fun is solving differential equations."

Morton took another sip of his bourbon. "It's not math, detective."

"What went on with you two, or should I say, you three? Sooner or later, I'm going to find out."

"Really, detective. I have no idea what you're talking about, but there are plenty of interesting characters who have been frequenting Anastasia's lately. Why don't you try checking into them?"

Hairston stopped writing. "What kind of people are we talking about?"

"Russian, and they're not tourists."

"What's that supposed to mean? KGB?"

"There is no KGB anymore. The Russian Foreign Intelligence

Service, or SVR, is like the CIA; they operate internationally, outside Russia, focusing on civilian intelligence and espionage activities. Lately, several SVR have been showing up at Anastasia's."

"How do you know that?"

"It's my business to know my clientele. It might be worth your while to look for a Russian missing a foot. He wears a prosthesis but can probably outrun you."

Hairston put down his pen and looked up. "You want me to find a Russian Long John Silver. C'mon, you expect me to believe all that?"

Morton put his elbows on his knees and shook his head, then he looked straight at Hairston. Dark circles under his eyes belied a lack of sleep. "I'm quite serious. He's SVR, and if you find him, then you may find Noreen's killer."

Hairston sat up. "You got a name?"

"Boris. That's all I know."

"No last name?"

"Unfortunately, no," he said.

"And what makes you think this is our guy?"

"Let's just say I have my reasons."

"Why didn't you tell me any of this when I was in your office this morning?"

"I didn't know if I could trust you. I'm still not sure, but I'll take a chance." He stood up. "Now, if you'll excuse me, I have to take Candy to work."

"I thought you said she was twenty-one."

"She's had a little trouble with the driver's test."

Hairston extricated himself from the couch and tucked his notebook and pen into his jacket pocket. "I'll be in touch."

Morton shook his hand and leaned in close. "Come by the club this evening. I'll point out a few more people you may find interesting."

CHAPTER 26
JOINT OPERATIONS

THURMAN REREAD the text as his sympathetic nervous system kicked into high gear, producing a full fight-or-flight response. He abruptly stood. "Let's go." He glanced at the door and threw down a wad of euros.

"What is it?"

He showed her the message. "They're coming. We have to get out of here." He reached out and grasped her wrist as Maria entered the dining room carrying a tray of food. "They know our location."

"How?"

"I don't know, probably Walters's phone," said Thurman. He pulled it out of his pocket. "Damn. It was on." *Stupid, I should have remembered to check it.* He powered it off.

Carmen spoke to her aunt. "We have to go."

"But you haven't finished." A puzzled look came over her. Then her eyes turned to Thurman. "Has he brought you trouble?" she hissed in Italian.

Carmen hugged her aunt and kissed her cheeks. "No, it isn't his fault, but some men may come looking for us. Don't mention you've seen us. They are not good people. Grazie, I'll come back."

Maria placed a palm to her forehead then crossed herself. "Be careful."

"Is there a rear exit?" Thurman asked.

Carmen led him through the kitchen and into a dimly lit alley. They exited onto a main road and stopped to get their bearings. Thurman pulled out his phone and called John Bristow.

"We need a pickup."

"Where are you?" Bristow answered.

He handed the phone to Carmen as she pulled his jacket sleeve and began walking. "We're on foot heading north. We'll be at the Orsanmichele Church in a few minutes."

Carmen handed back the phone. They hustled through the eastern edge of the Piazza della Signoria and continued on the main street north. She turned east a few blocks later. Thurman matched her pace. They strolled arm in arm down the stone street in front of Orsanmichele. Thurman scanned the area for potential threats. A car coming down the street slowed next to them. Thurman looked left. It was a Mercedes with tinted windows. "I think we have company."

The car pulled to the curb a few meters in front of them. Two men emerged. Both wore dark clothes. The man exiting from the front passenger seat stepped in front of Carmen, blocking her path. The rear passenger reached for something under his jacket. Thurman charged before he could show his hand and smashed his fist into the man's face. The man crumpled to the pavement. His pistol clattered to the curb. "Run!" yelled Thurman as the driver shoved the transmission into reverse and gunned the motor. The open door hit Thurman in his back, slamming him to the pavement. The man he'd punched leapt on him and swung a sap. Thurman saw a flash of light, and his head exploded in pain. He felt a tug at his jacket pocket.

The man in front of Carmen lunged, grabbing her shoulders. She planted her right foot squarely on his testicles. Air rushed from his lungs as he doubled over. She grabbed two fists of his hair and smashed her knee into his face. He buckled. Carmen shoved him backward.

The driver dashed from around the front of the car and began to draw a handgun from inside his jacket. Carmen dove at his ankles, taking him down. The driver rolled to get up and reached for the pistol.

Thurman scrambled to his feet and kicked it, catching the silencer with his toe. The gun spun across the sidewalk. People screamed and ran. The driver shoved Carmen, rolled away, and took a fighting stance.

Thurman squared off. The driver lashed out with a haymaker. Thurman ducked and moved inside, planting a fist under the man's chin and whipping an elbow to his face. A white incisor bounced on the curb. His mouth spewed blood. His head smacked the doorframe as he fell backward into the front seat, unconscious.

"Get off me!" Carmen hissed. Her first attacker, dripping blood from his nose, gripped her sleeve. She yanked it free. He punched. She ducked and charged. They went down and rolled on the pavement. She snarled like an enraged animal, scratching at his face, ripping an eyelid. He shrieked. Thurman stood over him and delivered the coup de grâce, a strike that caved his cheek. The attacker lay motionless, sprawled on the sidewalk. *That's for Steve.*

Sirens sounded in the distance. Carmen pulled at Thurman's arm. "We have to move. The police are coming." They took off at a sprint, but Thurman couldn't keep up. His head ached and knee throbbed. Carmen looked back and let up a bit so he could catch up. They passed the Apple Store on the piazza and stopped under the Roman arch. Blood dripped from Thurman's left ear. A car approached and stopped near them. Thurman whirled into a defensive stance. The passenger window rolled down.

"Get in, hurry." Bristow looked them over. "What the hell happened?"

Carmen briefly explained as she climbed into the back seat.

Thurman followed her. "Where the hell have you guys been? They almost had us."

Kearns looked over his shoulder. "Sorry, my fault. These streets all look alike, and the damn street signs are impossible to read."

Thurman wiped sweat and blood from his face as his breathing returned to normal. "Where were you this afternoon? You're supposed to have our six."

"We tried to save Walters. They got away," said Kearns.

"We saw you hightail it from the piazza," said Bristow

"This isn't a spectator sport," said Thurman. "How about a little help next time?"

Bristow chuckled. "We're trying. It's hard to keep up with you two. Anyone hurt?"

"Nothing serious," said Thurman, rubbing his knee.

"You look like hell," Bristow said, handing him a handkerchief.

Kearns turned onto a busy street and accelerated. "No one tailing us."

Bristow turned to face Carmen and Thurman. "They must be tracking a cell phone signal."

"They're tracing Walters's cell." Thurman patted his jacket pockets. "Shit. They took it."

Carmen's eyes widened. "They got it?"

"He claims it's loaded with valuable information."

"It must be," said Bristow.

"He said his life depended on keeping it safe," Carmen said. She gripped the door handle, her body tensing as Kearns made random turns through the city.

Thurman looked out the window at the Duomo lit up in the distance. "Walters said Noreen planned to meet Dario Benedetto after the conference. We need to find him."

———

The next morning Thurman stood at the podium and completed his PowerPoint presentation.

"Thank you," he said in response to the applause after the final summary slide.

"I think we have time for a couple of questions," the moderator said.

Thurman answered the audience's questions but kept his eyes on the two men standing next to Carmen at the rear of the conference room. He'd noticed them before starting his talk. *Damn it. Where are Bristow and Kearns?* Thurman sized up the men—two White guys in their midtwenties wearing dark suits. He half expected them to slip on sunglasses and start speaking into their sleeves. At the end of the Q&A

session, they made their way to the stage as the moderator introduced the next speaker. Thurman exited the platform. The two men stood at the foot of the steps. The tallest one stepped forward.

"Dr. Thurman."

"Can I help you?"

He produced a badge. "FBI, please come with us," he said with a New York accent.

"Really . . . here? Do I have a choice?"

The agent flashed the holstered handgun at his side. "Not unless you want to make a scene."

"I'm coming, relax."

They turned and walked toward the doors at the back of the room. As they approached the exits, he recognized Carmen's silhouette in one of the doorways. She came to his side and locked her arm around his.

"C'mon," the tall man said. "Car's waiting. We're late." The four of them marched from the hotel to a black Audi sedan. A valet opened the rear door. Thurman and Carmen got in.

The car crossed over the Arno River and wound through a labyrinth of streets, leaving the old city and entering the industrial warehouse districts. Thurman stared out the window as the scenery became more like downtown Durham, except the graffiti was in Italian. The Audi stopped in front of a gate. Through the iron slats Thurman could see an asphalt lot stocked with pallets of building materials. The driver spoke to the guard and the gate opened. The car advanced to a warehouse where a garage door rolled up and the car entered. Two Carabinieri with automatic rifles stood at the end of the garage bay.

Carmen leaned forward and spoke in Italian. "Are we under arrest?"

CHAPTER 27
CHEST PAIN

AT FIVE O'CLOCK, Detective Jack Ingram strode through the entrance to St. Matthew's Medical Center and stepped into a cavernous atrium. A grenadine-streaked sunset refracted through the three-story glass walls, illuminating the space with an evening glow. A woman in a red blazer occupied an information kiosk to his left; otherwise, the place appeared almost deserted. He located Hairston sitting on a bench with his legs crossed, looking at his phone.

"Jerry, wake up."

Hairston stood. "Hey, Jack. Any new developments?"

"We're still working on the photo from Chase's apartment. There's no record of anyone matching the unsub."

"This Dario Benedetto?"

Ingram nodded as they approached the elevator. "We asked the FBI for help; they contacted Interpol. Maybe we'll get lucky."

"That'd be a nice change."

"How about you?"

Hairston reported the events of the day. "I'm going to check out Anastasia's tonight. I have a bad feeling Morton's telling the truth. I don't know what Noreen Chase got herself into, but it's a lot bigger than drugs." They stepped into the elevator, and Hairston punched the button for the fourth floor.

"I think you're right," Ingram said.

The elevator doors opened as Hairston showed Ingram the rest of his surveillance photos. "This is what he drove this afternoon. Probably has less than ten thousand miles."

Ingram zoomed in studying the vehicle for several seconds. "It's the right make and model, it could be the one Thurman called in. Did it look like it had been in an accident?"

"It looked like he just drove it off the lot."

"Anything from the plates?" asked Ingram.

"It's registered to him through his business."

"Which one?"

"The dealership."

"It couldn't be the one that tailed Thurman, then. It ran into the back of his truck." Ingram pressed the buzzer on the door to the trauma ICU.

"May I help you?"

"Detectives Ingram and Hairston here." The lock clicked, and the doors swung open. The two men proceeded down the hallway, passing glass-fronted rooms with open curtains. A nursing station occupied the center of the unit. The ICU felt cold and smelled antiseptic. Ventilators hummed like mechanical insects. Glass walls permitted a clear view of patients lying prone on air mattresses.

Hairston glanced around as they approached the nursing station. "Feels like *Nostromo* with the crew in stasis."

"Huh?"

"*Alien*, the movie. *Nostromo* was the spaceship."

"Haven't seen it."

"You're kidding. It's a classic. Who hasn't seen *Alien*? You're a strange dude, Ingram."

A nurse stood behind the counter. "Good evening, officers. Mr. Drake is in room seven." She pointed directly behind them.

Yuri sat with the head of his bed raised about forty-five degrees. An untouched dinner tray lay on the rollaway table positioned across his thighs. The pelvic external-fixator frame blocked it from getting closer. The detectives knocked on the doorjamb and entered the room.

"Hello, Mr. Drake, I'm Detective Ingram from the Raleigh Police, and this is Sergeant Hairston from Durham PD. Do you mind if we ask you a few questions?"

"No," he whispered. He pushed the mobile table away from the bed. "I can't eat this crap anyway." The detectives moved closer. Ingram finished moving it out of the way. "Do me a favor, pick me up a cheeseburger the next time."

Ingram smiled. "MoJoe's is just down the street, best burgers in town."

Yuri gave him a thumbs-up. He looked pale and bloated. Dark circles surrounded his eyes, a result of his basilar skull fracture. The front half of his head was shaved, and an intracranial pressure monitoring tube protruded from the top of his skull like a recharging cord.

Someone had slicked down the remaining black hair, making him look like a pulverized Al Pacino with a receding hairline. "What do you want to know?" The raspy voice was more Marlon Brando.

"What happened the night of the accident?" Hairston asked.

"I don't remember. That whole last day before the crash is gone. I woke up in this place. They said my motorcycle crashed."

Ingram continued. "Did you know Noreen Chase?"

Drake nodded. "We are close friends."

"Are you in a relationship with her?"

His drooping eyelids retracted. "What?"

Ingram repeated the question. "Were you and Ms. Chase romantically involved?"

"Who told you that?"

"Just answer the question, please."

"I'm happily married, my wife's expecting our first child."

"A lot of people stray," Ingram interjected. "We're not judging. It has implications for the investigation."

"How does this have anything to do with a motorcycle crash?" Yuri said.

Ingram looked at Hairston as he cleared his throat. "I'm afraid that isn't what we're investigating at the moment," Hairston said. "Are you aware of Miss Chase's death?"

Yuri's head tilted. "Did you say Noreen is dead?"

Ingram gripped the side rail. "Someone killed her the night of your accident."

Yuri tried to sit up but stopped midway, grimacing in pain. "Noreen, murdered?"

The heart rate monitors beeped.

"Drug overdose," Hairston said.

Yuri rested his head on the pillow with eyes closed. "Then he must know . . . I've been betrayed," he whispered.

Ingram glanced at the cardiac display. Yuri's heart rate had doubled. *This ain't good.*

Hairston finished copying Yuri's words in his notebook. "Can you think of anyone or any reason someone would want her dead?"

Yuri pointed at a Styrofoam cup with a bent straw sitting on the rollaway table. "Water."

Ingram put it in front of him. With considerable effort, Yuri placed the straw between his lips and swallowed. Ingram took a second look at the monitors. Yuri's heart rate continued to accelerate. His blood pressure plummeted. Another monitor began flashing. "What are you afraid of? We can protect you."

Yuri coughed and held his belly.

"Call the nurse," Ingram said.

"Yeah—he don't look so good." Hairston started for the door. "Nurse!"

Yuri clutched his left arm and tried to speak. No sound emerged. His head slumped forward. Alarms went off. A nurse rushed in. She looked at the patient and placed her fingers over his carotid pulse. The erratic EKG tracing bounced all over the place. She leaned over his head, listening for breath sounds, then grabbed the phone clipped to her scrub pants while she pressed the button to flatten the bed. *"Code blue, code blue, trauma ICU room seven!"*

CHAPTER 28
SOLO

AS THE HOSPITAL personnel responded to the new crisis, Hairston and Ingram stayed in the corner where they watched the event unfold. Angie came over to them. "Do you guys always have this effect on people?"

"Only if you lie to us," Ingram said.

She wiped perspiration from her forehead. "I know you're trying to do your job, but no more questioning for a while."

"How long?"

"Check back in a few days." She escorted them to the TICU door.

Ingram and Hairston walked out of the hospital into the cool evening air. They made their way along the main sidewalk to the parking garage.

"You think he'll be all right?" Hairston asked.

"Hard to say, but I sure hope so." Ingram checked his watch. "It's a little early to go to Morton's club. You want to get a beer?"

Two hours later Ingram parked the unmarked black Charger next to a dumpster in an alley a block from Anastasia's. The sweet stench of rancid grease and organic rot greeted them as they exited the cruiser. "If anyone had told me police work was going to be this glamorous, I'd have listened to my mother and become an orthodontist," Ingram said.

"You should have taken her advice," Hairston said as he dodged puddles. "The army straightened me out."

Ingram looked over at Hairston. His eyes had a sad twinkle. "You too? No shit?"

"Military police, five years," Hairston replied.

They sloshed down the alley approaching Alston Street. "Then what?"

"Howard University on the GI Bill, then here. My wife's family is from Winston-Salem."

"Did you always want to be in law enforcement? Why not law or medicine?"

Hairston scanned the area, then shoved his hands in his pockets and walked on. "I lost my older brother to gang violence when we were in high school. I kind of went off the rails and didn't get back on track until boot camp."

"What made you straighten up?" Ingram said.

"A drill sergeant at Fort Leonard Wood helped me find my calling. We had a come-to-Jesus moment on the second day of basic training. After that I finished at the top of my class and went into MP training."

Ingram stopped walking. Hairston turned and halted but continued the story, his words floating down the alley. "They never found out who killed my brother, but I vowed to help others so what happened to him didn't continue—for Eddie."

"Wow," Ingram said. "I had no idea."

"I don't talk about it much," Hairston said.

"Why now?" Ingram asked.

"Sometimes I need to remind myself why I do this," Hairston said.

Ingram nodded understanding. "We all have those days. You spend enough time watching people dish out the worst shit humanity has to offer, and it takes a toll. Only priests hear more confessions." They both started moving again. This time, in silence.

They approached the pulsing glow of a neon sign. Hairston held the door and they entered.

"Twenty bucks cover, ten-dollar beers, twelve-dollar drinks, no empty hands," said the doorman, who bore a striking resemblance to the former Mr. Olympia Lou Ferrigno.

Hairston flashed his badge. "We have an invitation from Mr.

Morton."

The hulk scowled, then tilted his head toward the bar as he folded his arms. "In the back."

A whiff of cheap cologne assaulted Ingram's nose as he walked past and entered the arena. The bar ran along the right side of the room, illuminated by small halogen spotlights suspended on wires hanging from steel beams. A dance floor, outlined with brilliant stage lights, dominated the left side of the large open space. A topless woman wearing a G-string had one leg wrapped around the middle of three poles erected on the stage. Her body contorted in rhythm to techno music at a decibel level almost compatible with conversation. Patrons sat at tables near the stage, periodically holding out dollar bills. The performer reacted like a Pavlovian subject, releasing the poll and gyrating around the stage, tucking her tips under a garter belt.

"What can I get you, gentlemen?" asked the bartender. He was young, goateed, and muscular, over six feet tall with mohawked black hair in a topknot. The tattoo of a reptile wound about his neck above his shirt collar.

Hairston leaned over the bar. "Where's the manager?"

"Who's asking?"

"Just a friend."

He gave Hairston a skeptical look but motioned to the shadows at the rear of the room. "His office." He hailed a waitress clad in little more than a collection of well-placed sequins. Ingram wondered what kind of adhesive was used. "Take these gentlemen up to Solo's office." She slid her arm around Ingram's and felt the tension as his biceps contracted.

"My, my . . . doing anything later on?" she asked. "Buy me a drink?"

"Mr. Solo's office, please."

He slid his arm from her grasp.

"You're no fun," she said, giving Ingram a pout. She led them to a door at the end of the bar and pressed a button. After a buzz, she pulled the handle and led them down a dim corridor. Their escort moved with the grace of a runway model and half pirouetted, extending an arm toward a staircase like Vanna White on the *Wheel of*

Fortune. "Top of the stairs, gentlemen." She turned toward the bar and gave Ingram a wink. "I'm on stage next set, come see the show."

The tassels dangling from her pasties brushed against Ingram's folded arms as she strutted past. "Maybe next time, baby."

She blew him a silent kiss.

Hairston jerked his head, advanced up the stairs, and knocked.

"Come in," said a voice from a wall speaker. The lock buzzed and Hairston gave the door a push.

Bright lights illuminated an office space filled with dated office furniture and computer screens. The smell of stale tobacco smoke hung in the air. A bald white man who looked midthirties sat behind the desk. He wore a dark suit, a black crew neck shirt with several heavy gold chains, and a twenty-thousand-dollar Rolex. Two younger men who looked like extras from an early Scorsese movie sat at the desks on the opposite side of the room.

"What can I do for you?" asked the bald man as he stood and smoothed his tailored jacket.

"I'm Detective Hairston, this is Detective Ingram." He walked toward the desk and displayed his shield. "You the manager?"

The bald man leaned forward, right hand extended, and spoke with a Russian accent. "Artem Soloviev, but call me Solo, I run this establishment."

"All right, Solo. You know a guy by the name of Terry Morton?"

"Of course, he's one of the owners."

"How long have you known him?"

"Couple of years, he hired me."

Ingram walked around behind the desk and looked at the computer screen. Security camera video feeds ran in real time. Poor lighting cast some areas in shadows. "How many cameras?"

Solo pressed a key, and the screen divided into multiple images. "Six, we keep a close eye on the place. You know, to protect the talent." A man and a woman entered one of the pictures and approached the bar.

Ingram pointed to it. "Show me this one."

Solo's neck muscles tensed. He clicked on the image.

He nodded to Hairston. "Check this out."

Hairston moved closer to the desk and studied the image for a few moments. "I don't know the guy, but I met the woman today. She works at Morton's dealership. Name's Natasha."

"Tasha is one of our most popular dancers. She and Terry are . . . close."

Hairston squinted and pointed to the monitor. "Who's that guy?"

"Never seen him before," Solo replied.

Ingram studied Solo's face. *Liar.*

"Why are you here, detective?" Solo said.

"Relax, man. We were just in the neighborhood." Ingram watched the screen as Natasha walked to a table next to the stage and sat down with her back to the camera. A server brought drinks while another dancer began her routine. Ingram recognized the sequins. Two men entered the picture and sat at the table. One leaned over and kissed Natasha.

The man next to Natasha with his back to the camera turned around. His face appeared on the screen. Hairston blinked and leaned closer. Then he looked at Solo and pointed to the screen. "What about him?"

"That's Terry."

"I know who he is; the guy with his eyes glued to the stage."

Solo leaned toward the monitor and shook his head. "Don't know him."

Hairston glanced at Ingram.

"Ahhh . . . ahhhh . . . ahhhh*chu!*" Ingram sneezed right in Solo's face.

Solo was momentarily stunned.

"Oh, man. I am so sorry. My bad. That one snuck up on me."

Solo wiped his face with a handkerchief as Hairston stuck a dime-sized audio transmitter under the edge of Solo's desk. "C'mon, Jack, let's meet these guys. I'll introduce you to Morton and his friend."

Solo pushed a buzzer, and a man peeked his head in the door. "Kilo, show them the way."

"We can find our way," Ingram said.

"He'll keep you company." The guy had a long dark ponytail and a swollen lip.

The trio went down the stairs and through the back hallway.

"So, Kilo, what happened to your lip?" Ingram asked. "Someone punch you, or you been kissing your boss's ass too hard?"

A sneer appeared on Kilo's face. He pounded his right fist into the other palm. "The name refers to the weight of my fist when it connects with your face."

"Don't give me a reason, punk."

A gap-tooth smile appeared. "You want to find out?"

"I asked you a question. Who punched you?"

Kilo glared daggers, locking eyes with Ingram. "Sparring . . . a couple of days ago."

"There they are over there," Hairston said casually.

Ingram and Hairston strode through the door into the bar. Music pounded as two women moved like pros around the stage. The detectives approached the table where Morton was sitting with Natasha and the other men.

Hairston tapped Morton's shoulder, causing him to turn around. "Evening, Terry. Enjoying the show?"

"Detective, how nice to see you," he said. "We seem to be running into each other a lot lately. Coincidence?"

"I don't think so." *He's scared of something.* Hairston glanced across the table. "Hello, Natasha."

"Excuse me, Terry," she said. "I need a smoke." She took a sip of her drink, then stood and walked toward the entrance. Her eyes caught Hairston's.

"Sit down, gentlemen. Can I get you anything?" Morton signaled for a waitress and turned to Ingram. "I don't believe we've met."

"Jack Ingram, Raleigh homicide."

Hairston shook his head. "No drinks tonight, thanks. Who are your friends?"

Morton motioned to the man sitting next to where Natasha had just been. "This is a business partner of mine visiting from California, Bill Burke, and this is David Moore."

Hairston leaned over the edge of the table and shook hands. "Good evening, gentlemen."

Ingram remained silent and watched.

"What can we do for you?" Morton sipped his beer.

Hairston planted his palms on the table and leaned toward Moore. "What's an electrical engineer doing slumming in a strip club?"

Moore held his hand to his ear. "I didn't hear you."

Hairston repeated the question louder so he could be heard over the music.

Moore looked at Morton and almost shouted in response, "I like the entertainment."

"You have a problem with that?" asked Morton.

Hairston gripped Ingram by the arm. "C'mon, Jack, let's get out of here." He pointed at Morton. "We'll be in touch."

"Stop by any time," Morton said, raising his glass as the detectives left. The Lou Ferrigno wannabe nodded. They pushed open the front door and stepped onto the sidewalk. Natasha was standing a few feet away, smoking a cigarette.

"Good night, nice meeting you," Ingram said to her as they approached.

She took a deep drag, then dropped the butt and crushed it on the pavement. "You too," she said. Smoke whipped over her shoulders as she marched past, palming a note to Hairston, who slipped it into his pocket. She went back into the club while the detectives kept walking.

"Tell me you got it done," said Ingram as they entered the alley.

"Of course. By the way, you're getting good at sneezing."

Ingram chuckled. "Ever since COVID it really freaks people out. Where'd you put it?"

Hairston opened his door and slid into the car. "Under the corner near the wall. No one will notice it."

"We hope," said Ingram as he started the engine. "What's an ubergeek like David Moore doing hanging out with Morton?"

"It's more than just a coincidence." Hairston pulled out the note and unfolded it. "What do you make of this?"

Ingram turned on the interior light and read the note.

2745 East Birmingham Blvd, Friday, 0245

"Thanksgiving night. Where's East Birmingham?"

Hairston thumbed his phone. "Warehouse in the Triangle, near the airport. I'll ask around, see if any of our CIs have heard anything."

CHAPTER 29
FREEDOM FLIGHT

(Five Years Ago)

"IS EVERYTHING READY?" shouted the bespectacled, white-haired professor from the balcony of the particle accelerator's cantilevered control room, where the beam of ionized calcium would originate.

"Yes sir," replied Oganessian's brilliant protégé, Yuri Aleksandrovich Kogan who stood fifty feet away, double checking a piece of equipment.

Professor Oganessian looked out over his laboratory and smiled in satisfaction. Pipes and conduits of various diameters crisscrossed the room, connecting electronic instruments and computers. Scientists in gray coveralls scurried about, stepping over and around equipment carrying out their last minute tasks. The senior scientist raised an upturned thumb and retreated into the luminescent control room.

The Joint Institute for Nuclear Research, otherwise known as JINR, was located in the city of Dubna seventy-five miles north of Moscow. The centerpiece of its campus-like grounds was the Flerov Laboratory, where Oganessian and his team were about to conduct an experiment. Named after Russian nuclear physicist Georgy Flerov, it is the original facility for heavy ion research. The lab's enormous, chaotic conglomeration of pipes, wires, computers, valves, and switches had produced eight new superheavy elements over the last decade.

Yuri finished his preparations and started walking back to the control room. He stopped near the steps as Professor Oganessian, a woman wearing a long coat and fur Cossack hat, and a burly man dressed in a business suit and overcoat began descending the stairs. They stopped at the bottom. The woman's raven hair fell midwaist and framed her beautiful face. Yuri thought she looked bored standing behind the two men with her hands buried in her coat pockets.

The professor smiled and placed a hand on the big man's shoulder. "Yuri, I'd like you to meet Dimitry Stanov, a former student of mine who will observe today's experiment. Mr. Stanov is a generous patron of my research."

Yuri extended his hand. "Thank you, sir." After the handshake he looked at the beautiful woman being ignored by the two men. "Good morning."

She remained statuesque. Stanov and the professor exchanged smiles. Oganessian looked at Yuri. "This is a business associate, Natasha Vishneva."

Yuri smiled at the woman and gave a head bow. "It's a pleasure to meet you."

Stanov turned and gestured toward the control room. "Please tell me about the experiment."

The professor took over. "The ion beam will shoot approximately six trillion calcium ions per second. Once the calcium ions are fired, electrostatic deflectors turn the ion beam from the source into the cyclotron," he pointed to an enormous circular structure near the center of the floor. "A magnetic coil then bends the particle beam into a spiral, accelerating it close to the speed of light. Once it reaches the desired velocity, it's redirected through this pipe and shot into the target in the next building."

Stanov stood with his hands in his overcoat pockets and stared down the six foot diameter green pipe that ran the length of the laboratory and exited through a wall two-hundred feet away. "What's the target?"

"A thin film of the element californium. We will blast the target with the calcium ion beam for the next several weeks."

"Weeks?" asked Stanov.

Yuri looked at the floor and nodded. "Yes."

"Why so long?"

Oganessian stroked his chin. "Someone once told me a good analogy: Creating a new element is as difficult as shooting a machine gun at a needle in a haystack, trying to strike the very point of the needle so it fuses with the bullet, and then catching the fused piece as it ricochets, before it vanishes."

"That doesn't sound promising," Stanov said.

Oganessian smiled and again placed his hand on his shoulder. "With luck, several atoms will smash together in precisely the correct orientation forming a new element."

"The calcium and californium will fuse to form the element, oganesson," added Yuri, "named after the professor. Someday he will be awarded a Nobel Prize in physics for his work."

The professor sputtered and waved a hand. "Nonsense, let's get on with the experiment. Go to the control room, Aliya is waiting. The three of us will proceed next door. Fire the beam on my signal."

As Yuri started to the building, Natasha dropped a glove. They both bent down to retrieve it. She looked at him with piercing emerald eyes. Her gaze held him momentarily. "I can help you leave this place," she whispered. When he handed her the glove she discretely passed him a business card. "Call this number when you are ready."

He smiled and nodded, then climbed the steps to the control room. Aliya sat with her back to him at a computer terminal, her slender physique hidden by gray coveralls. "Have you checked the ion tube?"

"Everything is ready." He stopped and leaned over her shoulder. "You know this won't work. He'll never reach the Island of Stability."

Aliya turned to face him. "I know."

"I can build an accelerator that will."

"How?"

Yuri sat and pulled his chair close to hers and explained.

"That's crazy enough to actually work." Aliya said.

"It will work."

"Then why don't you build it?"

"How? There is no chance for me here. The professor laughed when I told him. He said we don't need another Lysenko affair."

Aliya's eyes widened. "He did not."

"I love you more than anything, help me make this dream come true?"

Aliya placed her arms around his neck and kissed him. "You are the most brilliant person I've ever met. Your happiness is what's important to me. I'll do whatever you ask."

Yuri's face brightened. "Then we must get out of here." He fingered the card in his pocket.

———

Six weeks later Professor Oganessian received the email he'd been waiting for. He ran his fingers through his white hair and picked up his phone. "I have excellent news. The final pieces of equipment have been completed. We will finish construction of the new ion collider on schedule."

"Excellent," replied Stanov.

"I'm going to Geneva next week. I plan to stop in Essen on the way to the CERN conference."

———

Noreen Chase stood in the lobby of Thyssenkrupp corporate headquarters in Essen and waved as Professor Oganessian, Yuri, and Aliya entered through the revolving doors a hundred feet away. She turned to Richard Gross, who buttoned his jacket and returned her smile. "Are you nervous, darling?"

"I'm worried about Natasha's message."

"Try to relax. Stanov needs this equipment. He's not going to do anything to stop it from being shipped to Dubna."

"It's not him I'm worried about."

"Yuri is committed, he's all in."

"How can you be sure."

Without changing his expression he whispered, "Because you're going to convince him we're his ticket out of Russia. Now, relax and remember your training."

Noreen smoothed her platinum hair and adjusted her sweater. "What about Yuri's fiancée?"

"Aliya will accompany Yuri. Focus on him, he is the key." They strode across the lobby. "Hello, Dr. Oganessian, thank you for coming."

"Hello, Rick."

"You remember my associate, Dr. Noreen Chase."

"Dr. Chase is difficult to forget." The professor kissed each side of her cheek.

"I hope your flight was easy," she said.

The professor frowned as he shook hands. "I'm certain that . . . that flying coffin we were on saw action in the Afghan war. My God, it was horrible."

Gross put his hand on the professor's shoulder. "Don't worry; tomorrow morning you will be seated in first class on the Swiss flight to Geneva, compliments of Thyssenkrupp." He addressed the group. "Please come with us. We have lunch and a short presentation by an engineer I'm sure you'll remember. Then we'll take you to the facility, where you will see what you've been waiting for."

———

After lunch the group of scientists and engineers boarded a Mercedes passenger van and drove across campus to a warehouse the size of a city block. Gross gathered them together as they disembarked and handed out hard hats then pointed them to several golf carts they would drive through the enormous storage facility to where the equipment was located.

Noreen leaned on Yuri's arm, holding him back from the others. "I think you will be impressed. Our engineers have done a wonderful job."

"I hope so. Without the instruments we can't proceed."

Noreen looked puzzled. "Do you think it will work?"

Yuri shrugged. "We will have to see. That's why it is called an experiment."

She placed her arm around his. "What would you do?"

"Build a different machine."

"Why do you say that?"

He stopped and faced her. "Because I would."

She slipped her hand into his. "Yuri, we've worked together for several years. We're friends. You can trust me. Whatever you tell me will be kept in confidence."

"Oganessian's design is flawed. I have a different strategy."

"I've heard you speak and read your papers. Your ideas are brilliant."

"Not everyone holds that opinion."

"Then they are blinded by their ambition and jealousy. Your theory on the plasma wakefield effect and its application for next generation linear ion accelerators is revolutionary."

"We may never know. I doubt if I'll get the chance to test those ideas."

Noreen once again slipped her arm around his as they resumed walking. "What if I could help you?"

"Do what?"

"Get a chance to test your theories and maybe change the world."

He whispered, "Tell me more."

"Ride with me. We can discuss the details."

Ten minutes later they parked the golf cart in front of a series of cargo shipping containers. Gross approached the closest one and swung open the doors. Yuri walked next to the equipment. "I have to see it work."

"A live demonstration?" asked Gross.

The professor turned and faced Yuri. "Is that possible?"

Yuri spoke up. "I want to observe the collection chambers connected to the control panels and the system turned on, fully charged with liquid helium. We've come too far to have the chambers shipped to Dubna only to discover problems. I insist on a test."

Gross ran his fingers through his hair and looked at his chief engineer, Dario Benedetto. "Can this be done?"

Dario thought for a moment before responding. "It will take the rest of the afternoon and most of the evening to set everything up. I can have it ready by noon tomorrow. Will that be acceptable?"

"I'd like to watch the assembly process," Yuri said, then clapped his hands. "Yes, that will be excellent. Benedetto, you are amazing."

"Prego."

"This is not possible," said the professor. "I have to be in Geneva by noon tomorrow."

"We need to be sure the equipment works," Yuri said emphatically.

Noreen spoke up. "Professor Oganessian can go to the meeting as scheduled. We'll have everything ready by tomorrow afternoon. Yuri can watch the setup and demonstration and then we'll fly him to Geneva on one of our corporate planes. He'll be there before dinner."

"I'll need Aliya to observe the tests," said Yuri. "She and I will be the ones operating the machines. Can you fly both of us?"

"Of course," said Gross.

Oganessian stood over the uncovered control panel. "The project has been delayed long enough." He looked up. "Very well, run the tests. You can catch up to me in Geneva."

Gross smiled. "Dario, take over here. Professor Oganessian, come with me back to the hotel. Dr. Chase will pick you up for breakfast at nine o'clock tomorrow morning, then take you to the airport."

———

At noon the next day the passenger van stopped at the warehouse. Yuri looked out his window at the empty golf cart. "Where are Noreen and Dario?"

"Calibrating the equipment," said Gross. As he exited the van, a black BMW pulled up. Two men dressed in jeans and lightweight zip-up jackets emerged.

"Who are they?" Yuri asked.

Gross shrugged and addressed them. "Can I help you?"

The terse reply came in Russian.

Yuri translated. "They're from the Russian Federal Security Service, the FSB. They want to escort us to the airport to take me and Aliya back to Russia."

"This is Germany. You have no authority here," said Gross.

Yuri translated. Then one of the men pulled a folded piece of paper from his inside jacket pocket and gave it to Gross.

"How considerate of Mr. Stanov and his associates at the Kremlin. They've convinced Interpol to issue a Red Notice." Gross returned the document.

"What's that?" asked Aliya.

"An international arrest warrant," answered Gross.

"That's ridiculous," said Yuri. "We've done nothing wrong." He turned to the agents and spoke in Russian. "What's the charge?"

The Russian replied and waved the document.

Yuri's color drained. He turned to Gross. "We're being charged with the theft and sale of Russian commercial trade secrets. We have to return with them to Moscow immediately."

Gross looked at the agents. "Your government has employed us to make these machines. No one has stolen anything. This equipment has been purchased by your country, and we want to make sure it's operating properly before shipping it. Can we at least complete the tests? It should take less than an hour."

Yuri translated and the head FSB agent responded in Russian, then took out a phone. "He will ask if this is okay." Yuri smiled as he listened to the one-sided conversation. The man slipped the phone back into his jacket pocket and spoke to Yuri. "He says very well, but afterward they will drive us to the airport. He also says they have authority to shoot if we resist."

Gross scoffed and led the group to the golf cart. He and Aliya slid into the front seat. "Yuri, hang on tight. Tell them the demonstration will be in section T-5. They better run or they'll miss it. Everyone in?" He glanced back. Yuri stood on the rear bumper, holding on to the frame while he translated Gross's instructions. Gross mashed the accelerator. "Hang on, there's been a little change of plans."

The FSB agents sprinted to keep up, but the cart sped through the warehouse, weaving in and out of aisles across the vast storage facility.

Yuri swayed with every turn as Gross drove between pallets of materials stacked twenty feet tall. Then Gross pulled a walkie-talkie from his coat pocket and spoke in Italian. Ten minutes later he stopped next to Noreen and Dario's golf cart. Noreen sat in front of a computer display. Gross called out, "Dario, everything ready?"

The Italian appeared from behind several stacked fifty-gallon drums, holding a large pipe wrench. "Buongiorno, everything is set." Gross walked to him and inspected the equipment.

A few moments later the two Russians appeared. Sweat dripped from their red faces as they gasped for air. Between breaths one yelled at Gross in Russian. He unzipped his jacket, exposing a pistol in a holster. He looked at Yuri and growled instructions.

"He says if you try that again, it will be unpleasant when we return to Russia."

Gross looked at Dario and asked a question in Italian.

"Certo, nessun problema," he responded, smiling.

———

"For cooling purposes, liquid nitrogen will substitute for helium in today's demonstration," explained Dario.

"It will suffice," said Yuri, glancing at Noreen.

Dario pointed to a digital clock. "The ion beam will be released on the count of ten." He started the timer. Ten, nine, . . ."

The FSB men watched the group.

"Five, four, . . ."

"What ion beam?" asked Aliya. "What's with the space launch drama?"

"Two, one." Gross touched his phone screen.

The cooling tank exploded. A deafening sound echoed through the warehouse. Smoking supercooled fluid sprayed from the insulated hose that whipped back and forth like an enraged silver snake. A wave of boiling liquid nitrogen over three hundred degrees below zero spewed across the floor.

"Get out of here! Run!" screamed Dario.

The wave of liquid washed over an FSB agent's shoe and leg,

instantly freezing his flesh. He screamed and tried to run, but his shoes stuck and he toppled to the floor. The other agent ran from the dancing hose that gushed anti-lava.

Gross grabbed Aliya. "Into the carts."

Noreen pulled Yuri's arm. "Hurry!"

The carts raced through the warehouse maze. Shelves of crates and boxes whizzed by in a blur. Yuri gripped the seat handle like a rodeo cowboy riding a bronc.

"Hang on," Noreen ordered. She maneuvered the electric cart in and out of aisles and broke into the open area near the front of the building. She slammed on the brakes and skidded to a stop next to the van. Gross walked to Noreen and leaned over to kiss her. "You and Dario call for an ambulance. I'll get them to the airport."

"I want to go with you," she said.

"No, you can't be tied to this. A nitrogen tank ruptured. It has to look like an accident. Meet me in London." Richard Gross stepped into the van. Before closing the door he looked at Noreen. "Help those poor bastards."

———

The van cleared the entrance to the Thyssenkrupp campus and soon merged onto the Bundesautobahn 40. Gross accelerated past numerous vehicles.

Aliya's eyes were wide. Her hands shook. "Where are we going?"

Gross ignored the questions and maneuvered into the left lane.

"The airport," answered Yuri.

Aliya gripped Yuri's arm. "Then where?"

Yuri brushed hair from her forehead and kissed it. "To freedom, a place where we can do our work without interference."

CHAPTER 30
EXTRATERRITORIAL CRIMINAL SQUAD

(Florence, Italy, Present Day)

THURMAN AND CARMEN sat in the back seat of the Audi sedan. It came to a stop next to a loading dock in a warehouse. Two Carabinieri approached with automatic rifles and belts full of ammunition magazines. Taking positions on each side, they heel-toe walked toward the vehicle and then stopped ten meters away. Another officer appeared from the shadows and gave commands in Italian. The guards lowered their weapons and approached the car, then each grasped a door handle and pulled in unison. They motioned for Thurman and Carmen to exit.

"Don't touch me," hissed Carmen in Italian at the officer who attempted to grip her arm.

The driver looked at the Carabinieri and shook his head. The man stepped back.

"You mind telling us what's going on?" asked Thurman.

"Follow me," said the driver. He led the group through a door at the rear of the loading platform and into the building. They walked single file through a series of hallways and up two flights of stairs. The driver proceeded to a wooden door with a frosted glass window. Etched lettering read ERNESTO D'ALESSANDRO & SONS, ANTIQ- UITIES IMPORT/EXPORT. The door opened.

"Greetings," said John Bristow. "We've been waiting."

Thurman exhaled, mumbled several profanities, and said, "How about a little heads-up next time?"

"Sorry, couldn't risk it." He embraced Carmen cheek to cheek, then followed her into the next room. "Thanks for keeping an eye on our guy."

Carmen smiled and glanced at Thurman. "From what I've seen, he can handle himself just fine."

Thurman gripped his friend by the arm and pulled him aside. "Who are these people?"

Bristow returned a tight smile. He spoke in hushed tones through clenched teeth, barely moving his lips. "The only way we could do this without causing an international incident was to get the FBI and the Carabinieri involved."

Thurman leaned closer and whispered, "This is an operational planning session? I thought we were being taken for some Italian enhanced interrogation techniques."

"Sorry about that. I wanted to tell you, but I couldn't. Complain to the FBI, it's their show."

Thurman let go of his arm and let out an irritated sigh.

Bristow stepped toward the front and addressed the group. "May I have your attention?" Everyone turned and conversations ceased. "The United States government thanks everyone involved. You have our deepest appreciation and gratitude. To set the record straight, we're here because of the kidnapping of three American citizens. Dr. Robert Walters, his wife, Gwen, and their daughter, Annie, were abducted and are believed to be in the area. A secondary goal is to recover a stolen prototype electric vehicle. At the request of the Italian government, a hostage rescue operation has been put together."

Bristow motioned to his right. "These are the individuals assisting us. Allow me to introduce Captain Alberto DiRienzo of the Cara- binieri. He's in charge of the Hostage Recovery Fusion Cell. Next to him is Special Agent Conner Jenkins from the FBI New York Field

Office and Special Agent Bonnie Pope, the assistant Legal Attaché here in Florence. She's been invaluable in helping coordinate this operation." With the introductions out of the way, Bristow proceeded to tell the story of Walters at the baptistery, the attack in Florence later that night, and the theft of the phone. "Now I'd like to turn things over to Special Agent Jenkins, who has been tasked with assembling what the bureau calls an Extraterritorial Criminal Squad. We'll keep it simple and call it C-11."

Jenkins stood about Bristow's height and except for his weapon, he resembled an American tourist. He wore trail shoes, hiking pants, a shirt made from fast-drying synthetic materials, and an unzipped lightweight jacket that flapped open to reveal a semiautomatic pistol and magazine pouches.

"Mr. Bristow, Dr. Thurman, and Dr. Black are part of a third-party intermediary, the private security company Trident Sentinel International. They are participating at the request of the State Department. A cellular analysis survey team has conducted a study on the phone calls made by our abducted engineer. The team acquired phone data from the last two years. Beginning two weeks ago, until his abduction, he made at least one call a day to Italy. Since then, there has been no activity. We tracked those calls to cell towers in the area around Poggibonsi."

Thurman raised his hand. "Where's that?"

Jenkins answered, "It's about an hour south of Florence, close to Siena. The CAST triangulated the signals and localized them to a recently renovated estate in the Tuscan hills owned by a Russian businessman named Dimitry Stanov. We believe Walters and his family, and perhaps the EV, are being held there."

Thurman exchanged glances with Carmen and Bristow.

"Stanov is a Russian billionaire collaborating with several Italian investors. They're in the process of building a high-tech campus in Poggibonsi focusing on a variety of futuristic industrial projects."

"Based on pirated technology," whispered Carmen.

Jenkins continued. "From what we know, Stanov has invested considerable capital into the local economy, he is well-liked, and the Italian authorities don't want to be linked to the raid, especially if our leads turn out to be wrong. Therefore, they have asked the FBI and TSI to do the heavy lifting. The Carabinieri will back us up in case this turns into a cluster."

———

The rotors of the Carabinieri Airbus H135 helicopter whirled on the runway at the Florence airport as the C-11 team piled into the transport bay and found their seats. The aircraft was outfitted for SWAT missions. Its twin sat fifty meters away, fully manned and prepared for departure. The flight would take less than twenty minutes after liftoff. Thurman looked at his watch, 0320 hours. He noted the tone of the engine and the sound of the blades. The Airbus produced a smooth whine that cut the air in contrast to the brute thumping of a Night Stalker Black Hawk. Thurman looked across the aisle at Carmen. "You ready?"

She shook her head. "Almost."

Thurman responded with a quizzical look.

She folded her hands, stared straight ahead, and began:

"Recognizing that I volunteered as a Ranger, fully knowing the hazards of my chosen profession, I will always endeavor to uphold the prestige, honor, and high esprit de corps of the Rangers.

"Acknowledging the fact that a Ranger is a more elite soldier who arrives at the cutting edge of battle by land, sea, or air, I accept the fact that as a Ranger my country expects me to move further, faster, and fight harder than any other soldier.

"Never shall I fail my comrades . . ."

A broad smile spread across Thurman's face as she continued reciting the Ranger Creed.

". . . Readily will I display the intestinal fortitude required to fight on to the Ranger objective and complete the mission, though I be the lone survivor.

"Rangers lead the way!"

Thurman raised his hand to the brim of his helmet in a salute.

"Now, I'm ready," Carmen shouted. "Hooah!"

CHAPTER 31
A TUSCAN VILLA

COMMANDS CAME OVER THEIR COMS, first in Italian, then English. "Gear check, LZ five minutes." Thurman didn't need to check his gear. He'd already triple-checked it, so he adjusted his night vision goggles one more time. There would be no fast roping on this mission. They would simply land and run.

Carmen pounded his knee with her fist and mouthed, "Ready?"

"Locked and loaded."

She read his lips and gave him a thumbs-up. The helicopter slowed and began a rapid descent, hovering for a moment before it touched down. He waited for the command, then hit the ground running. They'd landed in a clearing just outside the ancient walled compound. Thurman glanced over his shoulder as the helicopter settled and the pilot slowed the rotor rpms. He ran from the landing zone to a road lined with tall cypress trees leading up a hill to the villa. Carmen, Bristow, and Kearns waited.

"Come on, move," Bristow's voice hissed through his earpiece. Their four-man team ran and gathered next to the entrance gate. The other teams would enter from the rear. Kearns set the breaching charge. They waited against the limestone wall. Kearns held up a fist and raised fingers one at a time. When the third finger went up, the gate blew open. They ran into the courtyard.

Carmen pointed. "That's it." She and Thurman were to search the garage next to the main house. She ran to the entrance and turned the handle. The door opened. She looked at Bristow. "Seems too easy. Something's not right."

He nodded. "Let's go." They entered with weapons ready. Everything appeared in shades of green and gray through the NVGs. Two cars occupied the space, but neither was the one they were looking for.

"Here's a stairwell. I'll check upstairs. You go down," Carmen whispered.

Thurman followed and watched her ascend. He started down. A dozen steps later he came to a landing and turned a hundred and eighty degrees, then went down another flight, like descending to the bottom of a dry well. A metal door greeted him at the bottom of the stairs. He touched it and it slid open. He stepped into a large room. Someone had parked a Tesla Model X in the center of the subterranean space.

Thump, thump, thump.

Thurman crouched and scanned the dark room. It appeared empty through his NVGs.

Thump, thump, thump.

The noise came from the far back corner.

He crouched with his automatic rifle at high ready and maneuvered around the car.

"I think I have something," Carmen's voice came over his earpiece. "Can you assist?"

He didn't respond. Sweat droplets ran from his armpits. Sweat soaked the T-shirt under his body armor.

Thump, thump, thump.

Then he saw it, deep in the shadows. A door. The hair on the back of his arm stood up. He slipped his finger onto the trigger. He approached.

Thump, thump, thump.

The noise came from behind the door. He reached out and turned the handle. Then he pulled and ducked.

A wide-eyed prisoner sat tied to a wooden straight-backed chair.

Thurman relaxed. He lowered his rifle and reached for the tape covering his mouth.

Robert Walters gulped air. "Thank God . . ." *Gasp.* "Did you find my daughter?"

"Slow down." Thurman unsheathed his blade and sliced through the bindings that held him to the chair.

"He killed my wife and still has my Annie." Walters sobbed. "He's a monster. Please. You have to find my little girl." Thurman's stomach twisted. He tried to calm Walters. He knew what it was like to have a loved one in the hands of a psycho.

"We're working on it." He spoke into his mic. "Bravo Two, I found the car and have Walters. Repeat, I have Walters and the car."

"Bravo One, meet us in the courtyard," said Carmen. "Bravo Three has the child. No sign of the mother yet. I still say this is too easy."

"According to Walters, the mother won't be found," Thurman said.

Thurman helped Walters up. "We've recovered your daughter. Can you walk?"

"I think so, but I have to take a leak."

"Turn around and have at it."

Thurman deactivated his night vision and flicked on a light switch. The space lit up like an operating room. He inspected the vehicle. "Is this the car you drove, the one with the battery?"

Walters shuffled from the closet. "Screw the car, let's get out of here."

"Can we drive it out?"

"Not unless you have a key card."

Thurman thought for a moment. "How about the battery, can we take it with us?"

"Forget it. I want to see Annie."

"Can't. I've got orders. Grab a wrench. We just have to loosen these brackets and we can get out of here."

Walters gave in and grabbed a wrench. He leaned into the car. "Something's not right." He tried to lift it. "It's too heavy."

Thurman walked to the front of the car and opened the driver's door. A computer screen came to life and a digital timer appeared. It began counting down from five minutes. "Uh, what is this?" He returned to the back of the car and examined the case. Then he jerked his thumb toward the front of the car. "Check this out."

"Oh, shit," Walters said. "We have to get out of here." They both dashed for the door.

"This is Bravo Two, clear the area. Possible bomb in the lower garage. Repeat, bomb threat, garage. Clear the area." Thurman reached the handle and pulled. It didn't budge.

"Roger that, Bravo Two, clearing the area. Can you evacuate?"

He sprinted back to the car and looked in the passenger window. The timer read *4:15*.

Walters tried the garage door. Nothing.

Thurman ran over and helped. "Won't budge." He inspected the metal dead bolts that secured the door. "Stand clear." He retreated and aimed his rifle, then fired three rounds at the lock. Not a scratch. "Damn!"

3:45.

"We're going to die!" Walters screamed.

"Shut up and think. Can we drive this thing through the door?"

"There's no battery!"

3:22.

A banging sound came from the other side of the stairwell door. Carmen's voice came through his earpiece. "Hang on, we'll get you out!"

"Get out, save yourself. Three minutes. Go!"

"I'm not leaving. Ranger Creed, remember?"

"There's a garage door in the east hillside. Open it, but hurry."

He went over to the rolldown door and fired five more rounds at the bolt. Still nothing. The smell of gunpowder hung in the air, then disappeared.

2:45.

Ventilation. He looked up. A two-by-two-foot square metal screen covered an exhaust shaft in the ceiling.

CHAPTER 32
VESUVIO

"WILL THE CAR ROLL?"

Walters nodded. He shifted the car into neutral.

"Under the vent." They started pushing. The effort sent pain shooting from Thurman's right knee, but the car rolled into place.

2:14.

Thurman scrambled onto the roof and rammed the vent with the butt of his rifle. It didn't move. He knelt on the hood and fired at the retaining screws. The screen bounced off the car roof and clattered to the floor. "Get up here!"

Walters scurried onto the roof.

Thurman clasped his hands into a makeshift stirrup and squatted. Walters stepped up.

"One, two, three." Thurman stood, raising him into the ventilation shaft. He kept pressing his feet overhead until Walters disappeared inside.

"I can't turn around," Walters said. "I'm going forward."

"I'm right behind you."

1:35.

Thurman quickly hopped to the ground, then he sprinted onto the Model X's hood, ran onto the roof, and jumped toward the shaft. His grip faltered. He fell, rolling off the car onto the concrete. A shock of pain stabbed his right leg. *No time for pain.* He struggled to his feet. This would be his last shot. *Hang on, Steve, I'm not going to let you down.*

1:17.

He sprinted across the room, hurdled onto the hood and up the windshield, and leapt from the roof. This time his grip held. He chinned his head and shoulders up into the darkness. Groping forward, his fingertips found a metal seam. He pulled like a rock climber.

0:55.

He reached forward, alternating hands and knees to scramble forward.

"Walters! You there?"

A muffled voice called out. "Keep coming."

Memories of Steve and Noreen flashed through Thurman's mind. The air got cooler. He heard Walters banging on metal ahead.

"There's a grate. I can't get out!"

"Punch it!"

"I'm trying!"

Damn it. Too slow. We're never going to make it.

0:39.

"Hang on, doc." John Bristow's voice echoed down the shaft.

Then a light flashed. A thick rope slapped his face.

"Grab it, you navy puke!" screamed Carmen.

Thurman gripped it. "Got it." The line went taught and then ripped through his hands. "Throw it back." He inched forward.

0:26.

A few seconds later the rope landed next to his shoulder. Thurman wrapped it around his forearm and clamped with both hands. "Go!" He felt his body being propelled forward. In an instant he fell to the ground and rolled down a hill. Bristow and Carmen quickly pulled him to his feet. Walters was already several feet ahead, running away from the garage.

"Run!" Bristow screamed.

He didn't need to say it twice. They sprinted toward the sunrise.

The eruption lit up the predawn sky and slammed them to the ground. Dirt and rock rained like volcanic fallout. The blast reverberated, echoing off nearby hills. Dust and smoke replaced the morning air. Thurman coughed and spit mud. He half expected the ground to open and suck them down. His ears rang. Time slowed. He struggled to his feet and tried to look around. Breathing came hard. He peered into the haze. A few feet away Carmen sat up. She wiped her eyes and slowly moved her head from side to side. She gave him a thumbs-up then shouted, "Rangers lead the way!"

Bristow knelt beside him. "You okay?"

"Another fine Navy Day." The exhilaration of defying death surged through him. He stood and embraced his friend. "Saved my tail again."

"Barely. That was close."

Carmen came over and hugged him so hard it hurt. "I thought I'd lost you."

Thurman lifted her chin. "I did too."

Walters slapped dirt from his clothes and then stood up. "I owe you my life."

"You're welcome." Thurman turned back to Carmen. "How did you find us?"

"I radioed John, who grabbed a fast rope from the chopper, and we repelled down here." She pointed at the rope hanging from the wall. "When we heard Walters pounding on the grate, I cut the excess rope while John got the grate off."

"Now you know what it was like when Vesuvius erupted," Bristow said.

They walked up the hill toward the front of the villa. A Carabinieri jogged toward them. "Any casualties?"

"We're all right," Bristow said.

When they neared the helicopter, a little girl ran toward them. "Daddy!"

"Annie!" Walters gathered her into his arms.

A Carabinieri officer approached. Thurman recognized Captain DiRienzo. He motioned to them. "Come with me. The helicopter will take you to the hospital in Siena."

Thurman shook his head. "We're fine."

"Where's Kearns?" asked Bristow.

"Taken to the hospital," said DiRienzo. "I insist, you must be checked by our medical staff. It's only a few minutes by air."

"What happened to him?"

"Shrapnel from the blast."

Bristow began walking toward the helicopter. Carmen followed. After a couple of steps, she stopped and looked back at Thurman. "What are you waiting for?"

"I'm not going."

"Yes, you are." She marched back and stood toe to toe. "If I'm going, so are you."

"Forget it. You and I both know this game. Neither one of us needs to see a doctor."

Bristow placed his hand on Thurman's shoulder. "Let's at least find Kearns."

————

A purple glow highlighted the eastern hills as they circled the city, and in the predawn light Thurman recognized the bell tower and Piazza del Campo. The sun crested the horizon as they touched down at the University Hospital of Siena.

Hospital personnel met them and loaded Walters and his daughter onto gurneys and wheeled them into the emergency room. They brought wheelchairs for the others but they refused them. A nurse escorted the group to exam rooms, ignoring Thurman's protests. Carmen wasn't going to let him off the hook. The nurse stopped, pulled the curtain, and motioned to Thurman and gave him an exam gown. "Clothes off."

"Is that necessary?"

Carmen spoke to the nurse in Italian, then turned to her colleagues. "The doctor is required to do a physical examination and get screening x-rays. She'll be here in a few minutes. She needs you to get undressed and into a gown."

"I know the drill."

"This is a teaching hospital. Let her do her job."

Bristow shrugged and unbuttoned his shirt.

Thurman sat on the exam table. "I'm telling you, I'm fine."

"Just do it so we can get out of here," Bristow said as he removed his boots.

The nurse, who spoke some English, waved a finger at him. "Do this, please."

The emergency room physician opened the curtain. She looked younger and taller than Carmen and wore her long dark hair in a ponytail. The identification card attached to a lanyard hanging from her neck displayed her photograph and name. Carmen spoke to her in Italian.

A moment later both women burst into laughter and embraced.

Thurman looked at Bristow.

The laughter stopped and Carmen turned to them. "This is Dr. Castagno, but she says you can call her Julia since we are also doctors. She's a third-year ER resident, like me, and can speak English."

"What's so funny?" asked Thurman.

"She's from Siena. My family is from Arezzo. We are like sisters."

An hour later Thurman stared over Julia's shoulder at the x-ray of his right knee.

She pointed to a small dark circle at the end of his femur. "Does it hurt there?"

Thurman blinked but otherwise stood motionless. A mental abyss cracked open. He crossed his arms and nodded. *Recurrence.* His tumor had returned.

Julia turned around. "You need to get this checked out by a specialist."

"I will."

"This is serious," she said. "It needs to be biopsied."

"I know."

She changed the images to those of the entire right femur. The intramedullary rod went from his hip almost to his knee. She pointed to the area where his original tumor had deformed the bone. "I'm sorry, but this could be a recurrence."

"I'm aware."

"You already knew, didn't you?" Carmen said. Her expression was one of both anger and concern.

"Drop it. We can't stop to worry about it now. I'll get it checked out as soon as we get home." He turned away to avoid her gaze.

Carmen looked him in the eye. "Promise?"

He nodded.

Bristow broke the awkward silence. "One of our men, Bill Kearns, was injured and brought here. Do you know what happened to him?"

"His ankle is broken. He's in surgery."

Julia's phone vibrated. She pulled it from her coat pocket with the screen lit up. It drew Thurman's attention.

After a brief conversation she hung up and replaced the phone in her lab coat.

"May I see that?" Thurman asked.

A crease appeared across her forehead. "My phone?"

Thurman nodded. "The screen picture, your wallpaper. Can I see it?"

She withdrew the device and swiped it, illuminating the screen. It displayed a green-and-gold image with a bright blue border. A shield in the center depicted a crowned green caterpillar crawling on the stem of a rose.

"What is this?"

"It's the symbol of my contrada."

Thurman squinted, studying the pattern. It matched the patch on Yuri's motorcycle jacket and the flag in Noreen's photograph.

"Of course," Carmen said.

"The flag of the Noble Contrada del Bruco," Julia replied.

CHAPTER 33
CONTRADA BRUCO

THURMAN RETURNED A QUIZZICAL LOOK. "What is this Contrada Bruco?"

Julia concentrated as she sought the correct English words. "If you are Sienese, you are born into a contrada. They are the essence of Siena and have existed for centuries. Think of them as social or civic organizations."

"Like city wards or districts?" asked Thurman.

She frowned. "I don't know those terms."

"More like the clans of Ireland," Carmen said.

Julia tightened the elastic band holding her ponytail and continued. "In some ways, but the contrada are confined within the city, not spread out over the countryside. In the beginning they supplied troops for defending against invaders. Only seventeen exist today. The Noble Contrada del Bruco was formed in 1369. It earned this distinction after helping defend Siena against the army of the Holy Roman Emperor, Charles IV."

"That's a lot of history," said Bristow.

"They are our culture, our DNA. Each contrada is named after its symbol. Mine is the caterpillar; that's what *bruco* means, it represents the workers of the silk and cloth trade. The others have similar names representing their heritage—the eagle, snail, seashell, she-wolf, you see? The contrada are extended families with traditions and customs that have been followed for generations. Their unity and pride are displayed every summer during the Palio."

Bristow held out his hand. "Can I take a look?" Julia handed him her phone. He studied the image, then looked up. "What's the Palio?"

"The sacred, most important event in Siena. Twice a year, in July and August, Siena holds a horse race called the Palio," Julia explained. "These are huge festivals. Civic life revolves around them."

Thurman dug into the front pocket of his pants and produced his phone. "I want to show you something." He pulled up the picture from Noreen's apartment. "Do you recognize these people?"

"That is the entrance to the headquarters of Contrada Bruco." She pointed to the figures. "This is Dario Benedetto. I don't recognize the other two, but Dario and I grew up together."

"How well do you know him?" Thurman asked.

"We're friends. He and my older brother hung out when they were teenagers."

"Do you know where he is? We'd like to speak with him."

"May I ask why?"

Bristow handed her phone back. "The woman is dead, and the guy on his other side is in critical condition in a hospital. We can't tell you why, but it's imperative we talk to Benedetto."

Julia placed her phone in the back pocket of her scrubs. "How do I know I can trust you?"

Carmen placed her hand on Julia's forearm. "Dario's safety depends on it."

Julia glanced at them as if she was unsure what to do.

Bristow pulled out his phone and dialed DiRienzo to explain the situation. "Maybe you'll be more comfortable trusting him." He handed her the phone. After exchanging a few words with the police officer, she handed it back.

"We have a directory with everyone's contact information at the contrada headquarters. Let me make a few calls." She stepped out of the room, then returned a few minutes later. "I have a couple of patients left from last night. Rest in the waiting room while I finish their charts. Then I'll take you to Dario myself."

—————

After Julia checked out with the oncoming shift, the group squeezed into her Fiat and drove toward the center of Siena. They parked and began walking with Julia acting as their guide. After a short distance, they stopped at the end of a narrow street that opened onto a vast piazza paved with acres of red brick. Julia smiled and waved an arm as if making a presentation. "This is Piazza del Campo, where the Palio is run."

They followed her across the piazza as the sun peaked over a rooftop. Bristow slipped on his sunglasses. She led them into a small café, where they ordered espresso and croissants, then they continued through the maze of narrow streets lined with buildings constructed centuries ago. Merchants swept entrances and cleaned their store windows, preparing to open for business. After a ten-minute hike, Julia halted at a street corner near the top of a hill. "We're almost there," she called over her shoulder.

Thurman spotted a street sign hanging on the corner of a building: VIA DEL COMUNE. Buildings three or more stories tall lined both sides of the road, packed against each other without alleyways. He looked down the steep hill and spotted a familiar green-and-gold flag above an arched entrance. When the group stopped, Thurman glanced up at the stone plaque fixed to the wall with iron spikes. He read the inscription, NOBIL CONTRADA DEL BRUCO, and noted the crowned caterpillar carved above the words. A smile spread across his face.

Julia pushed her sunglasses on top of her head and rapped on the heavy wooden doors.

The group waited. She knocked again. A moment later the handle rattled, and the door cracked open. A curious eye appeared from the darkness, darting up and down to assess the strangers. An elderly female voice inquired in Italian, "What do you want?"

"We are here to see Dario Benedetto," Thurman said. Carmen translated.

"It's all right. It's Julia Castagno," said the resident.

"Wait." The woman closed the door.

"What now?" asked Carmen.

"She will get him," said Julia. "I have to leave you now. I need some sleep before my next shift."

"Thank you," said Carmen, kissing each cheek.

Thurman held out his hand. "We appreciate your help."

"Just keep Dario safe for me," she said. They waved as she walked back up the hill. Thurman saw her shoot them one last apprehensive look before she crested the hill and disappeared.

Bristow bent down and adjusted the Sig P938 holstered on the inside of his left ankle. The wind danced up the narrow street, snapping the flag that flew above. After what felt like an eternity, the hinges creaked, and the ancient wooden door swung open.

A man who looked in his midthirties, dressed in jeans and a T-shirt with a full head of shaggy blond hair, stood in the doorway. It was the man in Noreen's photograph. He glanced at them, then fixed his gaze. "Dr. Thurman, I presume?"

"Dario Benedetto," replied Thurman as he stepped forward, holding out his hand.

Dario shook it. "I've been hoping to meet you."

"Same here."

Dario smiled. "Noreen spoke highly of you."

"That's the reason we're here," said Bristow. Dario's smile faded.

"Is there a place we can talk? Privately?" Thurman asked.

Dario nodded. He led them through a passageway decorated with displays of mannequins dressed in green-and-gold contrada costumes from centuries past. Standards from Palio victories hung from the ceiling. He stopped and opened an ancient wooden door that led them into a dimly lit chapel. Thurman gazed upon the altar decorated with rows of candles in golden holders. Above these hung a painting of the Madonna and Christ Child in the two-dimensional flat style of the early Renaissance.

Dario sat down in the first pew. "We are alone. It is safe to talk here."

Thurman and Carmen both looked at Bristow. Thurman spoke. "I don't know how to tell you this, but Noreen is dead."

Dario slumped forward and muttered, "Oddio."

No one said anything for several moments, then Carmen placed a hand on his shoulder. "Are you all right?"

"What happened?"

"Narcotic overdose."

Dario's head shot up. "Impossible. She'd never do that."

"We believe she was murdered."

Dario covered his face with his hands. "Why would anyone want to kill her?"

"That's what we're trying to figure out," Bristow said. "We are part of an investigation. We believe her death is related to Yuri and Aliya's work."

"How? They died five years ago."

"We need information," Bristow said.

"Everything. Start from the beginning," Carmen added.

Dario stood. "Follow me. I need some air."

CHAPTER 34
DARIO'S TALE

DARIO LED THURMAN, Bristow, and Carmen through a back door that opened into a park encompassing several acres. The yellow-ochre brick walls of the Basilica di Francesco loomed at the top of the hill to their right. They sat at a picnic table in a grove of downy oaks and white poplars, Carmen at Dario's right, and Thurman and Bristow facing them on the opposite side. The temperature hovered close to sixty degrees, and a light breeze rustled leaves through the trees. Dario glanced about then interlocked his fingers on the wooden tabletop. "This is a beautiful place, don't you agree?"

"It's an oasis," replied Carmen.

Thurman folded his hands on the table. "How did you meet Yuri and Noreen?"

Yuri massaged his temples for a moment, then looked up. "My father had academic connections in England. I went to the university there and earned a PhD in physics at the University of Manchester. For my postdoctoral fellowship, I accepted a position at the Joint Institute for Nuclear Research outside Moscow."

"Where you and Yuri met?" asked Carmen.

Dario nodded.

"That's the connection," said Thurman.

Dario smiled during a moment's reflection. "For two years we worked together, Yuri, Aliya, and I."

"What did you do?" asked Thurman.

"We became friends."

"I meant research."

"We worked on projects for our boss, Dr. Oganessian, but on the side we designed a new type of particle accelerator."

"Did it work?" asked Carmen.

"Not like we wanted, but we made progress. When the fellowship ended, I needed a job. I went to work for a company called Thyssenkrupp."

"Where?" asked Bristow.

"In Essen." He told the story of his years in Germany culminating in the escape. "Richard arranged for Yuri and Aliya to take a private plane to England." Dario paused, then continued. "They almost didn't make the flight. I'll never forget that day. It was straight out of a spy movie." He recounted the warehouse explosion and the events at the airport. "Unfortunately, the plane crashed over the English Channel with no survivors."

"What happened to Gross?" asked Bristow.

"He died at the airport."

Bristow leaned forward. "We have some good news—the plane didn't crash. Yuri and Aliya are alive."

Dario's jaw dropped. "I'm sorry, what did you say?"

"The plane didn't go down, it flew to London. The crash never happened."

"But I attended their funeral."

Thurman smiled while shaking his head. "The caskets were closed, right?"

"No, they were in urns, the bodies had been cremated." Dario broke out in laughter, then said, "My God, this is a miracle."

"That's a hell of a tale," said Bristow. "Yuri is in deep trouble. Do you want to help him?"

"Of course."

"He's been gravely injured," Thurman explained his condition.

"The Russians know he's alive. They're coming for him. Just before she died, Noreen recorded a message telling us to find you." Bristow reached across the table and gripped one of Dario's forearms. "You know more about Yuri's work than anyone. It must continue to go forward."

"Come back with us," Carmen said. "Our government needs someone who can reproduce his work. You're probably the only person Yuri trusts with the knowledge and skill set capable of doing that."

———

Bristow tried the number again. After the third attempt, DiRienzo answered.

"Where are you, signore? I couldn't find you at the hospital."

"We met a friend who took us on a tour of Siena," said Bristow.

"You're safe?"

"Yes," said Bristow.

"Where are you? We need to bring you and the others in for safety and for your official reports."

"Fine," replied Bristow, "but when we're finished, I want to question Walters. You have him in custody?"

"Of course. My men are interrogating him."

"Hold him until I get there."

"Tell me where you are, and I'll send a car."

Bristow hesitated.

"Mr. Bristow, it's not safe on the streets. Dimitry Stanov has many eyes. Let me help, I'll send an unmarked vehicle. Where are you?"

CHAPTER 35
WIFE AND GIRLFRIEND

SERGEANT HAIRSTON SAT behind the wheel, sipping black coffee while waiting for the Raleigh-Durham Motorsports dealership to open. A hole in the clouds let morning sunlight beam through the windshield, causing him to squint. He reached for his sunglasses and pulled out the Thanksgiving grocery list Michelle had left for him. As the dean of student affairs at Wake Forest, her workload on top of keeping track of the girls made her schedule as hectic as his. Sabe, a third-class midshipman, wouldn't get home from Annapolis until Wednesday. Niayla was already home from college and was shopping with her sister, Lillie. He looked forward to having the family together again. A smile spread across his face as he read the list. *I'll get Niayla and Lillie to do some of this.* He'd begun composing a text of instructions when the rumble of a Harley-Davidson caught his attention. A woman decked out in leathers parked next to the entrance and removed her helmet. Hairston recognized her black ponytail. Natasha speed smoked the rest of her cigarette before crushing it on the pavement and unlocking the entrance.

"He won't be here until after lunch," she said the moment Hairston walked in the door.

"I'm not looking for him. I thought you might be able to—"

"Forget it." Natasha unzipped her form-fitting leather jacket and peeled it off, revealing a white Lycra long-sleeved shirt designed to distract.

"All I'm asking is for a little information."

Natasha scowled. "Are you trying to get me killed?"

"What are you talking about?"

"If you keep poking your nose around here, some unpleasant people are going to start asking questions."

Hairston eyed her closely. "So, what's with the note? What's going down on Thanksgiving?"

"I don't know what you're talking about. Do your job and leave me alone."

"I'm doing my job."

"Try harder. Talking to cops is bad for my health."

"So is smoking."

She tried to walk away.

Hairston blocked her. "You setting me up?"

She moved closer and whispered. "I don't know the details. All I know is Solo has something planned. Something big."

"Drugs?"

Her lip curled. "You really have to ask? Solo's crew controls distribution from Norfolk to Savannah."

Two customers entered the store. They looked like teenagers and walked to the motocross section. Each straddled a bike. Natasha surveyed them and frowned. "I got to go."

Hairston gripped her forearm. "Please, help me out."

"There's been a lot of meetings going on in his office lately with people I've never seen before. I've heard a few things about a major shipment coming in, so get your act together."

"What kind of people?"

"Guys from New York."

She looked over Hairston's shoulder and called out to the young men, "Hang on, I'll be there in a minute," then turned back to Hairston. She removed an e-cig from a hip pocket and took a drag. This time she turned her head as she exhaled the dense white plume of vapor.

"I'm trying to solve a murder. Do those people have anything to do with the death of this woman?" He pulled out a picture of Noreen Chase and handed it to her.

"Ice woman, all bling and no heart."

"You know her?"

"Noreen Chase."

"Did she and your boss have a thing?"

"Noreen and Terry? No chance, Noreen didn't love anyone but herself. They'd meet and she'd hang on him, but it wasn't anything serious."

"How long did they know each other?" Hairston asked.

She pursed her lips and expelled a vapor stream from her nostrils. "I'm not sure. It went back a few years. I remember when she first walked through the door. Terry looked stunned, like he'd seen a ghost from his past. I asked him about it later, but he blew it off. He didn't want to talk about it, so I let it go."

Hairston nodded. "What else can you tell me about Anastasia's?"

"You don't have any idea who you're dealing with, do you? I've already told you too much. Now leave or you'll be investigating my murder next."

CHAPTER 36
A RUSTY RING

DARIO INVITED the group into the kitchen, where the contrada staff had prepared a lunch of sliced meats, cheeses, dried fruits, and fresh bread, and opened a bottle of Vino Nobile di Montepulciano. "My apologies for a nontraditional noontime Italian meal. When we have guests, the menu is usually more lavish."

"The quality more than makes up for quantity," said Thurman, raising his wineglass.

Bristow stood at the sliding glass door that opened onto the backyard patio. After a few moments, he glanced at his watch. "Where is DiRienzo? It's been almost an hour. He said he'd be here in twenty minutes."

"Relax. They probably had a lot of questions for Walters." Thurman finished the rest of his wine.

"You think he staged the wonder car heist?" asked Carmen.

Bristow came back and sat next to her. "That's what we're going to find out. I want to know if Stanov double-crossed him."

"It's possible," said Thurman. "He's got a little 'splainin' to do, as we say back in North Carolina."

"Slow down on the vino, big fella," said Carmen.

Thurman smiled and held up his glass. "Try some."

"Don't overdo it," said Bristow. "We might need your skills."

Thurman leaned back so the front two legs of his chair were off the floor and placed his hands behind his head. "I've had enough excitement for one day."

"You're not the only one." Bristow resumed pacing until his phone rang. "Finally."

He answered the call, then turned to the group. "He's out front."

Bristow shook Dario's hand. "We'll pick you up at 1800. We have a flight to catch."

"I'll be waiting."

Outside the front entrance the unmarked police van waited. An officer in plain clothes stood next to the open sliding passenger side door. Two others sat in the seat at the rear. A younger man wearing sunglasses and a black leather jacket rode shotgun. Bristow and Carmen entered. She watched Thurman grimace as he stepped into the vehicle. Carmen shot him a concerned look.

"I'm fine."

The van pulled out and turned left. Thurman watched as the Porta a Ovile, one of the original entrances to the city, disappeared from view. The driver made turn after turn along the narrow streets in neighborhoods dating to the thirteenth century. Ten minutes later the van turned onto a highway and sped northwest, away from the city.

Bristow leaned forward and spoke to the driver through the plexiglass partition. "Where are you taking us?"

He smiled and spoke in Italian.

"He says to relax, we are meeting Captain DiRienzo and will be there soon," Carmen translated.

"If he understands me, then why doesn't he tell me in English?"

"Not sure," Carmen said, shooting Bristow a concerned look.

"We're supposed to be meeting DiRienzo at the police station," Bristow said.

Carmen turned and began speaking in rapid-fire Italian. "They say they're taking precautions."

The beautiful landscape didn't quell the anxiety building in Thurman's gut. "This is fucked up. Something isn't right."

The vehicle continued into the country. After negotiating a roundabout, it exited onto a two-lane road.

Bristow turned around again. "What the hell is going on?" He received another long-winded explanation in Italian from the officers, then looked at Carmen.

"They are holding Walters in a remote location for his safety. We are being taken there."

"That's bullshit," said Bristow, who then pounded on the plexiglass and metal screen partition separating the passenger compartment from the drivers. "Take us back to Siena. Stop!" He reached for the door handle and pulled. It was locked.

Thurman pulled on his handle. It was locked too.

"Be quiet and don't move," said one of the officers from the rear of the van. The Americans stopped and turned around. One guard pointed a nine-millimeter Beretta semiautomatic pistol at Thurman's face.

The other brandished a Taser. "You know what this is," he said with a thick eastern European accent. "Hand me your gun."

Bristow bent over and reached for his ankle.

A report echoed in the van. Bristow's body convulsed as the electrodes sunk into his flank. One of the men half crawled over the seat and snatched the pistol from Bristow's holster. The other looked at Thurman and Carmen. "Try something like that and I'll kill you."

Thurman yanked the electrodes from his friend and tossed them into the backseat as the van turned onto a dirt road that led into a forest. Bristow groaned. After a quarter mile, they broke through the tree line and drove across a field toward an old stone farmhouse that looked abandoned. The van made a sweeping turn and stopped.

A man in a leather jacket, holding a pistol, opened the sliding door and stepped aside. "Get out."

Thurman, Bristow, and Carmen got out of the van. Bristow wobbled from the effects of the electric seizure.

"Keep your hands where I can see them. Turn around, feet apart."

The two guards who'd been in the rear of the van searched each prisoner.

"Watch it," Carmen shouted as the guard fondled her.

The man laughed and yanked her hands behind her back, securing them with Flex-Cufs. He did the same with Thurman and Bristow. "Turn around."

The driver motioned with his rifle for them to move toward the house. "Inside." They walked between the cypress trees to the abandoned building. A single step led to the entrance. The stone walls were a foot thick. Inside the house, new boards had been placed over the windows, and the front door was solid oak with a dead bolt.

"Sit." They complied. A battery-powered lantern placed on the hearth of the mammoth fireplace provided light for the empty room. Bristow, Carmen, and Thurman sat on the floor in the middle of the space. "Lay facedown." They did as instructed. The guard who had bound their hands now did the same to their feet.

"Not her," said the Russian. "She'll need her legs free." He laughed and motioned to the other side of the room, where a rusty iron ring was fastened to the stone wall. "Tie her to that."

"What is this?" Thurman fumed. "Where's DiRienzo?"

"You'll find out soon enough," said the driver. They rolled Bristow and sat him up against the wall. They repeated the process for Thurman. The two sat ten feet apart, staring at their captors. Carmen stood across the room fastened like chattel to the iron ring.

"Why not just kill us now and get it over with?" asked Thurman.

Bristow's eyes widened a fraction. "Don't give them any ideas."

"He tried to blow us up this morning. What's changed?"

The driver came over to Thurman and squatted down. "We've been instructed to find out what the blonde woman told you."

"Blonde woman? Noreen? You murdered her."

"You will tell us what was on the thumb drive and where it is located." The driver stood and turned to his men and spoke in Russian. "That should hold them until the captain gets here. Boris will keep an eye on them." He looked at Boris. "I'll get you when the food is ready." The men walked into the kitchen and closed the door.

Boris lit a cigarette and sat down. He rolled up his pants leg, revealing a prosthesis. "See this?" He spoke in English with a Russian accent while removing the artificial limb. It made a moist sucking sound as it released. Boris wiggled the bony stump extending from his knee. He drew on his smoke while massaging what remained of withered calf muscles. "It hurts every damn minute of every day."

The three prisoners nodded, and Thurman asked, "What happened?"

"Liquid nitrogen."

Thurman recalled Dario's story and winced.

"It froze my foot like a block of ice."

He hissed as he removed his other shoe, revealing a toeless stub of a partial foot. "Along with these. The one who did this is going to pay."

"Who's that?" asked Bristow.

"A friend of yours. Yuri Kogan?"

"Doesn't ring a bell."

In a flash, he scurried to Bristow like a crab and pulled a knife from his pocket. The black blade snapped open. With Bristow's head pinned against the stone wall, he touched the point to his cheek a half inch below the right eye, just puncturing the skin. Blood trickled down his face. "Don't lie to me. I'll pluck that eye out and feed it to you while your friends watch."

"Boris?" The silhouette of the driver appeared in the doorway. "Come eat. DiRienzo is on his way."

Boris squinted as his savage passion subsided. He folded the blade, replaced the prosthesis, and stood. "I'm not finished with you." With that he turned and closed the door, but not before turning off the lantern.

———

"You all right?" Thurman whispered.

"That guy's a maniac," Bristow replied. "I'm fine."

"How about you, Carmen?"

"I almost have my hands free. The rust on this ring is like sandpaper," she said softly from the darkness across the room.

"You'd better hurry. DiRienzo may show up any minute," Bristow said. "And I've got a nagging feeling that he isn't on our side."

"What do you think I'm doing?" she hissed. One last hard pull and the wrist bonds broke. She flexed her fingers and rubbed her wrists. "I'm free."

The kitchen door handle rattled. Carmen froze and placed her hands behind her back in the darkness. Light appeared around the doorway. The younger man strode through the door as the room filled with light from the kitchen. He shut the door and placed his lantern on the hearth.

"I've come to check on my bella donna."

"I'm not yours, asshole."

The corners of his mouth curled. "You will be soon."

"Never." Carmen lashed out with her right foot, planting it squarely on his testicles. He crumpled to the floor and let out a scream. Her next kick landed on his chin, rocking his head. His body went limp. She dashed to the door and disappeared into the night.

CHAPTER 37
JUDITH BEHEADING HOLOFERNES

RANGER SCHOOL and Delta Force had trained her well. Carmen sprinted through the line of cypress trees and across the thigh-high grasses of the pasture. A brisk breeze blew from the west, bending the blades and rustling dead leaves. Moonlight illuminated the tree line, and she reached the woods as flashlights emerged from the farmhouse.

"Fan out, she can't get far," a voice she recognized as the driver called out. "Antonio, phone DiRienzo. Tell him to bring the dogs."

She didn't have much time. Underbrush crunched as she picked her way deeper in the trees. She stopped to listen and stepped on something round. It felt like a fallen tree branch but rolled beneath her boot. She bent down and grabbed it. An old axe handle, broken near the head. She gripped it like a baseball bat.

A flashlight beam swept twenty yards to her left. She stood erect, breathing slowly. *Come on, asshole, this way.*

"Shouldn't we just wait for the dogs? She could be anywhere," said the young man wearing the leather jacket.

"Keep looking. The faster we find her, the better," called the driver.

At least thirty yards separated the two men. Branches snapped and leaves rattled as they approached.

The noise brought a smile to Carmen's lips. *City boys.* She slowed her breathing and prepared for a fastball. *Come on, bring it.*

"Where are you, my little whore?" he said in Italian as he approached.

Carmen watched as he walked by, too far away for her to reach. She moved to keep the tree trunk between them and stepped on a twig. The snap sounded like a pistol report through the forest. Leather Jacket whirled around. "I have her!"

Carmen dashed toward darkness. A pistol shot cracked and the man in the leather jacket sprinted after her. Branches whipped her face and tore at her shirt. The flashlight beam followed. More gunshots. Tree bark bounced off her face. She ducked behind the trunk of a huge tree and held her breath.

"La mia piccolo puttana." His pace slowed as he sensed her presence. The light beam swept back and forth on either side of the trunk. "Come out, come out. Antonio has something very nice for you."

She held her breath. The barrel of the pistol appeared, followed by a hand and forearm. He came forward. His head appeared and Carmen swung hard. His forehead caved as the axe handle sunk into his skull. She didn't see the pistol, but she grabbed the knife from its sheath and ran parallel to the tree line as she heard the other man crashing through the brush.

"Antonio! Where are you?" the driver called.

She hid under a fallen tree that lay over a small creek. The gurgling of running water covered the sound of her breathing. She lowered herself into the creek bed and looked around. The driver's flashlight became brighter as he approached. She reached down and picked up a rock from the stream bed and tossed it behind her. The light stopped. She threw another. The beam came closer. She tucked herself into a tight ball and nestled against the creek bank under the downed tree. The trunk vibrated as he stepped onto it and began to cross. She tensed. As his foot landed above her, she reached up and grabbed his ankle.

The trunk rolled a quarter turn when the body struck. He fell, landing on his belly in the water. Carmen struck with the adrenaline-stoked ferocity of an enraged lioness. She leapt onto his back. In a blur of motion she grabbed a fist of hair, yanked his head, and dragged the knife across his throat. She pulled hard. The blade parted flesh until stopped by bone. Carotids pumped blood like twin faucets. She shoved his head into the running water and rode him like a saddle bronc until his body went limp. The only sound had been the rushing of the swollen stream—a silent death. A search of his body produced another knife, a pistol, ammunition, a flashlight, and keys to the van.

Carmen exited the forest and looked across the field toward the farmhouse. Clouds covered the moon. If DiRienzo and his men arrived, it would be over. She jogged across the field and circled around the house looking for the Russian and the other guard. There was no sign of them. She stopped at the cypress stand and scouted. *All clear.* She entered the building.

"Thank God you're alive! Are you okay?" Thurman asked in a whisper.

The lantern was still on the hearth, casting a soft glow across the room. She placed her finger to her lips.

Bristow noticed the blood stains on her wet clothes. She reached behind his back and cut the Flex-Cufs. They all looked up at the sound of a boot striking the floor.

"Don't move," said the guard. "Put your hands where I can see them." He glanced toward the door and shouted, "Boris, in here! I have them."

Carmen's back was to the door. She dropped the knife and raised her hands, casting her eyes downward. Bristow followed them and saw the pistol tucked into her waistband. "The safety is off," she mouthed silently.

With her shielding his arm movement, he snatched the gun. Carmen rolled away as Bristow aimed and fired. Three shots echoed within the stone walls. The guard's body fell against the doorjamb and slid to the floor. Carmen scurried to the body and grabbed the gun.

"Cut my feet loose," Bristow said.

"Roger that." She sliced through the restraints, then moved to Thurman.

"I can't wait to hear this story." He watched as she worked the blade between his skin and the cuff. "Careful."

She smiled. "Trust me, I'm a doctor."

Bristow examined the guard. "What happened out there?"

An image of *Judith Beheading Holofernes*, Caravaggio's masterpiece, appeared in Thurman's mind as Carmen spoke. "Remind me to stay on your good side."

The wounded guard who lay on the floor opened his eyes and mumbled. "I may be dying, but you'll soon join me." A dark stain spread across his shirt.

Thurman knelt beside him. "Not today. Where is Stanov and the battery?"

He coughed and grimaced with pain.

"Answer a few questions, and we'll get you to a hospital."

The guard nodded.

"Where's Walters?"

"Dead."

"You're lying. Stanov needs him."

The guard shook his head. His breathing became more labored. "He only needs Yuri. The woman . . ."

"Who? Noreen Chase?"

A weak cough was followed by a gasp and a whisper. "Yuri is the only one who matters. Now . . . hospital."

Thurman reached down and lifted the bloody shirt, exposing two bullet holes. The third was to the right of his heart in his chest. Air hissed from it with every breath. "He's in bad shape."

"We've got bigger problems," Bristow responded, peering through the open door past the gap in the cypress trees. Headlights broke through the forest. He reached for the guard's rifle and turned off the lantern. "Take the magazines from his pouch." He handed the pistol to Thurman, who tucked it into his belt behind his back.

"Come on," said Carmen, gripping the guard's feet and pulling the wounded man from the doorway. They stepped into the yard and closed the door as the headlights grew brighter.

A voice with a Russian accent came from the shadows. "Nobody moves."

CHAPTER 38
POPE INTERVENES

BORIS APPEARED FROM THE DARKNESS. "Weapons on the ground." His rifle erupted. The ground exploded near their feet. "Now!" He moved closer, sweeping the barrel of an AK-47 back and forth.

Bristow dropped his rifle, and Carmen squatted down with her pistol held at arm's length. She placed it on the ground.

"Good." He looked at Thurman. "You, show me your hands."

He held them up. "No weapon."

The car drove down the dirt road. Boris looked back at Carmen. "What's in your hand?"

She held out her hand. "It's just a flashlight. You're going to need it."

"Drop it."

Carmen flicked on the halogen beam and pointed it into the eyes of the Russian. He flinched. Thurman drew the pistol tucked behind his back and fired. Three rounds buried into Boris's chest. He rocked back and stumbled, his knee touching the ground before he collapsed into the dirt.

Bristow stared at the approaching headlights. "We need to get moving."

Carmen fished the keys from her pocket. "Into the van."

Bristow and Thurman scooped up the rifles and magazines and followed. The rear wheels sprayed a cloud of dirt as Carmen stomped on the accelerator. She headed straight for the oncoming vehicle and looked over her shoulder. "Shooters ready?"

"Ready," replied Bristow.

The approaching vehicle accelerated. Moonlight illuminated a pistol protruding from a passenger-side window. Its muzzle flashed in unison with gunshots. The van windshield spiderwebbed.

Bristow knelt in the seat behind Carmen. "Pass on their left!" Then he turned to Thurman seated two rows behind. "Aim for the driver, I'll get the passengers." He stuck the barrel of the assault rifle out the window and raked the car as they passed in a modern-day joust. Thurman unleashed a hail of gunfire. Bullets ripped into the car, puncturing metal and shattering windows. The vehicle steered an erratic course, veering left into the field before stopping. Smoke rose from the hood. Carmen drove on, following the dirt road into the trees. Thurman slid open the plexiglass partition. "The car's not moving, they're dead in the water."

"Get the hell out of here," Bristow said. "We don't know who to trust anymore."

"What about Jenkins or Pope?" Thurman asked.

"They're probably our best chance," Bristow agreed.

"Surely the FBI's on our side." Carmen turned onto the paved road and accelerated. Five minutes later she reached the highway and headed north. A sign indicated fifty-five kilometers to Florence.

"How do we contact them?" Carmen asked.

"With this." Bristow held up a cell phone.

Thurman leaned forward. "Where did you get that?"

"The dead guy in the farmhouse. I grabbed it when I searched his pockets."

"Do you remember the number?"

Bristow raised an eyebrow. "Do you?"

Carmen looked at them through the rearview mirror. "Call the US Consulate, ask for the office of the assistant Legal Attaché for the FBI. They can put us in touch with Pope."

"What about Dario?" asked Thurman.

Carmen eyed Bristow's reflection. "When you talk to Pope, ask her to round him up. He can meet us in Florence."

"Can we trust him?" Thurman said. "DiRienzo's men showed up at the contrada."

Bristow rubbed his jaw. "I've asked myself the same question. But there's no reason to think he betrayed us. I told DiRienzo where to pick us up when he called, and we watched Dario talk to him on the phone in the backyard. I think we have to give him the benefit of the doubt."

"We need him," said Thurman, "and we don't have much choice."

———

Carmen navigated the streets of Florence searching for the safehouse address Pope had given them. She found the warehouse and stopped the van at the rear gate. "Special shipment for Mr. D'Alessandro," she said into the speaker. The chain-link fence slid open, and the bullet-riddled van passed into the import/export storage yard filled with pallets of calacatta and travertine marble. The warehouse door opened. Carmen drove forward and parked by the loading platform. Special Agents Pope and Jenkins stood on the loading dock.

Jenkins surveyed the van. "Fuckin' Bonnie and Clyde. Is anyone hurt?"

"A couple of scratches," Bristow said.

"What the hell happened?"

Pope stood silently with arms crossed.

Thurman looked at her and asked, "Did you find Dario?"

"He'll be here soon," Pope replied as Thurman emerged from the vehicle. "I want the full story."

"Can we get some coffee first?"

Her face remained implacable. "Inside." She looked at Carmen's blood-stained clothing. "Afterward, change those clothes. Your suitcase is upstairs."

Carmen's head tilted. "Thanks, but . . . how did you pull that off?"

"Special Agent Jenkins checked you out of the St. Regis yesterday and brought your luggage. Dr. Thurman's too." Pope turned and went back up the stairs, leading them to a conference room that smelled of freshly brewed coffee. After filling their cups, they took seats around the table and told the story of the last twenty-four hours.

"DiRienzo, corrupt, I never would have guessed," said Pope.

"Believe it," replied Bristow.

Thurman slid his chair back and stood. "Look, I need to get back home. Our mission here is complete. Stanov's men are holding my cousin hostage. I can't help him here. Please get us on the next flight home."

Pope sipped her coffee. "Settle down, doctor. After last night, your photos will be everywhere. You're not flying commercial. Other arrangements had to be made."

Thurman sat back down.

"What happened to the battery?" Pope said.

"No idea. It could be anywhere," Bristow said. "Stanov has it."

"We'll find it and deal with DiRienzo," said Jenkins.

Pope reached for her purse on the floor by her chair. "In the meantime, you folks have a plane to catch in Aviano, compliments of the United States Air Force and the secretary of defense." She produced a phone from the handbag and gave it to Bristow. "This is safe to use. Call Admiral Jaggears and have him clear you to enter the base. There's a car downstairs. Jenkins will drive you." She pushed her chair back and stood. "Good luck."

A series of knocks drew their attention. Jenkins pulled his weapon and opened the door.

"Buongiorno." Dario entered, smiling.

Pope relaxed and looked at Bristow. "Tell your boss to add Mr. Benedetto to the list."

CHAPTER 39
DEATH OF A TWIN

HAIRSTON SAT at his desk and clicked on the email from the human resources department of Thyssenkrupp in Essen. The information he'd requested regarding Noreen arrived this morning. He sipped his third cup of coffee and began scrolling through the documents. She'd earned an electrical engineering degree from Purdue and a master's in Industrial and Systems Engineering from Georgia Tech. He already knew that. She'd been recruited by Thyssenkrupp during graduate school. *A good engineer with impressive credentials, but nothing that might explain why someone would want to kill her?* He continued scrolling.

She'd been involved in a number of successful projects. The email included several corporate newsletters documenting recognition Noreen received for landing several big contracts. He was almost ready to take a break when he saw the photograph. Noreen looked radiant as she accepted a framed award from a handsome man with white hair. Hairston leaned closer and enlarged the image.

I'll be damned, it's him. It has to be. A pale, thinner, white-haired Terry Morton shook Noreen's hand. The detective read the caption, *Senior Vice President of Operations, Richard Gross, awards the Silver Citation of Merit to Dr. Noreen Chase for her recent accomplishment.* He composed an email response to the company representative requesting information on Gross, then pulled his phone and snapped a picture of the image. He sent it to Ingram. Five minutes later his phone rang.

"He could be Morton's brother," said Ingram on the other end.

"It could be his twin."

"Maybe he is."

"Different last names." Hairston magnified the picture on his computer screen and leaned closer. "Or Morton and Gross are the same person, and the bastard's been lying to me from the start."

"What's he trying to hide?" asked Ingram.

"Whatever it is, I'm going to figure it out."

"You bringing him in?"

"Not yet. But I'm going to show him this picture and see what he says. By the way, Chase's DNA analysis is supposed to be ready this afternoon."

"Well, it's about damn time. Call me when you get it and give Mr. Morton my regards. What are you going to do if Natasha's there?"

"I'm not worried about that."

"Do you trust her?" Ingram said.

"I don't have much choice. Either she wants out and is on our side, or the warehouse is a setup."

"What do you have on the address?"

"The building is in the Research Triangle Park, it's owned by BASF, a big-time chemical company with a market cap over seventy billion. They distribute products to university and commercial labs all over the East Coast. They're also into fertilizers and pesticides. There are so many chemicals and drugs that pass through there, no one would bat an eye if another truck made a delivery or pickup. If Solo and his crew pay off the right guy, they have the perfect operation."

"Any unusual activity?"

Hairston shrugged. "Hard to say. The trucks have shipping manifests filled with names I've never heard of and can't pronounce. It's a drug dealer's dream come true."

"Any deliveries scheduled for Thursday?"

"Closed on Thanksgiving but it's business as usual Wednesday with a partial schedule on Friday. We have an eye in the sky and boots on the ground."

"You got anyone inside?" asked Ingram.

"Not yet. I've pulled aerials and blueprints of the building. We're working out the SWAT operational details."

"There goes Thanksgiving dinner."

"Eat early."

———

Natasha opened the front door. A cigarette dangled from her lips. She brought a lighter to it and flicked the flame. The tip turned bright orange as she inhaled. A moment later she tilted her head up and blew a long stream of smoke that passed over Hairston's left shoulder. The smell of burnt tobacco mingled with her perfume. She stared at him.

"Good morning. Terry around?"

"He's not up yet."

"I have something important to show him."

She leaned against the door in a classic noir pose with one arm folded across her chest, the other hand at shoulder height, wrist relaxed, with her cigarette perched near the ends of her long fingers. Smoke curled from the tip into the still air.

"Why don't you come back in a couple of hours?"

Hairston leaned forward. "Wake him up or I'll be back with an arrest warrant and make it official."

"Wait here." She flicked her cigarette, then shut the door. Hairston looked down and tapped his shoe toe, sending a bit of fallen ash onto the porch, then turned to admire the blooms on the camellias and Encore Azaleas. There wasn't a stray leaf on the lawn. *Morton's doing more than just all right.* Footsteps came from the foyer, then the door latch clicked.

Terry Morton stood in the threshold wearing his robe and slippers and a tight-lipped grin. His bleary eyes and disheveled hair confirmed he'd just woken up.

"Detective Hairston, what a wonderful way to start the day. Would you like some coffee?"

Hairston appreciated the sarcasm and looked at his watch, which read eleven fifteen. "Thank you, I'd love some. Late night?"

"Not really, typical weeknight. This way." Morton led them into the kitchen and motioned for Hairston to sit at the island. Natasha had disappeared.

"Very nice," said Hairston, rubbing his fingers over the ogee edge on the granite countertop.

"The previous owners had good taste."

"And a lot of money."

"I suppose. Now, what can I do for you?"

"Remind me again where you worked before you moved to Durham."

"In La Jolla, California. I was the sales manager for several car dealerships in the area."

"Which ones?"

"I started out at Del Mar Motor Cars, then moved to the Mossy Toyota Lexus dealership off Interstate 5."

Hairston scribbled a note. "How long were you there?"

"Three years."

"Ever worked overseas?"

Morton filled Hairston's cup with coffee and replaced the carafe on its warmer. "I've traveled to many countries but never worked outside the US."

"You've never been employed by a company called Thyssenkrupp in Germany?"

"The elevator company? No, never."

"They make a lot more than just elevators."

"Really? I had no idea."

"Take a look at this picture." Hairston handed him his phone with the photo displayed.

Morton's brow creased, his eyes narrowed, then he relaxed and handed it back. "Noreen, what a beautiful woman."

"I was referring to the man next to her, Richard Gross."

"What about him?"

"It's you."

Morton laughed and shook his head. "You're joking. I've never worked for Thyssenkrupp and I've never been in Essen, Germany."

"I didn't say where the photo was taken."

Morton shrugged. "You asked me if I worked for Thyssenkrupp in Germany."

"That's correct, but I didn't specify the city. How did you know the picture was taken in Essen?"

"I didn't. It was just a guess."

Hairston smiled. "This man presenting Noreen the award. He's a spitting image of you, don't you think?"

"He's at least twenty-five pounds lighter and has white hair." He pulled up the sleeve of his bathrobe and held out his arm. "My skin is much darker, don't you agree?"

"Tanning bed?"

"I don't think so. Look closer—no freckles, the hair on my forearms is dark. I'm not an albino, detective."

"Then you don't mind giving me a sample of your hair."

"Why would you want that?"

"For a color analysis."

"You think I color this?" He raked his fingers through his hair.

"How about it, Terry, care to give up a lock?"

"Not without a warrant."

Hairston stared at the picture. "This photograph was taken seven years ago, Richard, plenty of time to put on a few pounds."

"Excuse me?"

"Who are you, Terrance Morton or Richard Gross?"

"Knock off the bullshit, detective. This isn't doing either of us any good."

Hairston replaced the cup on the counter. "And why is that?"

"Because you're not going to believe anything I tell you."

"Try telling me the truth."

"I have been," said Morton.

"I see. Excellent coffee, by the way."

"Jamaican Blue Mountain, ground this morning."

"Natasha?"

Morton blew across the steaming surface. "She's a barista."

"A woman of many talents." Hairston took another sip. "Is there anything you can tell me?"

"Like what?"

"What about Natasha? Where did she work before she met you?"

"New York."

The corner of Hairston's mouth rose in a half smile. "Dancing on Broadway, I suppose?"

"She mixed drinks at night and worked at a café during the day. She immigrated from Russia five years ago and has an incredible work ethic."

"You're her knight in shining armor?"

"I wouldn't go that far, but we help each other."

Hairston sipped his coffee. "I've been doing a little research into Anastasia's. Two of your business partners, Victor Chenko and Alex Shukhov, have connections with organized crime in New York."

"Really?" Morton folded his hands. "Look, detective, you seem to have a vivid imagination. I'm just a motorcycle salesman and night-club owner trying to make a buck. Tasha is my employee and close friend. There's nothing more to it. As for Victor and Alex, they are business partners. I don't know what they do apart from our interaction with Anastasia's. Now, is there anything else I can help you with? If not, then I need to get a shower and change."

"I'm going to find out who killed Noreen Chase."

Morton's eyes narrowed. "Do me a favor and let me know when you do." He planted his palms on the granite surface and stood. "I have to get ready for work."

Hairston returned a tight smile and placed his coffee cup on the counter. "I'll let you get on with your day. My apologies for interrupting."

"No apology necessary. I'll show you to the door."

Hairston said goodbye at the front door and walked to his car. The sound of grating metal hurt his ears as he pulled the driver's door open.

"I can get you the name of a good body shop," Morton called from the front porch.

Hairston waved, got in, and grimaced at the repetition of the sound as the door slammed closed. *Got to get that fixed.* He took one last look at the house. Morton hadn't moved. He didn't look like a spy. He looked like a fat version of Hugh Hefner standing on the steps of his mansion. All he needed was a pipe to make the image complete. *This case just doesn't make any sense.* He checked his email. A message from the medical examiner's office appeared labeled DNA RESULTS. *It's about damn time.* He sat in the driveway for several minutes digesting the results. Once he was on the road, he called Ingram.

"How'd it go?" Ingram asked.

"It's him."

"He admitted it?"

"No, but he slipped up. It's him, I'm sure, he's Richard Gross."

"I hate to ruin a good theory, but I'm emailing you a newspaper article. It's from the *London Times*. Richard Gross died five years ago."

"What?"

"Shot and killed during a terrorist shootout at the airport in Essen, Germany. Read the article."

"You're sure it's the same guy?"

"Essen, Germany. Thyssenkrupp. It's the same guy, there's a photo."

"Scheisse. It gets weirder. The DNA report is back."

"And?"

"We got a hit from the military DNA database."

"That's great news. Who was it?"

"Your boy, Thurman."

"What?" asked Ingram.

"The vaginal and fingernail DNA matches that of ex-navy surgeon Dr. Mark Thurman."

"No way, no fucking way!"

"I'm giving you the facts. These tests are over 99.9 percent accurate. I have the official report in my hands," said Hairston.

"I don't care how fucking accurate they are, he didn't do it."

"Try to be objective, Jack. He doesn't have an alibi for the night of the murder. He claims he went home alone and watched college football then went to bed early. Then he goes for an unwitnessed two-hour run before sunrise while someone robs his house. When I investigate the scene, what do I find? Chase's missing earring."

"Why would he let you in his house if he kept a souvenir from the crime in his bedroom? The man's not an idiot by any stretch. He'd have known you'd find it. It doesn't add up."

"I agree, he isn't my first choice, but evidence is evidence. Those are the facts. Where is he?"

"I don't know. I haven't heard from him in a couple of days. He was supposed to meet me in my office but never showed."

"I'm putting out a BOLO."

"You're really going to arrest him?"

"Give me one good reason why I shouldn't."

"It doesn't pass the smell test," Ingram said. "You've been a cop for a long time. You know in your gut things don't add up."

"Look. I know he's your friend, but he's strong enough to pull it off. He knew the victim well. He's a physician with access to narcotics. We found her earring in his house. Most importantly, his DNA is all over her. What more do you want? Thurman is our prime suspect."

"It's too convenient, too airtight. You expect me to believe that the man goes from serving his country and saving lives to taking one? It just doesn't fit."

"You ever read *Dr. Jekyll and Mr. Hyde*? You might want to check it out. It's about this respected doctor with all kinds of repressed evil urges who disguises himself and goes around killing people."

"Give me a fucking break."

"I have no choice but to bring him in. If you want to be a good friend, you'll call and convince him to turn himself in so he doesn't get hurt."

CHAPTER 40
LAZARUS

THE C-17 GLOBEMASTER from Aviano landed at Seymour Johnson Air Force Base in Goldsboro, North Carolina, just before noon. A Black Hawk helicopter transported them to Pope airfield adjacent to Fort Bragg. A half hour later they sat in the conference room at TSI headquarters waiting to be debriefed by Jaggears. He entered at exactly 2:30 p.m. and took the chair at the head of the table.

Afterward, Bristow, Thurman, and then Carmen gave their accounts. Jaggears questioned Dario for another half hour, then stood up. "Thank you for a job well done. There are several minor details left to clean up, but the Italians aren't threatening to cut diplomatic ties. The caretaker at Stanov's villa is claiming the explosion was caused by an electrical short igniting solvents in the garage."

"More like C-4," Bristow said. "Tell them to look close, they'll find evidence of a bomb."

"Captain DiRienzo has been taken into custody, and Walters's daughter is on the way back to the US."

"What about Walters?"

"No sign of him yet, I'm afraid. Probably never will be. It's a shame."

"What about his daughter?" Carmen said, aghast.

"The wife's parents are going to take care of her for now."

Thurman remembered the engineer's face. Now a little girl might be an orphan. He felt a surge of anger and the overwhelming urge to shoot something.

"What about the battery?" asked Dario.

"At the moment, I don't have much to tell you. It's missing, presumably in Stanov's possession. Am I correct that you will be joining Yuri's team at Angstrom Industries?"

Dario nodded. "It's a dream come true; he's alive and made the most important scientific discovery of the century."

Thurman cleared his throat. "If you don't mind, sir, I held up my end of the bargain. Now what about my cousin?"

"Our intel suggests he's in the Raleigh-Durham area."

"Where?"

"If I knew, we'd be planning a rescue."

"They're going to call. I need the sphere."

"The sphere will be kept here. When arrangements for the ransom have been made, I will give it to you. We will, of course, take part in the swap. We'll get him back."

Thurman exhaled and placed his forearms on the table. "Thank you, sir."

"Now if you will excuse me, I have several phone calls to make."

After picking up Carmen's Jeep from Bristow's farm, driving to Raleigh, and getting Dario checked in to his hotel in Durham, it was almost six o'clock in the evening. Thurman and Carmen entered her apartment and tumbled into bed, succumbing to sleep before turning the bedroom light off.

A few hours later, Thurman grimaced when he rolled over. A brief jolt of pain shot from his right knee up his thigh. He thought of the small black spot on the x-rays taken in Siena, the lytic lesion eating away at his femur. He locked his fingers behind his head and stared at the ceiling as the pain subsided. The differential diagnosis was short. *Recurrence of Ewing's sarcoma, metastatic lesion, new primary . . . if it's any of those, I'm screwed. My days are numbered.* He'd get it checked soon, but not today. It didn't matter. He thought of Steve. *Hang on, I'm coming.*

Thurman looked around at Carmen's bedroom bathed in soft lamp light. The white bedsheets retained the fresh scent of fabric softener.

He noticed the mementos of Carmen's life. A framed army recruiting poster hung on the wall featuring two women soldiers. The slogan MOTIVATED, DEDICATED, EDUCATED appeared in large block letters. She'd placed a military shoulder patch in the bottom corner. A framed photograph of the West Point women's soccer team from her senior year hung next to the poster. Carmen knelt in the front row with her long dark ponytail draped over her shoulder. Thurman looked closer and noted the resemblance to the famous striker Alex Morgan.

Soft breaths drew his attention. Her eyes opened. Crystal-blue irises swept over his face. She pulled a fistful of covers under her chin and smiled. They stared at each other without speaking. He leaned closer, teasing locks away from her face and then running the tip of his index finger over dark eyebrows the color of her hair. *God, she's beautiful.*

"Close your eyes," she said.

"Why?"

"You're not allowed to see my bedhead and pillow face."

"Your bedhead and pillow face are gorgeous."

"You're crazy."

"No, I'm not." He leaned over and kissed her cheek. "Hungry?"

"Starving, but I'm not up for going out or cooking. What time is it?"

"A little after nine."

"There's a great pizza place down the block that delivers."

"I'm up for that."

She reached for her phone and ordered a large pie with the works and two Greek salads.

He swung his legs around and sat at the bedside facing the recruiting poster and pointed to the patch in the corner. "What's this?"

She smiled. "That's my regimental patch from the 75th Rangers."

He recalled her escape from the farmhouse and the two men she'd slain in the woods near the Tuscan farmhouse. He studied her angelic face. *A truly complex woman.* "Remind me to stay on your good side."

"No worries there." She stood and walked to the bathroom.

He watched the pointed undulations of her tank top and the rhythm of her gluteal muscles in silk briefs.

She stopped at the door glancing over her shoulder. "What are you looking at?"

"Nothing."

She bent over and wiggled out of the bottoms, then turned and peeled off her top. "You call this nothing?"

He stopped breathing.

She defiantly placed both hands on her hips. "Well?"

He stood, his face the picture of mock surprise. "Major Black, I didn't know you were so . . . brazen."

She crossed the floor and placed her arms around his neck. "There's a lot about me you don't know. Yet." Her soft lips touched his.

He wrapped her in his arms, kissing her with desire that had been dormant for months. She yanked his T-shirt over his head and ran her hands over his taut chest and shoulders. Her hand reached behind his neck and pulled him to her. A moment later she broke off the kiss and looked into his eyes.

He adjusted himself, then pulled her tight. Carmen felt his arousal and smiled. Her lips parted, and she tilted her head for another kiss. "It's about time," Thurman said. Her fingers slipped within the elastic waistband of his boxer briefs and peeled them off. She walked him backward to the bed until he sat on its edge. She pushed him onto his back and straddled his waist. Her lips kissed his face, neck, chest. Her breasts swayed back and forth, brushing her erect nipples over his chest. His hands cupped her breasts as she reached down and guided him. He let out a small gasp, and she placed her finger on his mouth, hushing him as she concentrated, carefully moving, changing her rhythm as the waves within her grew, then crested, and one after another broke, making her shudder.

Thurman pulled her to him, and they lay, breathing hard, wrapped together. Their eyes met and they kissed once more.

The front door intercom buzzed multiple times in rapid succession.

They looked at each other. *WTF?* Thurman thought.

Carmen looked at her silenced phone on the dresser. Several text notifications were displayed on its screen. "Pizza! I forgot. The delivery man is downstairs."

"Here, now?"

"Better check while I get in the shower."

Thurman pulled on his T-shirt and jeans and went to the door, activating the intercom for the delivery guy. After collecting the food, he opened a bottle of Rosso di Montalcino and finished his first glass by the time Carmen emerged from her bedroom.

"Your turn," she said as her bathrobe fell open.

He watched her walk from across the room. "Still hungry?"

She gave him a feline glance and reached for her glass of wine. "Starving."

"Pizza is warming in the oven if you can't wait. I'll be back in ten minutes." He took her into his arms and kissed her wine-stained full lips. "Excellent vintage."

She broke away and walked into the kitchen. The smell of fresh pizza filled the room when she opened the oven. "Better hurry if you want some."

———

After dinner, Thurman excused himself to call Ingram.

"Where the hell have you been?" Ingram said when he answered the phone.

"Out of town for a couple of days, just got back today."

"Your cousin's been kidnapped and you skip town? What's wrong with you?"

"Nothing's wrong with me. I didn't have a choice."

"What are you not telling me?"

"I'm telling everything I can."

"Well, you may want to rethink that. Chase's DNA report just came in."

Thurman froze. "And . . . ?"

"You sitting down?"

"Yeah."

"They ran the samples through the military DNA repository and got a match."

"That's great news. Anybody we know?"

"Yeah," Ingram said.

"Who?"

"You," Ingram replied.

Thurman's head buzzed with confusion. "That's impossible."

"Hairston's put out a BOLO on you. He wants me to recommend you come down to the station."

"You can forget that. If Hairston holds me, there's no chance on getting Steve back."

"Leave that up to us. We'll get him back."

"You can't get him back. Look, Jack, I can't give you all the details, but you have to trust me. I didn't kill Noreen, and I'm the only one who can get Steve back. If they arrest me, it's a death sentence for him."

"I had a feeling you'd say something like that, but half the Raleigh and Durham departments are going to be looking for you, and it's going to look bad if you run."

"My God, what has this come to?" Thurman let out a sigh. "I'm sorry, Jack, you know I'm innocent, and I have to get Steve back. Do your job, I'll do mine. Just do me a favor and give me a head start." He ended the call.

When he went back into the living room, Carmen was sitting on the sofa looking at her laptop. He leaned over and kissed her. "I'm sorry, but I have to get out of here."

"What's going on? I'll come with you just let me . . ."

"No," he said. "This one I've got to do alone." He grabbed his coat and walked out the apartment door. She was still sitting in stunned silence half an hour later when the police arrived.

CHAPTER 41
FACEPALM

DETECTIVES Hairston and Floyd followed a clerk through a maze of hallways in Raleigh's northeast police headquarters and stopped at Ingram's office. The clerk rapped at the door three times, then retreated down the corridor.

"No one's here," Ingram barked.

"Sorry we're late," replied Hairston as he entered. "You remember John Floyd, my new partner."

Ingram shut the file he'd been reviewing and extended his hand. "I remember. Have a seat."

All three sat. Hairston crossed his legs and leaned back in his chair. "Thurman still missing?"

Ingram nodded. "He's not answering my calls. I haven't seen him since last week."

Hairston sat up and leaned forward. "He's been missing since his house burned and his cousin disappeared. He's not behaving like an innocent man."

"Thurman isn't going to rest until his cousin is back. Nothing is going to interfere with that, even if it means being a fugitive."

"Hostage negotiation is our job, not his," said Hairston.

Ingram shook his head. "You don't know him like I do. He won't sit on the sidelines."

Floyd half raised a hand. "Can we table this for the moment? What about the warehouse and the drug shipment? Isn't that what we're here to talk about?"

"Fine." Ingram said, leaning back and folding his hands. "That note said 2:45 Friday morning. I'm calling out the SWAT team to cover the BASF warehouse Thursday night."

"On Thanksgiving? You're going to be one popular guy."

"It's lonely at the top. I'm not running a popularity contest."

"How do we know this isn't a setup?" Floyd asked.

"It's not a diversion. Two CIs corroborated the date."

Floyd's eyes narrowed. "How reliable are these snitches?"

Ingram scowled. "I wouldn't trust them to walk my ex-wife's dog, but something's going down tomorrow night. That date and address are the best leads we've got. Instead of turkey and stuffing, this year we get *Breaking Bad*."

Hairston looked up. "You know what I think?"

Ingram exhaled and rubbed his temples. "Sweet Mother Mary, here we go again."

Hairston ignored the comment. "It's all connected. Chase, Morton, the motorcycle wreck, the oligarch and his Russian mob, all of it. I just don't know how it fits together. Show me those photographs again."

"Which ones?" asked Ingram.

"Gross and Morton." Photographs of Richard Gross handing Noreen her Thyssenkrupp award and the Raleigh Motorsports website photo of Terry Morton appeared side by side on Ingram's computer screen. Hairston scrutinized them, then sat back in his chair. He pointed to the photograph of Morton. "He might be the guy Thurman saw in the bar at the Washington Duke Inn. The mystery man who met with Chase right before her death."

"So, ask him," said Ingram.

Floyd leaned closer to the computer screen. "The hair is darker."

"You ever heard of Just For Men? He dyed it."

Floyd shook his head. "This guy's twenty or thirty pounds heavier. Morton looks like a ginger-haired heart attack waiting to happen."

"There are drugs for treating albinism," replied Hairston. "I talked to a couple of dermatologists. The newest ones darken skin and hair color by making the body produce melanin."

Ingram's left eyebrow rose. "You're not going to let this go, are you?"

Hairston continued. "If Morton started taking one and put on the weight . . ."

Ingram frowned as he leaned closer to the screen. "No shit. They got drugs to do that?"

"According to the skin docs, albinos take them to prevent eye damage and skin cancer due to sun exposure. Look, I don't know if Richard Gross is albino, but they said if he took one of those drugs, it would darken his hair and give him a perpetual tan."

"Does he drive a BMW?" asked Floyd.

Ingram nodded. "Last year's model. A black 7 series, probably the one that rear-ended Thurman."

"Was it?"

Ingram shrugged. "We haven't located it, and according to this newspaper article, Richard Gross died five years ago."

Floyd blinked. "He's dead?"

Ingram rotated the screen toward Floyd, displaying the *London Times* newspaper article from five years ago. The headline read *Thyssenkrupp Executive Killed in Airport Gunfight*. The story gave an account of how businessman Richard Gross had been shot during a thwarted terrorist attack at a private terminal at the Essen/Mülheim Airport. He died en route to a local hospital.

"That's bullshit," said Hairston. "He may have been shot, but I don't believe he died, and he wasn't some innocent bystander. I'll bet he was right in the middle of it. I've asked the Essen authorities to check hospital records for anyone treated as a result of the incident."

Ingram turned his palms up. "What did they say?"

"They haven't said anything yet, I'm waiting for their reply." Hairston reached for the keyboard and began typing. Another *London Times* article appeared dated the day after the airport shooting. It reported the death of two prominent scientists killed in a private plane crash off the coast of England. "The plane took off from the same airport. The dates of the shooting and the plane crash match."

"Coincidence," said Ingram. "What are you driving at?"

"The names of the scientists are Yuri Kogan and Aliya Novikova. Think about it, Jack. Two world-renowned scientists depart from the same airport, the same day, and the same time of the shooting. Gross's collateral-damage death seems a little convenient, don't you think?"

Floyd face-palmed. "It makes sense. All parties are believed dead. Yuri and Aliya resurface as the Drakes. When did they start working at Angstrom Industries?"

"Why don't you find out?" said Hairston.

Floyd jotted a note. "Assuming Gross survived, then he comes back as Terry Morton."

"Don't forget who else worked there." Hairston switched the computer screen image and pointed to the photograph of Noreen Chase receiving her award. "Her and Thurman."

"I'll be damned," said Ingram.

Floyd rubbed his temples. "I thought we were investigating a bunch of greasy Russian mafia thugs."

"Who may be involved with the SVR or FSB," said Hairston.

Ingram's neck stiffened as he stared across his desk. "WTF?"

"The Russian Foreign Intelligence Service."

Ingram cut him off. "I know what it is. What makes you think that?"

"I sent a security camera photo of the hospital ER shooter to the FBI. This morning I received an email from Special Agent Jenkins, who's with the New York Field Office. They think the shooter is SVR, a Russian agent. He's coming down Friday to meet with us."

CHAPTER 42
RED STORM

FROM ANASTASIA'S in downtown Durham it usually took Natasha twenty minutes to drive home. She started the car and glanced at the dashboard clock, half past two in the morning. Fatigue seeped through her muscles; her feet and legs ached. She popped two Motrin and chased them with water, then called the number Hairston had given her.

At that moment, the detective sat in a black unmarked Suburban parked down the street from the gentlemen's club. He lowered his binoculars. "Hairston."

"It's Natasha, where are you?"

"Parked down the street. I just watched you leave the club."

"Good. Solo is expecting a phone call. After that, he and his men will be leaving. You'll want to follow them."

"What's going on?"

She told him about what she'd overheard in Solo's office earlier that evening.

"Why are you telling me this?"

"There are those who do not want Stanov to succeed."

Hairston chuckled. "Tell me why I should trust you."

"Don't be stupid. I'm your best option." She hung up, pulled a Marlboro Red from its hard pack, and cracked the window. Downtown

Durham had turned to suburban gated communities by the time she stubbed the butt in the ashtray. A couple of minutes later she pulled into Morton's garage and shut the door. Once inside, she walked to a kitchen window, lifted the edge of the curtain, and scanned the backyard. Empty darkness. A shiver went through her as an awareness came. *It's beginning.* She changed into her nightgown. Morton stirred when she slipped under the covers. He rolled over and lay facing the ceiling.

"Awake?" she whispered.

"I've been waiting for you."

She leaned over and kissed his cheek. "We have a problem."

"Just one?"

"I wish."

"What is it?" he asked.

"It has begun."

"What happened?"

She told him about the phone call between Solo and Stanov. "He plans to take Yuri."

"He screwed that up once. How's he going to do it?"

"I don't know, but it involves all of them—Yuri, his wife, and the Italian."

"They're working with Stanov?"

"How else could he pull it off?"

"Yuri too?"

She shook her head. "Never, but Aliya has arranged for him to be transferred to a rehab hospital in Wilmington."

"Can she do that?"

"She's his wife. She has the legal authority."

"Wilmington? Why there?"

"She says they have a condo at Wrightsville Beach where she will stay during his convalescence, but it just so happens Stanov's yacht arrived there this morning."

He sat up and swung his legs off the side of the bed.

"Where are you going?"

"To make a call." Morton walked to the closet and opened his safe. He withdrew one of the burner phones supplied by Jaggears and placed the call. He spoke the code words, "Red storm arriving, today, Wilmington." He hung up, dressed, and kissed Natasha. "Good work. I'm going out. I'll be back before you get up." He made his way through the kitchen, picked his keys from the rack, turned on the garage light, then stopped. A man stood next to his car. Before Morton had time to react, a pistol barrel pressed into the side of his neck. Morton raised his hands.

"Hello, Richard, it's been a while," said the man holding the gun. Morton recognized the Russian accent.

"Hello Boris, sorry about your foot."

The man next to the BMW rhythmically slapped a two-foot cylinder into the palm of his hand.

"Don't do anything crazy. I'm not armed. What do you want?"

Boris applied more pressure, causing Morton's head to tilt. "Time for payback. You owe me a leg, plus interest."

In Russian Morton said, "You piece of shit," then spun, knocking the gunman's arm and keying his face.

Boris stumbled backward.

Morton lunged. Pistol cracks reverberated in the garage. Two quick ones followed; a second later, a third. Then all was quiet.

Footsteps padded from the kitchen to the door leading to the garage. "Terry? What was that?" The door opened and Natasha's head appeared. "Oh, God." Morton lay motionless on the cement floor. She gasped and hurried to him. He lay on his back with blood saturating his shirt. Her hands went to her face. "What have you done?" she whispered.

"Natasha." She felt the pressure of the gun barrel on the back of her head. "Solo wants to talk to you."

"Don't touch me!" She stood and faced Boris. "Why?"

"Change of plans."

A man came up behind her and gripped her arm.

She yanked it from his grasp. "Let me get some clothes." A few minutes later they crossed the garage, and he pressed the door opener. A sprinter van was parked in the driveway. Two men dressed in black got out. Natasha remained silent. One of the men pulled the side door open and motioned for her to enter.

"I demand to know what's going on. Why did you kill him?"

"Get in, I'm just carrying out orders."

"Whose orders, Solo's?"

The Russian shook his head. "Stanov's. You'll see him soon. Maybe he'll tell you."

She spoke in Russian. "You idiot! You just killed one of the SVR's most valuable intelligence sources—destroyed years of work."

"That's why he wanted him eliminated."

—————

Hairston sat next to Floyd a block from Anastasia's in the unmarked SUV. He looked at his watch, 0245. *This isn't the way I wanted to spend Thanksgiving.* Hairston repositioned his headphones, which were beginning to feel like a vice, then leaned forward to stretch his back. He hated the monotony of stakeouts. The two detectives listened to the transmission from the bug he'd planted the night he and Ingram paid their visit. A phone rang and Solo answered. Hairston heard only one side of the conversation.

"I got it, the warehouse, four o'clock. You won't have a problem getting in. The gate guard has been taken care of."

Pause.

"Don't worry. We'll get the damn sphere. Relax, it's taken care of."

Pause.

"He'll deliver it."

Pause.

"We'll leave them both in the building. There won't be anything left . . . yes, sir."

Pause.

"Lunacy, right?"

Pause.

"I got this, just be ready to cast off when we arrive."

Pause.

"Yes, sir."

The sound of glass breaking came through the headphones, followed by Solo's voice. "Can you believe that asshole? After all I've done. He picks up ten million tonight and tells me to drive a fucking ambulance to Wilmington. That's bullshit."

Solo dialed again. "This is your last chance. Be at 2745 East Birmingham Boulevard in an hour. Stop at the front gate. Tell the guard you're making a delivery. He knows to call me. You better have it or your cousin dies." Hairston heard people moving about the room, then Solo said, "C'mon, let's get this over with." After a minute of silence, he removed the headphones and looked at the detective sitting next to him.

Floyd removed his headphones and placed them on the equipment. "What do you make of that? He said, 'You better have it or your cousin dies.' You think he called Thurman?"

"That's exactly what I think. It's the warehouse address and Emerson is his cousin."

"What's he supposed to bring?"

Hairston frowned. "The ransom, what do you think?"

"I don't know, but Solo didn't like his marching orders."

An ambulance driver? What that's all about? Hairston called Ingram.

"It's three o'clock in the morning. This better be good," said Ingram.

"Thurman just got his call. He's to be at the warehouse in an hour. Something's going down and it sounds like they're swapping his cousin for something."

"The SWAT team is in position. Send me a recording of the call."

"Check your email in a couple of minutes. You better get rolling. Good luck. I'll tail Solo." Hairston ended the call.

Floyd raised his binoculars and focused on Anastasia's lighted doorway. "Solo and two guys just left the building. They're getting in a Mercedes."

CHAPTER 43
SOLAR FLAIR

"WAIT," Thurman said, but the call ended. He called the number back and got the standard recorded message. His watch read 2:50 a.m. He researched the warehouse address, then dressed and went to the other end of the house. Bristow's face appeared at the bedroom door after Thurman's second round of taps. "Get dressed. I just received the call. We have an hour to be at a warehouse in the Research Triangle."

Bristow ran his fingers through his hair while processing this information. "Give me five minutes."

"I need a gun."

Bristow nodded and before closing the door said, "Coffee and filters are in the cabinet next to the refrigerator." Five minutes later he walked into the kitchen dressed in jeans, a T-shirt, and trail shoes. The handgrip of a Kimber .45 protruded from his inside-the-waistband holster on his right hip. "You got an address?"

"Birmingham Boulevard, the BASF warehouse." Thurman repeated the message and filled two travel mugs with coffee. "You ready?"

"I'm always ready." He reached behind his back and handed Thurman a P320 Legion XFIVE handgun and an extra extended magazine. He took a sip of coffee and smiled. "That do?"

Thurman gave him a tight smile and nodded. "Thanks, but we

have a big problem. I don't have the sphere. Jaggears wouldn't give it up. I don't think he'd give it up if they held the president hostage."

Bristow walked into the laundry room and opened a cabinet, revealing a wall safe. "Don't be too hard on the old man." He returned holding a silver sphere. He released it and caught it with the opposite hand as it shot to the ceiling. "You owe the admiral an apology."

"That old son of a bitch. I almost feel bad about everything I said."

"Don't, you aren't the first to call him an SOB."

"I don't want to lose this thing."

Bristow handed him a zip-up belt pouch the size of his wallet. "Use this. We'll both be in Jaggear's doghouse if you do."

Bristow led the way to the garage. They got into his Gator and drove to the barn a quarter mile away. Bristow parked and opened a door, revealing a black Tahoe. "My special-ops vehicle. Compliments of TSI." He raised the rear hatch and reached for the nearest of two large storage boxes. He lifted the lid and handed Thurman an armored vest, a throat mic, and an earpiece. "Put these on." He did the same. From the other box he extracted a suppressed MK18 rifle. He slipped on a chest rig with three ammo pouches loaded with thirty round magazines. He turned and faced Thurman and said, "Let us not prove unworthy of our brothers."

Thurman knuckle bumped Bristow's fist, then adjusted his vest and slipped on his jacket. "Let's get Steve."

———

Ingram keyed his mic. "This is Alpha One, we're ten minutes out. Give me an update."

The SWAT team second-in-command responded, "Check, Alpha Five here. The men are in position. All doorways covered. We have identified five males, two from a delivery truck and three from the warehouse. They've unloaded five pallets. Not sure what it is, no labels. Now they're loading the truck. So far, three pallets have been placed in the trailer."

"When they've finished loading, let me know. That truck cannot leave the area. Be ready to move in and secure the vehicle and anyone in the building."

"Roger that, Alpha One."

"Break, break, Alpha Two here, we have a situation," said another SWAT officer.

"Copy, Alpha Two. What is it?" said Ingram.

"A black Tahoe just pulled up to the front gate."

"What's happening?"

"He's stopped, talking to the guard."

"Copy, this is Alpha Five. We need to know what it does. Is there another player in the game?"

"You were right."

"Don't keep me in suspense, Alpha Two."

"Doc Thurman is driving."

"Repeat, Alpha Two," said Ingram. "I did not copy."

"Dr. Mark Thurman is driving the vehicle."

"Is anyone with him?"

"Negative, he appears to be alone."

———

After dropping off Bristow a block from the warehouse, Thurman drove into the industrial park and stopped at the gate. He lowered his window. The gate guard approached.

"Come back after eight o'clock," he grunted.

"I'm here for a delivery, check with your boss."

The man stepped back into the guard shack and made a phone call, then came back. "Show me the sphere."

Thurman produced it and let it bounce off the cab roof. He retrieved it and rolled it between his fingertips. "Seen enough?" Thurman replaced the orb in the belt pouch.

The guard nodded. "Now, get out."

Thurman complied. The man frisked him, then lit up the Tahoe with his flashlight, checking it from front to rear. Thurman stood back, motionless. The odds of him finding the XFIVE in its storage compartment were too small to worry about. A few minutes later, the guard made another call. "He's clean, the vehicle is empty. He's got it." A moment later he ended the call and replaced the phone in his front pocket. He looked at Thurman. "Drive around to the delivery dock in the back. They're waiting for you." The chain-link gate slid to the right. Thurman put the Tahoe into drive and proceeded. Even in the predawn darkness, the building appeared massive, as big as a Boeing assembly plant, over a hundred yards wide and long and at least fifty feet tall. He followed the road that made a wide arc into a wooded area, sloping downhill toward the rear of the building. A hundred yards away, through leafless trees and underbrush, Thurman saw the loading docks and a tractor-trailer rig illuminated like a movie set. A forklift made trips back and forth between the warehouse and the trailer. In the cover of the trees, Thurman stopped the SUV in the middle of the road. He adjusted his earpiece and keyed his mic. "I'm near the loading docks. Are you in position?"

"Roger that," said Bristow. "I've got a clear field of fire."

Just then Thurman's phone rang. He placed it on speaker and kept his mic open. The familiar voice asked, "Why did you stop?"

"Just getting my bearings."

"Proceed to the loading docks."

"Be there in a minute."

"Your cousin and I are waiting." The call ended.

———

"Alpha Two here, it's definitely Thurman," said the SWAT officer. "He got out and the guard frisked him then searched the vehicle."

"When this thing is over, arrest him. My ETA is two minutes," said Ingram. "Alpha Five, update."

"Copy, Alpha One, it looks like they've finished at the loading docks. The forklift operator is in the building. The guys with the truck are getting ready to close the rear doors. I don't see the other two."

Ingram white-knuckled the Charger's steering wheel as the warehouse came into view. "All units, hold your fire. This may be a drug deal, but it's also a hostage recovery situation."

Thurman withdrew the pistol from under the dash and wedged it next to the driver's seat as he drove to the back of the warehouse. A man stood in the center of the spotlit area and held up his hands, indicating for Thurman to stop. Thurman put the transmission in park, left the engine running, and got out. The man looked familiar. Thurman froze. His heart rate doubled. *It can't be.* The one-legged man he'd shot in the chest in a field in Tuscany now stood before him, an apparition from the dead.

"Dr. Thurman, we meet again." Boris smiled and withdrew a pistol from behind his back. "Show me the sphere."

Thurman raised his arms and produced the sphere pinched between the fingers of his left hand. "Where's my cousin? This thing is going into orbit if I don't see him in the next ten seconds."

"He's in the trailer." The Russian limped toward the tractor-trailer rig. "See for yourself."

The truck had been moved forward twenty feet from the loading dock. As Thurman approached, two men appeared from inside the trailer and jumped to the pavement. One wore a beard and a stocking cap; the other was hatless and clean shaven.

"Frisk him," said Boris.

Stocking Cap came forward. He padded Thurman's legs, torso, and arms. As he felt the left sleeve, he grabbed his fist with both hands. "I got it!" he yelled. Thurman reacted immediately, cracking him in the nose with a compact right. The man's head rocked back and his stocking cap flew into the air. He stumbled backward, then regained his balance and charged. Thurman flattened his nose with a jab then dropped him with a left hook.

"Try that again, asshole, and this sphere gets launched." He held his left hand above his head.

"Enough!" Boris waved him toward the trailer. Thurman followed. He came to the back and looked inside. Pallets of boxes filled the front half of the space closest to the cab. Ten feet from the doors Steve Emerson sat, tied to a chair with his arms behind his back. "Steve! It's me, Mark. Can you hear me?"

He blinked and nodded, but he didn't speak.

"What have you done to him?"

"I assure you he's in good health. He's sedated."

Thurman stood at the back of the truck. "Bring him to me."

Boris watched with arms folded, the gun clenched in his right hand. "If you both want to live, I'll take the sphere."

Thurman held it for him to see. "If I give it to you now, then what's to stop you from killing us both? You'll get this when he's out of this truck and in my car. Understand? Now get him out of there." The hatless man looked at Boris, who gave him a single nod for confirmation, then he vaulted into the truck and produced a pocketknife with a three-inch blade. He cut the cords binding Steve, then closed the blade. "Help me get him out of here," he said to his companion.

The bearded man with the bloody nose leaned over the back edge, swung a leg up, and rolled into the trailer. He struggled to his feet, then helped get Steve on the ground.

Thurman ducked under Steve's left arm and helped him stand. He spoke into his ear. "I've got you, now let's get out of here." They shuffled toward the SUV.

Boris remained silent and watched.

Thurman held out his left hand, showing him the sphere. "Shoot me, asshole, and this floats into the heavens."

"Let it go, and you're dead."

"So, we have a standoff. You'll get it when we're in the car; now get the fuck out of my way." He shuffled, half carrying Steve toward the Tahoe idling thirty feet away.

Boris walked past, opened the passenger door, and retreated a few steps. "Put him in and give me the sphere."

Thurman dumped Steve into the seat and lifted his legs to get him situated. Once Steve was in position, he leaned in and snapped the seatbelt. *This is it, now or never.* He reached for his gun wedged between the seats and stood, keeping his back to Boris.

"Hand it over. Don't let it slip."

Thurman gripped the sphere and half turned, keeping the pistol out of sight. He presented the sphere to Boris. "Hold it tight in your hand. Don't open it or you might lose it. Don't even look at it."

Boris's fingers closed around it. He smiled and while hypnotized by the gleaming orb that pulled at his fingers, he started to raise his gun.

Thurman stuck his gun barrel in Boris's face. "Drop it or I shoot. In the face this time."

The gun clattered onto the pavement.

"Smart move, asshole." Thurman moved the gun to Boris's back, keeping there as the two of them hustled around the front of the SUV. Stocking Cap stood ten yards away, holding an assault rifle. "Don't do it asshole," Thurman shouted at him. "Drop the gun." The rifle barrel turned toward the Tahoe. "Point that thing this way and I'll shoot him. I'll bet his fingers open up after I put a bullet through his spine."

"Put the gun down," Boris said as he placed the sphere into his front pocket while Thurman opened the driver's side door and climbed in. The engine idled almost silently.

Suddenly, Boris spun, broke Thurman's grasp, and sprinted away. Stocking Cap opened fire, spraying the hood and windshield. Thurman ducked and floored it. Stocking Cap flew over the hood, smashed into the windshield, and rolled off onto the ground. Thurman yanked the wheel, fishtailing one hundred and eighty degrees.

A barrage of gunfire crisscrossed the loading area. *A fucking death trap.* The SUV's window spiderwebbed. Bullets ripped into metal. The Tahoe accelerated as the rearview mirror exploded. Shards of glass ricocheted off Thurman's face. He reached over and pulled Steve to him.

The firefight reached a crescendo.

Thurman glanced in a sideview mirror and saw armed men scrambling toward the warehouse. Others retreated inside. A police SWAT vehicle coming from the opposite direction appeared in front of him. He veered around it and felt a rear tire blow, causing the Tahoe to became erratic. Thurman looked at Steve, who lay slumped over, motionless. The rear end fishtailed as Thurman tried to hold the road. Another tire blew, sending the Tahoe spinning. Trees came at him. The trunk of a pine tree the size of a light pole crushed the hood. An image of Carmen's face flashed as the airbags deployed.

Thurman tried to open his eyes. He blinked and turned his head from side to side. Then he pushed the airbags out of the way. Gunfire sounded in the distance. *Got to move. Get Steve to safety.* Thurman opened the SUV door.

Ingram ran down the road and grabbed Thurman. "Are you hurt?"

"I don't think so. Help me with Steve." He pointed to the passenger side.

Ingram tried to open the door, but the entire right side of the car had been crumpled by the impact. "This won't open. Let's pull him out from your side."

Thurman climbed into the darkness and released the seatbelt. "Steve, can you hear me?" He reached under his shoulders and pulled his limp body from the vehicle. Blood covered Steve's head and shirt. *This is not good.*

Ingram barked, "Come on, we have to get out of here."

"I'm not leaving him." Thurman's chest heaved. "Call an ambulance."

Ingram grabbed one arm and placed it around Steve's shoulders. Thurman had the other. They began jogging down the road with Steve's toes dragging the pavement.

"Alpha One, this is Alpha Five, do you copy?"

Ingram replied, "Go ahead."

"That truck just off-loaded five thousand pounds of ammonium nitrate. It's a trap."

"Muthafucker," Ingram whispered. He keyed the radio. "Alpha Five. Pull back. Get everyone out of there. Repeat, get out—now!"

"The truck's leaving."

"Let it go and get the hell out of there! We can follow it." Gunfire sounded in the background. "What's happening?"

"Receiving fire."

"Move it. This could be another Oklahoma City."

"What?"

"They delivered the same shit Timothy McVeigh used."

"Repeat? I did not copy."

"Get out of there, now!"

Thurman and Ingram stood in the road supporting Steve as the eighteen-wheel rig lumbered up the hill, shifting gears to gain speed.

Bursts of suppressed gunfire sounded through the trees. A muffled explosion came from the direction of the building.

"Hurry! That place is going to blow." They ran as fast as possible while carrying two hundred and twenty pounds of dead weight. Trees and underbrush on either side made leaving the road impossible.

Ingram spoke. "Alpha Five, where are you?"

"We have men still in the warehouse."

"It's going to blow. Get out . . . now!"

"Here they come. All accounted for."

"Get the fuck out of there."

The truck was bearing down, thirty yards and closing. The Kenmore shifted into a higher gear, picking up more speed.

Thurman glanced at Ingram. "Into the trees." They veered off the paved surface into the woods. The tractor trailer came on like a locomotive. The air pressure dropped as the behemoth passed. Then it happened. The night erupted into day like a solar flare on the surface of the sun. It was followed by a hot blast that blew Thurman onto the road. A hundred yards away the back half of the chemical warehouse disintegrated into a five-story fireball. He turned his head away from the heat and watched the eighteen-wheeler plow through the gate. Thurman lay stunned as the surreal events unfolded in slow motion. Another explosion ripped through the warehouse, lighting up the sky for a second sunrise. Heat washed over his body as debris rained down. The truck shifted gears. It picked up speed, turned left, and disappeared.

Thurman turned Steve onto his back in the dim firelight. His white face stared into the dark sky. His chest made no movement. Thurman felt no pulse. He placed his ear near Steve's mouth, listening for breathing. Nothing. Thurman opened his cousin's jacket. Blood soaked the lining. He pulled up the saturated shirt. Two bullets had pierced Steve's chest, shattering his sternum and instantly destroying his heart and great vessels. Steve's spirit had departed before they'd left the loading area. Thurman lowered his head and wept. The earth mourned with him as several lesser explosions shook the ground.

CHAPTER 44
ED AFTERMATH

INGRAM APPEARED at Thurman's side. "You all right?" The cold, damp ground soaked into his jeans as he knelt by Steve.

"He's dead. They killed him."

"I'm sorry." He placed his hand on Thurman's shoulder.

Thurman touched Steve's eyes and arranged his body, folding his arms and straightening his legs. He said a silent prayer.

"If you're up for it, we need your help. I've got casualties."

Thurman nodded. He touched Steve's arm one last time, then got up. "Let's go." They ran back to Ingram's Charger. Chunks of building debris lay on the crushed roof. Smoke came from under the crumpled hood. All the windows were broken. Thurman went to the trunk. The latch had been sprung. He pried open the dented metal lid and found a flashlight, then removed a medical kit and a SWAT-issue M16. He checked the rifle's magazine and made sure a round was in the chamber. He slung the first aid bag over his shoulder, gripped the rifle, then looked at the flames shooting skyward from the warehouse inferno.

Ingram reached into the trunk and took the shotgun. They jogged back down the road toward the building, climbing over downed trees. Small brush fires flickered in the woods, threatening to become a conflagration. It looked like a war zone. Halfway to the warehouse they saw the armored SWAT vehicle laying on its side in the trees.

Ingram stopped, stunned at the sight. "My God, that's a ten-ton vehicle."

A gust of wind carried smoke through the trees. "No telling what chemicals are in those fumes," Thurman said, rubbing his eyes and coughing. "Let's get those guys out of there."

"See what you can do," Ingram yelled. "I'm going to check the situation at the loading dock."

Thurman grabbed a rear door handle and pulled. It protested but opened. He swept his flashlight over the interior and counted eight men, his comrades. He'd been part of this band of brothers for almost a decade. They'd been on hundreds of SWAT missions, trusting each other with their lives. The wrecked vehicle and twisted, strewn bodies brought back memories of the IED attacks he'd treated while deployed in Afghanistan. *Slow, steady breaths. You've got a job to do.*

The first two bodies he checked didn't have a pulse. The third had a thready carotid ripple that faded fast. Thurman grabbed a lifeless body and pulled it from the wreckage. "Can anyone hear me?"

A voice groaned from the front of the vehicle. "Help."

"I'm coming, hang on." Thurman crawled over another dead body and reached the man in the front seat. A pair of eyelids blinked from under a helmet. "Trotter, can you hear me?"

He nodded.

"Can you feel your arms and legs?"

"Yes."

Thurman unfastened his seatbelt and felt his neck. "Does this hurt?"

"Everything hurts."

"It's important, does your neck hurt?"

"Not too bad."

"Can you move?"

"I think so."

"Show me." The injured man moved all four extremities. "Let's get you out of here." Thurman put Bob Trotter's arm over his shoulders and helped him to his feet. Together they made it out the door. They walked to a patch of grass by the roadside and sat down. "Rest here;

I'm going back," Thurman said. Five minutes later he returned with another officer and ran back in for more.

Inside the van the smell of leaking gasoline saturated the air. Thurman moved faster, making multiple trips. The last injured man moaned. Thurman pulled his arm around his shoulder and said, "Sorry, big fella, you're coming with me." Once clear of the truck, Thurman fireman-carried the sergeant the next twenty yards. Then the explosion knocked them to the ground. Flames engulfed the SWAT van. A moment later Ingram ran up the road from the burning warehouse.

"The warehouse is an inferno."

Thurman pointed to where uniformed shapes lay motionless in the shadows. "Three dead." He pointed to the bodies next to the road. "I pulled these guys out before it blew." He knelt by a figure who reached up and gripped his forearm. "Five survivors, all injured. I can't tell how serious."

"Help my partner, doc, I'm okay," said the officer on the ground.

"Did you call for ambulances?" Thurman asked Ingram.

He nodded. "They're on the way."

"Hold this so I can start triage." He handed him his flashlight and began assessing the first victim. After a moment he looked up at Ingram. "What are you guys doing here?"

Sirens sounded in the distance. A police helicopter began to circle overhead, spotlighting the terrain. Ingram watched as Thurman applied a tourniquet to an officer's leg. "We were tipped off. Some major drug deal from New York. What are you doing here?"

"They called about an hour ago. Told me to be here if I wanted to see Steve again."

"You brought a ransom?"

"You could say that."

Ingram stepped back a few feet from the flames. He wiped his forehead. "I told you to let me handle it. How much did they get away with?"

"We'll talk about it later." He moved to the next victim. "Shine the light over here."

Ingram adjusted the handkerchief covering the lower half of his face. "We need to pull back. That fire is burning some dangerous shit."

Thurman nodded. "My eyes are burning and it's getting harder to breathe. There could be more explosions."

Fire trucks plowed over the open ground in front of what used to be the building and began dousing the flames. Downed trees blocked the road, making it impossible for the trucks to reach the rear of the building. More emergency vehicles arrived and moved into position. An ambulance appeared at the guard shack, and the SWAT officer directed it down the road. Ingram stood waving his flashlight. Its headlights lit up the area as it came to a stop at the first downed tree. The crew hustled out, carrying a gurney.

Thurman waved them over. "I'm the SWAT team medical officer. This guy's ready for transfer. Open right femur fracture. I've applied a tourniquet and a makeshift splint. Blunt chest trauma and a head injury. I've started an IV. He's had a liter of saline." Two more ambulances came through the gate.

An hour later the sun had risen. All casualties had been given an initial field assessment and transported to various hospitals. Thurman climbed into the rear of the last ambulance and sat down next to the gurney as it pulled away. "Take us to St. Matthew's," he said to the driver as he rubbed his aching knee. He'd failed his cousin and SWAT team brothers. He'd lost the sphere and let down his best friend. He placed his face in his hands as the ambulance picked up speed and began to wail its siren. Suddenly he looked up. *Where is Bristow?*

Thurman attended to the man on the gurney as the ambulance sped through the city. With lights flashing and sirens blaring, it turned into the medical center. The patient's breaths now came shallow and quick.

"Stay with me, Marlow. Don't make me intubate you." Thurman placed the bell of his stethoscope onto the man's chest. "Deep breath. C'mon, you can do better than that. Breathe."

The ambulance stopped and the rear doors flew open. Cool

morning air washed in. Women and men in scrubs lifted the gurney. Thurman stumbled out. "Who's on call?"

A male nurse in black scrubs nodded in recognition. "Dr. Sherrod just came on."

"Where is he?"

The nurse shrugged as he changed an IV fluid bag. "He was at the triage desk the last time I saw him."

Thurman weaved through the crowd and strode through the sliding glass doors into the emergency room. He caught up with the emergency department chief and grabbed his shoulder. "Bill."

Sherrod turned, looking startled by Thurman's appearance. Thurman's clothes were dirty and torn. He wreaked of acrid smoke. Blood stains covered his gloved hands, shirtsleeves, and vest. "Where have you been?" asked Sherrod.

"At the scene. I came in on the last ambulance. I stabilized them as best I could." He pointed to the patient being rolled into the ED. "That guy has a pneumo and an open femur fracture. I gave him two liters of saline on the ride here. He's stable for now but will probably need a chest tube."

"Thanks. There are a couple of others ahead of him."

"Anything I can do to help?"

"This is a mass casualty. All hands on deck. We need all the help we can get." Sherrod shook his head and walked behind the trauma desk speaking to no one in particular. "We just admitted the fifth casualty from a chemical warehouse blast and our chief of orthopedic trauma is on administrative leave because of a personality clash with his director. Just great."

Thurman followed. "I'm sorry, Bill. Tell me what I can do to help."

"Start with triage. I've called Wynn. You can fill him in on the ortho injuries. Get a chest x-ray on the guy with the pneumo and reassess him. If he needs a chest tube, do it."

Thurman's expression tightened. "I'm on it." He looked for Carmen but didn't see her.

A half hour passed by the time the x-rays had been shot and the wounded officer reevaluated. Thurman helped a resident insert a chest tube into the patient's left plural cavity and hooked it up to a collection canister. He'd just double-checked the water seal when Dr. John Wynn pulled back the curtains and strode through the open glass door. Wynn halted when he saw his former boss in tattered jeans, a bloodstained shirt, and SWAT body armor. "What happened?"

"Hell of a start to Black Friday," Thurman said as he rose from the patient's bedside and began giving report. "This is Percy Marlow, sergeant Raleigh PD, SWAT negotiator, thirty-two years old, bomb blast victim. Four left rib fractures, pneumothorax, and right open midshaft transverse femur fracture. I've taken care of the pneumo; someone needs to rod his femur."

Wynn looked stunned. "I heard about the explosion on the radio, then my phone started blowing up. How many injured?"

"Not sure what the final tally will be; five were brought here. At least five didn't make it, including Steve."

"Oh my God. I'm sorry, Mark. The world has gone fucking crazy."

"A major drug deal gone bad. Mob cartel turf wars? I don't know."

"How did Steve get mixed up in that?"

"It's too complicated to explain now. Trust me when I tell you Steve's an innocent victim."

"I'm sorry."

"So am I," said Thurman. "Have you seen Carmen?"

"I left her upstairs finishing rounds about an hour ago."

Two nurses from the OR wheeled the patient into the hallway, and Wynn followed. Thurman checked each trauma bay, praying he wouldn't find John Bristow. As far as he could tell, he hadn't been admitted to St. Matthew's. He started checking the triage board for updates when his phone rang. A look of surprise came over him when he realized it still worked. Angie's name and picture appeared on the cracked screen. He tensed. She didn't call for casual conversation. "Is everything all right?" he asked.

"Yuri's been transferred."

"What? That's crazy."

"He's being moved to a rehab hospital in Wilmington this morning."

"That makes no sense."

"The ambulance picked him up thirty minutes ago."

"I've never heard of such a thing. Rehab facilities don't take transfers on holiday weekends. Who authorized it?"

"The department chief."

"Vogler? He's nuts. Does Jaggears know?"

"I called him as soon as I came on this morning and found out."

"Why wasn't this stopped?"

"I tried. His wife came in yesterday and insisted on a transfer. Yuri consented. Vogler said to move him out claiming he's ready for inpatient rehab."

"That's insane, the guy's barely out of the ICU. He may not survive the trip." Thurman shook his head. "Vogler must want him out of his ortho department. This way he turns into someone else's problem. Put Carmen on the phone. I need to talk to her."

"She's not here. When the ambulance personnel took Yuri she went with them to try and stop the transfer. That was about a half hour ago. I haven't seen her since."

CHAPTER 45
DEPLOYING THE WORM

DAVID MOORE HUNG up the phone and resumed his work. Dario and Aliya had passed through security and would be arriving in a few minutes. It took some doing, but he'd managed to fast-track Dario's clearance thanks to Yuri's validation. Everything was going to work out. It had to. *This will be a day to remember.* The Ubh production run Yuri started before his accident finished last night. The ion separator would continue to filter and concentrate the reaction products for another hour. He took a final glance over the email he'd composed, then hit send. Moore hadn't felt this optimistic since Yuri joined the team. His watch vibrated and he read the text signaling they'd arrived. A few minutes later he stood and spread his arms as they entered the lab. "Welcome, so good to see you."

"Good morning, David. You're looking well," Aliya replied.

"So are you, Aliya."

"This is my good friend, Dario Benedetto."

Moore extended his hand. "I've heard so much about you."

Aliya walked to her desk and slipped on the white lab coat that hung on the wall behind her chair. "Dario would like to see the latest results?"

"Of course. I thought I'd start by showing him the CLICs."

Dario's head tilted with a quizzical look.

"Compact linear ion colliders," Moore explained as he led the group to one of the golf carts Angstrom kept for navigating the underground network of laboratories. "In my opinion they are Yuri's greatest achievement. Without the CLICs, we never would've discovered stability island." Moore accelerated through the tunnel.

We? Aliya fumed. *You had little to do with discovering stability island.*

Dario managed to keep a straight face when he stepped through the door into the room—no small task. A glass wall encased a battery of computers. He stepped around the consoles and walked through a glass door onto a viewing platform overlooking an array of equipment two floors below. Eight identical tubular structures, each a meter in diameter and ten meters long, pointed to a large octagon structure at the center of the room. The arrangement looked like a gigantic mechanical spiderweb. The sterile metallic surfaces gleamed. "Please tell me what I'm looking at."

Moore stepped next to him. "We call it the web."

"What is it?"

"An array of eight identical wakefield ion colliders designed and built by Yuri. They are the tubular devices surrounding the central octagon. They're the CLICs."

"Miniature particle accelerators?"

Moore nodded. "Micro-colliders. The device at the center is the SHIP, the separator for heavy ion reaction products."

"Tell me about the CLICs," said Dario.

"Ionic plasma is created in the tubes and accelerated with ultra-short high-energy laser pulses that boost the total energy several orders of magnitude greater than even the Large Hadron Collider in Geneva."

Dario raked his fingers through his hair. "Genius." He clasped his hands behind his neck and exhaled. "He's done it?"

"Yes, he's done it, but what is truly genius is making it scalable," said Moore. "All eight run in parallel. We can now affordably build ion colliders for manufacturing new elements. Yuri plans to make accelerators even smaller. He plans to double the number of colliders in a given space by next year."

"Like integrated circuits?" asked Dario.

"Exactly, a new form of Moore's law" said Moore. "The next version will have fifty accelerators in the array, all feeding into a central SHIP in a room less than twice the size of this one—at half the cost. Production will scale a hundredfold when it's finished."

"Where is it?"

"It's being built next door." Moore laughed as he punched the air. "It's fantastic."

"You seem awfully happy," Aliya said.

"Why wouldn't I be? We're about to make history."

She looked at him and stepped back.

"I've figured out how he does it. I can replicate it."

Aliya's eyes narrowed. "Without Yuri?"

"It's not hard once you get into the system."

"Show us," said Aliya.

Moore led the way down the metal stairs to the device in the middle of the room. He flipped down a keyboard and entered a password. Aliya watched his fingers. A two-foot-square metal door slid open, revealing a window. Thirty seconds later he peered through the glass into the machine, then he stepped away so that Dario and Aliya could see.

"Where is it?" asked Aliya. "It's empty. I don't see anything."

"Look closer," replied Moore.

Dario took his turn and shook his head. "I don't see anything."

"Neither did I at first. Look up, at the top of the container."

Aliya leaned closer, turning her head. "It looks like a film, some type of material coating the roof."

"That's element 126. It resists gravity. The particles are drawn upward. Yuri almost cried when he first opened that window and didn't see anything. Walters figured it out."

"Open it," demanded Aliya. "I want to touch it."

Dario nodded in agreement. "Yes. Please."

A few clicks of the keyboard and the glass window slid open. Moore reached in and pulled out a small, irregular-shaped object about the size of a BB. "Don't let go of it," he said, passing it to Aliya. "We'll have a devil of a time retrieving it from the roof."

"Amazing," she said, feeling its pull.

Dario held out his hand. It almost slipped through his fingers. "Incredible."

"What makes it fantastic is its electrical properties." Moore took the specimen and replaced it in the SHIP.

Aliya reached into her purse and turned to face Moore. "I'll take that password now." She pointed a gun at his chest.

Moore stared at the gun in disbelief. "What are you doing?"

Aliya smiled. "I'm leaving and taking this with me." She waved the gun in a motion encompassing the entire laboratory. "You think Yuri did this all by himself? We've worked together for years. He built these machines with my help. He couldn't have done it alone. Now he wants to give it all away for free. For the benefit of mankind. Without asking me." She scowled. "What a fool. I'm not letting that happen. Element 126 will make us rich. No one's giving it away. Now give me the password."

Dario grasped Moore's shoulders and turned him around, then firmly pushed him toward the stairs. "No one has to get hurt. Just go to the computer and bring up the code."

Once back in the control room Aliya pointed at a computer. "The files, all of them."

"Fine. But put the gun down," Moore said. His hands trembled. "I can't think with that thing pointed at me."

"Copy the code," Aliya said. She placed the end of the suppressor against his head. "Hurry up."

His fingers fumbled, but after a few seconds the screen filled with code. "It's all there."

"Just in case." Dario took Moore's seat and began photographing the screens as he scrolled through the lines. Then he inserted a USB thumb drive into a port and began copying files.

Moore looked at Aliya, then back to Dario. He eyed the door six feet away then snatched the flash drive and dashed for the exit.

A pistol crack echoed in the room. Moore stumbled and fell. He tried to crawl but collapsed, clutching the right side of his chest. A pool of blood spread on the floor like spilt paint.

Dario stared at the body on the floor, then turned to Aliya. "Must you be so drastic?"

She let the gun drop to her side and retrieved the USB drive. "Stanov's orders, no loose ends. Are you finished?"

"Almost. What about him?"

"Forget about Moore, we'll be long gone before anyone finds his body." Aliya replaced the pistol in her purse and snapped it closed. "Did you deploy the worm?"

"By noon every computer in this facility will be locked up. Nothing will work, and we have the only key."

———

Thurman paused with his phone pressed to his face. He sat down in an empty chair oblivious to the activity in the ER. *Answer the phone, Carmen.* After two more failed attempts, he called Angie back. "She isn't answering. Did you reach her?"

"No, I tried three times."

"Keep at it." Thurman then called Bristow. No answer from him either. *Damn it!* He'd begun to dial Jaggears when Ingram's voice bellowed across the emergency room.

"Doc Thurman! Over here." Ingram walked next to a stretcher being wheeled into a trauma bay. He waved at him. "Hurry, Hairston's been shot."

CHAPTER 46
10-33

(Two Hours Earlier)

OFFICER FLOYD STARTED the SUV's engine and followed the Mercedes as it pulled away from the curb in front of Anastasia's. Hairston checked the time, 0310. Solo was driving the black S550 sedan, accompanied by two of his soldiers. Durham's streets were almost deserted this early in the morning. Floyd kept his distance as the Mercedes merged onto Highway 147 heading south.

"What are they up to?" Hairston muttered.

"We're gonna find out."

"Stay back, don't be too obvious."

Floyd didn't reply but gave a quick sideways glance.

Hairston got the message. "Sorry, you know what I mean."

"Relax, next time you can drive."

The car proceeded out of Durham city limits into the Research Triangle Park area and turned west onto TW Alexander Drive. The Mercedes turned off South Alston Avenue into an industrial park.

Hairston looked through a pair of binoculars as the van parked in front of a large metal building. The sign over the entrance read WAGNER'S AUTO SALVAGE. A garage door rolled up and the Mercedes entered.

Floyd backed into a spot near the entrance to a metal fabrication shop fifty yards from the garage. Forty-five minutes later Floyd squirmed in his seat. "I need to take a leak."

"Don't open the door. The light will give us away." Hairston reached behind the driver's seat and passed him the empty plastic milk jug they kept in the vehicle for just such stakeout emergencies. "Don't miss."

Thirty seconds later a boom like a clap of thunder sounded in the distance, followed by a tremor. Floyd fumbled the jug, cursed, and then brushed his trousers. "Damn it! What the hell was that?"

Hairston chuckled. "I told you not to miss."

"Son of a bitch, a freaking earthquake right when I'm taking a leak."

"I felt it." Hairston held the binoculars to his eyes. "Probably a sonic boom from the marines flying out of Cherry Point."

"That was a damn seven on the Richter scale." Floyd recovered the jug and finished his business, then dried his hand with a Kleenex from the storage box.

Hairston snickered.

"It ain't funny."

"Sorry, I can't help it. Bad timing."

"I don't want to hear no bullshit about this. It was just a few drops. Damn sonic boom or something."

They were silent for the next half hour. Floyd dozed while Hairston watched. The clock on the dash read 0442 when his phone vibrated. It was the station desk officer.

"What is it?"

"There was an explosion at the BASF chemical warehouse about half an hour ago."

"We felt it."

"Another item I thought you'd be interested in. A 911 dispatcher just received a call from a Colvard Farms residence, Terrance Morton's place. There's been a shooting. The caller said Morton is dead. Units are on their way."

"I'm tailing suspects and cannot respond." Hairston gave their location. "Keep me informed." He hesitated for a second. "Thanks for the update. . . . Who phoned it in?"

"Female occupant, gave her name as Candy Smith."

"It's a stage name. She's a Russian exotic dancer on a visa. Young, blonde, beautiful, and she'll probably be gone by the time anyone gets there. She and another woman, Natasha Vishneva, live at the residence. They work at the deceased's club, Anastasia's. Bring them in for questioning and hold them until I get there."

"Roger that."

———

An orange-and-crimson streak across the eastern sky hinted at the possibility of rain. The milk jug was half filled by the time the garage door reopened, revealing an ambulance parked in the bay. Three men and a woman dressed in EMS attire entered the vehicle while several others stood close by.

"Same three guys? Who's the woman?"

Hairston stared through the binoculars. "Well, well, well, I'll be damned. It's Ms. Natasha Vishneva."

"Who?"

"Morton's girlfriend. Things just got a little more interesting."

"Do we need backup?"

"Not yet." Hairston lowered the glasses and pointed at the ambulance. The vehicle exited the garage and passed by them. "Get moving, and don't lose them. Half the guys on duty are probably at the warehouse explosion. No need to spread them any thinner."

The ambulance did the speed limit heading toward the west side of Raleigh. They had no trouble keeping the vehicle in sight on the near-empty highway. Hairston noted the blue road sign with a single large white H. The ambulance's turn signal blinked, then the vehicle took the exit for St. Matthew's Medical Center. The driver passed the emer-

gency department entrance, taking the perimeter road to the rear of the
main building. He parked under a covered entrance.

"Where's he going?"

"It's where they bring patients for pickup after discharge."

Floyd glanced at him with a raised eyebrow. "How do you know
that?"

"It's where I picked up my mom on Monday. Park over there, in the
staff lot. Not too close."

Floyd stopped twenty yards from the ambulance. They remained in
the SUV, observing through its tinted windows.

"Let's see what happens." Hairston raised the binoculars.

"What are they doing?"

"What do ambulances usually do?"

"Transport the sick and injured."

"Very good, detective."

"Except that's not a real ambulance."

"Oh, it's a real one, but the EMTs are Russian thugs accompanied
by a stripper."

Two men exited the ambulance cab and opened the rear doors,
retrieved a gurney, and steered it into the hospital.

Floyd pulled at his chin. "What now?"

"We watch and wait. They'll be coming back, and I'm betting that
stretcher won't be empty."

"Want me to call the desk officer?"

"I want you to act like a damn detective. We got this under
control."

Five minutes later Natasha got out of the ambulance. She stood
next to the rear and lit a cigarette. As she exhaled the first stream of
smoke, the SUV caught her attention. She stared at it for a moment,
then took a few more drags before grinding out her butt and climbing
back in.

Hairston raised his binoculars. *What the hell is she doing?*

"Think she made us?"

"No," replied Hairston. *Whose team is she playing for?*

A November chill began to penetrate the vehicle by the time the hospital door opened and the EMTs wheeled the gurney back toward the waiting ambulance. A woman in a white coat was walking beside the patient. Hairston raised the binoculars.

Yuri Drake and Carmen Black. Hairston took several photos as they loaded the scientist into the ambulance. "Get ready, almost time to move." Floyd started the engine.

Dr. Black wore scrubs under a long white coat and had a stethoscope around her neck. The driver gripped her arm and stepped toward the rear of the ambulance. She pulled back, trying to break his grasp.

"Wait," said Hairston.

They watched as Black became more agitated. Another man grabbed her wrist and pulled a pistol from his jacket. He stuck the barrel under her chin. Hairston noted the suppressor. An EMT appeared from the ambulance and pulled her into the rear compartment, and the man with the pistol followed. Once they were inside, the driver shut the rear doors and then got behind the wheel.

Floyd looked at Hairston. "Should we round them up?"

"Follow them."

"We just witnessed a kidnapping in broad daylight. Those guys got some balls."

The ambulance pulled away from the hospital. "Don't lose them."

Floyd scowled. "It's an ambulance, for Christ's sake."

Hairston called the watch commander and requested backup.

———

The ambulance exited onto eastbound Interstate 40. It passed the exit for RDU International Airport and continued past several Cary exits.

Floyd placed a couple of cars between them, keeping his distance. "They're heading out of town. You going to let them?"

"Light 'em up. Let's stop this adventure."

"Backup's not here."

"Pull 'em over," Hairston said.

"I hate to remind you, but we're outnumbered and they're armed."

"We don't know what they're doing to that woman. The state patrol is on the way and I'm not waiting any longer." Hairston pulled his weapon, checking the magazine and peeking into the chamber before holstering. He adjusted his vest and slipped on his sunglasses. "Just do it."

The police lights began flashing and the SUV closed the distance to within a few feet. The ambulance braked and steered to the shoulder, stopping a hundred yards later. When the police vehicle pulled in behind, the ambulance driver got out and approached. Hairston and Floyd exited with shields visible and weapons drawn. Floyd stayed by the passenger door while Hairston advanced. "Police, halt. Stay where you are. Put your hands behind your head."

The ambulance driver stopped at the rear of the van. "What is this, officer?"

"Durham PD. Hands up, keep them where I can see them."

Both officers had their weapons at the ready.

"I'm transferring a sick patient," said Solo.

Hairston raised his gun. "Open the back, I want to see your patient."

The driver kept his hands above his head and slapped the rear doors, then stepped around the corner. The rear doors flew open. Two men stood in the opening, holding pistols.

The woman screamed. "Help! I'm being kidnapped!"

Hairston aimed at the one on his left. "Nobody move. You're under arrest. You have the right—"

The men opened fire. Rounds tore into the SUV's grill. Gravel flew from the pavement. Glass shattered. Bullets riddled the hood.

Hairston fell to the ground. He squeezed off rounds until his slide locked.

Floyd felt a sharp pain in his leg and ducked back behind the SUV. He returned fire until his slide locked back, then did a speed reload and kept shooting. The ambulance sped away with guns blazing until the rear doors slammed shut.

Hairston raised his head from the asphalt. "Floyd, where are you?" A second later he collapsed. Blood spurted from the side of his neck turning his white collar tomato red.

The ambulance disappeared down the interstate. Floyd grimaced as pain shot from his right leg. Below his knee blood soaked his trousers. He crawled to the passenger door, reached into the front seat, and gripped his radio. "10-33! Repeat, 10-33! Officers down. Need assistance." Then he crawled to his friend and placed his hand on the side of his neck. "10-33, 10-33! Emergency, officers need assistance!"

CHAPTER 47
RUDE MOOD

THURMAN BEGAN to inspect Hairston's wounds. "What happened?"

Ingram calmly replied, "We don't know the details, but it looks like Hairston and Floyd stopped an ambulance on Interstate 40 and the driver opened up on them. Floyd took a bullet to his leg. He's at WakeMed."

Thurman looked up from the patient. "An ambulance? What for?"

"Unknown, but it came from here."

A bullet had entered Hairston's right lower flank just below his body armor. Two potentially fatal chest wounds failed to penetrate the vest. Blood seeped from an anterior right shoulder entrance wound.

Thurman removed the front half of the cervical collar and a wad of bloody bandages. He felt a bounding pulse and glanced up at Ingram. "External jugular's been hit, it just missed the carotid."

Hairston's neck looked lopsided. An expanding hematoma bulged on the right side Quasimodo-like. Thurman looked at the EMT standing at the head of the gurney and reached for his wrist, placing it over the oozing neck wound. "Hold pressure here." He turned to the wall rack and slipped on a pair of latex exam gloves. "Did you get vitals?"

The EMT spoke up. "Yes; last BP was one hundred and ten over sixty, heart rate in the seventies and eighties. He's been breathing on his own, rate about eighteen to twenty per minute."

"Has he been conscious?"

"No, sir, unresponsive."

Hairston's breaths now came rapid and shallow. "I don't think the bullet struck his trachea, but the edema is affecting his airway. I need to intubate." Thurman opened a cabinet in the corner of the room. He pulled the top drawer and located an endotracheal tube and a 10cc syringe. He looked at Ingram. "Hand these to me when I ask for them." He reached back into the drawer and located the laryngoscope, then supported Hairston's neck and shoulders with his left hand. After opening Hairston's mouth, he slid the curved blade of the laryngo-scope to the base of the tongue and lifted the instrument upward. The vocal cords came into view. "Hand me the tube." Ingram placed it in Thurman's extended right hand. He slid it into the trachea and advanced it to the appropriate depth. "Now the syringe." He pulled the scope, then filled the syringe with air and inflated the cuff. "Reach into that top drawer and hand me a roll of tape." Thurman taped the tube to Hairston's face, then reached into the bottom drawer and retrieved an Ambu bag. He began ventilating Hairston's lungs while listening with the EMT's stethoscope. He looked at Ingram. "Thanks."

The EMT spoke up. "Sir, I think he has a head injury. He's been out since we picked him up at the scene."

Thurman examined Hairston's scalp and palpated a boggy scalp hematoma on the back of the head. Blood covered his glove. He placed gauze sponges over the neck wound, secured them with tape, and replaced the cervical collar. "He's suffered head trauma and could have a subdural hematoma. We've got the neck bleeding under control. His airway is secure. Get some oxygen and get him to x-ray. I want trauma films and CTs of head, neck, chest, and abdomen. I'll put the orders in the computer."

"You'll do no such thing, Dr. Thurman!" The curtains to the exam room flung open and Harold Vogler entered, followed by two hospital security guards. "You seem to have forgotten your hospital privileges have been suspended."

Ingram positioned himself in front of Vogler so Thurman could work.

"Move out of my way." Vogler pushed Ingram without effect. Vogler turned to the nearest security guard. "What are you standing there for? This man is interfering with hospital business."

The guard stood fast. "He's a police detective, sir."

"Dr. Thurman is assisting a fellow officer," Ingram said as he shoved his badge in Vogler's face. "I suggest you let him do his job."

"How dare you," said Vogler, swatting Ingram's arm away. "This is my hospital. I'm his superior! His privileges have been suspended, and he's not allowed on these premises. Now move out of the way!"

"Let's not get into this now, Harold," said Thurman. "This patient is Detective Jerry Hairston of the Durham PD. He's received multiple gunshot wounds in the line of duty. I'm taking care of him, so shut up and stop interfering."

"You're relieved, Thurman. I'm taking over his care." Vogler turned to the guards. "Remove Dr. Thurman from hospital grounds, immediately."

CHAPTER 48
LUNASEA

THURMAN'S FACE HARDENED. He stared into Vogler's blinking eyes and thought, *You are a true asshole.* But he held his tongue.

Vogler started to speak, but Ingram interrupted. "You're under arrest for assaulting a police officer." He looked at the guards. "You saw him hit me. I'm taking him into custody."

The security guards stared at each other. Neither seemed to want to act. Vogler's face shaded crimson, and his eyes blinked in rapid-fire succession. "I'll have your badge for this!" Ingram whipped out his cuffs and pulled Vogler's hands behind his back. Thurman heard them snap with a satisfying sound. A smile spread over his face.

One of the security guards grabbed Vogler by the sleeve. "This way, sir."

"I'll have your ass for this, detective! I'm calling the commissioner."

"Anything you say can and will be used against you in a court of law," Ingram said. After reading Vogler his rights, he turned to Thurman. "I'll take care of this clown. Save Jerry." Thurman nodded and began removing Hairston's vest.

Dr. John Wynn entered the trauma bay, momentarily stunned by the spectacle. He moved aside as Ingram led his prisoner from the room, then he stepped up to the gurney and began to help. "Have you seen Carmen?"

Thurman looked at his friend and shook his head. "The ICU nurse said she accompanied Yuri Drake to an ambulance for transfer."

Wynn looked puzzled. "Since when does a senior resident accompany EMTs to move a patient?"

Thurman shook his head. "You tell me, she's on your service."

"I didn't ask her to do that."

"Then who did?"

Wynn shrugged. "I don't know. Maybe she wanted to check things out. A holiday weekend transfer isn't standard procedure."

"When did you last see her?"

"A couple of hours ago. I had to go to the OR and left her to finish rounds." Wynn exhaled. "I'm worried. She wouldn't disappear without checking in. If you talk to her, tell her to call me. We're swamped. I have five admissions from that explosion, plus a full waiting room, and this guy needs to go to the OR."

"Good luck with this mess."

"You better get out of here. We both know what a vindictive self-righteous prick Vogler can be. If you see Carmen, send her my way."

"Take good care of this guy." Thurman shook Wynn's hand and walked out of the emergency department, checking for any sign of Carmen as he made his way through the busy facility. *Something's wrong or she'd be here in the middle of this.* He called her, again without luck, then shot a text to Ingram asking him to meet up at the coffee shop down the street.

After Thurman paid for two black coffees at the counter, he slid into a booth, waiting for Ingram to arrive. He watched steam rise from the two cups as he contemplated his situation. *Carmen, Yuri, and Bristow are missing, my SWAT team comrades are injured or dead, I lost the sphere, and cancer is eating my knee and probably metastasizing throughout my body. Maybe I should buy a lottery ticket.* He shook his head and stirred his coffee. *On the bright side, I might get a chance to see Steve soon.* Thurman looked around the coffee shop. A mounted television with muted audio played the local news. The newswoman stood on a pier in front of one of the most incredible yachts he'd ever seen. He recognized Wilmington and the Cape Fear River in the background and thought about his family's beach house on Bald Head Island. The closed-captioning streamed across the bottom of the screen.

One of Russia's wealthiest individuals, businessman Dimitry Stanov, paid an unexpected visit to the Port of Wilmington yesterday.

Thurman went rigid.

While making the autumn transit from Newport, Rhode Island, to the Cayman Islands, his superyacht, LunaSea, required minor mechanical attention, resulting in a brief port call. The camera panned to the spectacular ship. Its three-hundred-foot-long white hull gleamed. The name, *L U N A S E A,* glowed in blue neon lettering set into the superstructure amidships. The fantail sported a swimming pool with curved glass walls.

"Stanov, here in North Carolina?" Thurman muttered. His heart rate quickened as a sickening feeling expanded in his gut. Recollections of the ambush at his villa, Noreen's videotape, and Jaggears's briefing swept through his mind like a storm front. *The oligarch is making his move.* Ingram's text broke the spell. With his mind racing, Thurman rose and grabbed the cups. He met Ingram at the entrance. The detective was holding a clear plastic bag containing Hairston's belongings, given to him by the pre-op nurse.

"Come with me," Thurman said, handing him a cup of coffee and walking out the door.

"What? Where're you going?"

"C'mon, I have an idea."

"Hold on, you're a walking disaster waiting to happen. Warehouses blow up. Hairston and Floyd get shot by a couple of guys in an ambulance that left your hospital. I just found out the dude in the hotel bar the night Noreen was murdered turned up dead this morning. I need to know what we're into here."

Thurman stopped. "Did you find out why Hairston and Floyd were tailing the ambulance?"

"How am I supposed to know?"

"Probably not for speeding." Thurman walked toward the hospital. "I know where we can find out."

"Early this morning they were staking out Anastasia's."

"Anastasia's?" Thurman asked.

"A strip club in Durham, frequented by lowlifes. We had the place wired. Hairston got a tip about a meeting going down last night in the offices upstairs."

Thurman shot him a quizzical look. "What's that have to do with tailing an ambulance?"

"Hairston called me around three o'clock this morning; he'd overheard two phone calls. The first one came in to the club manager. A Russian guy named Solo. It confirmed the time and place of the drug deal. The second call Solo made to you. He told you where and when to bring the ransom for your cousin. Both events occurred at the same place and same time."

Thurman halted.

Ingram pulled out his phone. He opened Hairston's last email and clicked on the audio file he'd sent. The recorded phone call began. *We'll leave them both in the building. . . . Lunacy, right? . . . Just be ready to cast off when we arrive.* A few more garbled words were followed by the sound of breaking glass. *He picks up ten million tonight and tells me to drive a fucking ambulance to Wilmington!*

Thurman's blood ran cold as he heard the address and the voice telling him to be at the warehouse delivery gate.

"Those are the guys who had Steve?"

"We didn't know the connection until that phone call. You heard it, you were both supposed to die in that explosion."

Thurman listened to the recording two more times. "He's not saying L-U-N-A-C-Y." He took out his phone and pulled up the local news. A full-sized photo of Stanov's superyacht *LunaSea* appeared on the front page. "It's L-U-N-A-S-E-A."

Ingram scrutinized the image.

Thurman's phone vibrated. A text message from John Wynn. *Call me, I have info about Carmen.* He dialed immediately.

Wynn answered after one ring. "I'm in the security office. A camera caught Carmen being forced into the ambulance transporting Yuri Drake."

"Stay put, I'll be there in a minute."

CHAPTER 49
CHASING REDFELLAS

THE HOSPITAL SECURITY video clearly showed two EMTs loading Yuri into the back of the ambulance and forcing Carmen inside. Ingram pointed to the screen. "That's Morton's girlfriend, and Solo's driving. The guys pushing the gurney work at Morton's club. They're the rodents who shot Hairston and Floyd."

Thurman folded his arms across his chest. "Let's assume these guys work for Stanov. Solo gets his instructions and drives to St. Matthew's this morning, in an ambulance, to pick up Yuri. Angie, the ICU nurse, told me Carmen went with Yuri and the EMTs to the ambulance. She tried to stop the transfer, so they forced her to come with them. Hairston and Floyd must have tailed the ambulance here, watched it go down, and then followed when they left the hospital. They pulled it over on I-40."

"Solo and his men shot them," said Ingram.

Thurman's fingers raked his hair. "They're heading to Wilmington to board the *LunaSea*. With Yuri, Carmen, and the sphere. How fast can we get there?"

"I'll call the Wilmington police and the Highway Patrol. We can be there in an hour and a half if I drive."

Thurman stepped out of the security office and called Bristow. *Please answer.* The connection came on the third ring. "Where the hell have you been? I've been worried sick. I called you twenty times."

"Ten, but who's counting? Sorry I couldn't answer and I'm sorry about Steve."

"How do you know about that?"

"Drone footage. It got the whole gunfight. They saw you pull him from the vehicle. In later shots his body is covered. My condolences."

"Thanks, I appreciate that, but now we have to get Carmen back."

"We've been tracking Stanov. His yacht is tied up to a pier in Wilmington."

"I saw the news," said Thurman.

"Our intel photographed Walters on the bridge."

"What? I thought Walters was missing."

"He turned up in Florence. The Carabinieri had him custody awaiting extradition."

"I don't get it. Stanov tried to kill both of us."

"He must have been given a reprieve. Special Agent Jenkins reported Walters was released five days ago. He flew from Rome to Saint Thomas, Virgin Islands then took the ferry to Cruz Bay, Saint John, where a water taxi delivered him to Stanov's yacht. He was on board when it sailed three days ago."

"Destination Wilmington, North Carolina. What's your plan?"

"Be on the hospital heliport in twenty minutes."

"I need some hardware and clean clothes."

"I'll take care of it. See you then."

"We better move if we're going to get to Wilmington before *LunaSea* sails," said Ingram, who now stood next to him in the hallway.

Thurman slipped his phone into his pocket. "Can't they keep her in port?"

"They're going to try, but the ship is registered in Russia. We can't board and search her without official permission from the State Department."

"So call them."

"You think the Russians are going to cooperate? Plus, it's Thanksgiving weekend, government offices are closed."

"The police can't prevent her from getting underway?"

"Hard to believe, isn't it?" Ingram's face looked like he'd bit into a lemon. "Diplomats, lawyers, and politicians."

"I'm not going with you."

"What?"

"I have other plans."

"Don't pull that on me, man. What's up?"

Thurman headed toward the elevators. "Bristow is picking me up in twenty minutes."

Ingram followed him. "You're not leaving me here. I'm in. You and your buddy have pulled this bullshit before—it's not happening again. That's my friend and fellow police officer in the OR. Shot by the same scum who killed Noreen Chase and gunned down your cousin, and don't forget, I helped you carry his body. Those Redfellas are going down, and I plan on being part of the operation that pulls it off. Got that?"

Thurman limped to the elevator and punched the button for the roof. He looked at Ingram. "C'mon, I'll call Bristow up top."

"What's wrong with your leg?"

"Nothing. Must've dinged my knee at the warehouse."

"I'll add it to the list."

"What list?"

"I'm keeping score. A list of what we owe them—payback for Hairston, Floyd, Chase, Emerson, our SWAT brothers at the warehouse." The corner of Ingram's upper lip twitched.

"Carmen and Yuri," said Thurman.

"And Morton." He took out his phone and showed Thurman several crime scene photos from Morton's garage. "These just came in."

Thurman flipped through the images, then gave the phone back to Ingram. "Check that one out." In the foreground lay Morton's body in a pool of blood. Behind it was a black BMW 7 series with a crumpled front quarter panel. "That's the car that rear-ended my truck. I'll bet it's the one Noreen got into at the hotel and the one casing Steve's apartment."

CHAPTER 50
DEFIANT X

INGRAM PLACED a hand to his forehead to shield his eyes as he stared southwest. "What the hell is that?" A dark green Sikorsky Defiant X helicopter approached the rooftop heliport at high speed. As it got closer, its twin rotors became visible along with its rear push-propeller. It hung above the landing deck motionless for a minute. Then it descended and softly touched the pad. The passenger door opened, and a man ran toward them, covering the distance with his helmeted head tucked. As he got closer, John Bristow's familiar face broke into an easy smile.

"What do you think of the Defiant X, the army's latest addition to its air cavalry?"

Thurman shook his head in disbelief as the turbulent air whipped around them. "What are you doing in it?"

"Jaggears arranged a test ride."

Ingram shook Bristow's extended hand and introduced himself.

"I know who you are, detective. Unfortunately, I'm not authorized to take you along."

Ingram flashed his badge. "I'm authorizing you."

"I'm sorry, detective, it doesn't work like that. The people I work for don't care if you're with the police."

Thurman reached for Bristow's arm and gripped it tight. "John, look. You know Jack and I go back a long way. He's been on this case since the beginning. We may need him."

Bristow pulled out his phone and walked to the hospital entrance, disappearing into the doorway.

"What do we do?"

"Wait a minute. He'll be back."

Five minutes later Bristow returned. He looked back at Ingram and shook his head. "I'm sorry, detective, it's a no-go, but there is something you can do to help." He leaned close and spoke into his ear. Ingram nodded. Bristow grabbed Thurman's arm and pulled him toward the helicopter.

Thurman looked over his shoulder. "I'm sorry."

Ingram waved him off. "Go kill that one-legged son of a bitch. I'll see you soon."

CHAPTER 51
YOUR WORST NIGHTMARE

THE HELICOPTER STREAKED on a southeastern heading five hundred feet above the terrain. Thurman noted the aircraft's relative calm compared to the Black Hawks he'd flown in over the years. He peeked into the cockpit at the airspeed indicator. His eyes widened. The instrument displayed a velocity of two hundred and forty knots. They'd be in Wilmington in thirty minutes. He adjusted his headset and keyed his mic. "Bristow, I'm still waiting to hear how we're going to get on board."

"Don't worry. It'll be easy."

"Easy? How's that?"

"You're going to be a pilot."

"Are you nuts? I don't know how to fly." He could see Bristow laugh but couldn't hear it with his headset on. His voice came through a moment later.

"Not that kind of pilot. A riverboat pilot. The *LunaSea* is the size of a small freighter, over three hundred feet long. The North Carolina Port Authority requires all large vessels to have a pilot when navigating the Cape Fear River. Two pilots will be on board when it gets underway later today."

"One problem—I also don't know how to navigate the river in a ship that size."

"You've done it with your boat, right?"

"A thirty-five-foot fishing boat."

"Then you're familiar with the river. You won't have to do anything. You're my apprentice on a training exercise. I'm the pilot."

"You can do that?"

"I spent twenty-two years in the navy. I can drive a boat down a river. You just need to know where the next navigation tower is located and how to operate the GPS. The channel is five hundred feet wide."

"What about Ingram?"

"Another bird will pick him up shortly. He'll be with the Coast Guard ready to make arrests."

"What if shit hits the fan?"

"It might."

"Why can't Jaggears make a few calls and just seize the ship?"

"The Russian ambassador refused our requests. If we knew for certain Carmen and Yuri were on board, it might be a different situation, but we'd have to get a warrant, which would require a hearing. Impounding a foreign vessel, especially one flagged in Russia, against their government's wishes isn't easy, and it could spark a nasty international event with political retaliation. The secretary of defense would like to avoid an incident. That requires other options."

"Like what?"

Bristow smiled. "Like you and me."

"Now I'm worried."

"No need to worry; it's a piece of cake. We take the helm and secure the bridge. When we get past Frying Pan Shoals, I'll signal SOS. The Coast Guard will respond."

"From Caswell Beach?"

Bristow nodded. "They have a Maui class cutter with a .50 cal on the forecastle standing by."

"What about Carmen and Yuri?"

"That's your job."

"What are you talking about?"

"While I'm navigating, you slip on down below and bring them back to the bridge."

"What if I can't find them?"

"You'll find them."

"Someone could get shot."

"It won't be us." Bristow detailed the plan. "We'll drive to the Cape Fear Pilots Association office, and you'll get a ten-minute lecture on how to act like a pilot in training, and then we'll drive to the pier and board the *LunaSea*. Oh, and just one more thing."

"What?"

"Jaggears mentioned the navy spotted a Russian submarine patrolling off the coast."

"A what?"

"A Russian fast attack."

That hollow feeling in Thurman's stomach reopened. "What are they doing around here?"

"I don't know, could be standard patrol operations. Our subs patrol their coastal waters all the time." Bristow shrugged. "They're tracking something. Probably playing tag with one of ours."

"That's just great—outstanding." Thurman's helmet shook back and forth. "How can this get any better? Now we have to worry about the Red October."

"Relax, everything's gonna be fine."

"Where have I heard that before?"

———

Aliya entered the stateroom and sat on the edge of the bed. "How do you feel? Comfortable?"

Yuri stirred and murmured from his narcotic-induced stupor. "Where are we?"

"On a ship that will take us to our new home."

"New home?" He startled awake and tried to move, but his limbs wouldn't obey.

"Yes, darling, home to Italy. Where you can work without being controlled by the CIA or SVR. Dimitry and Dario have started building our facility. All we need is for you to get well."

He shook his head. "No. I want to stay here, where we are free."

"Don't be a fool. You will never be free, no matter what they say."

"What about our baby? Don't you want it to be born in America?"

"There is no baby. I lost it weeks ago."

Yuri's eyes narrowed as he struggled to comprehend her words. "You miscarried?"

She nodded.

Yuri shook his head and squeezed her hand. "Our baby?"

"The child is gone. Let's move on. I am tired of hiding, tired of being manipulated. We will start over in a new country. We will be wealthy beyond our dreams."

Yuri's eyes widened. "What have you done?"

She placed her hand on his chest. "Go back to sleep. You need rest. One day you will appreciate the sacrifice I've made."

He tried to sit, but she held him back. He tried to push her away. He grimaced.

"Nurse!" Aliya yelled. Alarms began beeping as Yuri thrashed.

A woman entered and held him down while injecting him with the contents of a syringe. The effect was almost instantaneous.

Aliya stood and looked at her husband as the drug took effect. "I've done what's best for both of us. In time you will understand."

———

Carmen felt blood roll down her hands as the wrist restraints cut into her skin. She strained against the ropes that confined her to a chair in darkness. A gag tore at the corners of her mouth. She struggled to shed the cloth hood encasing her head and silently repeated her creed: . . . *I am better trained and will fight with all my might. Surrender is not a Ranger word.* . . . Then she relaxed as the room gently swayed. She focused on her breathing. She heard machinery humming and felt an ache in her shoulder from the injection site. She had no memory since the ambulance gunfight and the Russian stabbing her with the syringe. After that . . . nothing. She'd lost track of time—a chunk of her life had been excised. It pissed her off.

A latch clicked and a door opened, then closed. Footsteps halted in front of her. A hand gripped the material covering her head and pulled, tearing hair from her scalp. The light hurt her eyes. She squeezed them shut but not before glimpsing at the man. Fear gripped her when she saw his face. The sting of his slap lingered on her cheek.

"Open your eyes, *shlyukha*. Look at me."

She opened them slowly and gasped around the gag tied between her teeth.

"Your worst nightmare has returned."

She cast her gaze on the metal deck and shook her head.

"You should have killed me in Italy."

We tried, she thought. She stared at the feet standing before her. One moved with the rhythm of the water, adjusting to the ship's roll, but the prosthesis didn't. It shuffled awkwardly. *Boris.* Two smaller feet appeared in her field of vision. She looked up.

"She is not a whore," Aliya said. "I wish to speak with her. Remove the gag and loosen her bonds."

In one smooth motion, Boris produced a four-inch folding knife from his waist and flicked the black serrated blade. It snapped open. Carmen felt the flat, cold steel pressed against the side of her cheek. He slid it under the material. She sensed the pressure of the knife being rotated and the release as the blade sliced through the gag. "Next time I will use this on that beautiful face. You will never want to look in a mirror after I'm finished."

"Shut up, Boris. You will do no such thing. You will be shot and thrown overboard if you lay a hand on her. We need her unless you can keep Yuri alive." Aliya turned to Carmen and placed the palm of her hand on her cheek. She spoke softly. "You won't be harmed, doctor, as long as you do as we ask. You are here for only one reason, to care for Yuri. There are medical supplies, everything you need to keep him healthy and speed his recovery. If he dies or if you do anything to harm him, I will let Boris have his way with you. Am I clear?"

CHAPTER 52
UNDERWAY

THURMAN WATCHED the blurred landscape as the helicopter streaked overhead. He'd finished threading his belt into the khakis Bristow brought him, then he tucked in the polo shirt, shrugged on a bomber jacket, and fastened his seatbelt. He sat in silence for the next quarter hour until the pilot's voice came through his headset.

"We're cleared for landing, ETA five minutes."

The airspeed slowed and the Defiant X hovered for a few seconds before descending. Its dual counterrotating rotors allowed it to gracefully touch down on the landing pad on top of PPD's corporate headquarters in Wilmington. The pharmaceutical research company had the only helipad near their destination. The moment its wheels touched ground, Bristow jumped from the cockpit and hustled across the tarmac. Thurman followed, running through the turbulence and instinctively ducking even though the coaxial rotors were well above his maximal height. A PPD security guard waited by the rooftop elevator to escort them to the ground. Once out of the building, they got into a black SUV and sped away.

Thurman knew the area well. His father had been stationed fifty miles north at Camp Lejeune during his high school years. His family had vacationed in the area for decades, and he and his brothers owned a house on Bald Head Island at the mouth of the Cape Fear River and kept a twin engine Pursuit center console in the Southport Marina. He'd fished these waters since childhood.

As the SUV sped over the bridge spanning the river, Thurman looked back at the familiar Wilmington waterfront. A half mile in the distance, moored across from the battleship *USS North Carolina*, a white superyacht, the size of a small cruise liner, strained at her lines. The *LunaSea* prepared to get underway. A tug idled in the river, waiting to help guide her from her berth. After crossing the bridge, their vehicle turned into an industrial park containing several dry docks with vessels on blocks undergoing repair. Thurman spotted another black SUV parked near a pier where tugs and a Cape Fear Pilot boat were docked. Several men were leaning against the Suburban. As Thurman's SUV came closer, he recognized Special Agent Conner Jenkins, who walked to greet him.

"Good to see you again," said Jenkins.

"Likewise. How'd you get away from New York?"

"The FBI likes closure. We have unfinished business. I'd like you to meet Will Rabon, the river pilot who'll brief you and Bristow. Afterward he'll drive you over to the *LunaSea*, where you'll embark."

Rabon looked to be in his late thirties and sported a full, brown beard. His broad chest strained the buttons of his shirt. He strode forward with his beefy, callused hand outstretched. "Nice to meet you, gentlemen."

Jenkins glance at his watch. "You better get moving."

Rabon chuckled. "*LunaSea* won't go anywhere without us." He began explaining river pilot responsibilities and led them onto the pilot boat. Inside the cabin Thurman and Bristow changed into shirts with the Cape Fear Pilots Association emblem embroidered on the sleeve. After fifteen minutes Rabon finished by saying, "If all else fails, act like you've been doing this for years. It's all about attitude."

"Take these," Jenkins said, giving them each a backpack, "compliments of the FBI. A Glock 19, a radio, and an EPIRB."

Thurman pulled out the cell phone-sized yellow device and turned it over in his hand.

Jenkins smiled and added. "Emergency position indicating radio beacon, in case you go overboard."

"I know what it is. I just hope we don't need them."

Rabon handed each a life vest. "For when you transfer back to the pilot boat at Frying Pan Shoals. Conditions are good today; not much wind and the tide is coming in. That should make for less chop. Swells should be less than three feet. Air temp is about seventy, and the water temp is about the same."

Bristow smiled and adjusted his ballcap. "It's a good thing we're not in the North Atlantic." He exited the cabin and stepped over the gunwale back onto the dock and walked toward the SUV. "C'mon, gentlemen, it's showtime."

Rabon parked on the pier fifty feet from the *LunaSea*. Bristow and Thurman exited and walked toward the gangway. They turned and waved at Rabon as he put the vehicle in reverse. A pelican stood on a bollard eyeing the two would-be pilots as they crossed the pier. The *Chemical Pioneer*, a rusty, green-hulled freighter with a white super-structure, rode at her berth next to *LunaSea*. The two vessels provided a study in contrasts.

Sea air hung heavy with hints of sulfur and diesel fuel. The tugboat still idled in the river, waiting to assist the superyacht as it moved from the wharf. A uniformed crewman stood on the quarterdeck awaiting their arrival. Thurman crossed over and instinctively turned toward the fantail, looking for the ensign. He caught himself before starting his salute.

"This way," said the sailor in good English. They followed him up three flights of stairs to the starboard side entrance to the bridge. He opened the door and stood at attention, allowing Bristow and Thurman to enter.

Bristow extended his hand. "Captain, I'm John Bristow, your river pilot. This is Mark Thurman, my assistant in training. Thank you for allowing him on board."

"Not a problem, Mr. Bristow. Glad to have you with us. We're ready to get underway when you give us the word."

Bristow examined the ship's instruments and entered information into the GPS system. A moment later he reached for the radio on his belt and spoke to the tugboat. Then he turned to the captain. "Cast off when ready."

———

LunaSea made ten knots as they departed. Soon the Memorial Bridge faded from view. They'd been underway for twenty minutes when Thurman turned to *LunaSea*'s regular captain. "Where's the nearest head?"

The captain pointed to the passageway at the back of the bridge. "On the port side down the stairs."

Thurman took his leave and found it, then went down another set of stairs that led to the deck below. The door at the bottom opened into the galley. It was empty. Another stairway led down to the main deck. At the bottom he walked to a side door and peered out a porthole. Several passengers were standing along the railing. He immediately recognized Dario. A woman with black hair turned and stared at him. She'd pushed her sleeves to her elbows, revealing intricate tattoos adorning her forearms.

A male voice came from behind. "What are you doing?"

Thurman spun. "Trying to find my way back to the bridge. I used the head and must have taken a wrong turn."

"Come with me." The sailor led him back up the stairs.

"Do you all speak English?" Thurman asked.

The young man looked over his shoulder. "We're an international crew; most speak English. Some of the Russian passengers don't. I'd stay out of their way if I were you."

They returned to the bridge. "I found him wandering on the main deck," the man told the captain.

"Sorry, I got lost," Thurman explained. "Beautiful vessel."

The captain glanced at Thurman, then raised his binoculars. "What are those cranes?" He pointed to twin cranes in the distance on the starboard shoreline. The cranes were identical to the ones used for transferring cargo in Port Wilmington. They stood at the end of a long pier that jutted into the main shipping channel. An armed patrol boat idled a few hundred yards from the end of the pier.

"That's Sunny Point," replied Bristow. "It's a marine terminal for one of the largest weapons and ammunition depots in the world."

The captain smiled. "Interesting." He kept his binoculars fixed on the ammunition pier.

Bristow watched him, then turned to Thurman and whispered, "Spies. Every damn one of them."

Thurman felt a breeze and turned as the starboard side door opened. The exotic tattooed woman entered. She spoke to the captain in Russian, then turned to Thurman.

"I noticed you looking around. Would you like a tour? It's not often one can see a ship like this."

"Thank you, but I'm training to be a pilot. I should stay on the bridge."

"There will be many trips up and down this river. You will never get another chance to see *LunaSea*. You don't mind if I give him a tour, do you, captain?"

The captain's attention remained focused on the Sunny Point Terminal. He took out his phone and snapped several photos of the facility.

Bristow looked at Thurman. "Go on, I've got everything here. Take good notes and get some pictures."

He smiled at the woman and introduced himself. "Mark Thurman."

She took his hand. "Natasha."

CHAPTER 53
BALD HEAD SHOALS CHANNEL

NATASHA LED Thurman from the bridge down four flights of stairs and then began moving aft. Once they descended to a level below the waterline, the ship's opulence diminished. The passageways looked clean and bright, but the polished wood, chrome, and glass changed to bulkheads of steel interrupted by watertight doors and decks covered with nonskid epoxy resin. This wasn't the part of the ship one would normally see on a tour.

"This isn't what I was expecting."

She cocked her head and looked over her shoulder. "What did you expect?"

"Staterooms, bars, home theater, gym, what every superyacht has."

"This will be more interesting."

"Where is everyone?"

"There is a crew of thirty-two, mostly men. Everyone has a specific assignment while the ship is getting underway. We won't be interrupted."

"Interrupted? What's your job?"

"I'm not a member of the crew. I'm a guest."

"You know your way around."

"It's not the first time I've been on board."

"You know the owner?"

She took out an e-cigarette and placed it to her lips. A vapor cloud streamed over her shoulder as they proceeded. "Dimitry and I have been acquainted for many years. I was twelve when he took me from an orphanage in Leningrad."

"Your stepfather?"

Natasha scoffed. "More like his Lolita."

"He's a pedophile?"

She halted and stared at him, her green irises practically obscured by the narrowness of her gaze. "Life in a Russian orphanage is not good. He rescued me, gave me a home, and provided for my education, but I'm not his daughter. I've been on this yacht many times. They weren't pleasant experiences. Billionaires don't live by the same rules as we do."

"Why are you telling me this?"

"Because I know who you are, Dr. Thurman. Terry told me about you."

"You knew Morton?"

Natasha nodded. "We worked together. I loved him, and this morning those bastards took him from me."

"I'm not sure I understand."

Natasha continued walking down the passageway. "Stanov had him killed this morning and brought me here."

"Why would he do that?"

"Terry knew too much."

"How do you know this?"

"Let's just say I do freelance work."

"You're a spy?"

"I work for the Russian intelligence service."

Thurman reached out and touched her shoulder. "Hold on a second. Your government set you up with Morton to spy on Stanov?"

Natasha nodded. "Our governments have a mutual interest in this case—both do not want Stanov to succeed. Terry tried to infiltrate Stanov's operation. It didn't work."

"Isn't Morton in business with Stanov?"

"That's what Dimitry believed. They shared ownership in a nightclub. With help from the CIA, Terry arranged to expand Stanov's East

Coast drug distribution network and gain his trust. The BASF warehouse is part of it . . . was part of it. Their competitors didn't approve."

"Why would the CIA do that?"

"For access to Stanov's organization. Solo is one of Stanov's primary lieutenants who could provide actionable intelligence. That's where I came in."

"You work both sides?"

She smiled. "It's complicated."

"Why would Stanov—"

She halted and turned to face him. "We don't have much time. Keep up with me." She began walking, and he hurried to catch up. "You know of the sphere?"

"Yes, I know what it does."

"That's the key. Yuri's element 126. Everyone wants it." Her face hardened. "Solo double-crossed Terry. He found out Terry and Richard Gross were the same person and about his relationship with Noreen. Solo told Stanov, who ordered Terry's execution."

"I'm sorry. Why blow up the warehouse?"

"To cut off Stanov's money supply. His Russian businesses have been confiscated. His only current source of revenue is profit from his organized crime interests."

"Drugs," said Thurman.

Natasha nodded. "The startup costs to produce Yuri's element are astronomical. The Kremlin wants Stanov starved of capital."

"Who blew up the warehouse?"

"His competitors."

"Who?"

"Does it matter?"

"It matters to me," Thurman whispered. She looked at him.

"Members of the Guerrero cartel. Stanov's new expanded distribution network was cutting into their territory. They wanted to put him out of business."

"Why not just kill him?"

"They've tried, but he's not stupid. The cartel tried to destroy a six-month supply of heroin and fentanyl. Enough to satisfy the demand from Philadelphia to Boston. They failed, the truck got away."

"I lost family and friends in that explosion."

"I lost Terry. Does that make us even?"

He paused to reflect, then tried a different tack. "What do you know about Yuri?"

"He's the reason Terry and Noreen set up operations."

Thurman stopped. "He told you that?"

"We had no secrets."

"I'm missing something. Why would the CIA want Stanov in the same city where they set up Yuri?"

"They didn't, but they knew someone at Angstrom was leaking information to Stanov. Your government needed to find the mole. Solo is one of Stanov's most trusted lieutenants. He managed the club and worked with Terry. They thought it was worth the risk to try and turn him in order to identify the leak."

"Morton thought he could recruit Solo?"

She drew on the e-cigarette and exhaled the vapor. "He tried. It cost him his life."

"Why are you still alive?"

"Dimitry loves me."

"Why are you telling me this?"

"So you'll trust me. We're on the same side."

"I don't have much choice."

"And I want you to help me kill them." She opened the cabin door and entered. Thurman followed, then froze.

———

Bristow kept his hands on the wheel and eyes on the range tower a mile in the distance. The captain stood three feet to his right. Bristow felt the vibration in his left front pocket and pulled out his phone. The text read:

Red October spotted offshore. You may have an escort, or it may be waiting to transfer personnel. Our friends are standing by at Frying Pan Tower ready to pick you up.

"Anything important?" asked the captain.

"No just a message from the pilot boat. It will pick us up once we're clear of the shipping channel."

"What is considered the end of the channel?"

"It's dredged six and a half miles offshore."

The captain nodded.

"If the channel isn't maintained, the shifting shoals will fill it. These waters are treacherous. We don't have an accurate count of the hundreds of shipwrecks that have occurred. Many are unrecorded."

"Be careful, Mr. Bristow. We don't want to be the latest."

"Yes, sir."

"What's next?"

"We're in Lower Swash Channel." Bristow pointed to a range tower in the distance. "Next is the tricky part, a big S-turn. We bear to port into Battery Island Channel, then turn starboard into Bald Head Caswell Channel past Frying Pan Shoals and out to sea."

The captain pointed to the port shoreline. "What's that?"

"Battery Island. Bald Head is behind it in the distance." Bristow pointed straight ahead at the blinking tower. "Caswell Lighthouse, and starboard we're approaching the city of Southport." Before he could explain anything else, Bristow heard laughing and then a knock on the door. He went slack-jawed when the familiar face appeared at the port-hole. The captain motioned to let the visitors in.

A breeze blew across the bridge as the port bridge door opened. A couple entered, and the man stepped forward and extended his hand.

"Good day, captain, I'm Dario Benedetto, and this is Aliya Drake. Mind if we have a look around?"

Bristow pulled the bill of his cap down and turned away.

———

Less than ten feet from Thurman, Carmen sat bound to a chair. The gag bound her head like a bridle and bit. Thurman leapt to her side and snapped open his knife. He cut the gag and she inhaled with a gasp.

"Water," she whispered.

He freed her hands and feet, then he surveyed the empty room. Natasha came to his side. Carmen rubbed her wrists.

"Are you all right?" Natasha asked.

She nodded and tried to stand.

Thurman caught her and helped her back to the chair. "Slow down. Stay seated and move your joints for a minute."

Carmen flexed and extended her arms and legs trying to restore circulation. "That maniac is here. The one-legged psychopath you shot in Italy."

Thurman stopped and stared at her. *How did he get here from the warehouse?* "You're sure?"

"He threatened to carve up my face less than an hour ago. You should have put a round between his eyes."

"He's harder to kill than a cockroach," he mumbled.

"Boris," said Natasha. "One of Stanov's . . . mechanics. He does his wet work." She glanced at Thurman. "You may have to shoot him again."

He thought of his cousin. "I hope I get a chance." Thurman removed his backpack and took out the Glock 19. He checked the magazine and pinched the slide to make sure a round occupied the chamber. Satisfied, he tucked the pistol inside his waistband behind his right hip. Then he located the two extra magazines and placed them in his left rear pocket. He looked at Natasha. "Where's Yuri?"

"Come." She walked to the door. Carmen stood, this time with better motor control, and followed. Thurman closed the door and for the first time noticed vibrations from the diesel engines. *The ship is turning.*

Natasha retraced their steps, stopping at passageways to check for crewmen. She led them to midships and climbed two ladders. At the top she turned toward the center of the ship, walked to the middle of the passageway, and stopped. She placed a finger to her mouth and an ear to the door. Thurman felt the return of the now familiar ache in his right knee as his heart rate accelerated. He wiped sweat from his forehead, then drew his weapon. Natasha listened for a moment longer, and when satisfied, she turned the door handle and pushed. They entered a stateroom more luxurious than any five-star hotel. Yuri Drake lay supine on the king-sized bed in the middle of the room. Tubing carried intravenous fluids into his arm from a plastic bag hanging from an IV pole next to the bed. He didn't move.

"Natasha, what have you done?"

They turned. Natasha gasped when she saw the figure standing in the doorway. "Boris."

He leveled his pistol at Thurman's chest. "Drop your weapon."

———

Bristow turned the wheel hard starboard, completing the complicated series of turns and bringing the vessel into Bald Head Shoals Channel, on course out to sea. Thurman and Natasha hadn't returned to the bridge, and he hoped they'd been successful. The dark-haired woman peered out the windscreen next to him, and Dario stood on her other side. Bristow noticed him staring at his reflection in the glass. His eyes widened.

"John Bristow!" Dario darted toward the side door. "Help!"

Bristow shoved the throttle to all-ahead full and gripped the wheel. The turbo diesel engines responded, accelerating the ship. Anything not secured flew toward the rear. Everyone on the bridge slammed into the rear bulkhead. He spun the wheel hard to port and dashed after Dario.

———

Thurman pinched the gun between his thumb and index finger and placed it on the edge of the bed.

"Put it on the deck."

He complied.

Boris smiled, took out a pair of handcuffs, and gave them to Natasha. "Cuff him with his hands behind his back."

"I'm sorry," she whispered as she placed them on Thurman, taking care not to make them too tight.

Boris stepped forward and punched Thurman square on the jaw, knocking him to the floor. Then he grabbed a fistful of Natasha's hair and yanked her to him. "I should kill you right now, but Stanov has better plans for you." He leveled the gun at Carmen. "You too. Let's go."

Yuri's eyes fluttered. "Wait. What are you doing?"

"Go back to sleep. It is of no concern."

Thurman began to stir. His eyes opened and as they began to focus, he saw Boris with the gun.

The Russian laughed at him. "Thanks for the sphere. How's your cousin?"

"He's dead."

"Good, saves me the trouble. Now you can join him." He raised the pistol.

"No!" screamed Carmen.

At that moment the ship surged forward. Everything not fixed to the floor shot rearward. Then the ship turned hard left. All sense of balance went askew. A deafening gun report echoed in the room as Boris flew over the bed and Thurman slammed against the bulkhead. The smell of gunpowder permeated the air. The Glock slid across the deck, landing against Thurman's leg. He scooted to it and gripped the butt behind his back, sliding his finger into the trigger guard as he struggled to his knees and stood. The ship accelerated at high speed. Thurman widened his stance and leaned forward to compensate. Yuri had been tossed against the headboard and Carmen lay next to him. *Where was Boris?*

Natasha crawled to her knees and reached for the doorknob, terror evident in her expression. She pointed to the other side of the bed. Boris rose from the floor, wobbling like a man afflicted with ataxia. Blood trickled from a gash in his scalp. He raised the pistol in his right hand. Thurman dove onto the floor just as flames erupted from the barrel. Natasha swatted for the light switch and the room went black.

"I'm coming for you, Thurman," growled Boris. "Then you're next, Natasha. Your fucking boyfriend took my leg. I'm going to send you to hell to join him."

Two more shots exploded from the pistol.

The room was inboard without windows, resulting in total darkness. With arms trapped behind his back, Thurman struggled to his feet, his legs bracing against the foot of the bed. He inched toward Boris and prayed the Russian didn't get lucky with another shot. Even with his cancer at stage four by now, he wasn't planning to die today. *I'm coming, Boris. Take your best shot.*

Two more shots rang out. The muzzle flash lit up the space. Thurman spun around to return fire but the ship's engines stopped, sending him tumbling onto the bed and pitching everything forward in the darkness. Boris fell to the floor on the other side of the bed, and Thurman was bounced from the mattress onto him. Both lay on the deck jammed between the bed and bulkhead, back to belly. Boris wrapped his arm around Thurman's neck and squeezed like a boa.

"Say hello to your cousin when you get to hell," he said, laughing as he pulled Thurman's neck.

Thurman inhaled; no air entered his lungs. His eyes bulged. *Not today, asshole, not today.* He gripped the gun in his cuffed hands. With his last bit of strength, he arched his back and jammed the barrel into Boris's flesh, then began squeezing the trigger. After five rounds Boris released his stranglehold and stopped moving. Thurman's back burned from the heat of the barrel. "Turn on the lights."

The ship once again began making headway. Light flooded the room. Thurman stood and surveyed the ghastly situation. Boris was sprawled beside the bed, entrails springing from his belly like roadkill. Thurman bent over, his cuffed hands behind his back still gripping the gun. Blood soaked the carpet and the back of Thurman's polo. The odor of bowel contents and spent gunpowder lingered in the air. "That's for Steve."

Natasha stood next to him. "Fuck you, Boris," she said, then she looked at Thurman. "Hurry, we have to get off this ship."

"Get these off me." He turned, showing Natasha his bloody hands. "Our rendezvous should be here soon."

She searched Boris's pockets, then shook her head. "There's no key."

"Shit." Thurman turned to Carmen, who was tending to Yuri. "You all right?"

"Oh, God," Carmen said. "Yuri's been shot." She peeled the blood-soaked shirt from his abdomen. A small, round hole was just below the right side of his rib cage. "If it hit his liver, he's in big trouble."

"He needs an OR," said Thurman.

Natasha wiped her forehead with the back of her wrist. "Then we better get him off this ship."

"I need my hands. Find me something small and flat like a bobby pin. What's in there?" Thurman nodded toward the closet. "Open the door."

Natasha turned the handle and peered inside. She rummaged through a couple of boxes. "Medical supplies." She held up a package wrapped in blue paper labeled SUTURE KIT. "How about this?"

"Open it."

Carmen came over and ripped it open. "What are you thinking?"

"Trying to remember my SERE training."

Carmen's eyes narrowed. "Your what?"

"Survival, Evasion, Resistance, and Escape course. Survival training, we learned how to defeat wrist restraints."

"What about this?" Carmen held up a needle.

"Too round." He looked at the contents on the deck. "Grab those forceps and bend one arm ninety degrees."

"We have to get moving," hissed Natasha. "They'll be coming."

"Give them to me," Thurman said. Carmen placed the bent instrument in his hands. He sat on the floor and concentrated. With his right hand he felt the shackle and slipped the flat end of the thin forceps between the teeth and the pawl. *Thank God for cheap-ass Russian cuffs. I hope these aren't double locked.* He advanced the bent bladelike end of the forceps until it wedged. Nothing. *C'mon.* He shoved harder and twisted. The blade advanced a millimeter. A second later the clamp sprung. "Got it! Fuck you, Boris." He pumped his freed fists into the air. The cuffs dangled from his left wrist as he scrambled to his feet. He popped the other wrist free, then bent over and retrieved his gun.

Natasha cracked the door and peeked into the passageway. "They're coming. Let's move."

"We can't just leave him." Yuri lay curled against the headboard moaning. "Dress that wound," said Thurman.

"We don't have time," said Natasha.

"I'm not leaving him." Thurman pulled a full magazine from his rear pocket, did a tactical reload, then tucked the Glock into his waist. He hoisted Yuri over his shoulder in a fireman's carry.

"You're going to kill him," said Carmen.

"He's dead if we leave him here." Thurman wrapped his left arm around Yuri's legs and walked to the door, then leaned out and scanned the empty passageway. "Right or left?"

"To the bow," said Natasha, ducking by his shoulder and dashing to the right.

CHAPTER 54
PLAYGROUND STANDOFF

BRISTOW SPRINTED ACROSS THE BRIDGE, grasped the handrails, and scrambled to the next level like a sailor called to battle stations. At the bottom of the steps, Dario lay sprawled on the deck. A gash had split his forehead. His blond hair, matted with blood, looked orange. The ship's surge had pitched him into the bulkhead. Bristow knelt and felt Dario's bounding pulse. He stood and shook off his backpack and withdrew the pistol and ammunition. A small device lay at the bottom. He recalled Jenkins's words. *The GPS transponder.* He put it into his pocket as a door opened twenty feet to his right. Two men with guns drawn turned to face him. They fired, but not before Bristow disappeared down the promenade deck. He stopped and took cover at the next corner, bracing himself against the bulkhead. When the muzzle of the first gun appeared, he leaned out and fired two rounds into the chest of the lead man. The other returned fire. Bristow felt the jolt of a round grazing his shoulder. He squeezed off a double tap that sent the man over the rail. Bristow leaned over and watched the ocean claim the body.

Bristow gripped his pistol with both hands and ran back to the door the crewmen came from. He entered and hustled forward to a stairwell. Voices came from the passageway below. He stood in the ready position, gun leveled at whatever target entered his vision. The voices became louder. A man armed with an AK-47 grabbed the railing and looked up. Bristow fired. The back of the man's head exploded, spraying the passageway with blood. Footsteps retreated. Bristow followed, sliding down the stairs. He scanned the space for threats, then tucked his pistol into his waistband and hefted the rifle. The dead man carried an extra magazine in his rear pocket. Bristow added it to his collection and moved on.

————

Natasha led them forward. "There's a small boat and Jet Skis in the bow of the ship."

"I'm not leaving without Bristow," Thurman whispered.

"Let's find the boat first," said Natasha.

"We can't launch them when this ship is doing twenty knots," Carmen said as she brought up the rear armed with Boris's pistol. His spare magazine protruded from her back pocket. "We can take a hostage and make them stop, then launch."

"Keep moving," said Thurman, his face showing the strain of carrying an unconscious hundred-and-eighty-pound man.

Natasha came to another set of stairs and descended. Thurman turned sideways and took the steps slowly, right foot leading, sweat beginning to trickle down his face. Pain sparked from his right knee with each step. It took two or three times longer than it should have. Once they were all down on the next deck, they proceeded toward the bow. Yuri remained as motionless and silent as a sandbag slung over Thurman's shoulder.

"Find them! Hurry," came a voice from down the passageway.

Natasha halted and peered around a corner. Then she turned, placing an index finger to her lips and motioning them to retreat. Carmen turned and began leading them back when a man appeared from a side passage. He leveled a rifle. "Stop, don't move. Put your hands up."

The women complied.

"Hands in the air," he repeated to Thurman.

"I can't," said Thurman. He turned, showing him his hands.

"Everyone on your knees." The man said, reaching for a walkie-talkie. Suddenly, the passageway exploded with the sound of gunfire echoing off the bulkheads. Within seconds the man's body began convulsing like he was having a grand mal seizure. Then he collapsed and went limp. John Bristow appeared and ran over to the dead man, kneeling beside him. He took the radio, then walked toward the group. "Good to see you." He clapped Thurman's shoulder. "C'mon, we need to get off this thing."

"You got a plan?" Natasha inquired.

"Not a good one," Bristow replied. "The Coast Guard is nearby. We may have to get wet. How's Yuri?"

"Not good," Thurman said. "Shot."

"Do you think he's going to make it?"

"He may have a better chance if he stays here than if he gets dumped in the ocean."

Bristow glanced toward the sound of men coming down the passageway. "Then leave him."

Thurman adjusted Yuri's body on his shoulders. "We'll take our chances. I'm not leaving him."

Natasha spoke up. "There is a small boat for transferring passengers to shore when the ship is anchored."

Bristow looked at her. "Where?"

"In the front, near the bow. A door in the hull opens, and the boat is lowered from there."

"You've been on this ship before?"

She nodded.

"Lead the way." Bristow motioned with his rifle.

The bulkheads began to narrow into the shape of the bow as they progressed. Natasha stepped through a watertight door, went another twenty feet, and stopped. She read a sign in Russian next to a door. "This is it."

"Open it."

She tried to turn the handle, then shook her head. "It's locked."

"Move out of the way," said Bristow. "Everyone step back and cover your ears." He looked at Thurman. "Get him out of the way." He raised the AK-47 and fired a three-round burst. The door handle disintegrated.

Bristow leaned against the opposite bulkhead and kicked the door. It sprang open, revealing a large open area. The anchor chain locker was to their left. On the far side of the room, a thirty-foot, dual-console boat with twin three hundred horsepower engines sat on a lift. Thurman put Yuri on the floor. He looked at the boat and the two Yamaha Jet Skis stored behind it. Water skis and wakeboards were secured in wall racks. "How do we get that boat in the water?"

"Look for a switch that operates the winch," said Bristow.

Voices yelled Russian commands. Footsteps pounded down the passageway. Bristow peeked his head out and listened. "Get ready. They're coming this way."

Natasha went over to the hull near the tender. She opened an electrical box and pulled a lever. The bow gave a shudder, then slowly a crack of sunlight appeared. A large section of the hull began to open. Wind rushed through the compartment. Sea spray from the bow wave showered the area.

"How do we launch this thing?" Carmen asked as she looked at the tender.

Natasha punched a button in the control panel. She cursed in Russian. "It won't work!"

Bristow looked at it. "The ship probably has to be stopped before the mechanism engages."

"That's just great," Thurman said, placing Yuri's body near the opening.

Bristow reached into the boat. "Grab some life jackets." He tossed one to Natasha and another to Carmen. "Put them on, now." He watched as they slipped their arms in and tightened the waist strap. He glanced at Thurman and handed him two. "Put yours on first."

Thurman slipped it on, then rolled Yuri to one side and put an arm through the opening. Then he rolled him and did the same for the other arm. He pulled the front strap snug.

Several men appeared at the door. "Halt! Don't move."

Dimitry Stanov's large frame momentarily blocked the doorway as he entered. When he saw Bristow's rifle, he ducked behind a steel support and spoke from behind his cover. "Give yourselves up. Stop this nonsense. You're killing him." From behind the metal support, he pointed at Yuri. "We will be in international waters shortly. There is nothing your government can do to stop us. If you surrender, we will release you when we get to Havana."

"No, thanks," said Bristow. "I've been there and don't want to go back."

Thurman looked up from where he was kneeling by Yuri's side. "You're the one responsible for his condition," he told Stanov. *And for Steve's death.*

"I'm just giving a friend a ride home."

"You kidnapped him and his doctor," Bristow shouted.

"She was brought to care for him. No harm would have come to her. She will be well paid."

"That's not what Boris said," Thurman said. He stood up. "Look, Stanov, if you want to do the right thing, then stop your ship and launch this boat with us in it."

Stanov waved a hand in disgust. "Shoot them."

Two men raised their rifles.

Thurman leveled his Glock and fired first. Rounds tore through the tight space. Fiberglass shards flew from the boat's hull and ricocheted off the steel bulkheads. A guard slumped to the deck.

Bristow ducked behind the boat and returned fire. Ocean spray showered him.

Carmen emptied her magazine. "Cold!" With the Makarov slide locked back, she ducked behind the bow of the tender, ejected the empty mag, and slapped in the other. "Hot!" She leaned around her cover and returned fire.

Thurman's ears rang. He saw Carmen's mouth move but couldn't hear her words. Then she grimaced and fell to the deck. She reached for her leg. He dashed to her and dragged her behind the hull.

Stanov's men stopped firing and retreated into the passageway. A man stepped into the doorway, holding a grenade.

"Grenade!" Bristow shouted. "Into the ocean!" He grabbed Carmen as Thurman slung Yuri over his shoulder and Natasha sprinted to the opening. They all jumped as the grenade rolled like a bocce ball toward them.

Blast debris exploded through the opening as they hit the water. The bow wake washed over them. Thurman swallowed salt water and coughed. *Get away from the propellers.* He slapped his arm across Yuri's chest and scissor-kicked as hard as he could. The stern passed by. Wake from the twin five-foot propellers tumbled them like clothes in a wash cycle.

CHAPTER 55
DROWNPROOFING

THURMAN'S HEAD bobbed to the surface. He exhaled panic and sucked in air. The salt water was cool, but not North Atlantic cold—nothing like in *Titanic*. Men appeared along the fantail and raised rifles. Bullets broke the water near them. Thurman rolled Yuri on his back and threw his arm over his chest. He swam like he had a chance to win an Olympic medal. The ship turned hard to port as it began executing a one-hundred-and-eighty-degree turn. Three-foot swells bobbed them up and down in a continuous rhythm. *This isn't a man-overboard drill; they're going to run us down. We're sitting ducks.* He kicked harder and pulled with his free arm. Yuri felt like a corpse leaking blood. The *LunaSea* had nearly made the full turn reversing course when Thurman heard the staccato gunfire of a .50-caliber machine gun. Thurman swiveled his head. On the horizon heading toward them he saw the orange-and-white hull of a U.S. Coast Guard cutter with a mounted deck gun on its forecastle. "Here! Over here!" Thurman waved while holding Yuri's head above water. The ship bore down on them. *They don't see us. We're going to be run over.* He scissor-kicked perpendicular to the cutter's path. A sailor at the bow began frantically signaling for the ship to turn. The bow cut the water like a scythe. Thurman saw the sailor motioning with both arms to turn away. At the last possible moment, the hundred-foot cutter turned hard to port, spraying

Thurman and Yuri with a five-foot bow wave. They bodysurfed to safety. The cutter corrected course, maintaining speed and bearing down on the *LunaSea*.

The superyacht continued its turning maneuver, making a full circle. Its twin props churned up a rooster tail as it sped away at full speed. Thurman watched as the Coast Guard ship tried to close the gap. He dolphin-kicked to keep above water but lost sight when he and Yuri dipped into a trough. When they rose on the next crest, he spotted the two ships in the distance. Then it happened. As he blinked and tossed his head to shake salt water from his eyes, a fireball twice the size of the *LunaSea* engulfed the superyacht. The sound of the explosion arrived a second later. In less than a minute, nothing remained on the horizon but the Coast Guard ship. No fire, no smoke, no *LunaSea*. Thurman scissor-kicked, treading water and looking in all directions. *What just happened?*

"Bristow!" he screamed. Then his head sank beneath the water. He kicked. When he regained the surface, he sucked in air and shouted, "Carmen!" Down he went again. The next time, "Natasha!" After several rounds of not getting any response, he gave up and concentrated on staying above water. He turned Yuri on his back. *Thank God for these life jackets or we'd be dead.* Then he felt something brush against him. His head whipped around in all directions. He spotted it circling twenty yards behind them, a gray triangle cutting along the surface. A dorsal fin.

What the hell are sharks doing out here in November? He lost sight of it. *Where did it go?* He looked around but didn't spot it. With Yuri floating like a hunk of meat, he felt like bait bobbing in the water. He recalled the training he received while in the navy. Jaggears had insisted he participate if he wanted to be the DEVGRU surgeon. Thurman had enthusiastically complied, but until today he considered it a SEAL torture session, a SEAL rite of passage. He silently thanked the good Lord that Jaggears made him do it. They called it the drownproofing. He just tried to stay calm and keep dolphin-kicking to the surface. Then he caught a glimpse of the fin again in his peripheral vision. He twisted to face it. It turned and streaked toward them. Thurman rolled onto his back and kicked. His heel struck the shark on the tip of its nose. It veered away. *Am I bleeding? No, but Yuri is, and Boris's blood is all over me! That fucker's still trying to kill me.*

He looked around for a dorsal fin and spotted it, circling. Thurman remembered news stories of a great white shark that patrolled these waters. Some marine biologists had tagged it. There was even an app where you could track the monster. *Just my luck it decides to show up today.* He pulled his pistol from his waist and pointed it at the fish. He felt like Quint in the movie *Jaws* as he pulled the trigger. Nothing. The gun didn't fire. *Shit.* The shark came at them. Thurman jabbed its face with the gun barrel. The beast veered away, its body scraping his arm like sandpaper. The fish disappeared into a swell, and he lost sight of the fin.

Then he heard it. The whine of an outboard motor.

He twisted in the water, searching. A moment later he spotted it. A Coast Guard RHIB deployed from the cutter crested a swell fifty yards away. He kicked so hard his chest rose from the water and waved both arms. "Over here!" The sailor at the bow pointed at them, and the boat turned in their direction.

The helmsman cut the engines, and the rigid-hull inflatable-boat drifted toward them. A life preserver landed next to Yuri. A minute later the boat came alongside. Two Coast Guard sailors grabbed Yuri's life vest and hauled him into the boat. Another sailor reached out to Thurman and yelled, "Grab my hand."

———

Thurman knelt by Yuri on the deck of the RHIB. His gunshot wound no longer bled. His chest didn't move. Thurman's hands were so cold he couldn't feel a pulse. He bent over and blew air into Yuri's lungs. Then he straddled Yuri's body, placed his hands on his sternum, and began chest compressions.

One of the sailors leaned over them as the boat rocked on the surface of the ocean. "Is he dead?"

"I don't know," said Thurman as he continued thumping Yuri's chest. Someone brought a thermal blanket. Thurman stopped and pulled it over Yuri's body, then mounted and resumed. A sailor who looked like a teenager made the sign of the cross and said a prayer.

A moment later Yuri's eyes fluttered. He coughed and a grimace came over his face. Thurman felt a faint carotid pulse. He stood and looked toward the Coast Guard cutter. "He's still alive. We need to get him on board and to a hospital." Thurman shivered. "He's hypothermic, do you have another blanket?" A sailor removed his jacket and placed it over Yuri. The helmsman put the motor in gear and headed toward the cutter. Thurman looked at the sailor next to him. "What happened to the ship?"

The sailor shrugged. "We raised her on the radio, and the captain ordered her to stop. Then we put a .50-cal burst over her bow, but she took off at full speed. We tried to catch her, but she pulled away. Then she just blew up, right out of the water; like a bomb went off." He pointed to the cutter. "They're looking for survivors."

"Five of us jumped from the ship. Two women and a man are still missing," Thurman said. The ship driver spoke into his radio, then turned the wheel and gave the engines gas. The bow nosed upward as the boat gained speed. He looked at Thurman. "I relayed the information about your friends. The captain wants you aboard. They located the two women."

———

The boat idled up to the Coast Guard cutter, nudging its hull. A group of men stood by the rail and lowered a litter. Thurman and the sailors placed Yuri's body in it and helped lift as it rose to the level of the deck. Someone dropped a rope ladder and Thurman scrambled aboard. Several hands pulled him over the rail, and he rolled onto the deck and lay there grateful to be alive. A noise caused him to turn his head. He blinked salt water from his eyes and focused on the smiling face standing over him.

"What the hell are you doing trying to swim this time of year?" Jack Ingram knelt next to his friend and let out a hearty laugh. "I thought you had better sense."

Thurman sat up. "What are you doing here?"

"Your buddy Bristow made a phone call before you ditched me in the helicopter. I flew into Southport and hitched a ride with the Coast Guard. I'd planned to arrest a few of those arseholes, but there's nothing left of them now."

He smiled at his friend and muttered, "Where're the others?"

"Dr. Black and the Russian woman are inside with Yuri. No sign of Bristow. Two Coast Guard patrol boats and a helicopter are patrolling. The navy is supposed to have a submarine around here somewhere. At least that's what I overheard. Dr. Black's been shot."

Thurman's smile disappeared. "Is she all right?"

"I don't know. You're the only doctor on this tub, so you better take a look."

"Give me a hand."

Ingram pulled him up.

Suddenly, crewmen clustered on the starboard rail. Ingram helped Thurman hobble over. "What's going on?" Thurman asked.

The young man pointed off the starboard bow. "A sub is about to surface. They radioed to make sure we were clear." A quarter mile away the nose of a United States submarine breached the ocean surface like a gigantic whale, shooting fifty feet into the air at a forty-five-degree angle. It splashed back to the surface, leveled out, and settled. The Coast Guard cutter turned toward the ominous black vessel and accelerated.

"Man, I never saw anything like that," whispered Ingram.

The sailor standing beside him said, "That's the USS *Jimmy Carter*; they picked up your guy." He handed Thurman a pair of binoculars. He focused them on the conning tower. John Bristow stood next to the captain waving. Thurman raised his arm, then saluted.

"How'd they do that?" Ingram asked.

Thurman felt wobbly and placed his arm on Ingram's shoulder. "The *Carter* is designed for special operations. It can deploy a minisub with a spec-ops team or a remotely operated underwater vehicle. I'll bet they used one to recover him. C'mon, take me to Carmen and Yuri."

An officer came over. "Which one of you is a doctor?"

Thurman raised his hand.

"Follow me. Your friends need medical attention."

Ingram helped Thurman to a door that led into the superstructure. A sailor held it and helped Thurman through the hatch. Natasha sat in a chair wrapped in a blanket with her long black hair twisted into a wet ponytail draped over her shoulder. He went to her. "Are you okay?"

She smiled. "I'm in one piece, no bullet holes, but I could use a smoke."

"Sorry, can't help you there. Where's Carmen?" She nodded toward a small group gathered around the crew's dining table in the middle of the mess hall. As he approached, he saw them, Yuri and Carmen, lying on separate tables. *Thank you, Lord.* Carmen lay supine with eyes closed and teeth clenched. Blood soaked her right trouser leg, and her thigh was at an odd angle. He moved next to her and brushed strands of wet hair from her face.

"Hey, it's me, how you doing?"

Her eyes opened and she whispered, "Thank God, you made it."

He bent down and kissed her. "It looks like the bullet broke your femur. I'll need to splint it."

"I must be a sorry sight."

"Not to me."

"Liar."

He smiled and squeezed her hand. "You're alive and beautiful."

"My leg is screwed."

"I've seen worse; so have you." He turned to one of the crewmen who looked like he had just graduated from high school. "You the corpsman?"

He nodded. "An HS, health technician. I just finished training."

"Where's sick bay?"

"One deck below, but it's a small space."

"We'll keep them here, then. You got a pair of scissors?"

He handed a pair of trauma shears to Thurman, who used them on Carmen's pants to create a half-pair of Daisy Dukes. Her thigh was swollen as large as a midsummer watermelon, with a dime-sized red hole at midthigh. Thurman carefully tried to roll her body to get a look at the backside. Carmen placed her arm over her eyes and moaned. "Don't do that."

He untied her shoe and touched the top of her foot. "Feel that?"

She nodded.

"Good. Move your ankle."

She moved her foot up and down.

"Excellent, your nerves all work." He looked at the corpsman. "What have you given her for pain?"

"Two Percocet."

"That's all? You got anything IV, like morphine?"

He nodded. "In the drug locker."

"Get it, and a syringe." Five minutes later he'd injected Carmen with six milligrams of morphine sulfate, and she began to relax. He grasped her ankle and gently pulled traction. The leg straightened, and this time she didn't cry out. He could see a larger exit wound on the back of her thigh about the size of a quarter. He removed her shoe and tickled the bottom of her foot. "Do you feel me touching you?" She nodded and wiggled her toes. He turned to the corpsman. "We need to stabilize this."

He nodded. "I have a Hare traction splint below."

"What about antibiotics?"

"Ancef and clindamycin."

"Get me two grams of Ancef. I'm going to wash and bandage these wounds, then we're going to splint the fracture. The bullet broke her femur. She's lost a lot of blood, so let's get an IV going. Any questions?" After the corpsman shook his head, Thurman walked to the head of the adjacent table. Yuri lay with eyes closed, his chest barely moving. His pulse felt thready. "Let's get an IV going. Load him with two liters of warm saline. Check his core temp. Get these wet clothes off him. Give me as many blankets as you can find. Where's the captain? This man's been shot and needs emergent medical attention."

CHAPTER 56
JAGGEARS

THURMAN SAT in the chair next to Carmen's bed as she slept. He put his book down and looked across the room when John Bristow knocked on the door and peeked in. "Mind if I come in?"

Thurman motioned for him to enter. After the Coast Guard cutter docked at the Caswell Beach Station, they'd been airlifted to New Hanover Regional Medical Center in Wilmington, where Yuri underwent emergent surgery. The orthopedic trauma surgeon operated on Carmen that night, stabilizing her fractured femur. The next day she'd been transferred to St. Matthew's Medical Center, where they were now. Yuri's injuries had so far required two surgeries and eight units of blood. He remained in critical condition on a ventilator in the ICU at New Hanover. Bristow pulled up a chair. "How's she doing?"

"She's super pissed about getting shot, so I'd say she's going to be fine."

After a moment Bristow reached over and slapped his knee. Thurman winced. "C'mon, man, get your jacket. Jaggears wants to talk to us."

Thurman squeezed Carmen's hand, then leaned over and whispered into her ear. "I'll be back in a little while." He waited until they were in Bristow's pickup before speaking. "She took a nine-millimeter round to the right thigh. It struck her femur, broke it midshaft. The orthopedic surgeon fixed it with a titanium rod. If it doesn't get infected, she should be discharged in a day or two. Barring any complications, she'll be walking without crutches in about six weeks."

"That doesn't sound too bad."

"It could have been a lot worse; no nerve or blood vessel injury. A broken femur bleeds a lot, so she lost a few liters of blood into her thigh while floating in the Atlantic. It's a good thing you handed her that life vest."

Bristow shrugged.

"They transfused her with a couple of units," Thurman said.

"Lucky your shark didn't find her."

"That goes for all of us. What happened to you?"

"When I saw that grenade, I knew our only chance was to jump. I grabbed her arm and dove in right after Natasha, but I got separated in the propeller wash and we drifted apart. A bullet grazed my head, and I blacked out." He pointed to a nasty gash right in the part of his hair. "I'm lucky I didn't drown. The Coasties found Carmen. The *Carter* picked up the signal from my transponder."

"You remembered to bring that?"

Bristow smiled. "I put it in my pocket right after I left the bridge."

"Did you see the explosion?"

"I missed it, but I'm sure the admiral has something to tell us about that."

Thurman raked his hair. "I hate these debrief sessions. I lost the sphere. He's going to rip me a new one."

"He'll get over it. You saved Yuri. He can make another sphere. You're a hero."

"Some hero."

———

They drove an hour south through North Carolina farmland until they reached TSI headquarters. The familiar throbbing in Thurman's right knee intensified as he sat in the truck. It felt like a toothache that needed attention. He looked out the window at fallow fields while rubbing his aching joint. *Maybe it's just a sprain.* When Admiral

Jaggears entered the conference room, Thurman stood. The knee pain made his teeth clench.

"Sit down, gentlemen," Jaggears said as he took a seat at the head of the table. He picked up a remote control and pointed it at the familiar video screen hanging on the wall. "Thank you for coming on such short notice. Your presence is appreciated."

Thurman sat with his spine erect. *Like we had a choice.*

"You'll be glad to know that as far as the US government is concerned, this operation never happened. You will not speak of these events to anyone. Is that understood?"

The two men nodded and responded in unison. "Yes, sir."

"The secretary of defense asked that I congratulate you both."

Thurman and Bristow exchanged glances.

Jaggears clicked the remote. A video began streaming on the screen. "You no doubt recognize this vessel."

"The *LunaSea*," said Bristow.

"This footage was shot from an air force high-altitude Sentinel drone. The ship is unmistakable."

"I can read its name on the hull," said Bristow.

"The camera optics are unsurpassed." Jaggears paused the video. "Any guess why Stanov made a visit to Wilmington?"

Thurman placed his interlocked hands on the polished table. "To pick up Drake and the sphere."

"Correct. The only sample and the only person capable of producing it."

"How did he find him?" asked Bristow.

"His wife, Aliya."

Thurman sat forward. "She's the mole?"

"She contacted Stanov a year and a half ago and has been feeding him information ever since. Fortunately, Yuri kept his process secret, even from her. Drake's linear wakefield micro particle-accelerator is the only device capable of producing element 126. Others tried to replicate his achievement but failed. He is a visionary determined to change the world for the better. He's currently developing a process to bombard spent uranium from nuclear power plants with ionized selenium to make his element 126. If he can do that, it solves the problem of nuclear waste. Imagine what that means to the nuclear power industry. Greed and power motivated Stanov. I doubt if he knows what altruism is. He dreamed of monopolizing the battery market. He approached numerous automotive, airplane, and locomotive manufacturers. Private equity firms began forming a long line to capitalize on Stanov's venture—if he could get Yuri to run it."

"What about Benedetto?" asked Bristow.

"Dario Benedetto thought he could do it. So did Aliya. She played her role as Yuri's wife, if that's what you call her, but betrayed him long ago. She worked alongside him her entire career and believed she could do anything he could. She and Benedetto stole what they thought was the information they needed from Angstrom, shot David Moore, and planted a worm in the computer system. They planned to run a production facility in Italy. We believe she always loved Benedetto and never forgave Yuri for taking her away from him."

"I wonder if Yuri suspected something?" asked Bristow.

"He made it a stipulation that Benedetto not be allowed to come with them when they escaped."

Thurman shifted in his chair and tilted his head. "How do you know this?"

"Most came from reports made by Richard Gross, known to you as Terry Morton, a veteran CIA case officer. In addition to his civilian engineering career, he recruited Noreen Chase when they worked in Germany. They got the Drakes out of Russia. When Yuri and Aliya settled in the US, SECDEF used his influence to have Noreen hired at Angstrom to keep tabs on Yuri's work. Noreen knew of Aliya's love affair with Benedetto but believed Dario was an ally with them against Stanov. Unfortunately, she paid the ultimate price for that mistake. By the way, before her miscarriage, Aliya was carrying Dario's baby, not Yuri's."

"How is that possible?" Thurman asked.

"Aliya betrayed him in every way. She contacted Benedetto right after she began feeding information to Stanov. They met secretly in Charlotte or Atlanta, occasionally Charleston. Noreen tipped us about several of these trysts. We trailed Aliya and bugged their hotel room. Benedetto wanted Yuri out of the way but needed him. He couldn't figure out how to build the linear accelerators even with the information Aliya slipped him."

"If you knew all this, why didn't you stop it?" asked Thurman. "It would have saved us all a lot of trouble."

"The CIA doesn't work that way. Its objective is intelligence—information is its currency. They wanted details on Stanov's network. Morton's job was to turn Artem Soloviev."

Thurman scowled. "What happened to him?"

"He remains free, for the time being."

Bristow leaned forward and folded his arms on the table. "So, Stanov planned to bring Yuri and Aliya to the facility he was building in Italy. He failed and caused the motorcycle accident?"

"Correct, Aliya wanted to go back to Russia, but Stanov had a falling out with Russian government officials and was persona non grata with the Kremlin. She had to settle for Siena."

"Walters too?"

Jaggears nodded. "Walters remained in Moore's shadow at Angstrom. His Achilles' heel was pride and ambition. Aliya recognized this and tried to turn him to their side. When he had second thoughts and tried to back out Stanov kidnapped his wife and child. He delivered the car and battery to Stanov, but his wife died trying to escape. After that Stanov believed him a liability and tried to kill him in the villa ambush. Benedetto convinced Stanov he needed him, so he had him released from Carabinieri custody. Walters disappeared from the ship when it stopped in Wilmington. His whereabouts remain a mystery."

"Who killed Noreen?"

"Soloviev. Morton and Noreen tried to get Solo to work for them." Jaggears shook his head. "He double crossed them. Morton suspected something and met with Noreen in the bar after her Angstrom presentation." Jaggears looked at Thurman. "That's when you saw them together."

"Then he picked her up in the BMW," said Thurman.

"Correct," said Jaggears. "Noreen suspected Stanov's desperation. She knew their operation had a leak but didn't realize it was Aliya. She voiced her concerns, and Yuri made copies of files and deleted them from laboratory computers. He hid the one copy with all the key information. The thumb drive he gave Noreen was a red herring, and so was the information Aliya and Benedetto stole from Angstrom."

"Did anyone find the original?" asked Bristow.

Jaggears shook his head. "Negative. Noreen made her video and put her copy of Yuri's incomplete files on the flash drive with her presentation. She planned to give it to doc but received Solo's urgent message to meet at the Duke Gardens. So, she gave the thumb drive to Emerson and told him to pass it to you."

Thurman folded his arms and leaned forward. "That's how Noreen wound up there."

"Solo gave her the lethal injection, then abused her."

"How do you know?"

"We have his DNA; samples from under Noreen's fingernails match."

"How did mine get there?" said Thurman.

"From a water bottle they stole when they broke into your house."

"They weren't after the sphere; they planned to frame me."

Jaggears nodded. "It appears that way."

"He murdered Noreen and shot Detective Hairston. Why isn't Solo in custody?"

"He's got a cell in the federal pen reserved. There's a joint FBI and police task force hunting for him as well as the cartel involved in the warehouse blast."

Bristow looked at Jaggears. "Was he on the *LunaSea*? I didn't see him."

"No," said Jaggears. "He delivered Yuri, and Natasha then drove back to Durham. He hasn't been seen since."

Thurman leaned back, crossing his arms. "Too bad he wasn't on board."

"He'll get his due."

"It can't be soon enough."

Bristow leaned forward and changed the subject. "Who blew up the ship?"

"The Russians torpedoed it," said Jaggears.

"Why do that? You'd think Yuri would be a Russian national hero for his discovery."

"Don't be naïve. We're talking about a complete disruption of the world energy market, the number one source of revenue for the Russian economy. Look at what happened in the electric auto industry in the early 1900s. People still believe a group of powerful countries, led by the US, sabotaged the electric vehicle industry to further the interests of the Middle East. History has a way of repeating itself." Jaggears resumed the video. "You witnessed the newest Yasen-class Russian submarine in action. The Kremlin wants Yuri and his invention destroyed. The navy suspected there might be a Russian sub patrolling off the Eastern Seaboard and started looking for it a couple of days ago. The USS *Carter*, other US Navy ships, and antisubmarine aircraft from the naval base in Norfolk participated in the hunt. Confirmation of its presence was never obtained. Once Stanov cleared US coastal waters and entered international waters, the *LunaSea* exploded and sank."

Thurman raised an eyebrow. "Sunk by a torpedo?"

Jaggears nodded. "Affirmative. Watch." The video image showed an aerial view of the *LunaSea*. "Here it comes." He flashed the top of the screen with a laser pointer. A faint white object streaked down and appeared to strike the vessel amidships. A fraction of a second later, the ship became engulfed in a fireball. Ten seconds later only ocean water remained. Then the Coast Guard cutter entered the picture and began circling, looking for survivors.

Thurman turned his palms up. "We let a Russian sub do that? Why? I don't understand."

"We didn't let them—they did it. We're not a hundred percent sure what happened. Even if we were certain, how could we stop a sub we couldn't locate? The news services reported an explosion occurred on board. It sunk with no survivors."

"That's bullshit," said Bristow.

"Maybe, but think about it. What would happen to the world economy if oil suddenly became worthless?"

"But it wouldn't."

"Once the production of 126 scaled up, the price of oil would drop to less than ten dollars a barrel within a year. Do you think the people who run Gazprom, Saudi Aramco, China National Petroleum, Exxon, Shell, BP, Chevron, Phillips 66, National Iranian Oil Company, ONGC . . . I could go on, but you get the idea. Those people weren't going to stand by and let Stanov put them out of business."

"That would have taken years. It may not have ever happened."

Jaggears chuckled. "Stick to fixing bones, doc. Get out of international politics. It's a dirty business."

Thurman stood. "You firing me?"

"I'm educating you."

Thurman's fingers stroked the three-day growth along his jawline. He shook his head in disbelief then said, "Our government is going to bury it, deprive the world of one of the greatest discoveries since the steam engine?"

Jaggears changed the screen image. A picture of Yuri's laboratory appeared. "Relax commander, don't get worked up. We have every intention of continuing Drake's work at Angstrom Industries, and so do the Russians. They have Dubna, we have Angstrom. Hell, the machines have been built. We just need someone to reverse engineer the process and write the code. SECDEF thinks David Moore is the perfect choice to head up the project. Aliya and Benedetto tried to kill him but failed. He's expected to make a full recovery and will be put in charge of the project."

"Why not Yuri?" asked Thurman. "He can resume his work once he recovers."

"He died this morning," said Jaggears.

Thurman sagged back into his chair, his head hanging. "He'd been doing so well. I spoke with his surgeon yesterday. He'd been extubated. What happened?"

"His body was taken to the morgue this morning and loaded into an ambulance."

Thurman's eyes narrowed. "An ambulance? You mean a hearse?"

"No, I mean an ambulance. It drove to an undisclosed location."

Thurman looked at Bristow, and they both smiled. "He's alive."

"I can neither confirm nor deny that information," Jaggears responded. "I can tell you the same mistakes won't be made twice."

Bristow gave Thurman a high five. "What about Walters?"

Jaggears nodded. "The FBI is looking for him. He's got a strong case. A good lawyer like your friend, Whitehouse could probably get him exonerated without too much trouble. We'll see. He's a smart guy, Moore could definitely use him."

"Natasha?" Thurman asked.

"She and Morton were married about a year ago. He left her a sizable estate. She's quit dancing and knows enough about motorcycles to run the business. She'll be fine."

CHAPTER 57
REFLECTIONS

THURMAN EXITED the elevator and turned right. The yellow tape no longer marked Noreen's door. Her apartment looked the same as all the rest. He inserted the key Ingram gave him and opened the door. Everything looked unchanged. He opened the blinds, sat on the couch, and imagined her walking through the bedroom door. Tears welled as he fought back emotion. Yesterday he'd returned from Washington after attending Noreen and Richard Gross's ceremony at Langley. He'd kept his promise and touched her star on the wall. It had burned too bright and had gone out too fast. Her memory made him recall the lyrics to *Candle in the Wind* by Elton John.

It's in here somewhere, he thought as he surveyed the spaces. *What did she say? "Look inside the artist's portrait."* The apartment's contemporary design felt austere. A lot of glass and metal. He preferred wood and stone, something more solid with warmth.

She had to be referring to M. C. Escher, her favorite artist. He'd done many self-portraits during his career, but Thurman couldn't find any reproductions in her apartment. He scanned her bookshelves and walls. Nothing in the kitchen or bathrooms. He wandered toward her bedroom.

The space was spotless. The pictures on her walls were modern, but no Escher. The nightstands were clear. Only twin lamps and a charging station lay on their surfaces. Nothing of significance in the drawers. A few engineering trade journals and the Winston Graham novel *Marnie*. His gaze wandered to her dresser, and he spotted it. A mirrored sphere about the size of a grapefruit resting on a chrome tripod. *That's it.* Escher's most famous self-portrait was called *Hand with Reflecting Sphere*. It was a lithograph of a hand holding a sphere with a mirror surface. The reflection showed Escher holding the sphere and his reflection as the self-portrait.

Thurman hurried around the bed and grasped the spherical mirror. He held it up and looked at his reflection much the way Escher would have. It revealed more than his image.

"I'll take that," said Solo. He stood in the bedroom doorway with a Makarov pointed at Thurman's back. The curved reflection made the suppressor appear as long as the barrel and the gun twice its size. "Turn around, put it on the bed nice and slow, then get down on the floor."

Thurman turned with the sphere held away from his body. "You couldn't have her, so you raped her in the garden as she lay dying."

A smile appeared on his face. "I gave her what she deserved and enjoyed every second of it."

"You're a sick psychopath." Thurman jumped to his right and whip-kicked the window. The glass shattered. Flame spit from the suppressor. Thurman felt a jolt under his outstretched arm, then pain around his shoulder blade. He gripped the sphere and thrust his hand through the broken window, suspending it in air. "We're on the twenty-fifth floor, asshole. Good luck finding what's inside this thing if I let go."

"Don't drop it. If you do, I'll kill you right here."

Thurman flipped him off and laughed. "I'm already dead." He coughed and spit blood-streaked sputum at Solo. His knee throbbed. "My body's rattled with cancer, so your threats mean nothing. We can meet in hell, but you'll never have this." He shook the sphere. Something inside moved.

"We may meet there one day, but you'll get there first. Now put it on the bed."

"First tell me how Noreen knew Aliya was pregnant with Dario's child."

Solo laughed. "She told her."

"Why would she do that?"

"Noreen loved her like the sister she never had." He moved toward the window.

"Stop, or it drops. Tell me more."

Solo snarled. "I'm going to put a bullet in your head in about thirty seconds, so I'll tell you. Noreen knew Aliya loved Dario. Aliya put up with Yuri because she needed to learn how to make the stuff. Aliya knew the bitch was a spy. She played it to her advantage. Aliya knew everything."

"I don't believe you."

"I don't give a shit what you believe. Hand over the ball, and we can make a deal."

"Did you kidnap my cousin?"

"You should have given me the sphere."

"I didn't have it."

"It doesn't matter." Solo laughed. "Boris wasn't going to let him live."

Traffic noise came through the window. Thurman couldn't hold his arm out much longer. Pain from the gunshot wound intensified. The weight of the ball made his shoulder quiver. He brought it to the sill and shook it. Something rattled from within. A grin broke across Solo's face momentarily.

"We'll sell whatever's in there for fifty million and split it. What do you say?"

Thurman glanced over Solo's shoulder and smiled back.

A deep resonant growl came through the doorway followed by a full-frame .45 model 1911 semiautomatic. "I say put the gun down. You're under arrest."

Solo whirled. Ingram hesitated with Thurman standing behind his target. He ducked behind the wall. Solo fired two rounds. The doorframe splintered.

Thurman threw the silver ball. It cracked off the back of Solo's head and shattered. He staggered. Thurman dove over the bed onto Solo's back. They fell to the floor. He snaked his right arm around Solo's neck. Solo turned the gun and Thurman grabbed the suppressor. It fired, scorching his hand. Pain seared through the right side of his chest. Solo gagged as Thurman locked his legs around his waist and tightened his hadaka-jime hold. Two more shots splintered the floor by Thurman's head. He contracted every muscle pulling with all his strength. Solo's face purpled. His eyes bulged. Thurman arched his body. He tightened his leg lock and pulled with his arm. Searing pain spread from his right knee. He exerted with maximum effort, then gave more. He felt the snap of dislocating cervical vertebrae. Solo's body went limp, and the gun fell from his hand.

"That's for Steve and Noreen."

"I couldn't shoot him with you on his back," Ingram said as he knelt beside Thurman. "I was about to put the barrel of this .45 against his head and blow his brains all over this room." He inspected Thurman's bloody shirt. "You need a doctor."

"How did you find me?"

"You been acting strange lately," he said, smiling, "even more than usual. When you asked for the key I decided to keep an eye on you. We've been looking for this dirtbag. He gave the Feds the slip, but we know the city better than they do. When I got the call that you both were in the building, I lit up the Charger."

"It's a good thing. I couldn't hold that ball much longer."

"You're bleeding all over. Let's get you to the hospital."

The left side of his shirt felt wet and sticky. Thurman touched his chest below his armpit and winced. Ingram helped him to his feet. His knee hurt and his left flank felt like it was on fire. "Wait." He knelt and brushed shards of the reflecting orb out from under the dresser. Then he peered under it and reached into the darkness. He gripped the small object and forgot about his pain.

"What's that?"

"Yuri's gift. He gave it to Noreen for safe keeping."

"What is it?"

"A memory drive."

One eyebrow rose, wrinkling Ingram's forehead. "I know what it is. What's on it?"

"I don't know for sure, but I'll bet this holds the secrets to a brave new world."

Ingram placed a big hand on his friend's shoulder. "I don't even want to know what that means. You'll just get me into more trouble."

Thurman smiled as he tried to stand. He felt lightheaded. A lightning bolt of pain struck inside his right knee. It gave way, and he fell to the floor.

CHAPTER 58
PRIME EDITING

THURMAN THOUGHT of the many times he'd ridden in an ambulance. He'd been the patient only twice. He lay on the narrow gurney with his arms strapped to his side. An IV tube placed into a forearm vein delivered saline from a bag above his head. The EMT administered a narcotic, and as the morphine molecules bound to opioid receptors throughout his body, it produced a profound feeling of comfort. He began to relax. The pain in his chest and knee faded into oblivion. He looked up at the woman wearing a blue shirt and trousers. "Where are we going?"

"The hospital, sir. You're in an ambulance."

"Which hospital?"

"Does it matter?"

He slowly nodded. "Take me to St. Matthew's."

"That's where we're going."

"Thanks."

"No need to thank me; it's where the detective said to take you."

"Hurry, please hurry," he whispered between short breaths.

"Don't talk, we'll be there soon." She placed an oxygen mask over his face.

———

He awoke to the feeling of choking. He couldn't breathe. Something blocked his airway. He tried to reach for his mouth, but his hands were restrained. His body convulsed as he tried to free himself.

"Get help!" someone shouted. "Dr. Thurman, relax, you're all right. It's Angie. You're in the ICU."

He coughed as she deflated the cuff and pulled the endotracheal tube. Air poured into his lungs. The panic subsided and was replaced by racking pain from the right side of his chest. He motioned to it.

"Dr. Naylor will be by shortly. I'll let him explain. For now, try to rest. You've been through a lot."

She wiped the IV port with an alcohol swab and connected a small syringe. He watched as she pressed the plunger. A minute later he began floating into a white cloud as the pain evaporated.

The sensation of pain returned and made him roll to his right. His eyes opened to the sight of Dr. Richard Naylor peeling foam tape and four-by-four gauze from his chest. He saw the stapled wound beneath.

"Hello, Mark, I'm glad you're awake. Sorry, I know this isn't pleasant, but I have to check your incision."

Thurman looked at him, confused. Naylor laughed. "You took two bullets, one to your left axilla and the other to the left side of your chest. Don't you remember?"

He conjured a mental image of Solo's face. He nodded.

"The first one just missing the brachial plexus. The second and more serious one entered your left chest wall, broke several ribs, and took out a chunk of your scapula. You had a hemothorax, arterial bleeding into your chest. You bought a chest tube in the ER, then a trip straight to the OR. I opened you up and got control of the bleeding. I even plated a couple of your ribs. It made me feel like an orthopod. I like drilling and screwing ribs back together. I'm going to assist you on a few cases when you get better. You can show me the finer points."

Thurman groaned.

Naylor looked over his shoulder at the nurse standing behind him and nodded. Angie reached for the control and elevated it about forty-five degrees. Thurman's right knee was wrapped in an immobilizer brace. He pointed at it.

"What happened to my knee?"

"I don't know. You'll have to ask Dr. Wynn about that." He turned to Angie. "The incision looks fine. Change this dressing. If he continues to show improvement, I'll pull the chest tube on rounds tomorrow morning. Have fresh bandage material ready."

"Yes, sir," she replied as Naylor strode from the room, his long white coat flowing like a cape behind him. When the door closed, she looked at Thurman. "Is he always like that?"

He chuckled. "He can't help it. We call him King Richard, the Lion-heart. He's a damn good surgeon."

————

Thurman lost track of time. When he awoke his untouched lunch tray lay on the table at the bedside. Sunlight radiated through his window, too strong to be close to evening. He looked to his right and pressed the bed control on the railing, and the head of his bed tilted upward. A cord with a plunger at its end lay across his waist. He grasped the device and pressed the plunger with his thumb. A few moments later, a voice came over the intercom. "Can I help you?"

"Yes, I need to go to the bathroom."

"You have a Foley catheter, Dr. Thurman."

He looked under his bedsheets. A tube protruded from the tip of his penis. He followed the tube to the plastic bag hooked to the side rail. It was half filled with clear yellow urine. "Can someone come and pull it? Get this thing out of me."

"If you can't void your bladder, we'll have to replace it."

"I don't care, I want this thing out!"

"I'll be there in a minute."

She appeared by his bed and withdrew the sheets. With gentle hands she gripped him, then swabbed the head with Betadine. With a syringe she deflated the balloon in his bladder and pulled. The long tube slipped out of him like a tapeworm. She held it for him to see. "There, that should be better."

Thurman exhaled. It hadn't hurt as much as he feared. "Thank you."

She tossed him a baby wipe. "You may want to clean off that excess Betadine; it can be irritating to sensitive skin."

"You're a regular Nightingale."

"I try my best, doctor."

"When are rounds? Where's my phone? I want to talk to whoever operated on my knee."

"I don't control their schedules."

"Who was the surgeon?"

"Dr. Wynn."

"Can you call him for me?"

"He wouldn't like that."

"I'd like that."

"They should be by soon, please be patient." With that she turned and retreated from the room. He turned his head on the pillow and fell asleep.

The next time he awoke, sunlight had almost disappeared from the window. He lay in semidarkness in his hospital bed and tried to lean forward, but the effort produced a surge of pain from his chest. He wanted the chest tube out as much as he'd wanted the Foley pulled. He looked up when a knock on his door sounded.

The door opened and the overhead lights snapped on. He blinked, then blinked again. "Claire?"

She approached the bed. Her long golden hair framed her face. She came close and kissed his cheek. "Mark, it's good to see you."

Her face began to blur as tears welled up in his eyes. "I thought you were in California."

"Until last week."

"You're back?"

"Yes. It's a work in progress . . . getting the lab set up again."

He reached out and took her hand. "Thanks for coming to visit."

"This is a little more than a social call."

"What do you mean?"

She looked at her phone. "Dr. Wynn will be here in a minute. I'd like for him to help explain."

"My knee?"

She nodded. "You're our patient."

John Wynn knocked as he entered the room. "Hello, Mark, how do you feel?"

"Better, I think. Tell me what's going on."

Claire pulled a chair from across the room. Wynn sat at the foot of the bed. "When you arrived five days ago, you were in bad shape. Not just from the gunshot wounds. You'd sustained a pathologic fracture of your lateral femoral condyle from a recurrence of your Ewing's sarcoma. It had metastasized throughout your body, even to your lungs. You were sick."

Thurman understood. "How long?"

"Excuse me?"

"How long do I have?"

Wynn chuckled. "Many, many years, I hope. You can thank your research partner for that. If what she says is true, then she's saved your life."

Thurman turned to Claire. "It wouldn't be the first time."

"I'll let her take over. I need to see a few more patients and will stop by in the morning. I'll talk to Naylor about getting rid of that chest tube." He stood and walked from the room.

Claire rose from her chair and took Wynn's seat on the side of the bed. "I went to California initially to learn how to edit human genes using CRISPR-Cas9 and later, prime editing. I spent a month at Berkeley at the Innovative Genomics Institute learning the methodology. Then I returned to San Diego and began experiments in Chris Peterson's lab. You remember Chris?"

Thurman nodded. "Of course."

She smiled. "Yes. We dated for a couple of years while he finished his postdoc at Duke."

"I remember."

"You and I began working together a few months before Chris left for San Diego."

"You said it was over between you two."

She nodded. "He started a successful biotech firm. When I

contacted him about a place to work, he hired me to help him on a few projects."

"I know. You told me, remember?"

"What I didn't tell you—couldn't tell you—is that one of them involves inserting modified tumor suppressor genes into osteocytes for the treatment of osteosarcoma and Ewing's tumors. The FDA fast-tracked the project last month. They gave it an experimental use authorization. That's how we used it for your knee. Dr. Wynn resected the tumor. I bioprinted a matching segment filled with your stem cells altered to contain the modified tumor suppressor genes. They've already started transforming into osteocytes."

"I'm a regular guinea pig."

"Index patient."

"You think it'll work?"

"I hope so. Yesterday's CT scans show over 80 percent tumor reduction. It's melting away." Claire paused for a moment. "Remember, we don't know everything about the technology, but I expect permanent remission. Of course, we'll need to keep track of you."

"No problem. What about chemotherapy, am I getting Endovancin?"

"You're receiving it daily."

"I feel good, sort of."

"You're responding remarkably well. It's miraculous."

"Just call me Hyperion." They laughed and he grasped her hand. Then he felt the ring and held up her fingers. "What's this?"

"An engagement ring."

"You and Chris?"

She nodded and blinked as a tear rolled down her cheek. "I'm sorry, Mark. We had a wonderful thing and it's still special, but I truly love Chris. My time with him in San Diego has proven that to me."

Thurman released her hand. "I'm happy for you," he said, but his expression didn't show it.

"We can still work together. Chris sold the company and has accepted a faculty position at Duke. He's moving back."

"When is the wedding?"

"Next June, in Sydney. You'll come, won't you?"

"Of course, wouldn't miss it," he lied.

"I need to go, but I'll stop by tomorrow."

He watched as she walked to the door. "Turn the light out, please."

———

Thurman spooned what looked like scrambled eggs into his mouth, then quickly washed it down with a swig of black coffee. The chest tube had been removed on rounds early that morning, and the pain in his chest was subsiding. Pulling it hurt almost as bad as when he'd been shot, but only for a few moments. A nurse came to the doorway.

"Dr. Thurman, you have some visitors."

"Who?"

"They're from the police, detectives Ingram and Hairston."

Thurman smiled. "Send them in." Ingram strode to the bed with Hairston two steps behind. A white bandage protruded above Hairston's unbuttoned collar. "Gentlemen, what do I owe the occasion?"

"Cut the crap," said Ingram. "We're just worried about you."

Hairston stuck out his hand. "Good job, glad you're getting better."

"You here to arrest me?"

Hairston smiled. "Not today."

"How are you doing?" Thurman asked, pointing to the bandage.

"Getting better every day, just a scratch."

Ingram scoffed. "A scratch my ass. The doctor said that if it'd been a millimeter closer, his carotid would have been severed."

"I've got a guardian angel watching over me," Hairston said. "I wanted to personally thank you for taking care of that asshole."

"My pleasure."

Hairston folded his arms. The motion caused his suit coat to open, exposing his gold detective shield clipped to the left side of his belt. "Anastasia's has been closed down by the Feds. Multiple interstate commerce violations, prostitution, drugs, you name it. The Russian mob will have to find a new place for business."

Ingram walked to the other side of the bed and placed his hands on the side railing. A beeping alarm sounded, and he let go. The alarm stopped. "What was that?"

"Escape alarm, it lets the nurses know if I'm trying to get out of bed."

This brought a smile to Ingram's face. "You need one of those."

"You were saying?"

Ingram pinched his chin. "Oh, yeah, the Feds are classifying the warehouse bombing as an act of terror. Those Redfellas and the Guerrero cartel are going to wish they never set up shop in the Raleigh-Durham area."

Thurman nodded. "Good riddance."

Ingram dug into his front trouser pocket. "One more thing." He produced the memory stick from the reflecting sphere. "I think you wanted this."

Thurman grabbed it and held it to the ceiling. "Thanks, I was wondering what happened to it."

"You know damn well no one was getting that from me."

"I wasn't worried."

Ingram sat at the bedside. "Your cousin was buried in Seattle last Saturday. I'm sorry about him."

"Thanks, I'll call his folks and see them when I go out there to pay my respects."

"I think that would be good for you." Hairston took a few steps toward the door. "C'mon, Jack, let's get going, he needs the rest."

Ingram stood and followed him. "Let me know when you're ready to shoot. You'll need to requalify after you're healed."

"Looking forward to it." Thurman waved as they left.

———

That afternoon the physical therapist helped Thurman into a wheelchair and rolled him down the hallway to the therapy room. With some effort Thurman managed to transfer from the wheelchair to a flat therapy platform about eight feet square with a four-inch-thick padded surface. The therapist had him lay flat and removed his knee brace.

"You ready for this?" she asked.

"Ready for what?"

"I have orders from Dr. Wynn to start passive range of motion on your knee and see if you can manage a walker without putting weight on your right leg."

Thurman nodded. "I'm ready." She lifted his leg and let gravity bend it about twenty degrees, then she straightened it. "How was that?"

Sweat was beading on his forehead. "Not bad. Let's do it again." She continued. Twenty minutes later she brought over a walker and helped him stand on his left leg, balancing with the walker.

"Can you hop?"

He demonstrated by hopping across the room and back. He'd move the walker a foot or so, then hop to it and repeat the process. It bothered his right side, but he tolerated it.

"Very good," she said.

Thurman turned at the sound of soft applause. Carmen Black stood in the doorway, leaning on a pair of aluminum crutches.

"Great work, keep it up," she said.

Thurman turned to the therapist. "Do you mind if I have a word with her alone?"

She smiled and stood. "I'll be back in ten minutes. Remember, no weight-bearing on that leg."

Carmen crutched across the room and sat on the therapy platform next to Thurman. "I heard you're getting better."

"Who's the informant? That's a HIPAA violation," he said, then smiled.

"Your orthopedic partner and former trauma fellow, Dr. Wynn. He keeps me posted on your progress."

"Former practice partner. I don't have a job, remember."

"I still can't believe that."

"Maybe it's for the best. I need a change."

"Me too." She reached out and gently touched his knee bandage. "Pretty amazing stuff Dr. Hodgson and her team are doing."

"Yes, it is, and I'm grateful. The alternative isn't very appealing."

"I'm just thankful you're okay. That was a damn close call." She turned and looked him in the eye. "Dr. Hodgson is your Claire, right?"

Thurman nodded.

"Good. I hope you two will be happy. Maybe we can get together sometime, the three of us." He caught the tremble in her voice.

Thurman looked at her and brushed the stray bangs that always seemed to fall into her blue eyes. "I kind of doubt that will happen."

She tucked the lock behind her ear. "Why?"

"She's engaged to another man."

"I'm sorry."

"Don't be. It's not in the cards. I've known that for a while now."

"Well, you can still stay at my apartment while you're healing. I mean, until you find a place. We can help each other."

Thurman smiled. "That ought to be interesting; between the two of us, we might have two good legs."

"Two left ones," she added, and they laughed.

"You should be able to get back to work in six or eight weeks," he told her. "It shouldn't set you back too much."

"I've already talked to my chairman and the program director at Hopkins. Everything should work out. I'll be able to graduate and start my fellowship on time. What are you going to do?"

"I don't know. I need to hire a contractor to rebuild my house. That should keep me occupied."

"I mean professionally."

"I was thinking locum tenens might be a nice change, you know, freelance work."

"Did you hear the news?"

"What?"

"Vogler was caught with a medical student in his office. She claims he was trying to fondle her. It was pretty damning, especially right after he got arrested for threatening a police officer. The hospital can't afford any more bad press."

Thurman laughed. "That's the best news I've heard in a while. Serves that lowlife right. Too bad that poor medical student had to go through that."

"She slapped his face and reported him immediately. I wouldn't worry about her, she's tough."

"Like someone else I know."

"Do you think you would come back to work here?"

"Maybe. No one's offered to reinstate my privileges."

"Let things settle out." She stood and leaned on her crutches. "When will Wynn let you out of here?"

"As soon as I can get around on this damn thing." He reached out for the walker and stood next to it. "Probably tomorrow, the next day at the latest."

"Get after it. Call me when you're coming home."

He leaned over and kissed her. "I will."

ACKNOWLEDGMENTS

This book would not exist if not for a team of extraordinary people. I am deeply indebted to one of the best thriller writers in the business, Robert Dugoni. He critiqued several early drafts. His talents as a writer and teacher are unsurpassed. Amber Meyers is a certified developmental editor who I had the good fortune to meet at one of Shawn Coyne's Story Grid workshops in Nashville. She tackled the task of shaping the manuscript with an abundance of skill and enthusiasm. I doubt if there is a copy editor any better than Christina Roth. We went through many rounds of editing to get the book into its final shape. She is the best. Once again I called upon retired Special Agent James Reightler for advice on SWAT and FBI topics. He has never let me down. Caroline Harberd is the talented graphic artist who created the frontispiece. Maxwell Roth's immense skill as a cover designer speaks for itself. I have also had the benefit of a number of experts and advisors who have volunteered their time to help me on a number of complicated topics. I am indebted to them for their support and take full responsibility for any errors or omissions.

No one deserves more credit than Vicky, my wife and life-partner. She read and reread the manuscript multiple times over the last two-and-a-half years. Her love and encouragement never wavered. For that, I will always be grateful. Thank you.

ABOUT THE AUTHOR

Thomas Kelso is the award-winning author of *Fractured* and *Hyperion's Fracture*. He lives on the southeast coast of North Carolina with his wife and continues to practice orthopedic surgery.

https://www.thomaskelso.com
Facebook: @ThomasKelsoMD

Made in the USA
Columbia, SC
17 November 2022

71290439R00207